D0094567

The Writing on the Wall

GUNNAR STAALESEN was born in Bergen, Norway in 1947. He made his debut at the age of 22 with *Seasons of Innocence* and in 1977 he published the first book in the Varg Veum series. He is the author of over 20 titles, which have been published in 24 countries and sold over two million copies. Twelve film adaptations of his Varg Veum crime novels have appeared since 2007, starring the popular Norwegian actor Trond Epsen Seim. Staalesen, who has twice won Norway's top crime prize, the Golden Pistol, lives in Bergen with his wife.

The Writing on the Wall

GUNNAR STAALESEN

Translated from the Norwegian by
Hal Sutcliffe

Arcadia Books Ltd
139 Highlever Road
London W10 6PH

www.arcadiabooks.co.uk

First published in the United Kingdom by Arcadia Books 2004
This B format edition Arcadia Books 2009
Reprinted 2010, 2013
Originally published by Gyldendal Norsk Forlag, Oslo as *Skriften På Veggen* 1995
Copyright © Gunnar Staalesen 1995
This English translation from the Norweigan copyright © Hal Sutcliffe 2004

Gunnar Staalesen has asserted his moral right to be identified as the author of this work in
accordance with the Copyright, Designs and Patents Act, 1988.

A catalogue record for this book is available from the British Library.

ISBN 978-1-906413-19-4

Typeset in Minion by MacGuru Ltd
Printed and bound by CPI Group (UK) Ltd, Croydon CRO 4YY

Arcadia Books supports English PEN *www.englishpen.org* and
The Book Trade Charity *http://booktradecharity.wordpress.com*

Arcadia Books distributors are as follows:

in the UK and elsewhere in Europe:
Macmillan Distribution Ltd
Brunel Road
Houndmills
Basingstoke
Hants RG21 6XS

in the USA and Canada:
Dufour Editions
PO Box 7
Chester Springs
PA 19425

in Australia/New Zealand:
NewSouth Books
University of New South Wales
Sydney NSW 2052

in South Africa:
Jacana Media (Pty) Ltd
PO Box 291784
Melville 2109
Johannesburg

*My Danish publisher and friend, Erik Vagn Jensen,
died before this book was completed.
It is respectfully dedicated to his memory.*

And if I had called,
and he had answered me;
yet would I not believe that he had
hearkened unto my voice.

Job 9:6

One

WHEN ONE FRIDAY AFTERNOON in February Judge HC Brandt, age seventy, was found dead in one of the better hotels in town, wearing nothing but flimsy women's underwear, rumours soon began to spread.

Each fresh revelation brought bursts of raucous laughter from the press tables at Wesselsttien Pub, and there was no shortage of details embroidered beyond all measure. I too received my fair share of speculations from my old school friend, Paul Finckel, also a reporter, over a quiet beer and a sandwich at the Exchange a few days later.

The fact that the judge had been found in women's underwear was bad enough in itself. There was no shortage of suggestions as to what colour the flimsy garments might have been. Pink and red were the firm favourites, although quite a few people stubbornly backed lime green. Yet in the end, the general consensus was that they were most likely black.

Who might have been with him in the hotel room was also the subject of intense speculation. Not a soul believed he'd been there alone.

One faction was convinced it must have been a man, since it was the judge himself who had been wearing women's clothes. But as nobody had ever heard the judge's name linked to the gay community, and as he was also married and a grandfather, if he did turn out to be gay, his cover as a closet queen was blown wide apart and no mistake. And who could say for certain that his putative partner didn't belong to the same group? If he did, the press tables weren't short of hunches as to who it might be but lacked any concrete proof.

Some were adamant that the judge had been having an affair for years with one of his female colleagues, and a whisper of hushed scandal ran through those present when the name was mentioned.

At tables with only male reporters a few women's names from their own inner circles were mentioned, among them a prominent journalist from one of the Oslo dailies and another, not quite so well known, from the Norwegian Broadcasting Corporation's *Today* programme.

Others merely shrugged their shoulders, suggesting that the judge had simply been there with a prostitute, male or female, who cared? Another half pint, please.

No one speculated any further as to the actual cause of death.

Most of them probably assumed it was heart-related.

Two

SHE WAS SITTING in the waiting room when I got back from the funeral.

It was one of those days in February of which there are far too many, even though it's the shortest month. February is a parenthesis in the year. The tax return has been handed in, the tourist season hasn't yet started, and there's nothing going on. Damp frost lay oppressively over snow-clad Bergen, pressing down so heavily that you could only just walk upright under the force of the depression. Greyish-brown slush lay in the gutters, and the mountains surrounding the city were barcly visible through a bank of fog so stubborn that it did not disperse even after gale warnings were forecast. Like the brass buttons on the waistcoat of an abandoned snowman, you could just make out the lights of the funicular railway running up the mountainside, and the street-lamps were lit even at midday.

The funeral hadn't exactly been a floorshow either. No one had danced on the coffin of Lasse Wiik, even though, at some of the darkest hours in my life, I could have imagined myself doing just that. But rather too many years had passed since Beate and I had parted company for the dcath of her new husband to make any deep impression on me now. And he wasn't all that new anyway. They'd been married since 1975, and she'd stuck it out a good deal longer with him than she had with me.

I stood right at the back of the queue of people offering their condolences after the burial. When I had given her a formal embrace and mumbled an apology, we stood there for a moment avoiding each other's eyes. – At least it was quick, I said. – He'd been on sick leave for almost a year, she countered.

Her face was the same, yet perhaps a little more pointed around the chin than before, almost like a caricature. – What were you thinking of doing now? I asked. Her eyes glanced past me down towards the lake, Store Lungegårdsvann, and the jagged silhouette of the tower blocks at Nedre Nygård. The large motorway intersection, completed in 1989, looked like some kind of vast instrument inadvertently left behind by a giant dentist. – I'm not really sure, actually … maybe just go back home. – Home? You mean … to Stavanger? – Yes …

I sidled up to Thomas and Mari, standing on the edge of a group of people I didn't know. – When are you two going back? I asked. – We're catching the night train this evening. There's a seminar I have to be at tomorrow, said Thomas. – Will the two of you have time to pop in for a minute before you leave? – His eyes flitted to his girlfriend. – That might be nice, actually. What are you going to do now? – I think there's going to be a little get-together for the immediate family…

February is a miserable month, the light as feeble as the will to do anything. Lasse Wiik had certainly chosen the right port to put to sea from. Winter still lay like a film over the fjord. Spring was only a distant hint of a life he, as a heart patient, couldn't fully participate in anyway. For a moment I almost envied him.

Then I'd formally taken leave of the mourners in their black clothes and strolled down to Møllendalsveien, where the car stood waiting for me, cold and chilly in keeping with the month. I drove into town, parked just around the corner from where I lived and walked down to the office. If I needed the car, it wouldn't take me more than ten minutes to walk back up again, and given the way the traffic patterns had developed in town over the last few years, it was in any case the best place to start from if you were driving anywhere.

I bought a couple of newspapers and almost dropped them in shock at finding someone sitting in my waiting room. Most people contacted me by phone, and those who came when I was out of the office rarely chanced waiting. The only conclusion was that it was something urgent.

As I came in, she quickly put aside the glossy magazine from 1974 and stood up. Seeing the magazine made me think I should perhaps consider paying a visit to the nearest antique bookseller and taking the whole lot with me. It might at least pay for some magazines from the nineties instead.

'Hello. The name's Veum,' I said, introducing myself. 'Were you waiting for me?'

'Well, I was hoping so. I mean, that you'd turn up.' She looked at me enquiringly but with a certain remoteness in her eyes. 'I'm Mrs Skagestøl.'

We shook hands, I opened the door to my office and ushered her inside. Her perfume smelled of lemons. She'd opted for a scent with an autumnal touch: a landscape you looked at from a distance in clear weather but never went walking in.

On entering my office she glanced quickly around. I motioned her towards the visitor's chair, asking whether I should put the kettle on for a cup of coffee.

'No thanks, that's – not necessary.'

I walked around the desk, sat down, opened the top drawer and took out a notebook and something to write with. For a few seconds we sat there looking at each other like two political opponents in a face-to-face encounter on TV thirty seconds before going on air.

She was in her early forties, fair-haired and wearing a waist-length brown and beige sports jacket, newly washed faded jeans and black ankle boots. She had a russet-coloured bag over her shoulder. Her face was distinctive, with arched light eyebrows, high cheekbones and a mouth that had lost the easy smile it once had, judging by the lines around her eyes. She was wearing discreet make-up and a simple gold chain around her thin neck.

She plaited her fingers and stretched out her arms, palms towards me: a fairly clear sign that she had no real desire to begin.

I pushed the notepad aside as though to give her a bit more confidence. 'I didn't catch ... your first name ... '

'Sidsel. With a "d".'

'And what can I do for you?'

Again her eyes had that hint of remoteness as she looked at me. 'I ... I never thought I'd find myself in a situation where I'd need to resort to the services of, er – somebody like yourself.'

'Let's call a spade a spade – you mean a private investigator.' I placed my hand on the left side of my chest and leaned back with a little smile. 'But in my heart of hearts I'm a sociologist.'

'Really? Is that your background?'

I nodded.

'I haven't told my husband that I ... In any case ... we're separated.'

'I see.'

'I don't really think he would ... Perhaps you've heard of him. Holger Skagestøl.'

'The journalist?'

'Yes, now he's – on the editorial board.'

'Oh, I see. Yes, I do know the name and who he is, but I don't think I've ever met him.'

'No, well ... ' She opened her handbag and fumbled for something before glancing round enquiringly. 'May I smoke?'

I opened the second drawer down and took out a little pottery ashtray Thomas had once made at school. 'Of course.'

'You don't smoke yourself, then?'

'No, I stick to the other vices.'

She gave a faint smile, put the cigarette in her mouth and lit it herself. 'I don't smoke much either. But ... '

'It wasn't to tell me this that you came, though, was it?'

She glanced at me surprised. 'No.'

Reassuringly, I nodded at her to continue.

'We have three children. Torild's sixteen, Vibeke fifteen and Stian's ten.'

'Mm. Is it about one of them perhaps?'

'Yes. Torild. That's with a "d".'

'A family tradition?'

She didn't even attempt a smile. 'Yes, you could say so.'

'And what's happened to her?'

She dragged nervously on her cigarette and exhaled as though intent on fumigating the room. 'She's disappeared. Hasn't been home for – nearly a week!'

'Oh?'

The fact that the cat was finally out of the bag also seemed to have loosened her tongue. 'I couldn't help noticing after we, well, after the separation, that she hasn't been, well, content, so to speak, but it's never, no, she has sometimes been a bit late home, but I've never waited up for her, till she came home, but last Thursday, I never went to bed at all, because she didn't come home!'

'Oh? Where was she?'

'Well, you see I thought that, but she hadn't been to school either, it turned out that she'd often been absent lately, without my knowledge. I ... Obviously, I thought she was at a friend's house, so I rang round, but she wasn't at any of those places either, not at any of them, so I thought, well, she'll come home when she's hungry, then it was evening, then night, and she just didn't come.'

'So what did you do?'

'Well, that Friday she wasn't supposed to be at school, in any case. It was an inset day. Then I called Holger.'

'And what did he say?'

'Well, obviously he started to ask me the same questions, whether I'd called this person or that, and why I hadn't let him know that she'd been in a bit of a strop, and that she might have a boyfriend ... '

'And might she?'

'Have a boyfriend?' She looked as though she scarcely knew what the word meant. 'Not a steady boyfriend. Not that I know of. But now I see that, well, then there are the others to look after as well, and it's not so easy, with all that happened with Holger and everything, it wasn't my fault that things went wrong!'

'No, I realise that.'

'Oh, how do you mean?'

'Well, I … But there is no boyfriend, is there?'

'Not as far as I know.'

'Have you asked her girlfriends about it too? They often know more than – '

'None of them has said anything at least!'

'Has she ever had anything to do with … Well … Drugs, alcohol, the police?'

'No, she … ' She glanced away momentarily. 'Well, of course, actually, there have been times when she's come home smelling of beer and it's a long time since she started to smoke.' She looked at her own cigarette with distaste; there was already only about half of it left.

'But I really can't say that she's ever been, well, drunk … '

'It doesn't sound all that unusual, alas. She's sixteen, you said?'

'Yes, her birthday was in January.'

'So she's in Class 9?'

'Yes. At Nattland School. We live in Furudalen, this side of Natland Mountain.'

'I see.' I had started taking notes.

She watched me write. 'The form teacher's name is Sandal. Helene Sandal.'

'Got it. Any particularly close girlfriends?'

'Well … Åsa.'

'Mm?'

She glanced at my notebook. 'Åsa Furebø. She and … her parents, they were friends of ours – of Holger and mine before … But it was Holger and Trond who were friends to begin with, so after … But I've met Randi in town, for a coffee, we talk to one another, she and I do, I mean.'

'And where do they live?'

'Down in … Birkelundsbakken. Not far from where the stave church was, before it was burnt down … '

'But you've talked to her, have you? To Åsa?'

'She was the first person I called.'

'And she didn't know anything either?'

'No, she wasn't at their place.'

'But … Thursday, Friday … That's nearly a week now.'

'Yes, I … At first I thought, well, the weekend, she'll surely come at the weekend, but then I thought, OK, school starts again on Monday, but … '

'Look, to be frank, a girl who's never been away like this before – or has she?'

'Torild? Been away? No, not like this.'

'Not – like this?'

'No, she's just come back late sometimes.'

'How late?'

'In the morning, but that's been from parties and I, well, she was grounded the first time but the next time, I mean, you can't lock young people in either, can you?'

'No, I don't suppose you can. Where had she been those times? Did the two of you talk about it?'

'No, I mean, yes, at discos and things, in town, and now and then at parties.'

'Recently – or before?'

'Er … Over the last year, in any case.'

'When she was still fifteen, in other words?'

'Yes!' There was a hint of irritation in her eyes now. 'You see, Holger wasn't often home till past midnight, that is, after he became responsible at work, as he so nicely put it, but who he was responsible for, search me, and in any case, I had the other two to think about, Vibeke's a completely different sort, much more homely in a way, and Stian, well, he's still little, and you just want to do the best you can for your children, don't you?'

'Yes, of course we do.'

———

'Do you – have … ?'

'Yes, a son. But he's grown up now.'

'And is he making out all right?'

'Yes. He's a student in Oslo.'

'Do you think you might be able to find her?'

'Er, I … But there's one thing I must ask you about … You have been in contact with the police, haven't you?'

'Yes, we … I mean … I got, Holger called from the office, every day, to find out whether anything had happened, you know, the way people do.'

'Yes, I understand, but – no proper investigation, then?'

'No, in the circumstances, Holger thought she was bound to turn up.'

'So you haven't talked to them?'

'To the police? – No.'

'But if your husband didn't want the police involved, how do you think he would react if I … '

'But you don't need to talk to him, do you?'

'Perhaps not to begin with, but … I can't guarantee it.'

'Just so long as you find her … Between Holger and me things are – well, whatever. It's not important.'

'I'll do my best, of course. After all, I do have a fair amount of training, especially in matters of this sort.'

She opened her handbag again. 'How much will it … '

'The bill? Er … Look, you haven't said anything about yourself. Do you have a job?'

'No, not any more. But I'm a kindergarten teacher by training, so I mean, I should *know*, shouldn't !?'

'About children, you mean?'

'Mm.' She nodded.

'But you never do, do you? Children are like adults, just even less predictable, that's all.'

She took out a chequebook. 'How much shall I put?'

'If it takes a few days, it'll soon mount up to five or six thousand kroner.'

I noticed her eyes widen ever so slightly. 'But look … Just put two thousand, as an advance. If we're lucky, that may cover it.'

She started writing out the cheque, tore it off and pushed it across the table to me, accompanied by a cheque card. I looked at the photo. Her hair had been longer then, and her cheekbones not quite so pronounced. But I made no comment.

I gave the card back to her. 'You don't have a photo of her, do you?'

'Yes, of course, I brought … ' She produced a page torn out of a newspaper and gave it to me with a slightly apologetic look. 'It was Stian who sent it in.'

I looked at the page. It was one of those congratulations columns which most newspapers have had for the past few years now, where you send in a photo of the person to whom you want to wish many happy returns, often with couplets that would make even the humblest occasional poet seem like a literary genius.

In this case the text was fairly sober: *Many Happy Returns on her Sixteenth Birthday to our big sister TORILD, from the little trolls Vibeke and Stian.* The photo showed a stern-faced girl looking straight at the camera in a photo booth.

'This is the most recent one we have,' said Sidsel Skagestøl apologetically.

'What colour is her hair?'

'Fair. But darker than mine.'

'And what's she like, otherwise?'

'She's rather slim, but … ' She blushed slightly, 'but quite shapely.'

After she'd gone, I remained sitting there for a while, looking at the little picture in the newspaper. There was no hint of shapely curves here, yet her look was confident enough, as if nobody was going to tell her how the pyramids were built, who Vasco da Gama was or the formula for ferrous sulphate.

I glanced out of the window. It was already getting dark. It struck me that February was a dangerous month to be wandering about alone, especially when you were barely sixteen and nobody was going to tell you what to do.

Just as I was on my way out of the door the telephone rang.

I went back to my desk, lifted the receiver and said: 'Yes. Hello?'

There was no reply.

'Hello? Veum speaking.'

Still no answer. But very faintly, almost like background interference, I could just make out … What was it? A sort of digital organ music?

'Hello?' I said again irritably.

And the tune … There was something familiar about it …

It was … 'Abide With Me' … Like at a funeral.

'Hello?' I said, a bit more cautiously this time as though the call was coming direct from the chapel. 'Is anyone there?'

But there was still no reply. Then the connection was cut off.

Three

THE FUREBØ FAMILY lived in a semi-detached house in that part of Birkelundsbakken where you never know what gear to be in when you're driving there. The woman who opened the front door was thickset, about five foot ten, with dark, short-cropped hair. Her face was round, her eyes brown, and she had worry lines at the corners of her mouth.

'Yes? We don't want any, if that's –'

'Mrs Furebø?'

She nodded. She was wearing a brown skirt, a light-green blouse and a reddish-brown, loose suede waistcoat. Behind her, I could see into a bright hall with yellow walls.

'The name's Veum. I'm a private investigator. I've been hired by Sidsel Skagestøl to try and find her daughter, Torild, and in connection with that, I'd like to have a word with – Åsa.'

'You mean she hasn't turned up yet? Sidsel called me … It was …'

'Last Thursday, I think.'

'Yes.' She looked at me sceptically. 'Do you have any identification?'

I gave her my driving licence. She fingered it as though it was a counterfeit note. 'Doesn't say anything here about a – private investigator.'

'No. But I can give you some numbers you can ring for references.'

She handed my driving licence back to me. 'No, I'm sure it's OK. But Åsa's not at home just now.'

I glanced at the clock. It was twenty past four. 'But … she's not still at school?'

'No. Trond, my husband, collected her from school. They – had an errand to do together.'

'When are you expecting them back, then?'

'Well, er ... '

She didn't reply. A white Mercedes swung into the drive and parked on the far side of the small lawn. The ignition was switched off, and a young girl opened the door and emerged from the passenger side. At the wheel I glimpsed a thin face beneath a silver-grey yet boyish quiff of hair.

The girl was very pretty with dark silky hair and naturally red lips. She was slim, wearing jeans and a very expensive burgundy leather jacket. Over her shoulder she had a light-brown satchel and was wearing white trainers. Yet she didn't move like a sporty type, more like a jaded office girl. Her blue eyes registered the fact that I was there but with no hint of curiosity.

'But ... ' I heard Randi Furebø mutter just behind me.

The other door slammed. A thin wiry man came towards us. He was wearing grey flannels, a brightly coloured pullover and an open beige windcheater. The youthfulness of the face was emphasised by prematurely greying hair as though he had once experienced the shock of a deep loss. The look he gave me was a good deal more inquisitive than the girl's.

'Here they come,' said Randi Furebø.

The girl walked straight past us and into the hail with nothing but a curt *Hi* to her mother, who followed her with a rather unfathomable look before glancing at me with a hint of resignation: *Teenagers* ...

The man stopped in front of me.

She said: 'Trond, this is Veum, he's a sort of private investigator, and –'

His face turned beetroot. 'What?! But we've just been down there now! Everything's sorted. All over and done with.'

'I don't quite follow,' I started to say.

'We've taken the leather jacket back, and *I've* bought her a new one myself!'

'Yes, I noticed,' said Randi Furebo.

'The manageress said she was more than happy with that solution. So she said there was no reason to contact the police.'

'But *that's* not why he's here, Trond!'

'Isn't it?'

'It's about Torild! She still hasn't come back … '

'Oh?' He relaxed visibly.

'Look Veum,' she said, 'this was something quite different; certainly just a misunder –'

'No need to go into the details,' Furebø interrupted, 'if that's not what it was about.'

He turned back to me. 'Sidsel's already talked to Åsa before. I doubt if there's anything else we can tell you.'

'But your daughter and Torild were best friends, weren't they?'

'Best friends … They've gone to the same school since the first form, and her parents and us have met socially for many years, her father and I are colleagues, but maybe you ought to ask –' His words tailed off.

'That's just what I was thinking.'

He glanced at his wife again.

'We must *help* him, Trond! Poor Sidsel, she must be going out of her mind. And when I didn't even … '

'Yes, yes … ' He turned to look at me. 'But not unless we're there too.'

'Oh, I see.'

I clearly didn't seem over-keen, as he quickly added: 'It's up to you. Either you talk to her with us present or not at all!'

'OK, thanks for the offer.' I glanced in the direction of the door. 'Well, perhaps we can … '

'Yes.'

Randi Furebø held the door open, and he walked in ahead of me.

'Can you fetch her? We can talk to him down here.' He ushered me into a door on the right. I entered a little TV room with a worn leather suite, family pictures on the walls, a bookshelf with a rather random collection of books and a small fireplace with a log basket and a pile of newspapers beside it. It felt cool and airless, with a slight hint of whitewash.

After hanging up his jacket out in the hall Furebø followed me in.

I turned to face him. 'So does that mean you're a journalist as well?'

'No, I work in graphics. In other words, I'm involved in how the newspaper looks.'

'I see. You're the one who makes conflicts into wars and collisions into catastrophes, at least where the presentation's concerned?'

His look suggested he'd heard this one a thousand times before. 'Wrong,' he said sharply. What he reminded me of most was a football trainer meeting the press in the dressing room just after his team has lost the cup. 'Those choices are made a few rungs higher up the ladder.'

'By people like Holger Skagestøl perhaps?'

'For example.'

Someone cleared their throat at the door, and Randi Furebø pushed her daughter in front of her into the room. 'Here we are – this is the man who'd like to talk to you, Åsa.'

She shook off her mother's arm without speaking.

I smiled and put out my hand. 'Hello, Åsa! The name's Varg. Varg Veum.'*

Trond Furebø stifled a snort.

She shook my hand correctly but almost without any strength in her grip. 'Hello.'

She stood there in front of me, looking nonplussed. She had taken off her leather jacket, and the white blouse did its best to camouflage the shape of her young breasts.

---

* *Translator's note*: In Norwegian, 'varg' means 'wolf' as well as 'miscreant' or 'culprit'. There is also a pun on his full name in Norwegian: Varg Veum as the expression 'varg i veum' means 'persona non grata' 'outlaw' or 'pariah'.

I took a step sideways and glanced down at the sofa, but no one suggested we should sit down.

Furebø looked at the clock, and his wife said: 'Yes, supper's ready.'

'It won't take long. You know what it's about, don't you, Åsa?'

She nodded.

'Your friend Torild. She's been absent from home since last Thursday. Have you any idea where she might be?'

She shook her head. 'No.'

'No idea at all?'

She shook her head again but this time without a word.

'Is she friendly with some boy or has she a boyfriend she doesn't want her parents to know about?'

She looked down. 'No.'

'Are you sure?'

She raised her eyes again. 'Nobody she's told me about anyway!'

'Quite sure about that, are you?'

'Look here, Veum,' Furebø broke in, 'if we're going to repeat every single question at least twice, this is going to take an awful long time!'

'Perhaps you two could just go up and start, if you're in such a hurry. Start supper, I mean.'

His face darkened. 'Like I said outside, Veum! You had two choices!'

'It's in the oven,' said his wife reassuringly.

He shot her a look of irritation but said nothing.

'That's OK, Åsa. I believe what you say. Just tell me, though … Have you and Torild spent much time together recently?'

She glanced sideways. 'No more than usual.'

'And what does that mean?'

'Oh, a few evenings a week.'

'And what do you two do then?'

'Oh… Sit at home talking. Go into town to see a film. Stuff like that.'

'Stuff like that. What else?'

'Oh … Go for a hamburger maybe. If we have any money.' A veiled glance at her father. 'Just walk around and check things out, look in clothes shops, record shops, places like that.'

'Down town, in other words?'

'Sure. There's nothing going on up here!'

'Just the two of you?'

'No, there are almost always some other girls too.'

'Who, for instance?'

'Oh, various people we know, girls from our class or some we know from before, from Guides and stuff.'

'Are you a Guide?'

'Not any more.'

'Nor am I, a Scout I mean.'

She looked at me without interest. 'So it's just girls, then?'

'No. We do sometimes meet up with a few of the boys.'

'The ones in your class?'

'No, well … they're so daft!'

'Older boys, then?'

'Yes.'

'But you girls know them, do you?'

'You do get to know people, don't you?'

'Well enough to know their names?'

She shrugged. 'Some of them, I suppose?'

'And where they live?' She thought about this one.

'Maybe.' Her mother fidgeted uncomfortably. Her father looked on with pursed lips. But neither of them said anything. 'Was it any of these – older boys that Torild was going out with?'

She looked ahead vacantly. 'Not that I've noticed.'

'But she *could* have been?'

She shrugged again. 'Mm, well … maybe.'

'What milieu were they from, these boys?'

'Milieu?'

'Yes, I mean, were they from school or – ?'

'Some of them go to The Cat School,' she blurted out.

18

'And the others?'

'There are a couple of them who go to the Tech. And others who don't go to school.'

'Unemployed?'

'Dunno. Haven't asked them. Are we done now?'

'I think so,' her father said. 'It doesn't look as though we're going to get much further.'

I glanced at Åsa. 'You can't think of anything at all that might help us to find Torild, can you?'

She shook her head silently.

'She's never mentioned taking off anywhere? To Oslo? Or Copenhagen?'

'No way! Where would she get the money for that from?'

'Oh, I don't know … She could hitchhike … It doesn't cost all that much … '

'Åsa's strictly forbidden to hitchhike!' said her mother sharply.

'Anyway, she's never mentioned anything like that!' Åsa broke in.

'In that case … ' I scribbled my name and phone number onto my notepad, tore it off and gave it to her. 'If you think of anything, please get in touch. That is, unless you talk to her mother directly.'

She took the piece of paper and put it into her pocket without looking at it.

As she was walking towards the door, I said: 'Bye!'

'Bye,' she mumbled and went out, leaving the door wide open.

Randi Furebø gestured vaguely, pulling a face that showed she was not sure what to do next, looked up at the ceiling and said: 'Mm, supper calls I think.'

We nodded a curt goodbye.

Trond Furebø accompanied me to the door. Before stepping outside, I turned to face him. 'It might be an idea if you and your wife had a word about these things with Åsa. Could be she'd be more open with you two.'

He did not reply.

'If that was so, I'd be grateful if you contacted me.'

He gave a curt dismissive nod.

'That business with the leather jacket ... '

'I said it was no concern of yours, Veum!'

'But it –'

'So long!'

We stood for a moment eye to eye. But he clamped his lips tight shut, and I saw that it would take physical violence to prise any more out of him about the matter.

As soon as I had stepped through the door it was slammed so hard behind me that I felt the rush of air on the back of my neck.

Before driving back home I made a detour along Sædalsveien and up to Furudalen.

The address took some finding. It was a large, dark, wooden detached house, which towered up on the edge of a rather steep uncultivated site, with a terrace on the side that did not get much sun on a late winter's afternoon but clearly had a very favourable situation from May to September.

The entrance was at the back, and Sidsel Skagestøl must have seen me from a window as she opened the door before I had time to ring the bell. 'Yes? Have you found out something already?'

'No, unfortunately, but I have talked to Åsa and just have a couple more questions.'

'Oh?' She half-closed the door behind her. 'Vibeke and Stian are home. Do you mind if we deal with it out here?'

'No, no ... It's just whether you can give me the names of any other close friends of Torild's besides Åsa?'

'Any others? No, I don't know ... There are some, of course, but none I thought was – closer.'

'You can't think of any names?'

'I can give you a list, of course, but I'd have to sit down and think about it. Can it wait till tomorrow?'

I nodded. 'The other question was ... It's perhaps a bit awkward.

But ... you haven't noticed whether Torild has come home wearing particularly expensive clothes recently, have you?'

'Particularly expensive clothes! You surely don't mean that – ?'

'I'm just asking.'

She looked at me slightly puzzled. 'But at least I think I can give you a fairly clear answer to that one. No, I haven't noticed it at all. And I *would* have noticed it! All her clothes are bought by me, or by both of us actually, together, unless it's just a pair of jeans or something like that which she can get herself. But apart from that ... no, nothing.'

'Fine.'

'But why do you ask?'

'Oh, I just had the impression there'd been – an episode ... Between Åsa and *her* parents.'

'Åsa! I'd never have thought so.'

'No. Well, that was all there was, actually. Unless you've thought of something else?'

'No, unfortunately not.'

'I'd thought of calling in at the school tomorrow, in fact. Could I pop by to collect the list while I'm up there?'

'I could make sure I'm in. About what time?'

'Sometime between ten and twelve?'

'Fine.' She stood there with one hand on the door catch. With the other she grasped my shoulder. 'I hope you find her!'

'So do I.'

She opened the door, and then she gave me a faint smile before disappearing back into the house.

I found my own way back to the car and drove home.

◆

Thomas rang at about half past eight asking whether he and Mari could call by on their way down to the station.

That gave us barely an hour; hardly time for a cup of tea and a glass of beer together. We didn't mention the funeral or Stavanger at all. I didn't know how much Beate had told them of her plans.

Afterwards I walked down with them and stood on the platform chatting until the train was just about to leave. When the light-brown sleeping car began to move and slid slowly past me they bent down to the window and waved.

As I left the station, I passed a group of teenage girls walking through the waiting room each clutching a bottle of Coke, a cigarette dangling from their mouths. The way at least two of them were walking suggested they'd mixed the Coke with something much stronger.

Children come and go. Before you know where you are they've grown up and flown the nest. Some over a period of time: others in the blink of an eye. Some take the train to the capital: others just take the bus into town. But the general direction is the same. They go away, and the parents are left behind wondering what actually happened. Or they contact someone like me to find out why.

Four

THE NEXT DAY there was a sharp frost in the air, greeting you first thing with a cold damp embrace.

The car had scarcely had time to get properly warmed up before I parked at Nattland School and stepped out. The squat school building stood at the end of the narrow valley linking Sædalen to Sandalsbotn, and February had etched its black and white runes into the steep slope opposite. The roads up here had names like Mars Way and Mercury Way as though they were expecting visitors from another planet in the solar system and had done all they could to make them feel at home.

It was break-time, and in the playground it was easy to tell the primary from the secondary school pupils. The former were absorbed in games; the latter prowled about circling one another, the girls arm-in-arm, the boys with their hands thrust as deep as possible into their pockets.

I found my way to the teachers' common room and enquired after Helene Sandal.

A brunette in her thirties, her face slightly marked by acne, wearing oval glasses, a red sweater and jeans, came out to the door.

I introduced myself and told her what it was about.

She nodded solemnly. 'Come on in.' She glanced in through an open door leading into a small office. 'We can go in here.'

The office contained a desk, two chairs and a phone. Beside the desk stood a bundle of about thirty exercise books for marking.

'It's Torild's mother who's hired me,' I explained.

'I see.'

'My background's in child care, so I've been involved in cases of this kind before.'

She glanced at the clock. 'How can I help?'

'First, I'd like your opinion of Torild, as a pupil and as – a person.'

She pursed her lips indicating that she was thinking about it. 'Well, she's changed.'

'How long have you been her form teacher?'

'Since Class 7. Nearly three years.'

'And ... '

'It's an important time in a young person's life, of course. You know this as well as I do. But ... ' She looked at me, hesitating. 'I don't know if Mrs Skagestøl told you about the situation at home?'

'Yes, she did. I know about it. Was Torild affected by it?'

'It's rather hard to say. I did have the feeling she was on the slippery slope before this happened.'

'What do you mean by on the *slippery slope* exactly?'

'Well, er ... when she came into Class 7 she was just an ordinary twelve-year-old girl, in the upper half of the class academically, no doubt about that, cheerful and happy – as I said, absolutely normal. In Class 8 ... It's quite a tricky transition. That's the year when kids with a tendency to get fed up of school do so with a vengeance. Primary school is behind them for good. The teachers demand more of them. But at the same time, there aren't really any important exams, and the end of Class 9, when they're fourteen or fifteen, seems so far away. I don't mean to say that Torild herself was fed up of school. She did her homework conscientiously, the written work at least. I had the impression they kept a good eye on her at home. But her oral work sometimes left a bit to be desired. What was more worrying was the impression that she – how shall I put it? – switched off? She was inattentive in class, and she ... Often I could tell from the look in her eyes that she was miles away.' She glanced out of the window. 'She would just sit there, looking out of the window.'

I followed her gaze. The trees in the valley leading down towards Sandalen were white with hoar frost. There was something permanent and unchanging about the view as though time had stopped and the frost would stay forever.

'I suppose you're all trained in … Did you have the impression she was taking drugs?'

She nodded gently. 'I wouldn't rule it out.'

'Did you inform her parents about it?'

'Yes. I had a talk with her mother.'

'Not with her father?'

'No. He couldn't spare the time.'

'Did anything change afterwards?'

'Things improved for a bit, maybe. She seemed to pull herself together. But then … it started again.'

'And did you have another word with her parents?'

'Yes, but … This time only by phone. After all, there's a limit to how much time I can give to each pupil. There are others, for example, who have far more problems with their schoolwork. And there are others with shaky family situations. We have a few immigrant children, and a child who's physically disabled but integrated. In other words … '

A school bell rang. She stood up. 'I have to go now. Was there anything else?'

'Yes, absolutely. Can you spare me a few more minutes?'

'OK, then.' She remained standing, to indicate that she couldn't spare many minutes.

'I just wanted to know … Did she have any close friends, any who might have influenced her; were there others you noticed with the same attitude?'

Her face hardened slightly. 'I can't be as explicit about others without their parents' permission.'

'I've already talked to Åsa Furebø. I got the impression they knocked about together a lot.'

'Yes. That's right, I think.'

'Were there other girls?'

'Astrid, perhaps. Astrid Nikolaisen.'

'What's she like?'

'As I said, I can't … But … ' She pointed at her wristwatch. 'Must dash.'

'Would it be possible for you to get Åsa and Astrid down here? So I could talk to them?'

'Åsa, maybe. Astrid's absent today.'

'Oh? Has she been absent for a few days?'

'Yesterday as well. All this week,' she said dryly.

'Torild wasn't at school either the day she disappeared. Was that something that happened often?'

'Sometimes. But she always brought a note afterwards.' With a bitter smile she added: 'But it turned out they were forged, according to what I've just heard.'

'I see. Is it OK for me to use this office?'

She looked around. 'If no one else is using it … Sure, all right. If you hang on, I'll get Åsa to come along.' With a quick nod, she left.

I stood waiting in the doorway.

The teachers' common room was practically empty. In the corner of a sofa sat a young man in a flannel check shirt and brown cords reading *Dagen*, a daily. On the tables lay a scattering of periodicals and a few more daily newspapers. The tables were decorated with small embroidered runners with an unlit square candle in the middle, and at the corner of one of them stood a hastily abandoned cup of coffee. For all I knew it might be Helene Sandal's.

The man reading the Christian daily scowled in my direction as though suspecting I might be a Russian secret agent who had sneaked into the school, pockets stuffed with condoms to start an all-out campaign targeted at the young impressionable souls.

There was a knock, the door leading into the corridor opened, and Åsa came in, her face full of curiosity. When she saw who it was, she couldn't conceal her disappointment.

'Hello again, Åsa!' I said with affected cheerfulness like the social worker I had once been.

She glanced at the teacher in the corner as though hoping he might release her from this embarrassing situation.

'I was thinking … There were perhaps a few things it might be easier for you to talk about without your parents present.'

'Oh?'

'Come on in here – we can sit down … '

'Can't I refuse?'

I paused before replying. 'Why would you want to do that?'

'Well, er … '

'Do you have anything to hide, then?'

'Like what?'

'You don't? Could there be any other reason for not answering my questions?'

She flopped down in the chair and sat there slouching, half turned away, which was certainly not going to do her back any good if it became a habit.

'I'm thinking of – what I asked you yesterday. You can be frank with me, Åsa. I won't repeat a word of it to your parents. All I need is information that can help me find out what's happened to Torild.'

She shot me a hostile look. 'Oh really?'

'So … When did you last see her?'

She sat there open-mouthed. 'When did I see her last? – It was the day we … She … ' She changed her mind.

'Well?'

'The day before she went missing.'

'Last Wednesday?'

'Yes, that's right, I think.'

'Where was it you saw her?'

'Where? How do you mean?'

'OK, let me put it like this, then … What were the two of you doing?'

She shrugged. 'We – went into town. Wandered about like we usually do.'

'I see. Do you remember where you went?'

'Mm, no … Nowhere in particular.'

'Not to the cinema?'

'No.'

'Did you go for a Coke somewhere?'

'No, I don't think so.'

'If you went for a Coke, where might that have been?'

'I don't know … Burger King … Or some other snack bar.'

'But you can't remember where it was?'

'No.'

'Were there just you two or were other people there?'

'Other people.'

'Who?'

'Er …'

'Was Astrid there?'

'Astrid Nikolaisen?'

'Yes.'

'Might have been.'

'Did you two spend a lot of time with her?'

'A lot of time?'

'Why do you want to know? Has Helene said something?'

'Like what?'

'Erm … '

'Do you know why Astrid isn't at school today?'

She snickered suddenly. 'It's not the first time.'

'The first time what?'

'She comes to school when it suits her.'

'Oh really? I see.'

'No, you don't!'

'Maybe not. What is it I don't see, then?'

She looked at me defiantly, without answering.

'Did you two go home together? You and Torild, I mean.'

'No, we … I went home earlier.'

'Was there a time you were supposed to be back by?'

'Yes. Ten-thirty.'

'And what did she do then?'

'I don't kn … I don't remember.'

'Really?'

'No!'

'And are you sure it was Wednesday and not – Thursday?'

'Y-yes, I think so', she said, glancing away.

I tried another tack. 'That business with the leather jacket, that your father –'

'Well, what about it?'

'Was it one you'd – stolen?'

Her gaze looked shifty, and her lips moved wordlessly as though rehearsing what she was going to say. Finally all she said was: 'Yes.'

'Was that something you lot were in the habit of doing?'

'No! Not expensive stuff like that anyway.'

'Just pilfering?'

'Doesn't everybody do that?'

'Do they?'

'Christ, are you thick or something? If you heard – !'

'What happened at home?'

'Oh … I was daft enough to take it home. I could always have left it … '

'Left it?'

'Yeah!'

'Where?'

She didn't answer.

'OK. So your parents found out about it. And then … '

She hesitated. 'My dad … he went crazy. Said I had to take it back, that we had to go back to that shop and tell them what I'd done, and then … Well, that's what we did.'

'Which shop was it?'

'The Leather Centre.'

'And he bought you a new one?'

She nodded. 'Mm.'

'As a sort of reward?'

'Yes, just imagine! A reward for going along with him of my own free will, for telling what happened, and because he ... he understood that I needed one, I suppose!'

'A new leather jacket?'

'Yeah!'

'I see ... '

'Oh yeah – ?' But this time she cut herself off. 'Is that all?'

'Not quite.'

I paused, and she looked at me impatiently. 'I have to get back to my lesson!'

I gave a faint smile as though it was the first time I'd heard a secondary school pupil say this. 'It *was* Thursday, wasn't it? The last time you saw her.'

She blushed. 'Must have been, I suppose!' She stood up and walked towards the door. Without turning around she added: 'If you say so!'

She tried to slam the door behind her, but its hinges were too stiff. It just slid to with a quiet sigh like a form teacher full of resignation.

Five

SIDSEL SKAGESTØL opened the door quickly as though thinking it was Torild who had rung the bell.

When she saw who it was, she stepped aside. 'Come in.' She looked at me questioningly. 'You haven't … ?'

'No, alas. Still nothing concrete. I – '

'Oh my God, I'm so scared, Veum! Where can she be?'

'That's what we must try and find out.'

'Yes … Of course. Forgive me.'

'I understand you completely. Don't get me wrong.'

She was wearing jeans and a white blouse, only the collar and cuffs visible under the ribbed blue woollen sweater. Her hair was light and fluffy as though she'd just washed and blow-dried it, and she moved across the floor with a sort of girlish elegance, a mixture of shyness and sensuality.

She pointed to a coat rack. 'You can hang your coat up there.'

I did as she said, followed her through the L-shaped hall, past the door into the kitchen, which looked out onto the back of the house, and came into a large, open-plan living room as luxuriously furnished as a showroom in a furniture store. A plum-coloured leather suite occupied the space in front of the picture windows facing south and east, while a dining table and chairs in dark-brown oak was the focal point at the other end of the room, just in front of the door to the kitchen. In the centre of the room there was also an L-shaped sofa and three chairs, all in dark-green material, set around a low black coffee table. The fact that the room didn't seem too full gives some indication of its size, and there was still plenty of floor space for the children to play. Just now the place was as spick-and-span as an operating theatre.

Cheerful morning sounds poured forth from a radio in the centre of a large dark wall unit. She had set the coffee table for two. 'I've made a couple of sandwiches, and the kettle is on. I'm just going to make the coffee, so … if you'd like some?'

'Yes please.'

'There are – some papers … ' She pointed to the two Bergen newspapers that lay folded up beside the white coffee service as though she was my secretary and had prepared lunch for the boss.

I leafed through one of the papers, while she was in the kitchen making the coffee. There had been a drugs raid in Møhlenpris, and two fifteen-year-olds had robbed a post office in Åsane at three-thirty the previous day. The raid had resulted in ten people being charged with possession of various amounts of drugs, mainly hash and tablets. The two fifteen-year-olds had been arrested an hour and a half later, having spent only eighty kroner on hamburgers and Cokes at a roadside café. Two new cases of AIDS had been registered in Bergen over the previous year, both in drug circles, and the health authorities stressed that heterosexuals had no cause to feel safer than homosexuals on that score.

So the cartoons were a lot more fun.

Sidsel Skagestøl came back in carrying a white coffee pot in one hand and a small dish with open sandwiches in the other. She put the dish down and poured out coffee for us both after I'd declined the offer of brandy in mine.

For a moment we sat in silence. Then she nodded in the direction of the dish. 'Help yourself.'

'Thanks.' I took one with a brown goat's cheese and beetroot topping. 'You haven't heard anything from her, I take it?'

'No, I haven't … And you? Have you – managed to have a word with anyone?'

I nodded. 'Åsa and her parents and Helene Sandal.'

'And … has anyone said anything?'

'So far I've more questions than answers.'

'Such as … '

'That list we talked about last time, of her friends. Have you made one?'

She looked past me, towards one of the shelves in the wall unit, where there was a collection of family photos. 'No, I … When I started going through the list of her class, it dawned on me that – I didn't know. If it had been a few years ago, at primary school, I could have given you five or six names straight away. When she was in the Guides. And a few more besides. But now … It suddenly occurred to me how little I knew her, in that way. I mean – who she spent her time with. Actually, I don't know of anyone apart from Åsa.'

'What about a girl called Astrid Nikolaisen?' I asked, taking a bite of the open sandwich.

'… Astrid Nikolaisen … Er … For me she's nothing but a name. She's never been here. I know she's one of Torild's friends from her class, I mean, since she started in Class 7 when she was twelve, but … I don't think there's any more I can tell you.'

I swallowed my food. 'Do you have her address, by any chance?'

She glanced at the wall unit. 'Yes, I think it's in the class list … But why … ?'

'Listen, Sidsel … Is it all right if I call you by your first name?'

She nodded.

'Helene Sandal suggested that Torild may sometimes have looked as if she was on drugs … '

She reached out for her coffee cup then changed her mind. 'Oh, that … It was never … We never got to the bottom of that.'

'But she called the two of you in to a meeting.'

'Yes. But only I went.'

'Your husband … '

She pursed her lips slightly. 'Holger was busy. It was in the evening anyway, and he was usually working late.'

'But it didn't lead to anything?'

'No.'

'Did you speak to Torild about it afterwards?'

'Of course! But she consistently denied it. She said it was just something Miss Sandal had dreamed up because she didn't like her. Or because she wasn't satisfied with her schoolwork. I couldn't … ' She looked at me with her large blue eyes. 'I couldn't *force* an answer out of her, could I?'

'Did she call you again later?'

'Yes, she did, and we got the same lecture as before, with the same results.'

'Didn't all this make you suspicious?'

'Suspicious? I was anxious, obviously! After all, you had … You obviously know what it's like yourself. Waiting up at night wondering whether she'll come home or not, where she is, who she's with. Thinking the worst, as we always do in such circumstances … I can't count the times I've seen her in my mind's eye, bleeding, beaten up, victim of a rape or a car crash.'

'And when she does finally get back, you're so pleased nothing's happened that you forgive her for being late, that she smells of beer and cigarettes, and that you've no idea where she's been. Because when you ask, she just replies … "Here and there."'

'Different places, you mean?'

'Yes. A party. Disco. Hamburger joint.'

'No pattern?'

'No. And you think of her when she was little, how happy you were when she was born – she was the first, after all! – the clothes you got for her, the first shoes, the gold lacquer ones over there on the shelf … '

I glanced over at them. They were no larger than a doll's.

'All these photos – I must have at least twenty albums altogether, Veum! The first day at nursery school, then at primary school, always happy and smiling, but then … Her confirmation last year, when she insisted on a civil ceremony, and Holger was so cross he hardly spoke to her for six months. You can almost see it in the picture we took. The flash of defiance in her face. Triumphant defiance.'

She stood up, walked over to the bookshelves, picked up the photograph and stood there for a moment looking at it, before she brought it over to me. As I examined it, she fetched two more and sat down beside me.

'Look at this', she said, holding one of them up. It showed a girl three or four years old, with blonde, slightly curly hair and a little summer dress with flowers on it, taken on a bench in a park somewhere with her small legs sticking straight out in the air and such a happy smile that you could almost hear her gurgling with laughter. 'That's how she was then. And here … '

In the next picture she was older, about ten or eleven, wearing a Guides uniform, looking slightly more self-conscious perhaps, her hair a touch darker, but with just as big a smile.

'But then … ' She pointed at the photograph I had in my hands. It showed a serious-looking young woman, with short scruffy hair, with no hint of a smile around her sullen lips and a darkness in her eyes that had not been present in the other photographs.

The three stages of childhood, like in a painting by Edvard Munch. And in the last one, she was already almost an adult.

I helped myself to another sandwich. 'I think I asked you this yesterday, but … She hasn't had any boyfriends yet, has she?'

She blushed slightly as though the word awakened unpleasant memories. 'She's never had … I don't know, do they still call it a steady date?'

'Goodness knows. But at least *you and I* speak the same language.'

'I suppose she must have had her crushes like everyone else – but she's never mentioned them here at home.'

'Didn't she confide in her mother?'

A hint of coldness flashed in her eyes. 'No, fancy that – she didn't.'

'So we can't come up with any names, can we?'

She shook her head.

'Did I understand correctly, on my visit to Åsa's house, that they'd been in the Guides together?'

'Yes they were, right from Brownies up to Class 7 or 8. Then they both suddenly packed it in.'

'Any idea why?'

'No. They just said they were fed up of it. That they'd grown out of it.'

'Maybe I could talk to one of the Guides leaders from that time?'

'I can't imagine it has anything to do with – with all *that!*'

'No … probably not. But is there a name you could give me?'

'Of one of the Guide leaders? Er … The one we had most to do with in the last years was called … what was it now? Yes, I've got it! Sigrun Søvik.'

I noted down the name. 'And Astrid Nikolaisen's address – do you have that?'

She nodded, stood up, went across to the wall unit again and pulled out a drawer. She leafed through a pile of papers before taking out a photocopy and bringing it over to me. 'This should be this year's.'

I looked at the class list, running my eyes quickly down the names until I got to Astrid Nikolaisen. I glanced up. 'I couldn't keep it for a bit, could I? In case any other names turn up?'

'Do you expect them to?' she asked anxiously, as if she'd suddenly started to wonder whether I was keeping anything back from her.

'It's just so I don't have to bother you each time I – '

'You're not bothering me! I'm paying for it, aren't I?'

'Yes, if it comes to that … But … ' I held the list up, repeating the question with my eyes.

'Of course you can keep it! – I've got last year's anyway. There aren't many changes.'

I drained my cup of coffee. 'Anything else I should know?'

She shot a glance at me. 'Like what, for example?'

'Oh, I … How long have you and your husband been separated?'

'Since August. It was during the summer holidays that things finally fell apart.'

'Classic.'

'Not how you think. We made the mistake of never going on holiday together. There was a lot of trouble down at the paper, as you'll no doubt remember, blank pages and things, so he couldn't go anywhere before school started again. And by that time we were already … Then eventually he took a week in London, or wherever it was, on his own, and when he got back home … ' She shrugged her shoulders. 'Things like this don't happen overnight anyway. They build up like a thunderstorm.'

'And Torild was out at sea, in an open boat?'

She looked at me perplexed. 'What?'

'What I mean is … how did she take it? Did she react in any particular way?'

She gazed wistfully ahead. 'No, I … Well, as I said yesterday, I suppose she did become a bit more distant. It was as though she'd opted out from what was left of family life. She went out more in the evenings, never brought anyone home and … would come home late herself.'

'The other children … did they react in the same way?'

'No, that was it.' She shifted her gaze to the window and looked out.

When she looked at me again, you could see the fear in her eyes. She held her clenched fist against her breast. 'Of course, you do ask yourself, when things like this happen: is it my, or our, fault? Where did we go wrong? But the others have had just the same upbringing! Stian, well he's only ten, so I mean … He's completely dependent on his mummy and daddy. As for Vibeke, she's managing fine – she's registered the situation and is doing just as well at school as ever. So what can the reason be?'

I threw up my hands. 'Genes. Environment, and here I'm not necessarily thinking of the home environment. People who became her friends. The teachers. There's an incredible number of possible influences. So the guilt can very seldom be laid at any one door. There are always several different factors at work.'

―――――

She nodded. 'Yes, I suppose there are.'

'And what about your husband, have you spoken to him today?'

'Yes, I speak to him every day now about all this.'

'Have you told him about me?'

'No, yes … He's started to say that we … That the police should be involved.'

'I can quite understand that.'

'But you said yourself – '

'Let me put it like this. The police have something I don't have – a whole apparatus. In other words, they can put out a general call over their entire network, to the other Scandinavian countries as well, with a cover I could never even begin to approach. On the other hand … Before it's been established that something serious has happened, the police will seldom have time to conduct the sort of detailed investigation I'm engaged in now.'

'So … '

'I would absolutely advise you to get the police to investigate her disappearance but let me carry on with what I'm already doing. That is, unless you two want to save yourselves the expense.'

'The money's no problem,' she said quickly. 'What's important is to find her and that … she's all right.'

'I ought to speak to your husband himself at some point.'

'If he has time,' she said somewhat tartly. 'Anyway, I think I can almost guarantee you're wasting your time. There's nothing he can tell you about Torild that I can't tell you.'

'Isn't there? But there could be something you've – overlooked – that he might think of … '

'Hm,' she said in a tone that indicated she didn't have much faith in that.

I stood up with a final look at The Three Stages of Torild still on the table in front of us. 'Well … in that case, I'd better … '

How mysterious people were. Could we ever get to know another person – properly? Or would they always keep something or other hidden from us, something we ourselves had perhaps known once but had gradually forgotten over the years?

She came with me to the door. 'You'll ring as soon as you – have any news, won't you?'

'Of course.'

Down at the lights that control the traffic in the narrowest part of Sædalsveien, I waited at red. It struck me that certain situations in life are just like this too. You sit waiting at red, and when the light eventually changes to green, an articulated truck squeezing through on amber slams straight into you without giving you the faintest chance of avoiding it.

When the light changed to green it was with the greatest caution that I drove around the first blind bend.

Six

THE PEOPLE WHO LIVE in Mannsverk have never liked hearing the district called by its original name of Toadsmarsh. But at the end of the fifties, when we were in competition with some boys from that district over a couple of girls from Fridalen, we never called them anything but toads, which unleashed such a back-lash that we very soon had to leave the Fridalen girls to their own devices and turn back to the more central parts of town, where it was us who were cocks of the walk.

Astrid Nikolaisen lived in the thirteen-storey block of flats that serves as the landmark for the whole district. The thoroughfare running beneath it became a veritable wind tunnel when the wind blew from that direction.

I found her surname on one of the letter boxes beside the entrance to the lifts but had to search floor by floor along the external walkway to find the right apartment. In addition to the two lifts, there was a staircase at every corner of the building, and I zigzagged my way up to the sixth floor, where I found the same name on a door and rang the bell.

The woman who opened the door looked younger than I'd expected. Despite the heavy make-up, she didn't look much older than her early thirties. She was wearing tight-fitting slacks and a striped, brightly coloured woollen sweater that seemed long enough to serve as a sort of miniskirt. Her hair was so dark and neat that it almost looked like a wig. 'Yes?' she said and clamped her dark red lips together in a kind of turkey-mouth.

'Veum. I'm from … It *is* Mrs Nikolaisen, isn't it?'

'You can drop the *Mrs*. But my name is Nikolaisen, yes.'

'Is Astrid Nikolaisen at home?'

She sized me up. I added: 'Perhaps she's your sister?'

In spite of the layer of make-up, I noticed she was blushing. 'Yes, no, she's my daughter. Just a second, I'll see if she's home.'

She closed the door and I stood outside waiting. From here I could see straight down into the depot of the Bergen Tram Company. The rather random collection of workshops and tower blocks didn't exactly make Mannsverk a showcase for fifties town planners if they could put up with something like this.

The door behind me opened again.

It was the same woman. 'What's it about?'

'Actually, it's about a friend of hers, Torild Skagestøl, who's been missing from home for nearly a week.'

'And what's Astrid got to do with that?'

'Nothing, probably. I just wanted to ask her a few things about – Torild. Who she was with and things like that.'

She still looked a bit suspicious. 'Are you from the police?'

'No.'

'Child Welfare? Social Security?'

'No, nothing like that. I'm here on behalf of the family.'

'She's just got up … But OK then. Come on in.'

As I followed her in, I stole a glance at the clock. It was eleven-forty. Did that make Astrid Nikolaisen a member of social group B or C?

The hall was papered with red lilies on a violet background. Through an open door an advert blared loudly from a local radio station.

She knocked on a door. 'It's Gerd. Can we come in?'

I could just make out a muffled 'yes' through the door. The woman opened it and stood aside to let me in. As I passed her I caught the scent of perfume: heavy, like lily of the valley kept far too long in an airless room.

The girl inside was just zipping up the front of her tight jeans, not without some difficulty, the whiteness of her plump midriff emphasised by the black bra, which was all she'd had time to put on. The look she gave me was brazen and provocative, and her slightly heavy face was a puffier version of her mother's, except that it was even more heavily made up, if with slightly blurred features since it was all too obviously the mask she'd been wearing yesterday.

'Astrid! Put something on!' said her mother over my shoulder.

I turned to face her. 'I can wait out here ... '

'No need. Put your sweater on!'

'Yeah, yeah, bossy britches!' said her daughter. 'I'm sure he's seen a bra before!'

I waited for a few seconds before turning around again. Now she'd pulled on a maroon sweater and was just straightening her dark, slightly red-tinted hair. 'What's he want?'

'To talk about Torild Skagestøl,' I said.

'Go on in.' The mother pushed me gently into the room. 'Tell him all you know, Astrid. I'm tidying up in the sitting room if you need me.'

Then she left us.

I glanced round. It was quite a small room, furnished with an unmade bed and a cross between a chest of drawers and make-up table in white. There were two beanbags on the floor. By the bed stood an old-fashioned Windsor chair and on the floor beneath the window lay an untidy pile of comics and pop and fashion mags and a handful of pulp fiction. Various items of clothing were strewn about the room as though she'd been looking for something, but I knew from experience that this state of untidiness was very often just how teenagers marked their territory.

She turned her streaky face towards me with a slightly too cynical look for her age. 'What's up with Torild?'

'Aren't you going to sit down?'

She sat down on the corner of the bed and nodded in the direction of the two leather beanbags. 'Park yourself there.'

'I think I'd rather stand, actually,' I said leaning against the doorframe.

She made a sucking noise between her teeth and shrugged her shoulders without insisting any further.

'You two are friends, aren't you?'

'Oh, I wouldn't go that far. We meet up in town now and then but not much more than that.'

'In town?'

'Yeah, at Jimmy's and places like that.'

'Jimmy's, that's an amusement arcade, isn't it?'

'Yeah, you can play the machines if you like. I just go there for a burger and to hang out with folk there. There's always some all-right guys there.'

'Oh? Know any of their names?'

'No, why should I? What's it to do with you anyway?'

'But Torild used to go there too, did she?'

She nodded.

'And Åsa?'

'Yeah, she did too. There was *loads* of us.'

'What … ' I thought better of it. 'Listen, places like that are expensive, aren't they?'

'So what's free then apart from coffee and cake at church and stuff like that?'

'Where did you all get the money from?'

She gave me a look of contempt. 'From home, of course. Pocket money. A few of us have part-time jobs. I have a Saturday job at the Mecca now and then.'

'On the till?'

'Nope, stocking shelves.'

'Do you sometimes steal things?'

'What's the idea? Thought it was Torild you were supposed to be asking about!'

'Åsa had to take back a leather jacket she'd stolen yesterday.'

Her expression became slightly less cocky. 'Oh?'

'Her dad took her down there.'

'What a pillock!'

'You mean it was OK?'

'Well, I've never stolen nothing anyway!' But she avoided my eyes as she said this.

'And what about drugs, can you get them down there?'

'Down where? At Jimmy's? In the loos you can buy anything you like, even at Hotel Norge!'

'Is Torild on drugs?'

'Is she on drugs? Don't make me laugh! That stuck-up tart!'

'At school they said that – '

'Oh, at school maybe! Who was it you spoke to? Spotty?'

'But her parents also thought … '

'Well she probably was on drugs then, just to try it, like everybody does. But she's not a smackhead, I can guarantee that!'

'Hm?'

'Yes, I mean it.'

'Do you know where she is?'

'Nope. Didn't even know she was missing!'

'When was the last time you saw her?'

'The last time? Hey, Inspector Morse, what do you think I am, an elephant?'

'I can't bloody remember, can I? Probably sometime last week.'

'Thursday, Friday?'

'It wasn't Friday, that's for sure. I was at a party.'

'Thursday though?'

'Yeah … Can't be dead certain she didn't call in at Jimmy's that day. Her and Åsa. And some guy or other.'

'A – guy?'

She looked shifty again. 'Dunno. Could have imagined it. Nobody I knew at any rate.'

'It could be important, Astrid!'

Suddenly the doorbell rang: three short rings.

She rolled her eyes. 'Oh Christ, what a bloody din!'

We heard the door being opened outside and immediately after the sound of a man's voice.

'I'm off! It's Kenneth, there'll be a right song and dance.'

'How do you mean?'

'They'll be at it! So the whole street can hear! Get it? Tidying up, was she? You're not kidding. I bet she'll be changing the sheets after yesterday ... '

'Was Kenneth here too, then?'

'No, it was some other guy, wasn't it?'

From the doorway there was the sound of someone clearing her throat. The woman who'd let me in glanced from me to her daughter. 'I think it's time your friend was off now, Astrid.'

'And me too!'

'But ... don't you want anything to eat?'

'I'll grab a burger or whatever – in town!'

'OK, if you like ... ' Her mother stepped aside to let me pass.

Out in the hall a well-built, athletic-looking man, in a black T-shirt, dark trousers and with tattooed arms had just hung up his black leather jacket on a clothes hanger. He was in his thirties, hair slicked back and glistening with gel; he had a muscular face with deep lines running down from his nostrils.

'All right, Astrid?' he said with a cocky smile.

'All right,' she said in a clipped neutral tone.

'She's on her way out!' said her mother quickly.

'She can stay as far as I'm concerned.'

'She's on her way out, I said.'

He gave me a hard look. 'And who's this guy? Her lover?'

I looked him straight in the eye. 'The daily help.'

He rushed at me, one hand clenched in a fist. 'I'll give you daily help!'

Gerd Nikolaisen stepped between us. 'He's on his way! Him as well ... He's just a guy from the... '

'From the – ?'

'A guy who's looking for a friend of Astrid's who didn't come home.'

'Torild Skagestø,' I said. 'Maybe you know something?'

For a moment he was on uncertain ground. 'Know something? I … what d'you mean?'

'You don't? In that case, you can just go right on into the sitting room. We've nothing to say to each other.'

He turned to the other two. 'Hear the way he just spoke to me? Who's out of order, *him* or me?'

Gerd Nikolaisen took hold of his arm. 'Come on, Kenneth! Let's go into the sitting room … They're off anyway.'

He shook himself free. 'I heard! If you don't watch your mouth, I might clear off too.'

I could feel my stomach muscles tightening, moved to the door outside and, addressing Astrid's mother, said: 'If either of you hear anything about – Torild, we'd be glad to hear from you.'

'I doubt it … but where can I … ?'

The fellow by the name of Kenneth lit a cigarette with a deft movement of the hand, eyes still flashing with anger.

'You can ring her home. They're on the class list. Skagestøl. Up in Furudalen.'

'Shagherstill more like,' muttered Kenneth.

I passed close enough for him to blow cigarette smoke into my face. Of course, I could have stuck my elbow right in the middle of his ugly mug. But I had better things to do with my time than spend the next few hours in the waiting room at A&E.

'Sorry to have troubled you,' I said and left.

Astrid followed me out. On the way down to the lift she said: 'What an arsehole! He thinks he's God's gift just because … '

'Just because?'

'Oh, forget it.'

Outside the block of flats I asked her whether I could give her a lift anywhere.

She gave me a look suggesting I'd proposed something more than a friendly lift. 'Where to?'

I sighed. 'Well, where are you going? Into town?'

'Maybe. Yeah, that'll be fine.'

I unlocked the door on her side before going round to mine. When I climbed in and sat at the wheel, she was already installed in the front seat beside me. 'If you try anything on, I'll roll down the window and bawl my head off!' she said with a dopey grin that made it look more like an invitation than a warning.

Seven

I TOOK THE QUICK ROUTE up over Leitet and Brattlien, with the centre of Bergen like a deep incision in the terrain to our left. When I parked in Øvre Blekeveien she looked round suspiciously. 'What are we doing here?'

'Parking the car.'

'Why didn't you say first off that you were going to the country, then I could have caught the bus instead?'

'It'll only take you five minutes to walk down to the Fish Quay.'

'I wasn't going to the Fish Quay!'

I leaned past her and opened the door on her side.

She squeezed back into the seat 'Hands off!'

'Take it easy. I wouldn't even touch you with rubber gloves on.'

With a snort she got out of the car. As I was locking the door, she stood there looking round. 'What's this street I'm on?'

'Never been up in the mountains before, then?' I pointed in the direction of Telthusmauet. 'That's the quickest way. But if you want to enjoy the view … ' I pointed up the street, ' … you can always walk over Skansen.'

'Up yours!' With a look of contempt she took the first option.

I didn't attempt to accompany her. She walked with the slightly knock-kneed gait of a young girl who'd skipped all PT lessons the past five years. Not even the humblest pensioner walking into a strong head wind would have the slightest difficulty catching up with her. But I had the feeling she wasn't that keen on my company any more.

◆

When I got to the newspaper office I asked for Holger Skagestøl in reception on the ground floor. The receptionist was a polite gentleman with a well-trimmed grey beard and an open visitors' book in front of him.

'Do you have an appointment?'

'No, I'm afraid I don't.'

'And could I have your name?'

'Veum.'

He punched in an internal number, spoke with someone and efficiently dealt with the enquiry.

Then he glanced up at me. 'Skagestøl's asking what it's about.'

'His daughter.'

It got me through the barrier. The concierge gave me a plastic guest badge to pin onto my overcoat lapel and told me what floor to go to. When I got there Holger Skagestøl was standing in front of the lift, waiting for me.

'Veum? Private investigator? What business have you got with Torild?' he barked even before the door had closed behind me.

'I've been hired by your wife to look for her.'

'What?' He looked at me as if to say it was the most ridiculous thing he'd heard in his life. 'In that case … you'd better come on in.'

I followed him down a long corridor with blindingly harsh strip lighting, a symbol of the powerful beam the hive of activity in the newspaper's offices was supposed to train on life outside. Yet there might still be a few dead flies up there like little beauty spots in the light fittings.

Holger Skagestøl was a thin ungainly man, over six feet tall. His light brown Terylene trousers were held up by a tight leather belt, and his silvery grey tie was loosened from the collar of his white shirt with thin blue stripes. His hair was brownish in colour yet completely white at the temples and round the ears, like an Irish coffee with a bit too much cream in it.

He ushered me into a narrow little office with a view of the other side of Nygårdsgaten, where a group of youngish women were doing a cross between gymnastics and ballet exercises in a lit-up hall with large windows looking onto the street. 'We can borrow this,' he said as if to emphasise that he was not inviting me into his own office. 'Take a seat,' he added, pointing to a chair on the other side of the desk.

Before speaking again he looked at me, shaking his head slightly. 'I've rung the police myself, but Sidsel ... Oh well ... '

'So you've reported her missing?'

'No, not officially. But one has one's contacts. I've made a few enquiries, so to speak, and given the problem a certain amount of attention.'

'The problem?'

'Yes. That Torild's run away from home, of course.'

'Run away from home? Is that how you'd choose to describe it?'

'Yes, what other term could I use?'

'Run away where, according to you?'

He licked his thin lips. 'Well ... I don't know.'

'But you are concerned about it, aren't you?'

'Of course I am. Didn't I just say I've contacted ... ? Look, what is it you want, actually?'

'Listen, Skagestøl, I've been put on this case by your wife, and so far I've been gathering bits and pieces to give me an impression of Torild's life before she disappeared, who her girlfriends were, the places she went to, things like that. In connection with that, I assumed that her father – '

'Yeah, yeah. The last thing I need is a lecture. I've had a bellyful of that at home. So ... what is it you want to know?'

'Er, what can *you* tell me about Torild?'

'Tell you? What are you after? Her life history? You've probably already got that from Sidsel.'

I felt my solar plexus start to tighten and had to make an effort to maintain the same calm tone of voice. 'Just tell me something! Doesn't matter what ... '

'Well, she ... ' He looked out of the window. 'In my profession

… She's always been a nice girl. There've been a few hiccups at school the last few years, but it hasn't – I don't think it's been any worse than anything they all go through. They get sick of it, don't they? If school can't hold their interest, how are we parents supposed to?'

'But – the two of you did keep an eye on her progress?'

'To be frank, Veum, it was Sidsel who dealt with the children. I took care of earning our bread and butter and made all the major practical decisions – '

'Er, *major*?'

He looked at me irritably. 'Yes, such as when we bought the house, money in general, the summer we went over to Disneyland, stuff like that. But everything to do with the house and the home, I mean, all the *domestic* side, including the children, was Sidsel's pigeon. There has to be some division of responsibilities, doesn't there?'

'Yes, but – '

'Look, don't come the sexual moralist with me. We both agreed about dividing up our responsibilities like this. And don't talk to me about neglected kids either, because Torild got a lot more attention than many others. Just look around you, Veum! Look at all the single parents; how much time do you think they have for their children?'

'Some children maybe need more attention.'

'Not Torild.'

'Didn't she?'

'Things were reasonably OK at school. She had lots of hobbies, played handball, was in the Guides – '

'But she's packed that in, hasn't she?'

'OK, then. But right up to last year, wasn't it?'

'Was it? So why do you think she's taken off'

He threw up his hands. 'What does one really know about one's children?'

'Exactly.'

'She's at the rebellious stage now, though. Maybe she's clashed

with her mother – she can be rather wearing, I can tell you that …
You know what kids are like, girls especially perhaps … '

'What are you thinking of in particular?'

'At that age, Veum? More – emotional, eh?'

In the gym on the other side of the street, the ballet group had
finished their practice session for the day. The participants were
now standing around in small groups talking, but some were
already on their way out to the changing rooms. I shifted my gaze
back again. 'So you think it's a result of the upheaval of puberty, in
other words?'

'Yes.' He looked at me aloofly. 'And, of course, the family situation at present, well, I assume you know about it.'

'I know that your wife and you have separated, yes.'

'That obviously hasn't helped.'

'No. What do the police say?'

'Oh, you know how much they say. So long as no one has officially been reported missing, then … '

'Who was it you spoke to in the police?'

'Oh, I'm not sure I really want to divulge my contacts to you.'

'Afraid I might steal them, are you?'

'At any rate, they're people in very responsible positions, Veum.'

'So … there's nothing else you have to tell me, in other words?'

'Not that I can – think of.'

'Do you know the names of any of your daughter's boyfriends?'
He shook his head.

'Girlfriends, then?'

'No, I … apart from Åsa, that is; they've been friends since they
were little.'

'Yes, I realise that. What about a girl called Astrid?'

'No, can't remember that one … '

'Well, in that case, I won't trouble you any further.' I stood up.

He accompanied me to the door. 'You're not troubling me,
Veum! Don't get me wrong … I'm just as concerned as Sidsel
about Torild's disappearing act … '

Just as concerned? I thought.

' … but I – it's not my area of responsibility, as I've told you, I just can't, there are so many other things I have to … And it'll all turn out OK in the end, won't it?'

'Yes, it probably will.'

'Who … er, has Sidsel enough money to pay for this? I mean, your fee … '

'Yes.'

'Oh, because if not … I'll have a word with her. Don't bother about it, Veum.'

'To tell the truth, Skagestøl, that's the least of my worries.'

'Oh?' We'd stopped in front of the lift. 'Well, then … Good luck. And if there's anything else, just get back to me!'

'Thanks.'

He gave me a quick smile and was already on his way back to his office before the lift arrived.

When I came out onto the pavement I noticed a woman coming out of a door on the other side of the street, red in the face and with her hair all over the place. She looked furtively both ways before buttoning her coat collar round her neck and rushing off almost as though she was coming from a secret rendezvous. But it was probably just the end of the ballet lesson.

Eight

THE LEATHER BOUTIQUE was in two sections. One was targeted at young people and people on middle incomes with special offers for under a thousand kroner. The other part was super exclusive and literally on a higher level than the rest of the shop.

The girl to whom I explained the purpose of my visit was in the lower part and shook her head, saying she knew nothing about it, quickly directing me to the manageress, who inhabited the upper sphere.

The characteristic smell of suede and leather grew stronger with every step I took into the shop. As I climbed the four steps to the domain of the upper classes, I noticed another less identifiable smell that reminded me ever so slightly of formalin and probably came from the furs of which there were several racks here. I located the manageress in a cross between an office and a glass showcase at the far end of this part of the shop.

She was one of those well-turned-out women, with pale skin and a hint of red in their hair, who never seem older than their late forties. She looked as though she'd been born and grown up in a beauty salon, a creature of luxury whose true place is lounging on a sofa with a fur jacket slung casually over her shoulders, a glass of champagne in her hand, rather than spending her days in something so vulgar as a boutique. The russet leather skirt and the light-green silk blouse hinted that she probably had very exclusive tastes in underwear too. Perhaps this is why I suddenly thought of Judge Brandt ... Where did he buy his stuff? I wondered.

The look with which she sized me up put me straight into the category of middle-aged deliveryman. Her voice was crystal clear and cool as she stood up behind the narrow dark-brown desk and said: 'How can I be of assistance?'

'The name's Veum. Varg Veum.'

I put out my hand, and she gave me a perfunctory handshake as cool as her look and didn't even bother to introduce herself.

'It's about this theft from the boutique ... '

She raised her eyebrows. 'What do you mean exactly?'

'Er, there was a father in here yesterday, wasn't there? To smooth things out after a theft by his daughter?'

'Oh, you must be thinking of ... ' Two tiny rosettes appeared on her prominent cheekbones. 'It was extremely unpleasant. And even harder to fathom.'

'Harder to fathom?'

'You've come here.... Who reported this? *We* didn't at any rate ... '

'Actually, it's about another girl from the same milieu ... '

A pensive frown appeared on her brow and remained there, almost like the symbol for infinity. She paused in front of one of the clothes racks. 'Look at this. Considering the value of what we have on display here, we've installed the most sophisticated security measures.' She took out one of the items of clothing, a short green leather jacket with extremely fine stitching at the waist. With long white fingers and nails the same reddish tint as her skirt, she showed how the garment was chained to the rack. 'We do this so no one can just come in, snatch a garment and run off. Apart from this, every single item has a security tag that sets off an alarm if you try to leave without paying.'

'And does it remain there even when garments are being tried on?'

'Of course. Besides ... we always size up our customers.' Here she looked at me sharply. 'In this trade you soon learn to be discerning about people.'

'So how did Åsa manage it then? The girl I mentioned.'

'Oh, one asks oneself, doesn't one?!' She looked at me with raised ironic eyebrows.

'Yes, I am asking – you.'

'It definitely wasn't a theft.'

'Wasn't it?'

'We spoke to the assistant who had sold her the jacket. She recognised her straight away. She'd been struck by the fact that a girl so young had so much cash on her.'

'So she bought it, in other words?'

'She did.'

'But how ... what did she have to say about it?'

'That's just what's so incredible. She denied it! She hadn't bought it, she said, but had stolen it. And her father insisted she was right!' Her pearl grey eyes flashed. 'Can you imagine?'

'But they went back home, with a new jacket?'

'Which her father paid for, yes! In addition to the fact that they returned the other one ... '

'But why ... couldn't they just have paid for the one she claimed she'd taken?'

'*She* wanted to do that. But her father wouldn't. If she wanted a jacket, all she had to do was choose another.' She lowered her voice. 'Even though it was more expensive, actually – well, for us it didn't make any difference,' she added. 'We were paid twice, after all.'

'Hm.'

'Yes, strange, isn't it? But in any case it can't be a matter for the police, can it?'

'No, not as such ... It would have to be the finance section in that case ... '

'The finance section?'

'Yes, to see how you've entered all this in the books ... '

I smiled gently as I left. If nothing else, at least I'd given her that to chew on.

Nine

THE PLACE that went by the name of Jimmy's was in a side street in the city centre, close to one of the most traffic-congested parts of the Central Ring and less than five minutes from Bergen Cinemas' main fleapit in the Concert Palace, which now smacked of neither concerts nor palaces but was distinguished by its trendy new abbreviation CP, with the numbers '1 to 14' added to it.

I vaguely remembered the place as a slightly dated snack bar from the sixties and seventies, always at least a decade too far behind the times to appeal to the youth of today. It was not until the end of the eighties, when they staked everything on the new electronic games machines, that the place looked as though it had found its true clientele: few people under ten but even fewer over thirty. Yet they'd kept the old name – it had originally been called after James Dean – through both hard times and good, so stead-fastly in fact that it had long since become a landmark. Everybody knew where Jimmy's was.

It still more or less functioned as a sort of snack bar, even if it steered well clear of such new-fangled things as kebabs and fresh salads. What you got here was hot dogs in defrosted bread and hamburgers from the microwave, glistening with fat, and smeared in mustard, ketchup and onions, the only available accompani-ments. If you had time to wait, you could always get hold of a cup of coffee there too. Mainly, people drank Coke and similar soft drinks.

Despite the fact that it was as gloomy as a cathedral in there, I still felt like a canary at a cat show when the door slid shut behind me, and a few phosphorus-coloured teenage faces looked up at me from their seats round the garish noisy games machines. It was as though a caste mark had been daubed on my forehead, the number fifty flashing on and off, on and off so everyone could see what team I played for. The only individuals who didn't honour me with a look were those in the middle of a game. The others soon lost interest, even though I couldn't help noticing that some of them cast furtive glances in my direction every time I moved, unsure what organisation I might represent.

The games machines were marshalled into four rows, two facing each of the sidewalls and two back to back in the middle of the place. Once I'd grown accustomed to the light I soon got my bearings in the rest of the room.

Behind the counter at the far end sat a great lump of a chap in his late thirties, with bulging biceps beneath the originally white but now ketchup-spotted chef's smock. He had a mousy little moustache, a cigarette stub at the corner of his mouth and a bad-tempered, jaded look which did not bode well for would-be troublemakers. He was reading a paper in the light from the open back door. As I came in, he threw an expectant look over the edge of the folded newspaper, his only reaction being a hint of suspicion, causing an involuntary twitch at the corner of his mouth before he could control it.

In front of the counter were a couple of bar stools and in the corner at the far end I could just make out two unoccupied round tables. Somewhere between fifteen and twenty youths were gathered round the games machines, four of five of them girls. One of the girls was playing a machine with a friend. It was Astrid Nikolaisen.

I jingled a few loose coins in my pocket and stood at one of the machines, looking at the trailers boasting the merits of the game, supposedly tempting me to throw myself into battle to find and release the abducted bank director's daughter somewhere in the ghetto of a large American city such as New York.

The block letters of the title were lit up in garish colours like in a second rate fifties B-movie: *RANSOM!*

'Gonna play?'

I looked down at the young lad who had come and stood beside me. He had long, wispy locks of smooth fair hair. 'Yeah, maybe. Can you show me what to do?'

'Got any money?'

'It's on me.'

He edged me gently aside and pointed. His shiny blue bomber jacket had a big green and orange dragon on the back. 'Stick the coins in there. One player or two?'

'Er … one.'

He grinned. 'It'll be just me, then.'

'You're going to be fighting against heavy odds.'

'Bah! Know where they pop up from, don't I?'

And he did know. After choosing which character he wanted to be, his weapons and which qualities would be the most important (brute force, intelligence, speed), he was suddenly in a back street in the ghetto. Armed gangsters popped up all over the place, from behind the corners of buildings and dustbins, at upper floor windows and from manhole covers. The lad shot them down at a rate of knots, and the points total soared in the top right-hand corner before further hordes sprang out.

As he stood there playing, and I pretended to look on, I kept watch out of the corner of my eye to see whether anything worth noting was happening anywhere else in the room.

The man behind the counter was once more engrossed in the paper. A couple of new players had come in now; a few others stood fumbling with their money to see whether they had enough for another go.

Suddenly I met Astrid Nikolaisen's eyes, as, pulling a face, she turned away from the machine now flashing *GAME OVER* at her.

It was a few seconds before she recognised me. Then she set off in my direction with a great yawn as though keen to show off her new fillings. 'What the bleeding hell's this? Are you tailing me or what?'

The man behind the counter looked up and put the paper aside. Calmly I said: 'Take it easy. It's a free country, isn't it?'

'Not for the likes of you!' She turned towards the counter. The guy who'd been sitting there was already coming out from behind it. 'Hey, Kalle! We've got a snooper here!'

An infernal din was coming from the machine beside me. I looked down at the screen. A colossal giant filled the end of the back street, where he was peppered with machine gun fire from my brave combatant, until his whole silhouette flashed before finally collapsing into a pulsating figure on the tarmac: *1000, 1000, 1000!*

The man she had called Kalle stopped in front of me. He looked even bigger now that he was standing up, and his breath stank of onions and cigarettes. 'What's the idea?'

'Better ask the young lady, hadn't you? I've come here to play the machines.'

The lad beside me looked up. 'He's with me! It's my uncle, innit!'

Kalle glanced suspiciously from the lad to Astrid Nikolaisen.

'He was at our place a few hours ago – said he was looking for Torild!'

'Tor ... '

'Just ask Kenneth!'

He turned to face me again. 'That true?'

'Why shouldn't it be?'

'He's my uncle!' said the lad. Now he'd come into a massive warehouse and let loose a no-nonsense burst of machine gun fire at one of the gangster bosses.

'Don't talk bollocks, Ronny!' snapped Astrid Nikolaisen. 'You haven't got no bloody uncle!'

'Who says I haven't?' – Rattatattataaaat! – Four or five gangsters hit the deck in a hail of bullets.

Kalle scowled at me, head slightly on one side. 'So which is it, law or social worker?'

'I'm qualified as the latter.'

'So what Astrid says is straight-up, then?'

'Yes, it's true that I called at her place and asked her a few questions about a friend of hers in the same class. One of the places that came up in our conversation was this one here.'

He looked crossly at Astrid.

'Yeah? So what's wrong with that?'

Ronny was over the moon. The final picture on the screen showed the bank director's daughter in a clinch with her saviour, as the message *BONUS 10,000, BONUS 10,000, BONUS 10,000!!!* flashed across the screen.

Kalle pointed a podgy finger at him. 'As for you – don't you ever show your ugly mug in here again!'

'Don't talk to my nephew like that!' I said.

'Come again? You really mean … ? I'll say what I like – don't give a bugger who it is!'

'What are you getting your knickers in a twist for?' I asked quietly. 'Paid for the game, didn't I? Got something to hide, have we?' Hamming it up for all I was worth, I cast a searching look round the room.

A few of the youths had gathered round us now, most of them just nosey parkers, but a couple of them looking as though they were dying for a chance to pitch in if he threw me out.

'Got an eyeful now?'

'It was Astrid who mentioned the name of this friend of hers. Torild. Know her, do you?'

'I don't know the name of every bugger who comes here!'

'Oh no?' I turned to Astrid. 'Maybe you could explain who she is to him?'

She looked at me hesitating. 'Torild … That girl who … One of the girls I usually knock about with.'

He coughed disgustingly. 'Doesn't make any odds, I've nothing to tell you about her. If she's done a runner, then … ' He shrugged his shoulders.

'Did I say she'd done a runner?'

He looked sideways. 'Oh? Wasn't that why you … ?'

Astrid looked at him vacantly. Neither of them was much good at lying.

Bonny tugged at my coat sleeve. 'Fancy another game, uncle?'

I shook my head. 'Not now, Bonny. Another day.'

'Is that a deal?'

'Yes.'

'See you, then!' A touch uneasily he shuffled back to the pals he'd come in with.

Just then the phone rang behind the counter. Kalle looked at me and nodded towards the exit. 'There's the door.'

I didn't budge. 'I can see that.'

For a moment we stood there glowering at each other, and I could see his biceps tighten. Suddenly he turned to the counter. 'Yeah, yeah, yeah, keep your hair on!'

I followed him, and the group of youths surrounding us slowly moved aside. As he picked up the telephone he turned and flashed a smouldering look straight at me.

'Jimmy's! Yeah. No, not now. No. I'll explain later. Yeah. OK. See you!'

He threw the receiver back down and barked: 'Is that it?'

'A hot dog with ketchup only, thanks!'

He planted his great big fists hard against the counter as though about to leapfrog right over it.

'On second thoughts,' I said, 'think I'll skip it. I'm not all that sure about … ' I ran my eyes over the counter. 'A while since you've had a visit from the health inspector, is it?'

'If you don't get your arse out of that door double quick you'll be the one getting a visit from them. Got it?'

'Got it … This town ain't big enough for the both of us. That means – '

'I've seen the film.'

'Me too. But did you see the credits?'

'Credits … '

'They say who wrote the script. And it sure as hell wasn't you, Kalle!'

With that, I turned and walked towards the door. But I threw a quick backward glance to make sure that a missile bearing the words 'THE END' was not winging its way towards the back of my head.

Ten

ONCE OUTSIDE JIMMY'S I paused for a moment to take stock.

So far I hadn't made much progress to speak of. I could call it a day, go down to the office and just fill in the blanks on my form with Tippex. Or I could take up a spot in the nearest doorway and hope Fate would intervene before I rotted away.

I looked around. A high greyish-white sky lay over the town. It was still only four-thirty and another hour before it got dark. On a corner a block and a half away the golden glow of a small café-cum-patisserie beckoned invitingly. I decided to give Fate half an hour.

In the café I bought a mug of hot chocolate with cream and a bun with generous sprinklings of cinnamon round the edges before taking a seat at one of the tables by the window facing Jimmy's.

Not long after I'd sat down, Ronny came out, turned towards the door and gave two fingers to somebody or other before looking around and making off fast round the nearest corner.

Otherwise, not much else happened apart from the build-up of traffic leaving town. The rear lights of the cars daubed red stripes along the steamed-up windowpane as they drove past, and along the pavement there were suddenly empty metered parking places.

When my allotted half hour was up, with Fate the loser, I stacked my plates together and carried them over to the counter with a crooked little smile at the plumpish lady behind it as though we'd shared a secret moment together that Thursday afternoon. The smile I received in return suggested that was exactly what we had done; it was just that I hadn't realised it.

Outside the air was cold and raw, and I thrust my hands deep into my overcoat pockets. I had just decided to take a little stroll past Jimmy's again before calling it a day when the door suddenly opened.

Two of the girls emerged, their heads close together and slightly huddled against the biting wind, which forced its way like an unwelcome guest through the narrowest part of the street. Neither of them was Astrid Nikolaisen.

Both of them were wearing tight-fitting jeans and anoraks a size too large. One of them had a broad red headband around her dark hair; the other a dark corduroy hat with a wide brim turned up in front. Right outside Jimmy's they stopped under the yellowish--white glow from a swaying street lamp. The girl wearing the hat held out a scrap of paper. Open-mouthed, her friend looked into her face as though not quite able to restrain her sense of shock – or perhaps it was anticipation.

The girl with the hat said something, and the other one nodded. They linked arms, and as the traffic paused for a breather, they crossed the street.

A quick decision was needed.

I decided to let Astrid Nikolaisen paddle her own canoe for now, waited until the two girls had disappeared from view round the corner of a block of houses then followed them, at a safe distance.

There was no need for caution in fact. They didn't seem to have the least suspicion that anyone could possibly be following them.

Five minutes later they suddenly stopped. They put their heads together again, looking as though they were studying the front of the large lit-up building on the opposite side of the street. The girl with the hat suddenly seemed different, more keyed up, and her friend looked around carefully as she spoke.

As for me, I remained glued to the spot in front of a shop window, pretending to read the front pages of the day's three tabloids, two from Oslo and one local one, not that there was much to distinguish them, apart from the colours.

Now the two girls split up. The girl with the hat crossed the street, while her friend stayed put, following her with her eyes for a moment; abruptly, she turned on her heel and shot off in my direction.

I scrutinised the banner headlines about yesterday's trivial events even more intensely. A national politician railed against unfair treatment on the *Today* programme, and a skating star had hit top form one Wednesday in February. Haukeland Hospital was in crisis, and there had been a traffic accident in Lindås. So what else was new?

The girl sailed past me without so much as a glance. I breathed freely, relieved that she was still at an age where she barely noticed people over twenty. Then I set off quickly in the opposite direction.

Her friend was just rounding the next corner, so I stepped on it.

As I turned the corner myself, I caught sight of her back disappearing through the main entrance of a classy hotel.

I went after her. Through the huge glass panels facing the street I could follow her every movement as she went straight through reception and into an open lift without so much as a glance at the reception staff.

The lift doors slid shut behind her and I watched the floor numbers as they lit up on the panel beside the lift: fourth, fifth, *sixth* floor.

I looked at the clock. It was five-twenty p.m.

I cast an involuntary glance up over the building as though I half expected her to appear at one of the windows and wave down at me.

The name of the hotel was displayed in large neon letters above the entrance.

For the second time that day I caught myself thinking of Judge Brandt. This was the hotel he had met his death in barely a week ago.

Last Friday, wasn't it?

But it was on Thursday that Torild Skagestøl had gone missing, at least from home.

My head brimming with sudden thoughts, I set off back to the office.

I opened the letter box in the entrance and flipped quickly through the pile. A brochure, another three mail-shots, two bills and a completely plain white envelope with my name printed outside.

I binned the junk mail, stuffed the bills into my inside pocket and inspected the back of the envelope as I waited for the lift.

No sender's name, but a Bergen postmark.

On the third floor I emerged from the lift, went along the corridor and let myself into the office.

The answerphone was blinking. Somebody had actually taken the trouble to leave a message.

I hung up my coat, sat down at the desk, grabbed a letter-opener and slit open the white envelope.

It contained a single folded sheet.

I opened it out.

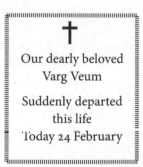

Our dearly beloved
Varg Veum

Suddenly departed
this life
Today 24 February

Someone had made a simple standard death notice on a computer:

I almost fell off my chair with the shock, automatically glancing at the clock. Today was February 18th. The 24th was next Wednesday.

Then came the delayed reaction. My whole body started to

tremble, and the hand holding the sheet of white paper began to shake involuntarily as though I was an elderly patient in a senile dementia ward. I was overcome with a feeling of intense nausea, and the letters danced in front of my eyes before, by sheer force of will, I managed to focus again.

I took deep breaths: one, two, three …

It was obviously a joke. A macabre one but a joke nonetheless. Or also …

A warning?

But in that case, from who?

And why?

Hardly able to summon the energy, I rewound the tape on the answerphone to hear what glad tidings might be lying in wait there.

There was only one message: the same digital-sounding organ music as the previous time. 'Abide With Me'… And now I suspected I knew whose funeral they had in mind.

Eleven

BEFORE LEAVING THE OFFICE I called Karin Bjørge, my long-standing girlfriend at the Population Register Department, and asked her whether she had any plans for the evening.

She had. 'I promised Eva … She had two tickets for a concert at the Grieg Concert Hall, and I … I think she needs some company.'

'I see.'

She caught the undertone in my voice and quickly added: 'But I can certainly change it, if you … '

'No, no, course not. Heavens above!'

She hesitated. 'We can meet up tomorrow, can't we?'

'Course we can! Is it the usual wind orchestra recital?'

'Yes.'

'Well, hope you enjoy it!'

'Thanks.'

So I went back home by myself after all.

I checked the front door carefully before letting myself in, went cautiously from room to room, opening the doors fully and turning the lights on before stepping in.

The flat was as empty as a Scout's promise twenty years on.

I rustled up a Veum special: leeks fried with chopped tomatoes, beaten eggs poured over it to make a sort of omelette, a bit ragged at the edges, but it went down a treat

I made a cup of proper filter coffee and sat watching a TV debate that was about as meaningful as a free number on the Reeperbahn. Then I poured myself a glass of aquavit, put on a Ben Webster CD and went to fetch a book from the pile waiting to be read on my bedside table.

But I couldn't concentrate.

I sat there with a kind of bad conscience, the feeling I'd been so accustomed to during the years I'd worked in Child Welfare. In fact, I should not have been sitting here taking it easy. I ought to have been out on the streets looking for Torild.

The old boy on the floor below was as quiet as a mouse. He'd been widowed a few years before and since then, all I ever heard from below was now and then the tinkle of a bottle cap when he opened a beer or the sound of the radio on the rare occasions he put it on a bit too loud at six a.m.

At eleven-thirty there was suddenly a ring at the front door downstairs.

I went over to the window, opened it carefully and looked out. It was Karin.

'Hi,' she said, smiling up at me in the darkness. 'Can I come in?'

I went down and unlocked the door. She came in and gave me a quick hug. 'You sounded as though you could do with some company.'

We went upstairs and she hung up her dark coat in the hall. Underneath, she was wearing smooth black corduroy slacks, a white blouse and a dark-brown suede jacket that emphasised her slim waist. 'I've brought my toothbrush,' she said with a little smile.

I kissed her tenderly. 'A toothbrush and good spirits. That'll do for anybody.' A slight hint of red wine lingered over her. 'Can I get you something to drink?'

Beaming at me, she returned my kiss full on the mouth. 'Yes … '

In the bedroom we slowly undressed one another. I lay her back across the bed, ran my tongue in a gentle line gently down over her belly, carefully parted her labia and kissed her again passionately. She sighed, opened her thighs even wider and devoured me in great mouthfuls as though after a long fast.

Afterwards she said: 'Eva and I went out for a glass of wine after the concert. Her husband's left her for a girl who could easily be their daughter.'

'A cleverer man than me once said: When you get older, and if you're reasonable, the women you fall for will grow older as you do.'

She snuggled in under my armpit, kissed me below my ear and said: 'So that's why things are so good between us, is it … ?'

'Mm.'

The next morning she kissed me again, and we went into town together. That's why I didn't see the front page of the paper until I was back at the office, and then the main headline hit me smack between the eyes:

GIRL FOUND DEAD ON FANAFJELL

Twelve

SIDSEL SKAGESTØL answered the telephone at the first ring as though she'd been sitting there waiting. Her voice was strained and shrill: 'Hello?'

'It's Veum.'

'Oh.' The change in her tone was so obvious it was almost palpable. 'Er … I thought it was Holger.' Then it quickly altered again. 'Is there anything new?'

'No, alas. I haven't found her, if that's what you mean.'

'Yes, I … Holger's down there now.'

'With the police?'

'Yes. He … ' Her voice tailed off.

'I saw the headline in the paper.'

'But it's not certain it's *her*!'

'Course it isn't. She … The girl has to be identified first, in any case.'

'Yes.'

'Is there anything I can do for you?'

'Not now.' Weakly she added: 'Have you found out anything about her at all? About where she might – be?'

'No, but I'm working on it.'

'I think I'm going to have to ring off, Veum, so the phone won't be engaged when he rings.'

'If anything at all crops up, don't be afraid to get in touch with me. If the case has already been – cleared up, then I'll actually owe you some money. I'll write out an itemised – '

'That's all right, Veum. We'll keep in touch.' With no further formalities she hung up.

I carefully replaced the receiver and sat there looking out of the window.

A few sparse snowflakes were falling over the city, like ash from a giant campfire somewhere high above. The layer of cloud above the mountains was ashen grey too, without a hint of a glow even though it was already after sunrise.

I picked up the paper and read the short notice again.

A young, so far unidentified, woman was found in a road-fill roughly midway between Fanaseter and Nordvik, on the eastern slope of Fanafjell Mountain. She was partly undressed, and there were clear signs of violence. However, it was still too early to say whether she had also been the victim of a sexual assault. The cause of death had not been established either. The person leading the investigation, Detective Inspector Dankert Muus, stated that, for the moment, the police were concentrating on establishing the young woman's identity and also securing the scene of the crime and combing it for evidence.

I got up, went over to the sink, filled a glass of water straight from the tap, drank it, went back to the desk, sat down, cleared away some piles of papers in front of me and counted slowly to ten before lifting the receiver, dialling the number of the police station and asking to speak to Dankert Muus.

He was out.

I hesitated slightly. 'It's about the body found up on Fanafjell. Could you put me through to someone else?'

Yes, she could. I was put through to Eva Jensen after about twenty seconds.

'It's Veum.'

'Oh, hello … '

'It's about that girl you've found. Has she been identified?'

'Er. No. Muus is down at forensic at the moment, with a man who – '

' – could be the father. Holger Skagestøl, right?'

'That's something I can't – '

'OK. The fact is that – I've been working on a case. A girl who's been missing about a week, Torild Skagestøl. So far I've found very little trace of her, so when a girl suddenly turns up dead, I'm – worried, if you see what I mean.'

'We haven't many details either yet, Veum.'

'When Muus is back, could you ask him to give me a call?'

'By all means, Veum.'

After our conversation, I sat there staring vacantly ahead.

It was dead time, literally speaking. On the sheet of paper I wrote out the names I'd noted down in connection with Torild Skagestøl's disappearing act:

Åsa Furebø (Trond, Randi)

Astrid Nikolaisen (Gerd, Kenneth?)

Helene Sandal, Nattland School

Sigrun Søvik, Guides leader

Jimmy's: Kalle? (Ronny)

What about the hotel I'd tailed the two girls to from Jimmy's? Almost without thinking, I added a new name to the list:

Judge Brandt

Then I called Paul Finckel.

His voice was gravelly as though he'd got up early – or already started his weekend.

He beat me to it. 'Varg? Don't tell me! You don't have something to do with *this* killing as well, do you?'

'Not necessarily. Know anything about it?'

'She still hasn't been identified.'

'I know. But do you have any – particulars? Anything about her condition?' I could hear him leafing through some papers. 'Was it delicate, d'you mean? Not guilty, your honour.'

I waited.

'A good laugh makes you live longer, Varg. Haven't you heard that?'

'Yes, I have. But my days are long enough as they are.'

'Here, let's see … She was found yesterday evening. At about ten o'clock. It was a jogger who, er, had to answer a call of nature and scrambled down from the road up there. God knows whether he'll ever go jogging again.'

'Joggers don't give up the ghost that easily.'

'In any case, he came across something lying there, under some bushes, went to take a closer look and, well, you know the rest.'

'No more than what's in the papers.'

'And there isn't much more than that to tell either. Her clothes were in a mess, but the police are still unable to say whether she'd been raped or was the victim of some other kind of sexual assault, as the expression goes.'

'Cause of death?'

'Nothing so far. Do *you* know anything else?'

'Not yet. But I've been on the trail of a girl for a couple of days and still not found her … '

'What's her name?'

'Er … But if it's *not* her … '

'A hundred per cent on the QT, Varg.' His voice took on a harder note. 'One good turn deserves another. Next time you ring, you might find I'm busy.'

'Strictly between us, then, Paul. Her name's Torild Skagestøl.'

I trotted out with her surname quickly and casually, but he immediately seized the connection. 'A relative of Holger?'

'His daughter.'

'Exactly.' I heard him making a note of it. 'Anything else?'

'Not yet. But if I receive confirmation that it is her, I may come back to you with more information.'

'Can't we deal with it now?'

'Have to check it myself first, Paul. To be quite frank, I've hardly found out anything.'

'Starting to feel your age, are you, Varg?'

'No more than you, I hope. Anyway, thanks a lot.'

'Same here, old wolf.'

I hung up and shifted a few piles of paper about again. One

page floated down to the floor. As I bent down to pick it up, the phone rang.

I grabbed the page, placed it in front of me, lifted the receiver and answered: 'Hello?'

'It's Muus. I heard you'd rung.'

'Yes, I … Has she been identified?'

He cleared his throat. 'I think you should get down here, Veum.'

'When?'

'I'm already expecting you.'

'Be there in five minutes.'

As I hung up, my eyes fell on the sheet of paper in front of me. I jumped. In all the fuss, I'd almost forgotten.

What I was looking at was my own death notice, dated five days hence.

Thirteen

WE HAD SO CONSISTENTLY AVOIDED each other the past few years that when I met Dankert Muus that day I was struck by how much older he looked.

Not only had he put on a fair amount of weight, he'd also become greyer, and his hair was thinning. The grim set of his mouth was more pronounced; on the other hand, a kind of peace seemed to have settled over him. No longer did it look as though he might leap over the desk and grind you to a pulp if you contradicted him; on occasion, he could even throw his typewriter after you.

Through the open door he signalled a rather heavy handshake. 'Come in, Veum. Have a seat.'

I did as he said and shot a quick glance round me. The office bore clear signs of the fact that, in a year's time, the whole department would be moving into the new wing now going up on the corner of Allehelgens Street and Nygaten. It hadn't had a lick of paint in the last five or six years, at any rate. And in a way Dankert Muus looked a bit like that too.

He looked at me dispiritedly. 'Jensen said you'd been trying to find this girl?'

'I have been looking for a particular girl, yes, that's right.'

He breathed in deeply then slowly exhaled. 'I'm afraid I can confirm it's the same person … if the name Jensen had noted was correct.'

I felt numb, as if I'd stayed too long in the water after a dip too early in spring. 'Torild Skagestøl.'

He nodded. 'Her father's just identified her. I went up with him to the Institute of Forensic Medicine, and we got a provisional statement from him before he had to go back home to – his wife.'

In a flash I saw before me Sidsel Skagestøl in the large east-facing sitting room. That view would lose something of its charm for her now and for a good many weeks to come. Indeed, it might well never regain it.

'He said she's been missing since the end of last week, and that his wife had engaged you to look for her.'

'Yes, but not till Wednesday, and it wasn't till yesterday that my investigation really got off the ground.'

'And what did you find out?'

'Not much. I talked to a few of the girls in her class. They were in town together last Thursday, raking about, window-shopping, probably went to a place called Jimmy's. Know it?'

He nodded.

'They were seen there, her friend Åsa, herself and an – escort.'

'Åsa… ' His ballpoint was at the ready.

'Furebø. They were old friends and still knocked about together. I don't think Åsa told me everything she knows. For example, she could definitely give you people the name of that "escort".'

'Anything else?'

'There was another friend, also a girl from her class, Astrid Nikolaisen … ' I paused as he noted down the name and the exact address. 'That was the one who said she'd seen these three at Jimmy's, probably last Thursday.'

'And her escort … '

'That's a loose end I hadn't even begun to tie up. Now I probably never will – '

'No, probably not.'

'No?'

'No!' He swivelled partway round on his office chair, looked at a place on the wall and pointed with a finger as chubby as a sausage. 'See that calendar, Veum?'

'Yes.' A traditional-looking annual calendar hung on the wall; it had no illustrations and was divided up into squares, like a sort of window on the future, which at that point in the year it was in a way. One of the days had been circled by a dark-red felt-tip pen.

'See that date ringed there?'

'March 1st?'

'Exactly.' He moved the corners of his mouth to one side, baring his teeth in something that just resembled a smile. To me, though, it looked more like the leering grin of a wolf. 'Liberation day!'

'Isn't that still May 8th?'

'*My* liberation day, Veum! The day I reach retirement age!'

For a moment I seemed to feel the breath of time on my neck like frost smoke on a cold winter's day. – Life without Muus? Was that possible? And how come I didn't feel even a momentary surge of joy at the thought of it?

'You mean you're – sixty?'

'On February 27th!' He smiled, proud as a six-year-old kid.

'Maybe that should be the retirement age for private investigators too.'

'Sixty?' said Muus dryly. 'Most give up at fourteen.'

'And what are you thinking of doing for the next few years? Court usher or town crier?'

A new look came over his face, a milder and completely different expression from anything I'd ever seen on it before. 'I've always been very fond of flowers, Veum.'

'Oh … ?'

'At Easter my wife and I are off to Holland for the bulb season. And later this year I'm going to be out in the garden every hour God sends.'

'Sounds – very nice.'

He looked at me sharply. Then the dreamy expression on his face was gone, and he returned to what was still the humdrum daily grind. 'So what I mean, Veum, is this. I've no intention of seeing the last few weeks of my life here at the station wrecked by you getting under our feet and playing the big private investigator at the expense of us ordinary overworked civil servants! Is that clear?'

'It never occurred to me to – '

'Is that clear?'

'Yes.'

'And I'm not planning to come to a sticky end like Vegard Vadheim either.'

'No, *that* I can understand.'

'Just one thing before you go, Veum … '

'I'm not in any hurry.'

'But I am!' He picked up a large white envelope and put it down again.

'During your investigations … did you come across anything …?' He hesitated.

'Yes?'

'I mean … ' He looked almost embarrassed. 'Anything linking her with – you know, these so-called Satanist circles?'

'No, absolutely not, but … why do you ask?'

'Oh, just a thought. You see, the place we found her in, it's not all that far from the old Lysekloster monastery, and … well, it was rumoured that – what do they call them? – black masses were held up there.'

'Yeah, there were certainly goings-on involving people getting togged up, but … is that your only reason for asking me?'

He looked at a spot a few inches above my head. 'Yes.'

As I left his office I still hadn't quite recovered from the shock. Flowers? Muus? The only plants I could imagine him liking were cacti.

On the way out, I stuck my head into Eva Jensen's office. She was on the phone, nodded curtly and turned her back on me to show she'd no time at all for knights errant.

A new chap had moved into Vegard Vadheim's office, a great brown-haired bear of a chap in his mid-thirties with a dark beard, a good-natured smile and an apparently optimistic view of life.

He glanced up through the open door, gave me a one-fingered salute in greeting, and I stopped.

I noted a sudden look of uncertainty come over his face, as he realised he couldn't quite place me. 'We – I don't think we've met properly.'

'No.' He stood up and came out from behind the desk. 'Inspector Atle Helleve,' he said in an unadulterated Voss accent.

We shook hands. 'The name's Veum. Varg Veum.'

'Oh … It was you who … I've heard about you.'

'That's what I was afraid of. If it wasn't from Vadheim, then … '

'Er, I … ' His face darkened. 'I never met him before … ' He made a vague gesture with his hand.

I sighed, and he regained his composure. 'Was there anything else?'

'No, I – just wanted to say hello as I was passing.'

'Hello.'

I nodded, gave a wry smile and carried on my way out of the building; and no one came running in hot pursuit to stop me, place me in custody down in the basement or make me some other offer I couldn't refuse.

Fourteen

IT WAS WITH A HEAVY HEART that I parked my car in front of the steep wooded plot in Furudalen. Slowly I walked through the gate and up to the entrance. I hesitated slightly before ringing the bell.

Holger Skagestøl answered the door himself. His gaunt face was deeply lined now, and there was a grimness about the mouth that had perhaps never been there before. 'Yes?' he asked testily before he'd recognised me. 'Oh, Veum.'

'I hope I'm not intruding.'

He looked at me without expression.

'I just wanted to say how – sorry I am. It's so terribly sad when this happens, at such a young age.'

His mask did not flicker.

'I ... Could you tell your wife that I called ... ?'

All of sudden he seemed to come back to life. A slight shudder ran through him, he stepped aside, opened the door wide and said: 'You can tell ... just come on in, Veum.'

I stepped cautiously into the hall. 'I really don't want to – '

He closed the door behind us. 'No, no, it's quite all right. Just go on in.' He nodded in the direction of the sitting room.

Sidsel Skagestøl was sitting on the same dark-green sofa as the last time I'd been here. She didn't notice the ash falling from the cigarette in her mouth down onto her white sweater.

As I went into the room, she looked up at me with the glassy stare of someone who had taken a large dose of tranquillizers and still wanted more.

I approached her and put out my hand. 'Mrs Skageststøl ... '

She took the cigarette from her mouth with one hand and gave me the other as though not quite sure where to put it.

Her hand was cold and damp, and I put both my hands round it. 'I can't find words to say how terrible this news is.'

I heard Holger Skagestøl make a movement behind me, a little uneasy, as if unsure what she might come out with.

She opened her mouth. Her lips looked dry, and she ran the tip of her tongue over them before speaking. 'Torild, she … '

'Yes, it's all right, Sidsel. Veum knows everything,' said Skagestøl.

'She's dead.' Sidsel Skagestøl went on as if he had not spoken.

'I'd hoped I might find her before – anything like this,' I said.

'We were too late contacting you, Veum. The damage was already done,' said Skagestøl.

I turned partway towards him. 'Have they given you – the time of death?'

'No, no!' he said quickly. 'But … it was a few days ago at any rate. The pathologist was absolutely categorical about that.'

'Well, you went up there yourself and … ?'

I looked down at Sidsel Skagestøl. She sat there dragging heavily on her cigarette, with a sunken expression on her face.

I moved a few paces away from her and lowered my voice. 'You saw her … '

He nodded and moved almost over to the picture window. 'She didn't look – a pretty sight. That isn't how one wants to see one's … ' His voice broke, and he had to regain control of himself so he could finish the sentence, '… daughter.'

'No.'

'She … ' He put one hand over his face. 'Her face was completely bloated and there was bruising on the skin.'

I looked at him. He was struggling to keep control of his facial muscles. 'It was horrible! They showed me pictures of the place where she was found … Her clothes … they'd been pulled up … her skirt, her jacket and her pants had been pulled down, and she was na … had nothing on under … Was lying on her stomach facedown and … Here, Veum, just here … ' He placed his hand behind his hip, on the far right-hand side. The look he gave me was a mixture of fear and bitterness. 'Here, someone had carved a mark into her flesh!'

A shudder ran through me. 'A mark?'

'Like a branding mark on a cow!'

'But what ... what did it look like?'

'A bit like – an inverted cross.'

'I see.'

'Do you, Veum? Do you really?' He almost hissed the words at me.

It sounded so sharp that his wife turned to look at us again and said in a pathetic little voice: 'What are you two talking about?'

Skagestøl rushed up to her. 'Nothing, dear, nothing.'

'No – thing?' she repeated as though it was a word she had never heard before.

I remained standing by the window and looked out. For a moment I wondered who was looking after the other children. Maybe they hadn't been told yet. Perhaps they had not yet come home from school.

I got my answer quicker than expected.

'I want to see it!' Sidsel Skagestøl exclaimed behind me. 'I *want* to, Holger! I *want* to!'

'There, there, Sidsel,' he said, trying to calm her. He looked up at me apologetically, as I turned towards them again.

'I want to see the place where she was found!'

'But we have to be here ... Vibeke and Stian will be home soon, and we ... '

'I don't want to be here! What shall I tell them?'

'You don't need to ... I'll – '

'I ... ' She stood up abruptly. 'Get me a taxi!'

'A taxi! But ... '

She tossed back her head. Suddenly she had the look of a woman rather the worse for wear at a very boozy follow-on party suddenly deciding she's going home. 'You can't deny me that, Holger!'

'No, I can't ... '

'We're no longer even married!'

'Just separated,' he muttered.

It was as though it only now dawned on her that I was there too and, looking at me, she said: 'You can drive me, Veum!'

'Me! But I ... Don't think you should ... ?' I looked at her husband. 'She ought to lie down.'

He made as if to take her arm gently, but she pulled away from him dramatically. 'I said no! No, no, no! I'll scream.'

'It might perhaps be best ... ' Holger Skagestøl said softly. 'It might do her good, and I'll have a chance to talk to the children alone – first.'

She looked at me with the same agitated expression, as though she hadn't heard what he had said at all. 'Well? Yes or no?'

I threw up my arms. 'All right, then. Of course I'll drive you up there, if you think ... ' I lowered my voice. 'But I'm not at all sure the police are going to like it.'

'The police? What have they got to do with it?'

'Well, in any case it's become a police matter *now*, hasn't it?'

'But she's our ... she's *my* daughter, isn't she?'

I nodded. 'Yes, of course she is.'

'Shall we go, then?'

Without waiting for an answer, she turned to the door and set off. I trotted after her as obediently as a little dog, with an apologetic backward glance at the hapless trainer who was staying behind to wait for the children. The *other* children.

Fifteen

I HELD THE CAR DOOR OPEN for her. She got in and had dutifully put on her seatbelt before I'd walked round to the other side and sat behind the wheel.

As I turned on the ignition, she asked: 'Do you know where it is?'

'More or less.'

Then she said nothing further until we sat waiting for the light to turn green at Paradiskrysset. 'You'd have thought a crisis like this ought to repair a broken relationship.'

I shot a sidelong glance at her. 'Often it does.'

'Hm,' she said pensively to herself rather than anyone else.

I turned right at Hopskiftet and took the motorway to Rådalen. The white snowflakes gave the landscape a grey tint like in an old copper engraving.

She sat quiet as a mouse beside me: her breathing calm and regular. She seemed to have left the pent-up hysteria behind at the house in Furudalen. Now we were more like a couple approaching middle age, with nothing more to say to one another, on the way to some shopping centre or other.

In Rådalen, the stench from the landfill site suggested it wouldn't be long before the refuse dump, now almost thirty years old, would be so full that the contents would start spilling out over the sides. Then we were out on the open farmland between Stend and Fanafjell, where the wind from the sea drove the snowflakes obliquely in across the landscape like dramatic flourishes in the copper plate. Fana Church, with its medieval-looking grey stonework, stood there like a reminder of life and death at the foot of Fanafjell, and I changed down so the car would smoothly take the first sharp bends on the way uphill.

As we neared the highest point on the road, she suddenly placed her hand on my arm and pointed left. 'Can you drive into the parking place there, Veum?'

I did as she said.

She took hold of the door handle. 'I think I could do with some fresh air before … '

I nodded and turned off the engine.

There were no other cars parked there. It was so utterly out of season that the café at Fanaseter was closed, and even if they still had any animals in the enclosures there, there were no kindergarten or other kids visiting them at this time of the year.

Sidsel Skagestøl walked ahead of me towards the old vantage point, where the base of a panoramic telescope still stood, the view long since obscured by the fast-growing conifers. She walked on over the rocky outcrops facing north until she finally felt she was high enough and paused, her gaze sweeping round in an arc, the wind tugging at her blonde hair, so that she had to gather her dark green coat tight round her to keep out the cold.

I climbed up and stood beside her, following her gaze. To the south-west Korsfjord cut its way through between Austevoll and Sotra, where the Lia Tower rose up to a height of 1120 feet above sea level. In the north-west, on the other side of Nordåsvannet, lay the collection of houses at Bønes like a scar in the landscape along the narrow elongated western side of Løvstakken, and beyond that Lyderhorn's highest point at 1300 feet. Behind the mountains the horizon could just be made out: a barely perceptible line between grey and white somewhere far out in the maw of the open sea.

'Life is something you lose,' she said in an undertone. 'Bit by bit.'

'Yes, I suppose so.'

'Childhood – a distant memory. You're young and frisky, full of expectations of life, and then – then suddenly that phase is over. You find love, or you don't find it, in all its various guises. And before you know where you are, that's gone too. The children you bring into the world … ' She swallowed and blinked back the tears as though the wind had become too biting for her. 'Suddenly they've gone too.'

'But life *does* go on, Sidsel.'

She seemed not to hear me. 'There are those who would say life is something we build stone by stone until by the day we die we have a complete edifice.'

'Mm.'

'I'd put it differently. The edifice is what is given to you when you're born: a beautiful edifice into which you are invited. But it's not long before they start to tear your fine edifice down, bit by bit, until at last there you sit, quite alone, on the empty plot. And some houses,' she added with sudden vehemence, 'are not even torn right down! They stand there for ever, like incomplete … lives.'

She turned abruptly and looked east, where the broad channel on the far side of the Hardangerijord lay like a diminutive duvet between the mountains at Fusa. 'And there – lies Folgefonna glacier, just as it has for thousands of years. *It* will never die.'

'Hm, glaciers are like people. They come and go too. They just take a bit longer, that's all.'

She started to walk back down. 'Shall we – carry on, now?'

'It's up to you.'

We got back into the car again.

The valley on the eastern side of Fanafjell is covered in conifers right to the top of Lyshorn, and the road descends in a succession of narrow bends down towards Nordvik and Lysefjord. On a bend a mile or so from the top, two cars were drawn up at the side of the road: a patrol car and a private vehicle. A uniformed policeman stood midway between the cars almost as though he was parked there too.

He followed us with his eyes until I pulled in to the side and parked behind the other two cars. At which point he immediately set off in our direction. As we got out of the car, he said: 'I'm sorry, but this is a restricted area for police only.'

'This is the deceased's mother,' I said with a small gesture of the hand in the direction of Sidsel Skagestøl.

The young constable blushed. 'Oh, I see … I'm really sorry, but I still can't let you through … Of course, you can *look* … ' He cleared his throat. 'I mean … Obviously you understand … we're still carrying out technical investigations down there. To make sure we have all the evidence,' he said, addressing Sidsel Skagestøl directly.

She nodded but looked at neither of us. Her gaze was directed towards the steep slope on the far side of the concrete kerb. With the look of someone afraid of heights she moved gingerly towards the edge of the road, leaning slightly back as though afraid of being sucked in by the downward air currents.

I followed at a discreet distance, conscious of the constable's eyes on the back of my neck. He said nothing but would certainly let us know if we made any attempt to step over the red-and-white tape cordoning off the police's preserve around the scene of the crime.

From the concrete kerb we looked down a steep slope towards an area of newly planted conifers. Under the road a concrete channel had been built to carry one of the streams running down from the mountain behind us. Around the mouth of the tunnel two plain-clothed individuals were carrying out a meticulous examination of what I reckoned must be the actual place where the body had been found, partly beneath the road itself.

I saw it straight away. There was something that didn't add up.

I turned and looked across at the far side of the road. There, the mountainside sloped gradually up towards the top of Fanafjell, the trees like tall dark sentries reaching right down to the edge of the road.

Slowly I redirected my attention to Sidsel Skagestøl. Tall, erect and silent, she stood there, apathetic almost, staring down the slope not unlike someone contemplating suicide on a bridge, wondering whether to jump or not. Beneath the surface, her feelings were no doubt in turmoil, wave upon wave dashing against the rocks so hard that the spray was visible in her eyes. But she did not jump: just stood there, alone and dignified as though already at the cemetery saying her last farewell before the body was interred.

She glanced quickly sideways, as if to reassure herself that it was me standing there. 'I just can't imagine it.'

'I'm sure it's best like that,' I said gently.

'This isn't where she died ... '

'Probably not.'

'It's just a – place where ... her body was kept. She's never actually been here herself. Not what *was* Torild.'

'You're quite right about that. Now you've seen it, I think you should sort of erase the image of this place – not from your memory, because I don't think you could do that, not for a long time anyway, but from your consciousness, from the place where *you* are – and where, in a way, your daughter will also always be.'

She turned to face me. For the first time today she looked me straight in the eye, and the trace of a smile flickered over her mouth. 'Was that the sociologist in you speaking?'

I smiled back. 'Probably. But he's the one who's usually right. Inside me, I mean.'

During the drive back one thought kept coming back to me: *Surely the police must also have seen it? The thing that didn't add up?*

I drove her right back to the door. 'Shall I come in with you?'

'I don't think that's really necessary.' She glanced at the door, where Holger Skagestøl was already coming out to meet us.

'How are you feeling, Sidsel?' he asked. 'Did you manage all right?'

An involuntary twitch ran across her face. She became a paper cut-out someone had suddenly crumpled up. 'Why shouldn't I have managed? It was just a place, wasn't it? Why don't you go up there yourself? You won't find Torild – not there either!'

He made an awkward gesture of the hand and looked dejectedly at me before turning to her again. 'The children are taking it – well. Alva is with them just now. I called her and asked her to – '

'Oh! I have to put up with *that* too, do I?!'

'The children can spend the night at their place, Sidsel. Then you can get a proper rest.'

'Who is Alva?' I asked.

'My sister,' said Skagestøl curtly.

'It might be best for Sidsel to be with the children.'

'And what business is that of yours, Veum?'

'None, strictly speaking, but she's been a hundred per cent calm now, during our drive.'

He grew red in the face. 'A hundred per cent calm *now*! What are you implying?' He rushed up to me as though about to hit me.

I immediately took a step or two back.

'For goodness' sake, Holger! Don't be such an idiot! Listen, we can't leave Alva in there on her own, can we? She'll wear the children out.'

Holger Skagestøl controlled himself, cast a final look of irritation in my direction before turning his back on me and following his wife inside. 'She's *reading* to them, Sidsel!'

Neither of them took the time to say a formal goodbye to me. My duty as a chauffeur was done; and I hadn't been much of a sleuth either. In fact, the only thing I could be credited with was that I'd more or less just happened to be there.

I got into the car, turned in the driveway, and then drove slowly down the steep slope to Sædalen, thinking: *Surely the police must have seen it?*

Sixteen

SHOULD I CHANCE IT and call Muus straight away, at the risk of receiving a thorough bollocking as soon as I opened my mouth? Or should I do as he'd told me: mind my own business?

The problem was that I didn't have any business at the moment, and the devil makes work … The death notice I'd received in the post lay there smouldering away in my desk drawer, a sword poised over my head, and I preferred to push it out of my mind.

I called Paul Finckel.

'Oh my God!' he groaned. 'Is this the big "Be nice to Paul" day or what? Or have you got something new to tell me?'

'No … It's just that I've been up to the place where the body was found.'

'What? So you didn't go right down to it?'

'No. No, I didn't.'

'No, because it's supposed to be a restricted area for everybody!'

'It was.'

'Well, did you go up there alone or what?'

'No, with the girl's mother. It was she who asked me to do it.'

'With the mother, you say? How did she take it? You do realise this could make one hell of a headline, Varg?'

'You know me, Paul. I don't want to appear in the paper!'

'You *are* a news item, Varg! You can't help it.'

'I can help it if you want anything more out of me, though.'

'OK, only out with it – '

'She took it well, Paul. Shocked and upset, of course, but – quite normal for a mother who's just lost her daughter. There's nothing to say, Paul. Nothing to tell you.'

'So why the hell did you call me, then?'

'To ask you one more question.'

'Well, didn't I just know it?!' He fumbled with the receiver. 'Come on, don't hold back: spit it out and tell uncle!'

'You press people always run something on the witnesses. This jogger who found the corpse, have you got his name?'

'His name? I don't even know what type of trainers he uses! The police haven't given us a scrap of information about him.'

'But it *is* a man?'

'Well, he was certainly referred to as *he* the first time I talked to them at the station.'

'But you must have some sources down there, surely? No leaks?'

'Not a drop, Varg, not one … Pretty amazing, actually, don't you think?'

'Right. That's just what I thought too.'

But afterwards I felt reassured. The police had seen it too.

◆

If nothing else, idleness led to restless pacing to and fro across my office floor.

I glanced at the Nordnes calendar on the wall. Maybe I should take a leaf out of Muus's book: circle in red the date which Anon had chosen as the day for my final curtain: Wednesday, the following week.

Was I to conclude that today was consequently my last Friday ever and make it a Friday to beat all Fridays? Ought I to book a suite at the Solstrand Fjord Hotel and invite Karin to come along for a winter weekend she'd never forget? Or, struck by the paralysis that would overcome anyone who received such a message, should I lie down and abandon all hope … ?

For several minutes I racked my brains trying to think who on earth could have thought of sending me such a message. It *could* be a sort of sick joke, of course, but the only person in my circle of acquaintances who had both the imagination and the lack of taste to do such a thing was the man I'd just talked to on the phone, and in that case, he'd hardly have lost the chance to make some small hint about it. In the course of almost eighteen years as a private investigator I'd obviously trodden on a good many toes but not, I hoped, so hard that anyone would want to go to such drastic lengths to pay me back. At any rate, not if they were thinking of carrying out the threat. In my situation I was afraid it wouldn't be much use reporting it to the police either. They'd probably ask me to deal with *this* particular case myself.

Think about something else: that would be best.

Twice yesterday I'd caught myself thinking about Judge Brandt. And that was the murder case that Muus had expressly forbidden me from investigating. But he'd not said a word about H. C. Brandt, had he?

No death notice had appeared in the paper yet, but the rumour factory suggested that, owing to the particular circumstances, the funeral would be a very quiet affair.

A visit to the widow to express my condolences would hardly be considered tactful or good manners. Yet no one could deny me a visit to the hotel where he'd met his death.

Seventeen

BERGEN WAS GOING THROUGH a new building boom, not
unlike the one in the seventies. Then it had been banks that had
mushroomed on the corner of every block. Now it was hotels.
Some people might be tempted to say that tourism had taken
over where finance had left off. But if you looked closer at who
owned the hotels, it was clear that, in reality, it was only a matter
of changing horses. The people behind it all, and the money with
which they speculated were still the same.

The hotel where Judge Brandt had spent his final hours had
always been looked upon as one of the best in town, even though
a string of different owners over the past few decades had taken
a bit of the shine off the reputation it had enjoyed during its
heyday. I walked through reception, heading for the restaurant
on the first floor, but carried on up the stairs, passed the cloak-
room attached to the sitting rooms on the second floor and from
there continued on up.

Considering it was a Friday, there was a good deal of activity
in the corridors. It was clear that the last business guests of the
week had hung on to their rooms as long as possible, and that a lot
of guests were expected for the weekend, perhaps attending some
congress or other.

The chambermaids hurried past, trolleys piled high with bed
linen, clean and dirty, stacks of towels and freshly opened cartons
of cleaning materials. At strategic points along the corridors stood
red plastic crates that quickly filled up with empty bottles from the
vacated rooms.

I stopped one of the chambermaids, a sturdy red-haired
piece with freckles and a smile that soon became a frown when,

assuming my most official voice, I asked: 'It was you who found Judge Brandt dead, wasn't it?'

'Me? No way!' she said, her alarm emphasising her Sognefjord accent. 'It was Annebeth, but she's not in today!'

'Oh?'

'She's been off sick ever since ... '

'But – '

'Have a word with Gro Anita. They're flatmates!'

'And where can I find her?'

'On the fifth floor. She's a big dark lass ... '

I thanked her and went off in search of her workmate, two floors above.

I ran into her emerging from one of the rooms, her arms full of bed linen. She was not only large and dark but also very pretty with a flattened out southern accent, making it hard to place.

Her brown eyes looked at me apologetically as soon as I appeared in the doorway. 'Is this your room, sir? We're running a bit behind, see, but reception told me you two wouldn't be checking in before three.'

'I'm not a guest, actually.'

She pulled a face, pouting slightly with her full lips. 'So where are you from? Department of Employment?' She squeezed past me into the corridor and turned right.

I followed her. 'No, I'd like to have a word with Annebeth.'

'She's off sick!' she said, disappearing through an open door.

From the door I saw her chuck the dirty linen into a large basket and with quick movements of her hands start to take down a clean set from the shelves along the walls. 'Yes, so she's in hospital, is she?'

'No, she's at home.'

'But in that case, she surely ought to be able – '

'Mind your back!' she ordered. 'Look, I'm really pushed!'

I stepped aside and trotted after her back to the room she'd just come from. Without so much as a glance at me, she began to make the bed.

'It's quite important.'

She paused for a moment, straightened up and grimaced as she placed her hands in the small of her back. 'Who for? You haven't even told me your name yet!'

I smiled apologetically. 'No, I'm sorry, but you – I haven't had time. My name's Veum. I represent Judge Brandt's insurance company, and it's just a few details about the death that we – '

'Whether he took his own life, eh?'

'Well … '

'Then his old woman wouldn't get a penny, right?'

'Yes, of course, but that rule only applies – for the first two years after the papers have been signed … but … '

She looked at me defiantly. 'Yes, well I can't help you!'

'Not even with Annebeth's address?'

'Oh, all right then … ' She looked me up and down in the practised way of someone accustomed to fending off heavy advances from travelling salesmen who were still half-asleep. 'We share a small flat in Steinkjellergaten.' She gave me the number and the floor.

I smiled. 'We're practically neighbours, then.'

'Hope that doesn't mean we're going to be stuck with you hanging round the door every evening from now on!'

'Are there a lot who do that?'

'Enough to be going on with!' Sighing, she leaned over the bed again but not as a prelude to any dalliance; it looked more as though she was on the rack to judge by her expression.

I shot out of the door before she had time to ask me the name of Brandt's insurance company and whether I had any identification.

◆

Steinkjellergaten is at the end of the old road into Bergen from the north. New sets had been put down, but the buildings along Steinkjellergaten still retained a historic look, and the gradient was unchanged.

The address I'd been given was in the narrowest part of the street. The two girls shared a flat on the second floor according to a handwritten cardboard sign that said: *Gro Anita Vebjørnsen and Annebeth Larsson*. The last three words had been added later with a different biro.

The varnished door was newer than the house. To the left of it was a narrow window. The light from the hall inside was just visible through the ribbed frosted glass.

I pressed the white button on the black doorbell.

After a while I heard hesitant padding footsteps within as though the occupant were an old lady. Then silence. No one made any attempt to open the door. It was as if she was just standing there waiting, hoping that whoever had rung the bell would go away.

But I'd rung too many doorbells in my life to give up that easily. This time I got an answer. 'Who is it?' asked a muffled voice behind the thick door.

'My name's Veum. I'm from – the insurance company.'

After a moment's thought there was a rattle in the lock and the door opened a crack to reveal a narrow female face peering anxiously at me. 'What do you want?'

'It's about Judge Brandt. We need to clear up a few details.'

She had wispy blonde shoulder-length hair, unbrushed, and she peered at me over her large gold-rimmed glasses that had slipped a little too far down her nose. She was pale with slightly feverish rosy cheeks and wasn't wearing much more than a blue-and-white quilted dressing gown. 'Have you any identification?'

I gave her my driving licence, and she studied it carefully. 'It doesn't say anything about an insurance company here,' she said suspiciously.

I took out one of the visiting cards I'd got a printer friend to run me off before he went bust and set fire to the whole shooting match. If she was pernickety enough to ring to check the number on the card, she'd get no further than my answerphone, which neutrally recorded everything that came in, from funeral dirges to doomsday trumpets. In that case, I hoped she would understand that the Nemesis Insurance Company was one of the smallest and that the telephone operator was at lunch just then.

But she was not that pernickety. She handed both driving licence and visiting card back to me, swung open the door and muttered faintly, 'I hope it won't take too long. I'm off sick.'

I went into the hall, waited till she had closed the door behind us and followed her into what turned out to be a kitchen looking out onto the back, where a February pigeon sat pecking forlornly at the window frame in the hope of finding some insects that had survived the winter.

She had been sitting at the kitchen table with a magazine open at the crossword and a half-empty cup of coffee beside it. I pulled out a wicker chair, sat down and had a quick look round the room before taking out my notebook and assuming an official air.

The room had a sort of half-hearted feminine look about it, with clear signs that it had been furnished by two different people with utterly different tastes. One of them had a preference for large flowery patterns in the curtains, the other for a kind of simple, almost cryptic style, represented in the wallpaper.

'Would you like a cup of coffee?' she asked, and when I nodded, I had the pleasure of seeing her stretch to take a mug from one of the shelves in the kitchen cupboard. Under her dressing gown she was wearing tight-fitting teenage-style pyjama trousers in pink cotton with small flowers, and she had stuffed her bare feet into deep red slippers with big pompoms on them, borrowed from some diva she had forgotten to return them to. Unless, that is, it was Gro Anita they belonged to. I wasn't in any particular doubt about which of them liked flowers and pompoms, and which had the simpler style.

She poured coffee from a pale yellow flask, pushed the magazine out of the way and looked at me inquiringly.

I nodded towards the half-finished crossword. 'That's just what a sudden death is like. A long row of unanswered questions and a form you have to fill in bit-by-bit, down and across, until – if you're lucky and have a good dictionary – you've completed it. Filled out what actually happened.'

She shifted uneasily. She felt her forehead with the back of her hand as though to emphasise the fact that she had a temperature. Her lips were dry and cracked with white blotches against the darker flesh.

'And there are still some clues we haven't found answers to,' I went on.

She fluttered her eyelashes, not from any attempt to make an impression but rather like someone suddenly emerging into very harsh daylight. Yet still she said nothing.

'As I was saying … not to beat about the bush … You were the one who found him, weren't you?'

She nodded, shifting her gaze to the window. The pigeon was no longer there, as if it had sensed danger. The same snowflakes fell steadily over the city as though from a never-ending supply, but did not stick, because the thermometer was still a fraction above zero.

'Can you tell me what happened?'

When she eventually spoke it was so softly that I had to lower my head to hear what she said. 'I don't know what had gone on in there … I just – found him.'

'Yes, I see, but … You knew he was there, did you?'

'Yes, we'd been told that the room was taken till two o'clock.'

'Was that normal?'

Her gaze shifted again. 'Y-yes … It often happens that guests need the rooms a bit longer.'

'Yes, but I meant … you'd seen the judge before, hadn't you?'

'Yes, he … they said he often had important meetings there … conferences.'

'Mm.' I looked reassuringly at her.

'So … I'd seen him there before.'

'And … did you see who he had these – meetings with before?'

'Er, sometimes … Yes.'

'Was it – men?'

She did not answer.

'Women?'

She nodded.

'Different women?'

She shrugged her shoulders. 'Er, maybe.'

'Young women?'

She pursed her lips.

'*Very* young?'

A further nod. 'I'll say!'

'Oh?'

'No, I just meant, you wouldn't have caught me doing it! Even if they paid me a fortune!'

'Yes, that's probably what most people would think.'

'The old pig! He got no more than he – ' She stopped herself abruptly, horrified at what she had just been about to say.

I took out the newspaper cutting showing a picture of Torild Skagestøl, put it on the kitchen table and pushed it over to her. 'This girl here, was she one of them?'

She glanced quickly at the picture, almost as though she was afraid of being recognised. She nodded faintly. Then she leaned closer and had a good look at it before nodding with much greater conviction. 'Hair a bit different maybe, and a much more brazen look on her face but – yes … ' She looked me straight in the eye. 'I'm sure it's her!'

I leaned forwards. 'Sure it was her the day we're talking about as well?'

She looked uncertain. 'Er, I think so, but … I didn't see her so clearly that day, but – it was nearly always her! Quite a few times. I'm sure of it now … When she passed me, well, us, in the corridor, she just looked straight at us with the most brazen look you can imagine – as if we, as if we didn't get what she was up to in there, as if we didn't know what she was!'

I felt a strange buzz, a mixture of satisfaction and fear. Satisfaction at what I'd already figured out; fear at what it could only imply. 'But ... OK. Let's go back to the day we're talking about – last Friday, right?'

She confirmed it with a faint nod.

'Tell me how it was that you ... that you found him.'

She pushed her large glasses back up the bridge of her nose but hadn't got many words out before they'd slipped back down. 'It was her I saw first ... She was ... she seemed in a real hurry because on her way to the lift she was still tucking her blouse into her slacks, but when she – saw me ... '

'Yes?'

'I was just coming out of a room at the end of the corridor, and ... when she saw me, she turned straight back as though ... ' She searched for the right expression. 'Well, she didn't want to be seen, in a way. Then she disappeared round the corner where she must definitely have taken the stairs instead.'

'Did her behaviour strike you as unusual?'

'Yes, but not in that way ... '

'Was that when you went into their room?'

'No, no, it wasn't two o'clock yet, and they had the room ... ' She lost the thread of what she was saying.

'I see. And then?'

'Then – I did the other rooms.'

'What time was it when you got to Brandt's room, then?'

'I didn't look at my watch – twenty past two, something like that, according to what the police said. At any rate it was twenty-five past two when they were telephoned from reception.'

'Tell me what happened.'

'Nothing *happened*. When I went to the room I knocked and waited, the way we're always supposed to. But he could have gone while I was doing one of the other rooms, so ... when there was no reply I let myself in with the key.' She put her hand over her mouth as though the memory of what she had seen there was so strong that she involuntarily had to go through her own physical reactions again.

'First it was so quiet that I was sure he'd left. But there was a smell, a smell I couldn't identify ... and when I got right into the room, there he lay, on the bed, in a really contorted position, wearing just, just ... I had to be sick, so I dashed into the loo, but nothing came up. It was just my stomach turning, my whole diaphragm heaving, it hurt so. I think that's what made me sick now I come to think of it.'

'That's not impossible.'

'I never wear any stuff like that myself ... I mean, black, it seems kinky to me.'

I didn't comment on that aspect. 'Was there anything in the room to indicate what had been going on there?'

'Well, it looked as though there'd been a party. They'd helped themselves to beer from the mini-bar, and there were pillows – on the floor, one of the chairs had been knocked over, and in the bathroom ... '

'Yes?'

'Just behind the toilet bowl, I saw it when I was bending over to be sick, there was a bottle lying on the floor, an empty – bottle of tablets.'

'What did you do with it?'

She looked at me wide-eyed. 'Do with it? I told the police, of course!'

'Was there anything on the label?'

'Do you really think I looked at it? It was all I could do to stand up. What I needed was – well ... '

I drained my coffee. 'Was there anything else in the room you particularly noticed?'

'Nothing except what he'd ... He'd tried to write something on the wall ... '

'What? He'd tried to write something?'

'At first I thought it was blood that he'd smeared around, but then … There was no blood apart from that, and I … then I realised it was lipstick.'

She looked at me with an air of intense unease. 'He'd *painted* himself, worse than the worst … ' She ran her fingers round her lips as though to show what she meant.

'So he'd tried to write something, with the lipstick?'

'Yes.'

'What was it?'

'First it looked just like a few squiggles, but later … it was a letter.'

'A letter! Which one?'

'A big – "T".'

Eighteen

SOURCES ARE, if anything, more important in my line than they are for the press and protected by just as strict a code of confidentiality. Maybe that was why I had so many useful contacts in the dailies.

The editorial world was a labyrinth, and a well-lit one, not so much because it was supposed to be difficult to find one's way through it but to make room for as many people as possible in the currently available space.

I found Laila Mongstad in a little cubicle at the far end, with half a window facing the back of the Social Sciences block in Fosswinckels Street and the Catholic school in the next building. It was almost four years now since, at a surprisingly late stage in her career, she had been poached from the paper's more radical cousin in Christian Michelsens Street and had long confirmed her reputation as a such a first-class reporter on social affairs that the paper had already been in the dock twice to answer libel charges following some of her revelations.

Perhaps it was all the dirt she spent her time digging up that had made her previously generous smile slightly frayed at the edges; or perhaps it was just age claiming its due. She'd kept up quite a pace over a career of thirty or forty years in newspapers, and, despite the fact that her blue-grey eyes were still full of energy and dynamism, I quickly calculated that she'd certainly turned sixty since we'd last had something special going. And we'd never really got any further than that.

The smile she gave me betrayed nothing. Her eggshell-blue silk blouse emphasised her large breasts, but I noted that she had done up the lower buttons of her red cardigan, most likely to camouflage the size of her waist above the tight-fitting dark-blue slacks.

'How are you?' I began cautiously.

'Is this a friendly visit, or is it work?' she answered, swivelling her chair away from the computer keyboard she was using.

'Both.'

'In that case, you'd better sit down.'

'Thanks. Which shall we start with?'

She gave a crooked smile. 'Which'll take longer?'

'I'm sure you know about – that girl they've found up on Fanafjell … '

'Holger's daughter. It's dreadful. But … '

'She'd been missing for a whole week, and I … I was hired two days ago to try and find her.'

'I see. You got there too late?'

'I wasn't even close – but I did find something out.'

'Oh?'

'One of the places I learned she'd hung out in a good deal is an amusement arcade called Jimmy's.'

She pulled a face. 'Jimmy's … '

'Know the place?'

She pulled out a drawer in her desk. 'How did you find out that she hung out there?'

'One of her girlfriends said so.'

'It doesn't necessarily mean anything, of course, but … '

She had taken a large beige envelope out of the drawer. Now she opened it and tipped about twenty black-and-white enlargements onto the desk. 'One of our photographers took these from a parked car at the beginning of January.'

She pushed four of the pictures over to me.

I looked at them. They showed the entrance to Jimmy's. A young girl was coming out. In the next picture she was walking along the pavement, as the dark shadow of a moving car came into the picture from the right. In the third picture she stood half leaning over, looking into the car, and in the fourth she was climbing into the passenger seat beside the driver.

The car's number plate had been touched up and was quite legible. I glanced up at Lalla Mongstad. 'Have you checked out who the car owner is?'

She nodded.

'And – ?'

She looked around and leaned so close that I caught a hint of her perfume, a fresh, sap-like scent. 'A not entirely unknown local politician … You know who Hallstein Grindheim is, don't you?'

'The Christian People's Party man?'

'Unfortunately, you can't see the driver.'

'You mean you don't know who the driver was?'

'No.'

I looked at the other pictures. 'Are there more like these?'

She leafed through a few pictures before taking three out and pushing them over to me.

One of them was almost identical to the first one I'd seen. It showed another young girl coming out of Jimmy's. The next one showed her walking along the pavement in another street. I had to look closer at a couple of the hoardings to identify where it was. The third showed her going through the main entrance of the same hotel I'd visited myself a few hours before.

'And then?' I asked.

She shrugged her shoulders. 'There's a limit to how far we can follow this up, but … a rendezvous in one of the rooms?' She handed me a fourth picture. 'Here she's on her way out two hours later.'

'Where did she go then?'

'To the bus station and then took the last bus home.'

'But your paper hasn't written about this yet, as far as I recall.'

'No. At the moment we're just gathering background material. When we come out with this stuff we must have cast-iron evidence to back it up.'

'Excellent. What more do you know? I take it your people have been poking around at Jimmy's too?'

'You know who owns the place?'

I hesitated. 'No, but since you say it like that ... it's Bjørnstjerne Bjørnson, isn't it?'

'No, but you're on the right track. The initials are the same.'

'Birger Bjelland?'

'Mm.'

'Does this mean, in other words, that something can be pinned on the guy at last?'

She pouted sceptically. 'Mm. Maybe we should put it like this ... A long time ago he showed that he has as many lives as a cat. We can possibly shorten his life account by one if this really nails him.'

'What about Hallstein Grindheim? Have you confronted him with the pictures?'

'Not yet. But if we can only get him full frontal, he's going to find it on the front page!'

'With clothes or without?'

She bared her teeth, and I noticed how pointed her eye teeth seemed. 'Without as well ... '

'But to come back to Jimmy's, have you lot been to take a look around there?'

'I'm too old and the wrong sex, in any case.'

'But – ?'

'Sure, I do have younger colleagues with the right calibre between their legs.' She looked at me provocatively as though to intimate that I perhaps didn't match up to her standards in that department. 'But it's hard to put your finger on anything specific. From the outside it looks like a normal amusement arcade. Most of those playing the machines are boys, and, of course, we don't rule out the possibility that there might be some – traffic there too, but ... it looks as though girls are the speciality, especially teenagers. They probably recruit the grown-up girls from some-where else.'

'The bar at the Week End Hotel, for instance?'

'That hotel's also changed its name recently, so … yes.'

'Oh really? Very recently?'

'Somebody's bought out the family.'

'Somebody?'

'And it's not Bjørnstjerne Bjørnson either.'

'I see. So what do they call the hotel now? The Secret Garden?'

'Is it a while since you ate?'

'Yes.'

'Pastel.'

'So they've painted it as well, have they?'

She nodded.

'I'm going to throw up.'

'That's why I asked … '

'Mm. Well … ' I threw up my hands. 'In other words, you're strongly suggesting that Jimmy's operates as a sort of procuring joint?'

'Yes, I am – unfortunately.'

'And how does it all work?'

'Via a phone call to whoever's on duty behind the counter. He writes something on a pad, and after a while the message is discreetly passed to whichever of the girls is in line for an – assignment.'

'Then some of them are fetched by car, while others meet at a prearranged rendezvous?'

'Something like that.'

I leafed through the photos again, trying to read the expressions on the faces of the two young girls. You could see from their build that they were two different girls, but the photos were too indistinct to make out who they were.

I put aside one of the photos from the series ending at the hotel entrance. Then I pushed it over to her. 'Could this be – Torild Skagestøl?'

She looked at me thoughtfully before picking up the picture and holding it away from her. 'I don't think I've ever set eyes on her … but some of the others could be … ' She glanced back at me. 'Do you think there's a direct link between this and the fact that she was killed?'

'It wouldn't be the first time a … ' I was reluctant to use the word. 'That something like this has happened to a – prostitute, would it?'

'No, you're quite right there.' She suddenly looked worried. 'Ought I to inform the editorial board about this?'

'For the sake of the girl's reputation – and the parents – I'd rather we kept it between ourselves for the moment.'

'I'll have to think about it,' she said, suddenly looking official.

I pointed at the picture of the front of the hotel. 'Doesn't this ring any other bells?'

'Should it?'

'Last Friday at the same hotel.'

She snapped her fingers. 'Brandt!' Her eyes flashed. 'Do you mean … ?'

'It was rumoured that he'd had a female visitor in his room, wasn't it?'

'And he did have, Varg, no doubt about it!'

'Precisely.'

'A municipal judge – and a man from the Christian People's Party. It's starting to add up to something … '

'And it wasn't exactly a book club meeting, was it?'

'But … strictly speaking, this is a police matter, isn't it?'

'Sure, but then I haven't said … I mean I was looking for Torild Skagestøl before she was found. I told the police what little I knew, but now you've got a lot more dynamite on Jimmy's … '

She looked at me doubtfully. 'But I'm not sure I want to publish all that yet. Besides, I'm sure the police checked out these activities long ago.'

'Checked them out – and didn't do anything?'

'Are any of the girls under age?'

'Well, no, not any of the ones I've spoken to.'

'Exactly. So evidence has to be found that someone's making money out of them.'

I thought for a moment. 'Who knows most about prostitution in this city at the moment? I mean *outside* the police?'

'In that case, I'd have a word with one of the people behind the most active Women's Lib groups.'

'Can you suggest anybody?'

'Someone you could talk to and who also knows what she's talking about professionally is Evy Berge.'

'And who's she?'

'A nurse in A&E at Haukeland Hospital.'

'Do you have any phone numbers?'

She turned to her computer and clicked the mouse. As the list of phone numbers came up on the screen, she said: 'Some of these girls have had to go ex-directory ... Evy too, actually. That means you have to keep it to yourself.' She wrote down something on a yellow message pad. 'Here's the number of the department as well, in case she's on duty. Actually ... ' She started ferreting through the bundle of papers on the left-hand side of the desk. 'Didn't she give me ... ? Yes, here it is!'

She handed me a circular on which, under the title RECLAIM THE NIGHT!, a demonstration was announced for eleven p.m. the following Monday in C Sundts Street.

'Will you be there?' I asked.

'No, I'm still keeping my distance from that, er – particular matter. But it might do you some good,' she added with a pointed little smile.

'Does this mean we're onto the *friendly* part now? Is that it?'

She leaned forward and came a little closer, looking into my eyes with a rather ambiguous twinkle and said softly: 'Still got any friendliness left, Varg? Is that a glimmer of belated love I see deep in there?'

The worst of it was that she almost made me blush. 'Er – belated?'

'Yes?' She leaned a little closer still and took my hands.

We got no further. The door into the corridor flew open, and we heard the sound of hurried footsteps rushing into the room before a loud voice shouted: 'I'm bloody well not having it! Buggered if I am!'

Through the shouting, I immediately recognised the voice. It was Holger Skagestøl.

Nineteen

LAILA MONGSTAD let go of my hands as though she'd scalded herself, and in unison we stood up and looked over the partition to the source of the racket.

Holger Skagestøl was herding a group of eight or nine colleagues into the room.

A man in his thirties with slightly dishevelled blonde hair, a short leather jacket and a large camera-bag over one shoulder was first, followed by a chap of the same age in a leather waistcoat and blue denim shirt. It was Bjørn Brevik, one of the journalists on the paper, who was doing his best to keep Skagestøl away from the photographer. Close behind Skagestøl followed Trond Furebø and a handful of others, a couple of them intent on pouring oil on troubled waters, the others there out of pure curiosity.

'I want that film, do you hear?! I want it!' yelled Holger Skagestøl so the whole editorial office reverberated.

'Better take it up with the desk, then!' replied the photographer.

'Goddamn it, you lot can't treat me like – like – like any Tom, Dick or Harry! I work on this paper, too, you know.'

'So is that supposed to give us preferential treatment?' Bjørn Brevik cut in.

'Preferential treatment?' Skagestøl seized Brevik by his lapels and pulled him close to his face. 'I'm talking about normal protection of personal privacy! The "Be Fair" code for journalists. Ever heard of it, you little upstart? I'm damned if I'm going to have my private family affairs splashed all over the front page!'

Brevik raised his voice a few decibels too. 'Let go of me!'

Skagestøl looked as though he was actually tightening his grip, if anything.

Trond Furebø seized him by the arm. 'Holger ... '

'Let go of me! Do you hear? I – '

Brevik pushed his elbows up and released himself from his grip so roughly that a shirt button ricocheted over the desks. 'There's no question of splashing any family affairs over the front page. It's a news item!'

'News! They've already arrested the guilty party! Why don't you use a picture of him instead?!'

'It's a perfectly normal illustration!' the photographer piped up his voice rising to a falsetto.

'Illustration! Do you want me to shove that camera down your throat, eh?'

Trond Furebø cut in: 'Holger! This is no good. Let's go and see the editor ... '

Skagestøl was starting to calm down. There was a sudden change in his face, and when he spoke again he was dose to tears. 'Surely you can understand ... Bjørn. This is about my daughter.'

Bjørn Brevik nodded. '*Your* daughter this time; somebody else's tomorrow. What would you have done in my shoes?'

'I'd have made allowances ... '

'*Would* you?'

Skagestøl had tears in his eyes now. 'Well?'

'And what if it didn't concern you personally?'

Trond Furebø came up beside Holger Skagestøl, stepped around him and stood face-to-face with Bjørn Brevik. 'We'll take it up with the boss, OK?'

Brevik gave him a look of contempt. 'OK by me.'

The group broke up. Those who had merely been curious withdrew, visibly disappointed that the drama was over. The photographer was still trying to keep Brevik between himself and Skagestøl, and all of them headed for the door.

Trond Furebø ran his eyes over the rest of us, standing there like tin soldiers in our boxes in a rather nondescript toyshop sale.

'What the hell are you lot gawping at?' he spat out to no one in particular.

When he caught sight of me, he changed his tack slightly and raised his voice. 'Satisfied now, are you? Bloody nosey parker!'

The door slammed behind him, and those left turned towards me as though only just realising a new specimen had been added to their collection.

I sat down and looked at Laila Mongstad. 'Any idea what all that was in aid of?'

'No, but we'll find out in due course.'

'But what was that about … have they made an arrest?'

She reached for the phone. 'If you hang on a second, I'll ask … ' She dialled a number, asked the same question and sat listening. 'Oh … I see … No, it was just … Thanks a lot.'

She replaced the receiver and nodded. 'Apparently it's that jogger who found her. But so far he's still a witness.'

Exactly. They had *seen it then.*

She kissed me quickly on the mouth when I went, as if to show what good friends we still were, unless it was just an expression of her overall generosity.

Twenty

ON SATURDAY MORNING I went down to the main door early to collect the paper.

There was no missing the article. The editor had apparently come down on Bjørn Brevik's side.

The headline read:

PARENTS IN SHOCK –
Friend of victim helping police with enquiries.

There was a large photo showing Holger and Sidsel Skagestøl being led out of the police station by a uniformed policeman. Holger Skagestøl was in the foreground, slightly too close to the flashbulb, and his overexposed face expressed in the clearest possible terms that he did not like being photographed. Sidsel Skagestøl was partly hidden behind him but was looking straight at the photographer, caught off her guard and anxious, like someone suddenly jumped on in a dark back street.

'We didn't even know she had a boyfriend,' said Sidsel and Holger Skagestøl when, at midday yesterday, they were informed that the police had called in a friend of the victim, Torild Skagestøl (16), for further questioning at police headquarters. Detective Inspector Dankert Muus, who is heading the investigation, will not comment other than to say that the young man has been summoned as a witness. From another source, this newspaper has received confirmation that the witness is none other than the young jogger who reported having found the body

late Thursday evening. The police are still refusing to comment
on whether the victim had been the object of a sexual assault
either before or after she was killed. Torild Skagestøl's friends
and family are deeply shocked at the murder. Friends and
teachers describe her as a good friend and a positive student.
No one has been able to suggest a motive for the murder yet.

That was all there was to the article, which, because of the early
hour it had gone to press on Friday evening, was considerably
briefer than would normally have been the case on a weekday.

After a similarly brief breakfast I rang Karin and asked whether
she was ready.

The weekend was not spent in a suite at the Solstrand Fjord
Hotel but in long steady sex on the island of Sotra in a cottage I
sometimes borrowed from a second cousin who didn't have much
use for it in February anyway.

As soon as we crossed the Sotra Bridge we noticed that the wind
had swung to the north-west, that the thermometer was rising and
that the weekend would be best suited to indoor activities.

The cottage faced straight into the maw of the sea, and when
the wind strength had increased significantly it felt like being in
the middle of a gigantic conch, with the constant sound of the sea
in your ears. The chasing clouds took on a leaden hue, and we had
hardly lit the fire when the first flash of lightning dashed white
stitches across the horizon, where the sky was about to rip apart.

The ensuing clap of thunder sent Karin straight into my arms,
and even when the thunderstorm had moved off it was no easy
matter to get her to shift. With a pot of tea simmering on the hot-
plate, we unrolled our sleeping bags, making one into a sheet and
the other an eiderdown and, like two bears still drowsy from their
long winter slumber and shunning the first cold dip of the year,
went back into hibernation.

We made love like a couple of seventeen-year-olds on their first
camping trip.

Afterwards we drank some tea, ate rough hunks of bread with thick slices of cheese and chatted. The advantage of being lovers at our time of life was there were so many stones to overturn, so many branches to pull aside, so much distance covered to talk about.

Late that night, with the gentle sound of her regular breathing beside me, I lay on my back, thinking. Was this happiness? Was this how life was supposed to have been the whole time? And, if so, how long would it last? Who the hell had sent me the death notice in the post?

Twenty-one

ON MONDAY EVENING I reported to the police station. I had come of my own free will, and no one threw me out before hearing what I wanted.

The Sunday papers had been much more sensationalistic in their reports, not least because they had more details to go on than the authors of Saturday's report. ANOTHER SATANIST MURDER? one of them asked. SACRIFICED TO THE DEVIL? asked another. Neither of them had any pictures of Sidsel and Holger Skagestøl on the front page, but both had got hold of a photo of Torild from a class picture and given it a prominent place.

It was the mark cut into her flesh and the fact that the body had been discovered near Lysekloster monastery that formed the main grounds for this speculation. The papers had dug up old rumours about black masses and sacrilegious orgies in the hallowed ruins of the monastery. These were stirred into a somewhat speculative brew with not many ingredients, judging by what I already knew about the case myself.

The Monday papers focused on another angle: CASE SOLVED? said one of the headlines. 'WITNESS' BEING QUESTIONED, said Holger Skagestøl's own paper with prominent quotation marks. SLAIN BY LOVER? asked Paul Finckel in his newspaper. (Had he tried to get in touch with me during the weekend? I wondered) Surprisingly, none of the papers gave the name or age of the much discussed 'witness' or any photos of him, merely saying that he was apparently a young man from among the victim's closest friends.

Muus was not in his office, but when I looked in on Atle Helleve, there he sat with a selection of the same newspapers spread out on his desk.

I knocked on the doorframe. He looked up, recognised me and gestured towards the headlines. 'Seen these? You'd not find wilder improvisation at the Voss Jazz Festival!'

'Can I come in?'

'Take a pew before someone else does.'

'How much is there to what they're writing about?'

'Not a lot, I can promise you that.' He scratched his beard. 'Why do you ask?'

'It could be I have a bit of – additional information. Something I've turned up.'

'Oh?' He looked at me with natural scepticism in his eyes.

'But I can't see how this so-called jogger fits into the picture.'

'Can't you?'

We sat there looking at one another for a few seconds, but he wouldn't take the bait.

'You first.'

'Well … when Judge Brandt died last Friday, was there a post-mortem?'

He sat up in his chair. 'There's a padlock on that case, Veum! If a single word gets out to the pre – '

'The press already know most of what there is to know about this case, Helleve. Since they haven't given us any descriptions of the judge in black silk underwear yet, they're hardly going to do so later, are they?'

'But how in – '

'Not all bulkheads are watertight in this office either. Rumours about this have been circulating for so long that this case is actually already dead. Unless they're given something new … '

'Something new? What do you mean?'

'Well, *was* there a post-mortem?'

'Yes, there was. A massive heart attack, from which he died.'

'A heart attack caused by … '

'At the judge's age, you know, and considering what he seems to have been up to at the time … I'll say no more, I'll say no more.'

'And the writing on the wall, was it investigated?'

'The writing … The sign or whatever he'd tried to make … ' He shook his head. 'There was nothing to suggest anything criminal had gone on there, Veum. What people do in their free time – '

'Wasn't it in office time though?'

' – and what clothes they choose to wear is their affair. It's not a police matter at any rate.'

'Wasn't it a large "T"? The letter he'd scrawled with his lipstick?'

'Could have been.'

'"T" for Torild, for example.'

He mulled it over for a few seconds. 'Are you trying to suggest that the girl … that she could have been … ?'

'Maybe … I don't know, Helleve, to be honest, but I'm sorry to say I have a few clues indicating that could have been the case.'

'That she and Brandt … That he was simply her client?'

'Could have been.'

'In that case, we … we need to look into it a bit closer. And it mustn't get out to that bloody pack of wolves, Veum!' He pointed, superfluously, at the newspapers spread out in front of him.

'The bottle of tablets that was found in his room … '

'Where did you get *that* from?'

I shrugged. 'A reliable source. Have you found out what was in it?'

'I don't think we've got the results of the analysis yet. It wasn't seen as all that important. I mean we know he had a visit from a prostitute, and we know they often take tablets. Which tablets exactly isn't all that important.'

I nodded towards the newspapers. 'This Satanist angle, is there anything in it?'

He threw up his arms. 'She has a sort of mark, behind here, on one of her thighs, but … '

'No other marks?'

'No.'

'And the cause of death?'

'She was suffocated. Everything points to the fact that someone held a pillow or something like that against her face. Sure as we are that Judge Brandt died a natural death, if you can speak of "natural" in a get-up like that, we're just as certain that we're dealing with a regular murder here.'

'Any sign of sexual assault?'

Helleve glanced at the door and leaned forward. 'Muus says you're a dicey bugger. Other people here say you're straight up.'

'So, in other words … '

He sighed. 'No. There's no sign of rape. But … '

'Yes?'

'Semen was found in her, after recent intercourse.'

'Enough for a DNA analysis?'

'More than.'

'How long will it be before you guys get the results?'

'No idea, really. It's a very time-consuming procedure.'

'But in this case the person whose semen it is doesn't necessarily need to be the perpetrator. I mean, if it really *was* Torild Skagestøl who was with Brandt – '

'You're jumping to some very hasty conclusions there,' he cut in. 'For starters, we don't know if Brandt *did* have intercourse; we don't even know if it was Torild Skagestøl he was with – '

'I'll come back to that!'

'We don't even know if Torild Skagestøl was a – prostitute, or whatever we should call it at her age.'

'Is there a nicer word?'

'No, but frankly, Veum, I have a daughter of my own. It's only two or three years since she was in the Guides … '

'Yes, so I heard, But she dropped out.'

'Most of them do in the end.'

'She didn't have any needle marks?'

'Not as far as we could see.'

'But a blood test would certainly show whether she'd taken anything from the bottle of tablets.'

'We haven't got that yet either!'

'But I didn't finish setting out my hypothesis, Helleve. Because *if* she'd had sex with Brandt, and this boyfriend of hers had somehow found out about it … then the idea of a crime of passion provoked by jealousy or just pure rage isn't all that outlandish, is it?'

'Know anything about this boyfriend, Veum?'

'This much,' I said, indicating a tiny amount with my thumb and index finger. 'I didn't even know she had a boyfriend. How did you lot find out about him?'

'One of her girlfriends gave us his name.'

'Åsa Furebø?'

He shrugged. 'The rest was just peanuts. He'd sort of put himself in the limelight anyway.'

'I hope you lot had the same reaction as I did up where the body was found?'

'Which was … ?'

'Well, if he wanted to answer a call of nature while out jogging, why would he clamber all the way down a rough slope to a place with hardly any trees, when he could just have walked over to the other side of the road and gone in between the dense conifers?'

'Exactly. But that's what he says … that he wanted to avoid the headlights of any passing cars.'

'Do you mean … ? Does he deny it?'

'Sure he does! The fellow's a hard nut, I'll say! Why do you think he's still only a "witness"?'

'Hm. Is there anyone I could talk to, do you think? Åsa? Anyone else? Sometimes people find it easier to talk to a – layman … than to you people.'

He scowled at me. 'Well, there's only … No, I don't think you ought to do anything else, except … This prostitution angle, how did you turn that up?'

I told him all I knew both about Jimmy's and the traffic in young girls to cars and hotel rooms, with a nod to sources in the press I couldn't name and chambermaids I *did* think I could reveal.

'This girl, then, who you got to say far too much, was she sure it was Torild Skagestøl who was with Brandt that day?'

'As good as ... '

'I think we're going to have to have a word with her in connection with this too. The last time it seems to have been a bit too cursory.'

'This place called Jimmy's,' I said, 'reminds you a bit of those places in the fifties or sixties that were exposed as procuring joints. Know who's behind it?'

'No.'

'Birger Bjelland.'

'That hypocritical Stavanger creep! If only we could get something on *him* ... '

'It's not that easy, evidently.'

'He walks a very fine line between his legal activities and what we're all quite sure is the illegal stuff he's got his fingers in.'

'He's crossed *my* path often enough in the past few years.'

'But without your being able to link him with anything illegal, right? I mean in the sense of something that would stand up in court.'

'No, alas. But what about ... Al Capone was caught on a tax matter in the end, wasn't he?'

'Waste of time. He has a first-rate accountant and sends in immaculate tax returns and annual accounts on time every single year.'

'But one of these days he's going to make a slip, Helleve, and then ... '

'Then we'll stand at the door here and wish him a pleasant stay at His Majesty's Pleasure, you can bet on that, Veum!'

'Is it OK if I see what I can dig up on what you call the prostitution angle, working on my own?'

'Provided you keep strictly to that, and I don't mean as a client, Veum. But if you start to get close to the murder, even by half an inch, then that's it. Then you're under an absolute obligation to report it right away – either to me or the nearest police authority. !s that clear?'

'Message received. Over and out.'

'And not a word in the paper, Veum!'

'Cross my heart and hope to die, Scout's Honour,' I said and left.

Twenty-two

JIMMY'S OPENED at twelve o'clock, and it was just after ten past as I approached the door.

When I looked in through the window I saw the silhouette of a man clearly outlined against the bright light in the room at the back. Behind the counter sat 'Kalle' in the same unwashed chef's smock as before, but with a fresh newspaper and hopefully freshly brewed coffee in his cup. As I opened the door and went in, I heard the sound of another door being closed. When I looked up the man who had been standing in the doorway of the room at the back had gone.

Kalle shot a sullen sideways glance at me.

I took a quick look around. At the far end, hunched over a machine, was a lad with a lock of long fair hair falling over his eyes. He scowled in my direction, obviously bothered by his conscience, missing school as he was, and for all he knew I could be from Child Welfare.

Kalle slammed down his cup and stood up behind the counter. 'What do you want?'

'Actually, I was looking for my – nephew.'

'Nephew. Kiss my arse!'

'Ronny.'

'Daren't show his face here any more. I told him that was it. You'd best look for him somewhere else.'

I moved towards him. 'Er ... Kalle ... I didn't catch your surname.'

'Persen,' he said, a bit surprised. 'What's it got to do with you anyway?'

'I was hoping to have a word with Bjelland actually.'

'Bje – ' He glanced involuntarily towards the back door. 'What for? It's me who's business manager here.'

'Diploma from Bergen Business School, I suppose? Does Bjelland know about the scam you're running from here, or is it something you started off your own bat?'

He looked even more sullen. 'What scam?'

The lad in the corner glanced at us for a second, before dropping in a coin and starting a new game. The hollow tinny sound of the introductory music echoed through the room.

'I think you know what I'm driving at. Young girls and – boys … I hung around for a while outside this place on Thursday, and it wasn't all that hard to find out where at least one of them ended up. Same place as Torild Skagestøl last Friday, right?'

Kalle Persen leaned forward over the counter so abruptly that I stepped back. He waved a podgy index finger in my face and snarled: 'Look, mate, if you don't want to spend the rest of your life with broken kneecaps, I suggest you watch your mouth – and no mistake. Got my drift?'

'Can I have that in writing so I can take it down to the police station in Domkirkegaten and show them?'

'You can have it for real some night when you're least expecting it.'

'Better be before Wednesday.'

'Before Wednesday? How d'you mean?'

'Forget it. In other words, you're suggesting I should speak to Bjelland in person, are you? Where can I find him?'

'He's in the phone book.'

'So, he's not the one hiding in the back room, is he?'

A sort of smile broke out beneath the mouse fur on his upper lip. 'You can go and take a look if you want … '

'It's not *that* important.' I walked towards the door. 'Have a nice day.'

'Kiss my – '

'I didn't do it last time, and I'm not going to this time either.'

I left the door ajar when I went out, so he'd have the pleasure of coming out from behind the counter and walking across the floor to shut it again after me.

◆

It wasn't time for a visit to Birger Bjelland yet and perhaps never would be.

Instead I went back to the office and, not without a trace of anxiety, went through the mail. But today's contained no death notices.

I tried to get hold of Evy Berge. There was no answer at her home number. And when I called her department at Haukeland Hospital, she was in theatre. – Could they ask her to call me? – But I preferred not to leave my name. You could never tell. It might end up in their database, and next time I was taken to hospital, they might discover I'd donated all my internal organs to the Institute of Pathology.

I ought to talk to one of the girls.

Astrid was the hardest nut to crack, but Åsa was probably harder to get hold of, at least, if I wanted to avoid having her parents there.

I leafed back through my notes with the feeling that there was another lead I'd meant to chase up before …

The Guide leader … *Sigrun Søvik*. I'd made a note of it.

When I called the office of the Girl Guides Association at Vetrlidsalmenningen I was given her work phone number: a development company with offices in Søndre. And if I still wanted to go to Karin's in Landås, it wasn't much of a detour.

◆

The district of Mindemyren is the coldest place in Bergen. In winter, the frost smoke never quite loosens its grip there. If you leave your car parked for long, you can have trouble starting it.

The development company had offices on the first and second floors over a warehouse, behind large grey steel Venetian blinds. I found Sigrun Søvik in a red check flannel shirt and grey pullover, totally absorbed in a computer screen, where she was slowly rotating a construction, with technical data listed here and there, deftly touching certain keys. The walls around her were covered in technical drawings. On a couple of them I thought I recognised the same diagram as on the screen.

She looked up at me vaguely as I stood in the doorway of her tiny office. 'Yes? What, er ... ?'

She was a stocky woman with medium fair hair, shorter at the back than in front, staring eyes and a strikingly broad bridge of the nose, as if it had once been broken. Her mouth – she was not wearing lipstick – seemed slightly too small for her large face, and when she pursed her lips rather primly, it looked out of place, like a transplant after some terrible accident.

'The name's Veum.'

'Yes? Do we have an appointment?'

'No, I've come to see you in connection with a death.'

She swung the chair right back round and stood up. 'A death? What do you mean?'

'I don't know if you saw it in the papers ... Torild Skagestøl.'

'Oh, Torild ... ' For some reason she looked almost relieved. 'For a moment I was afraid that ... But why have you come to see me?'

'Because I thought that maybe you knew something about Torild, I mean that you knew another side of her than – her parents did.'

Her mouth became even smaller. 'Another side? Who are you actually?'

'I'm a private investigator who was looking for Torild the week she was – went missing.'

'A private investigator? But I still don't understand ... Why have you come to see me?'

'You were her Guides leader, weren't you?'

'Yes, I was leader of the troop she was in – but it's … I mean she hasn't attended since – spring last year.'

'Is that when she stopped?'

'Yes, er … just before summer, as far as I remember.'

'And Åsa Furebø stopped at the same time, did she?'

She scratched her forehead as though to jog her memory. 'Yes, that's probably right … They were – best friends, you see.'

'You say that as though it was somehow – suspect?'

She smiled, but not from the heart. 'Suspect? I just meant … best friends tend to be in league with one another. Follow in each other's footsteps, so to speak. When one of them stops, the other one often does too.'

'So there was no special reason they stopped just then?'

'Special? Have they said anything themselves?'

I purposely held back my answer and noticed how the pause made her uneasy, as if afraid of what I would say.

'Er, no. They haven't … '

This time she answered straight away. 'No, because in our experience, that's exactly the age – either they carry on or they stop, and then they carry on right until they become Head Guides. But as you can well imagine, many of them develop other interests at that age.'

'Yes, I'm sure … I was in the Scouts myself once – and stopped at just about that age too.'

'Yes, well, there you are, that's what I … '

'But actually, that's not what I was trying to find out. How long were these girls Guides?'

'Torild and Åsa?' I nodded. 'Oh, er … seven or eight years. Right from when they were at primary school.'

'You must know them quite well, then?'

'Yes, as far as … Over such a period of time they change quite a lot, you know.'

'Yes, of course, but – what was your impression of them?'

'Oh, er … they were perfectly ordinary nice young girls from good homes.'

'Hm. Does that mean you also met the parents?'

'Yes, I did. You see we sometimes had events that were attended by the parents. Usually at Christmas, or if we were planning a trip; and when they took the Guides' Promise of course. The last few years we didn't see all that much of them. When the girls had started to grow up, so to speak.' She hesitated a little. 'Apart from ... '

'Yes?'

'The last time we were at camp, at Whitsuntide, north of Radøy, not all that far from Bøvågen, Torild's father and Asa's mother paid us a visit one morning.'

'Torild's *father* and Åsa's *mother*? Wasn't that a little – unusual?'

'No, they would normally come down together, all four of them, but Åsa's father was away on a trip, as we'd already been told in advance, and Torild's mother didn't feel well, so ... '

'And how did the girls react to that?'

'Nothing special. There's always a rather awkward atmosphere when the parents visit. Children need to be free from parental supervision sometimes as well, you know!'

'As well?'

'Yes!' she said defiantly.

'Yes, I suppose so ... ' I nodded at her to carry on. 'And then?'

'Well, we gave them a cup of coffee made over a campfire, had a tour of the camp and went down to the cove where we used to swim, then they left. That was it.'

'And in August of that year Torild's parents separated.'

'Oh? I didn't know. But ... the girls had already dropped out then, hadn't they?'

'So there's nothing else you can tell me that might shed any light on what happened to Torild?'

'No, I ... I must admit, I got a bit of a shock when I saw it in the papers, but ... And if it's really true that she'd got involved in – Satanism ... she'd moved a long way from the Guides in the space of just one year, I *must* say.'

'If I told you she was taking drugs – and was also maybe involved in prostitution … would that surprise you?'

Her features alternated from shock to disbelief and – something else I couldn't quite pin down. When she eventually replied her voice was shaking slightly: 'Yes, that really would have shocked me, Veum.'

'They never gave any hint of that while you – '

'They were *children*, Veum!' she cut in. 'Children.' She turned to face her computer screen as though it might offer a more complete answer to what I'd asked her than she herself could provide.

But she remained silent. She did not share the answers with me, if any there were.

Without troubling her with further questions, I nodded goodbye and left her, as silently as the passage of time, as silent and unremarkable as the sometimes sudden transition between childhood and adulthood in a young life: long before expected and completely unbidden.

Twenty-three

THE VIEW OVER THE GARAGES in Sporveien and the workshops in Mannsverk was the same as before: so much so that I couldn't even tell if any of the buses had actually been moved.

I stood and waited after ringing the doorbell where Astrid Nikolaisen and her mother lived.

The curtains were drawn. And it was quite a time before there was a hint of movement in one of them, as if somebody was taking a careful peep.

Then there were muffled footsteps and the door was opened the tiniest crack.

Gerd Nikolaisen looked older than on my last visit. Now she seemed not far off forty. Her hair was untidier, as if she'd just got up, and she was also wearing nothing but a loose-fitting, dark-red dressing gown. The thick layer of make-up did not conceal a nasty swelling round one eye and on her lower lip on the other side, giving her whole face a tragic clown-like air.

She looked at me blankly. 'What d'you want?'

'Don't you remember me? It's Veum, I called on Thurs – '

'Yes, I do. Astrid's not home.'

She was about to close the door, and I leaned carefully forward. 'Where is she then? At school?'

'I doubt it.'

'Where then?'

She shrugged her shoulders with a jaded air. 'Haven't a clue.'

'Have you read what happened to Torild?'

She nodded but didn't say anything.

I glanced quickly both ways. 'Listen … might I come in for a moment?'

She shrugged again before stepping aside. It made no difference to her. She apparently had nothing better to do.

I followed her through the dark hall and into the living room.

The room was spartan, dominated by chrome-plated tubular steel furniture with black, slightly grubby fabric cushions. In a corner stood a TV and on the floor below it a VCR, surrounded by a fair number of video cases. A rack contained a radio, a twin-deck cassette player and a gaping hole where the CD player should have been. The loose leads behind suggested it had once been there.

From the radio, a commercial station blasted its semi-hysterical ads out over the ether into Gerd Nikolaisen's living room. She walked across and turned down the sound with a gesture of irritation. As she turned back to face me, she gathered her dressing gown more tightly about her waist, yet not so quickly that I didn't glimpse her naked breasts.

I remained standing. 'These girls ... Have you any idea what sort of company they keep?'

She nodded towards one of the chairs to indicate that I should sit down and followed me, placing herself on the sofa on the other side of the low table. The tabletop was black Formica, with the same tubular steel frame as the rest of the furniture. 'Have you any idea ... what are you driving at exactly?'

'I mean ... do you *know* what sort of people they knock about with when they're in town?'

She took a pack of cigarettes from the table, shook one out, stuck it in her mouth and looked around for something to light it with.

I picked up a barrel-shaped lighter, ignited it and held it towards her. Her thin fingers shook as she leaned forward with the cigarette between them, and I couldn't help noticing how she'd gnawed the skin raw towards the bottom of the pink nail varnish.

'Well, I ... You can't keep an eye on everything, especially as I've had to bring her up alone the whole time.'

She leaned back in the chair, crossed one leg over the other so that her dressing gown parted and inhaled the smoke so deeply that you'd have thought it might soon start seeping out between her legs. Then slowly it was exhaled the usual way. Through the bluish smoke I could just see her eyes. They were dark-brown, almost black, as though consisting of nothing but pupils.

'But doesn't it – scare you when stuff like this with Torild happens?'

There was a faint movement at the corner of her mouth. 'Astrid can take care of herself. Better than *I've* ever taught her to.'

'How do you mean?'

'Nothing.'

I sighed. 'Tell me, shouldn't Astrid actually have gone to Ulrik School?'

'Well … she crossed swords with the teacher they had down there, so she was transferred to Nattland, that's when she was about ten, in Class 5, I think.'

'So that was when she met Torild and Åsa?'

'Åsa?'

'Åsa Furebø.'

'Oh? Yes, it probably was.'

'Wasn't she in the Guides?'

'In the Guides, Astrid?' Her upper lip curled up in a crooked grin that revealed her slightly irregular teeth. Then her brow furrowed. 'No, actually, she did try it for a couple of weeks.' She leaned forward and flicked the ash into the already overflowing ashtray.

'But when it came to buying the kit, the shirt and stuff, it was too expensive. Anyway, she wasn't interested.'

'So what was she interested in?'

She looked at me, baffled. 'Well, er … What are girls interested in at that age? For a while she used to go up to the riding centre, but we hadn't really … Then all she did was walk alongside while the others rode, lent a hand with mucking out the stable a bit then she packed that in as well.'

I sat waiting for her to continue.

'Apart from that … pop music and films and larking about in the evening.' With a slightly bitter look she explained: 'She started going out very early with boys who were … '

'Who were … ?'

'Well, a good bit older than her! I suppose that's how she got into – the habit … '

'Habit?'

'Yes.'

Every time I asked a new question she looked at me as though I was utterly dense. Now she uncrossed and crossed her legs again, with the result that a bit more of her thigh showed. Yet there was nothing seductive in this shifting of position; it was more like an expression of utter disinterestedness. 'Me and Astrid … we're not like mother and daughter to each other, really, more like mates. That's why she calls me Gerd. Remember, I was so young when I had her.'

'How young?'

'Sixteen.'

'But you were saying about *the habit*?'

She looked at me blankly.

'Oh yes. Well … since we're practically the same age … ' She paused for a moment, as if waiting for me to protest, but I didn't say anything. 'It sometimes happened her boyfriends were my type too … and vice versa.'

'Hm?'

Quickly she added: 'Yes. I don't mean we … you mustn't think we swapped. But sometimes – situations arose which led to – jealousy, right?'

I put my hand up to my eye and nodded towards hers. 'These marks you've got here … and here … ' I moved my hand to my lower lip. 'Are they the result of such a – situation?'

She pursed her lips, and her eyes flashed. The hand holding the cigarette was shaking even more now, and before she said anything, she inhaled deeply through her nostrils.

The words slithered out of her mouth like creepy crawlies from under a stone. 'I came home … yesterday… I'd just been down to hire a video and buy some fags … so they thought they could get in a quick one … '

I waited.

'I didn't ring the bell, just let myself in … then, of course, I heard the creaking from her bed right out here on … ' She nodded towards the front door. 'She was starkers, and he'd just – pulled down his pants. But they were at it like rabbits … Just like rabbits!'

The only sound that could be heard as she breathed was the muffled, but nevertheless relentless, blare of commercials from the radio.

There were tears in her eyes. 'You'd think they'd have had enough shame not to do it … here in my own flat … when I could come in any moment. But that's just what he's like, doesn't give a shit! And as for her … '

'What happened then?' I asked quietly.

'There was a hell of a row, obviously. I don't mess about when my back's up!'

'No, I'm sure you – '

'She got dressed like greased lightning, and I haven't clapped eyes on her since. But him … ' A hurt look came into her eyes. 'He just let fly, as though I was the one in the wrong … Here … And here … And look at this … '

Abruptly, she opened her dressing gown and pulled it down over her shoulders baring her top half. She had big blue bruises both around and between her breasts.

She looked down at herself. Her small breasts looked rather pathetic. 'How can I help it if mine aren't … if I don't have big boobs like her? If it was lamb he was after, couldn't he have taken himself off somewhere else?'

'Who are we talking about, anyway?'

'Who? Kenneth of course!'

'What else is he called besides Kenneth?'

'Kenneth Persen! Do you know him?'

'No, but … I bumped into him just as I was leaving, the last time I was here.'

'That's right … ' She threw up her hand before pulling the dressing gown back round herself.

'Do you think Astrid could be at his place?'

She looked bitter. 'Well, good luck to her if she is, that's what I say … '

'Do you know where he lives?'

'What for? Are you going to go and see him?'

I shrugged. 'It's Astrid I'd really like to have had a word with right now.'

'He lives in a dump of a flat in Nedre Nygård. In Jonas Reins Street.'

'Listen … Astrid and Torild … would it surprise you if I said that they were maybe involved in – prostitution?'

The last spark of life went out in her eyes. 'No. Nothing can surprise me now … nothing. I think … '

I stood up.

She accompanied me out into the hall. She only managed to raise her eyes as far up as my chest as she said: 'It did me good to talk to somebody.'

I took out my wallet and handed her one of the visiting cards that only gave my name and office phone number. 'If you think of anything else, or need to talk to somebody, call this number. If I'm out, you can leave a message.'

'Thanks,' she said, looking as though she had to turn the word over in her mouth, unable as she was to remember when she'd used it last.

'It's the least I can do,' I said and left.

Twenty-four

SUDDEN DEATH affects us all. If nothing else, it makes us older.

Randi Furebø also bore the traces of the past few days' events, if not as visibly as Gerd Nikolaisen. Her firm body seemed somehow to have shrunk. Her shoulders were slightly hunched over, as if she had made a vain attempt to disappear into herself in order to keep reality at bay.

She was wearing the same brown skirt but this time with a black blouse and a grey and white cardigan tightly buttoned up in front. Instinctively, but unnecessarily, she adjusted her short-cropped dark hair as she scrutinised me. 'Veum?'

'Yes. I'm sorry, but I'd like another word with Åsa ... '

'She's at school,' she said coolly. 'Besides, I really thought ... '

'Yes?'

'That it was the police who were looking into this case now.'

'Of course it is. I'm just making a few background enquiries.'

'And whose background is that, may I ask? Shouldn't it be Torild's family you're visiting?'

'Perhaps not so soon – afterwards. Maybe the people they sometimes used to go about with instead ... '

A hint of curiosity appeared in the brown eyes. 'The people ... You don't mean ... ? Does it have to do with ... ?' She glanced down the hill, where the Fantoft stave church had stood before it was burnt down.

'Perhaps I could come in for a moment ... '

She looked at me doubtfully as though I'd been a Jehovah's Witness and she was not sure how she would get rid of me again. She stood aside, with a slightly irritated look. 'You can hang your coat up in here.'

This time I was allowed upstairs. The living room was simple and stylish with parquet floors, green plants at the windows, shelves containing books and discreet ornaments and a slightly formal-looking piece of furniture in red and mahogany which proved very comfortable to sit on. On one of the walls hung a set of family photographs, including a photo of what looked like the first day at school, showing Åsa beaming optimistically at the photographer as though no ill could ever befall her.

I looked at the clock. 'What time are you expecting Åsa home?'

'Trond was supposed to be fetching her. We have to keep a special eye on her just now. Otherwise, I'm afraid … this thing with Torild has obviously affected her a lot.'

'Of course it has. I'd rather thought she might have stayed at home.'

'Well, we – and her too actually! – decided it was best to carry on as usual, to go to school as though it was just an ordinary day and behave as though nothing had happened … '

'Yes. Not a bad idea, I'm sure.'

She seemed like a woman in full control of the situation, so I came straight to the point. 'Listen, Mrs Furebø, when I first started working on this case … I quite quickly stumbled upon circles where it looks as though there was a certain amount of – prostitution with young girls.'

She paled visibly. 'Not Åsa!' she exclaimed loudly. 'Absolutely not!'

'No, there's nothing I've found that points to that … '

'Oh!' She let out a sigh of relief. 'But why did you … say it as though … '

'But there's everything to suggest that Torild was involved, and she and Åsa were best friends … '

'Yes, *were*! But I had the impression they were a lot less so, that they spent a lot less time together than – before. Åsa would never…'

'There was that episode with the leather jacket.'

She looked at me slightly surprised. 'Leather ja – . Yes, but … it was a real shock for us, of course, that Åsa was involved in pilfering … '

'*Pilfering?*'

'All right, shoplifting, if that's what you want to call it! But from that to … Anyway, *that* matter's over and done with now!'

I ran my hand over my forehead. 'Let's hope so.'

'Yes, well it is. But what are you getting at actually?'

'Er … according to what you say, Åsa and Torild were spending a lot less time together than before.'

'Yes, Åsa didn't say much – loyalty's always been important in our family but I did understand that Torild … that she was skipping school a lot, that she had other girlfriends, and boyfriends – well, boys who were a good bit older than her, from what I gather… In other words … she moved in other circles.'

'But Åsa went into town too sometimes, didn't she?'

'Course she did. What century are you living in, Veum? It's no good keeping them locked in, however much one would like to!'

'But as recently as last year, at Whitsuntide, they were on a Guides trip together.'

'Yes, they were – but that was when they were still … '

'Then they suddenly dropped out, the pair of them. That was very sudden, wasn't it? That they stopped going, I mean?'

'Yes, perhaps it was. But they'd grown out of it. Both Åsa and … '

'You went to visit them at their camp … '

'Did we? … Yes, perhaps so, we usually did … if it wasn't too far away, that is.'

'And you didn't notice anything about the girls then to indicate that they would so suddenly … '

'Notice anything? I really can't remember.'

'It was yourself and Torild's father who visited them … '

Her expression hardened. 'Is there anything unusual about that?'

'No, I ... '

'Trond was on a hiking trip over Folgefonna Glacier at Whit, and Sidsel was just not feeling too great that day. You're surely not suggesting that ... Where did you find out all this, anyway?'

Before I managed to reply, she continued. 'Sidsel and Holger and Trond and I, we've been close friends for – for nearly twenty years now. We've been on holidays together, we've spent several weeks on the same sailing boat, we've taken saunas together, we've been the closest of friends without it ever occurring to us, even for a moment, that we might, that there might be anything ... Is there something wrong with that?' She looked at me accusingly.

'Of course not! Did I – ?'

'But nowadays, everything is so fixated on sex that two close friends, such as Holger and I, can't even drive up to Radøy and visit our girls at Guides camp without people starting to talk behind our backs. Because it's certainly not from Sidsel that you got this, and if it is ...

'No, no. I assure you it's not – '

'Listen, Mr Private Investigator! You're probably used to spending your mornings on visits to women who'll go to bed with you, if you just turn on that charming smile of yours – '

'Now, now ... '

'But me, I wouldn't look twice at somebody like you, even if you paraded about and posed right here on the carpet in nothing but your swimming trunks!' She broke off her own tirade as though suddenly overhearing herself and, with bright red roses on her cheeks, tried to shrug it off with a false-sounding laugh.

'There wouldn't be much cause to carry on like that, I agree.'

'Well, let's say no more about it. But let me tell you *this*, Mr Veum ... if it's a family on the verge of breakdown you're looking for, take a trip up to Furudalen. It was that relationship that broke down, not the one between Trond and me, even though we're obviously the first to regret it. I mean, everything's changed now. I can still meet Sidsel, and Trond and Holger work together, don't they? But we four, we can never do anything together again, and I miss that, I really do.'

'You don't work?'

'No, and I don't miss it either! But good friends I do miss.'

I nodded. 'Have you talked to any of them since Torild was found?'

'Yes, I called as soon as I heard and spoke to both of them. It was Holger who answered the phone, he'd – just popped in … But what can you say? To lose a child, can there be anything worse? They're so young, still developing, and you've looked after them for such a long time, with all your love and affection, then suddenly – they're not there any more!'

She glanced anxiously at the clock. 'The way I see it, you just can't imagine it until it happens to you personally. They must be going through hell. I only hope … '

'What?'

'That the guilty party is arrested, of course!'

'Naturally. Åsa never mentioned the names of any of these friends of Torild's, did she?'

She shook her head gently. 'Not that I recall.'

She accompanied me sadly down to the front door.

At the top of Birkelundsbakken I encountered a white Mercedes on its way down. I caught a glimpse of Trond Furebø at the wheel. On the seat beside him sat Åsa.

For a moment I wondered whether I should turn round and drive back after them but soon decided that the family was scarcely ready for yet another visit from someone who, strictly speaking, no longer had anything to do with the case.

I turned right and headed towards Sædalen instead.

Twenty-five

SORROW BECAME SIDSEL SKAGESTØL. A kind of serene beauty had permeated her features, and she almost seemed taller, as if straightening her back against the harsh wind that was blowing.

I followed her into the large sitting room.

It was curiously silent in there. No radio, TV or CD-player was on, and the house was so far from the main thoroughfares that not even the distant roar of the traffic could be heard up here. It was as though she had decided not to let anything upset her contemplation of the situation she suddenly found herself in.

I almost felt embarrassed by the creak of the plum-coloured leather chair as I sat down, while she sat on the far side of a little round table with an inlaid, hand-worked brass plate in the centre, covered in some sort of hieroglyphs.

Sidsel Skagestøl was wearing a mixed grey, long-sleeved acrylic top with loose-fitting black trousers. With a quick sideways glance she took a cigarette from the edge of an ashtray, checked it was still alight and inhaled so slowly that her eyes almost seemed to take on the colour of the smoke.

With a sad smile she said: 'We think we have them forever. But it's a lesson we have to learn. We don't.'

'No.'

'There's something special about the oldest. She who was the only one for a while. I can still remember ... I stood there watching her while she slept. Stood there listening to her breathing. Saw the little bump under the eiderdown with teddy bears on it.' Her voice rose in intensity. 'So innocent! So unblemished by – anything at all! And now, sixteen years later, here I sit, and she ... She is ... ' She made a vague movement of the hand holding the cigarette, making a kind of smoke ring, as though her daughter was somewhere in the room, invisible to us, but still present.

'This must have been a very difficult time. I mean, even more difficult maybe, because of the press reports.'

She gave me a strangely distant look. 'Oh, those … It was probably worse for Holger. Me, I've shut all that out in a way. But Holger … '

'Did he take it hard?'

'When the first report was published, I don't know if you saw it, the one with the photo … he started to weep. And I mean weep, really weep. I hadn't seen him do that since his father died, and that's nearly twenty years ago now. He couldn't even bring himself to weep over *Torild*, but that report shocked him so deeply that … Afterwards he talked about sorting them out then all he did was put me in a taxi and go off himself – to the paper, I assume. When he came back, he was ashen-faced. He looked ten years older as though it was only *then* that it had really hit him.'

'Where is he now?'

She shrugged. 'Back at work. With the police. I don't know.'

'But he's offered to help you, I mean, the last few days, hasn't he?'

'He offered to sleep here, yes. But what good would that do? That's all over anyway.'

'For good?'

She nodded silently, leaned forward and tapped the ash from her cigarette.

'A situation like this can often patch up that type of conflict.'

'Not this one.'

It was not the right moment to ask why. Besides, strictly speaking, it was no business of mine. Instead I said: 'Anyway, the police have detained – a witness.'

'Yes, Helge … Hagavik, isn't it?'

'That's right. I haven't yet found out … Does it ring any bells?'

'No.' She shifted her gaze out through the large picture window, where we could see the western side of Gulfjellet Mountain, the new housing developments in Sandalen and the slightly more established one in Midttun and Øvsttun. 'But I'm starting to see that my daughter ... that Torild had a life, outside home – one I knew nothing about.'

'Has somebody said something?'

She made a vague movement of the head. 'Said anything about – what?'

'Erm, I was thinking of ... that young man. It was apparently someone she knew, wasn't it?'

'Apparently.' She sighed. 'Now, afterwards, you think of all the times you *didn't* show up. You think that – maybe that's why it happened – that if only you'd gone to that handball match, taken part in that cake raffle, in the election for the parent teachers committee at school, everything would have been different.'

'Like when you didn't go to visit her at Guides camp in Radøy last year?'

She looked at me puzzled, frowning in thought. 'Radøy ... But I was ill then, wasn't I?' She placed her hand on her stomach as though she could still feel the discomfort there.

'Yes ... '

She was suddenly more focused now. 'What on earth made you bring that up now?'

'Oh, er ... nothing.'

'On the contrary, I'm asking you for an answer!' she said sharply. 'This is no time to beat about the bush.'

'I'm sorry, it's just something that came up, I had a word with the Guides leader, Sigrun Søvik, and she happened to mention that it was just your husband and Randi Furebø who came to visit them.'

'Oh yes? And with that dirty private investigator's mind of yours, you immediately spied a – source of conflict?'

'Oh no, I – '

Suddenly she laughed. But it was not genuine laughter. 'To be honest, you look as though you've been caught with your pants down! Now I really regret having contacted you. If this is the result, then … I can assure you that if Randi and Holger had been up to something – inappropriate during that trip to Radøy, something I couldn't imagine in my wildest dreams, the chemistry between those two has always been *so* good, I can promise you at any rate that that wouldn't have been enough to tip me over the edge. The reasons why Holger and I are drifting apart go much deeper than that … ' She touched her temple with her finger 'The whole way we think, our entire personalities, do you see? And that's all I have to say about the matter. All!'

She stood up. 'Now I think it's time you were going.'

I threw up my arms as I rose from the leather chair. 'You must believe me when I say that I had no intention of – '

'Don't bother to come back, Veum. I hope this is the last time I see you, is that clear?'

My face seemed to freeze and instead of an apologetic smile all I managed was a grotesque grimace.

In the outer hall I turned to face her again for the last time. 'In that case, I wish you all the best for the future … '

'Sincere thanks from all the family,' she said with biting sarcasm and closed the door ostentatiously behind me.

As I walked down the short garden path I heard a sound I couldn't quite make out behind me: as though she was banging her fists against the wall, stamping on the floor or writhing about in convulsions.

Then a door slammed so hard that the whole outer wall shook.

She could not have emphasised it more clearly. *Partir, c'est mourir un peu*, as the French say. But this was a full-blown execution.

When I got into the car it was with a feeling that something absolute and irrevocable had happened. It was just that I hadn't grasped what it was yet.

Twenty-six

ONCE BACK IN THE OFFICE, I tried to call Evy Berge again. But she was in a meeting, they said, for the rest of the day.

I made a note to remind myself to try and call her at home a little later.

My answerphone was in hibernation. No one had tried to call me, not even to record some melodious funeral music.

I opened the drawer containing the homemade death notice. Again I turned the envelope over and looked at the back as though the sender's name had been written in invisible ink and might only become legible a day or two later.

The postmark was Bergen and the date February 17th. If I took it along to the police station and asked them to put it under the microscope, they might find some prints on it: mine, the post-man's and those of the person or persons who had handled the letter in the postal service. Whether they would also find a further, hitherto unknown, fingerprint I was not at all sure.

With a shrug I put the letter back in the desk.

The bottle was in the drawer below.

I took it out, unscrewed the cork, held the neck of the bottle to my nose and breathed in that incomparable smell of aniseed and caraway.

I couldn't resist the temptation but stood up, went over to the sink to fetch the beaker, came back and poured myself a couple of fingers of aquavit, the water of life.

– Does the condemned prisoner have a last wish?

– One last glass, Mr Executioner. Granted. (Glugglug)

– I raise my glass to all who are still alive here on earth; I raise my glass to the children whose lives are before them and to the adults who have stuck it out so long. I raise my glass to priests and firemen, presidents and plumbers; to all those who – '

– It was supposed to be a glass, not a lecture.

– Oh, I'm sorry… (Glugglug)

The rest is cunning. Blessed are the simple, for on earth they are fleeced. Victorious are the unscrupulous.

I banged my glass down on the desk. As hard as Sidsel Skagestøl had slammed the door to the rest of her life on me. As hard as someone had torn their daughter from the soil she had been planted in and hung her up like a hunting trophy, somewhere on the dark side of a star where you can search for her till kingdom come and never find her. As hard as they stamp a misdirected letter: *Return to sender. Address unknown.*

I talked to Karin on the phone.

'Got anything lined up for this evening?' she asked.

'Have to go to a demo at eleven o'clock – people who use prostitutes.' As she didn't immediately say anything, I added: 'A demonstration against them, of course …'

'I got that.'

'I'm meeting a lady who probably has some information on the case I'm – well, doing some background work on at the moment … Want to come?'

'Do you mean it?'

'You know I don't like involving you in the practical side of the way I earn my living, but … They might find it easier to talk to me if you were there.'

'Shall we have dinner first, then?'

I pushed my glass away firmly. 'Sure. When can I meet you?'

We fixed a time.

Before I left the office Sigrun Søvik rang. Her voice was hesitant and nervous, as if she was not sure she was doing the right thing.

'If you're trying to recruit me into the Scouts, you're a bit late,' I said, trying to strike a lighter note.

It fell flat. In a hollow voice she said: 'It's about the two girls.'

'Oh? Torild and Asa?'

'Yes, it's something I thought of that perhaps – that you ought perhaps to know, but I don't want to rub salt into the wounds … of the family, I mean, so … '

'Do you want to tell me now over the phone, or – ?'

'Could we meet tomorrow sometime, over a cup of coffee?' she said quickly.

'Sure, why not?'

We agreed a time and place, she hung up, and I made a note of the details.

Be prepared: wasn't that their motto? But for what? Maybe that was the question. *To be or not to be – prepared?*

I shook off these speculations and carefully locked the door as I left for dinner with my lady friend from the Population Register Department.

Twenty-seven

THE EAST SIDE OF NORDNES is not exactly the warmest place you can spend a Monday evening in what is already a chilly February.

A handful of demonstrators had gathered on Sunnhordland-skes Quay and were huddled close together, as if guarding their banner, but probably just trying to keep warm.

They viewed us with suspicion to begin with. But when they saw we were walking hand-in-hand, and as there were also a few people I was on nodding terms with from my Child Welfare days, they became friendlier and admitted us to the circle.

The banners they were carrying bore such obvious slogans as: NO TO PORN! RECLAIM THE NIGHT!, END SEX AND BODY TRADE – ENOUGH IS ENOUGH! and PORN = THEORY – RAPE = PRACTICE.

A couple of girls with spiky punk hair and rings in their noses and various other places were holding banners with the much more eye-catching slogan, FREE BLOWJOBS!, which no one appeared to take offence at.

There were very few men. I counted three besides myself. One of them looked a bit like a hired bodyguard. The other two looked as if they'd been tamed in the early seventies and were only allowed out alone on very special occasions.

The women covered the whole spectrum. Some would not have had so much as a finger laid on them even if they'd turned up stark naked at a Hell's Angels midnight mass in deepest Norway. Others would have been lucky to get away from a morning meeting of the Priests' Association without being groped. The ages ranged from secondary school kids to grandmothers. Yet all of them stood out by their burning commitment to the cause of their sex, with an absence of make-up bordering on self-effacement.

In the cold north wind they shook clenched fists at the occasional cars driving down C Sundts Street, heart of the red light district, that Monday evening, chanting 'No to whoremongers! No to the sale of women's bodies! No to whoremongers! No to the sale of women's bodies!'

Evy Berge turned out to be a large woman, an inch or two taller than me, with broad, almost Slavic features and short-cropped fair hair. She was in her late thirties, and the look she directed at me was steely blue, with a hint of violet.

'Laila Mongstad suggested I should contact you. I've tried to get hold of you all day.'

'We're terribly short-staffed in our department. There's never a break.' She nodded at Karin as though they were fellow conspirators. 'The lot of women's professions, right?'

Karin nodded. 'You can say that again.'

'I know you can. Just take a look around you! Who's under ever-growing pressure with ever-shrinking budgets? Nurses, teachers, postal workers – '

'The police,' I interjected.

'OK, but that's the only one! And who do you think it is who spends Monday evenings driving about in cars rounding up prostitutes?'

'Nurses, teachers and postal workers?!' I said.

'Don't listen to him,' Karin started to say.

'Directors … '

'It's just the way he – '

'Shop managers and heads of departments … '

'– talks.'

'Chief surgeons and politicians. Male … '

I nodded. 'I know.'

'In other words, the power apparatus! The people who occupy positions of power in society at large also have to be in a position of power when they buy sex too. They have to feel secure and feel they're on top, literally, so they won't be challenged just where they feel most vulnerable, if you get my drift.'

'You speak with exemplary clarity. No room for misunderstanding there. That's exactly why I need to talk to you.'

She glanced round. 'Here? Now?'

'There's not much going on, is there? It'll pass the time.'

'OK, I suppose so.' She shrugged her shoulders, and we went a few yards away from the others, like a little breakaway group of three who perhaps didn't do it for nothing, after all.

'What is it you're after, actually?'

'To come straight to the point: I've worked in Child Welfare, and I've also been a private investigator for nearly twenty years now. So I have a fair idea of the traditional profile of prostitution in this city. But I've just been working on a case that has updated it again … The girl who was found murdered up on Fanafjell … '

She nodded. 'I see.'

'So I'm trying to find out whether there arc any new elements in this business, new places where people meet and violins are not exactly playing, yet somebody rakes in money from it. For example, I've come across a place called Jimmy's … '

'The amusement arcade?'

'Yes. And Laila Mongstad is looking into it as the basis of a major newspaper report.'

She smiled. 'Great! Brilliant!' She lowered her voice. 'Of course, we don't find out much ourselves on our own. But people contact us, some of the prostitutes themselves, actually.'

'So, what's the market like at the moment?'

'Well, you obviously know why we're out here this particular evening, don't you?'

I nodded. 'It's common knowledge. The street prostitution of the fifties that has now moved over here from Strandkaien. The girls from Ole Bulls Plass who have now moved over here.'

'Up to a point, yes. What's new, of course, is the recruitment from among drug addicts, often really young girls, operating in completely new places. The area round the central station, for instance, and sometimes in the middle of Torgalmenningen Square, in summer at least.'

'The school holidays?'

'A tough time for a lot of kids.'

A van with a large company name emblazoned on the side drove slowly past the group, whose numbers had now swelled to about thirty. The driver leaned over and aggressively gave us two fingers.

The voices rose in a slow, ragged chant: '*Kerb* crawlers! *Kerb* crawlers!'

He put his foot down, sending out a cloud of exhaust fumes from his rusty rear end, screeched his back tyres and vanished in the direction of the next block without so much as a backward glance.

'That's the crudest form of prostitution, of course – and the most visible one. Folk who take an hour longer to get home from work, or just "pop out for a little drive" while the kids watch Children's TV.'

'As early as *that*?' asked Karin, surprised.

'Oh yes. Business is brisk on the girlie market at that time in the evening, dear,' said Evy Berge. 'A quick drive out to Tollbodkaien and the car parks round there, the quick relief of a hand-job,' she made a few telling gestures 'or … ' she raised her hand to her mouth, 'maybe even a quick one in the back seat, if they really want to push the boat out.' She pulled a disgusted face as she looked at me. 'Men!'

'Not all of them,' I said.

'Course not, sweetheart. Not all of them!'

Karin looked as though she was about to say something, but I beat her to it. 'OK, but the girls who are hired in other places often end up in a hotel room, right?'

She looked suddenly tired. Then she held her hand out and, in the teacherly style that was no doubt typical of her, counted on her fingers. 'There are the following main types of prostitution in this city. *One*: The sort that goes on out here. *Two*: The sort that operates through contact ads in newspapers, magazines and Internet chat rooms. For example: *Shapely blonde, 24, seeks well-to-do gentleman for morning meeting. Complete discretion required and guaranteed.* They're girls who live alone, have beautifully furnished flats and finance their studies or leisure activities by prostitution. These are the ones who appear in newspaper interviews where they claim they have a professional attitude towards what they do, that they do it of their own free will and have no scruples about it. They are, as they see themselves, the good Samaritans of other people's love lives, and are going to retire early too.'

'Perhaps they're just that.'

'And perhaps we live in a depraved society! A society in which everything is for sale, including love.'

'We're talking about what some people call the oldest profession in the world, aren't we?'

'Men are older, if you ask me, and a rotten bunch they are too!'

'Yes, I suppose so, if you're a fundamentalist as regards the story of creation.'

She overlooked this observation and continued with her list. '*Three*: Hotel prostitution. This is the hardest one to stamp out. Who can tell the difference between acquaintanceships that are *really* struck up on the dance floor or in a hotel bar and those that are just part of supply and demand? Who can really control what goes on in hotel rooms at night without resorting to closed circuit TV in every corner?'

'No, that's true.'

And lastly, *four*: What shall we call it? Institutionalised prostitution – the one that's concealed behind other forms of economic activity. The much-discussed massage parlours, of which there are some examples here too. They change addresses about once every six months, but it's the same people who run them, and the same people who're behind them, putting up the money. I can give you the addresses of at least two regular brothels in town.'

'But what about the pimps in all this? This is something the police could deal with.'

She looked at Karin as she replied. 'I can guarantee that, in nearly all cases, men are behind it or at least are pulling the strings. The girls in this district all have their so-called protectors. And if they haven't, they soon get one. If not, they're hounded out. Simple as that.' After a short pause she added: 'The worst thing is that they almost all need it. Some of their clients are real swine, and in that case it can pay to have somebody nearby to call on for help.'

'Oh my God!' said Karin with feeling.

'Some of the ones who operate from hotels also have their – backers. Sometimes just the owners of the hotels.'

I raised my hand. 'Oh? Anyone who's making a name for himself on that score just now?'

'Remember the Week End Hotel?'

'The one now called Pastel.'

'It had been quite decent for a few years under the new owners. But last year the hotel was sold again, and now … Now it's back to its old ways again. All that's new is the name – and the bartender.'

'The bartender?'

'One of our taxi driver contacts tells us that a popular phone number at the moment is a direct line to the bar at the Pastel. You just have to remember to ask for Robert.'

'Robert, I'll remember that! You can count on it … '

Suddenly everything fell silent round us. Evy Berge looked up. She sniffed the air with her nostrils like an animal trying to catch the scent. 'Talk of cockroaches, and they crawl out from under your boots! There's just the sort I mean.'

I followed her eyes. Karin immediately took a few steps back, and I felt her hand grip my arm.

Two chaps came shuffling across the street. One of them had his hair in kiss curls I'd hardly seen since the fifties. The white shirt, the pale blue jeans and the black shoes protruding from beneath the long black wool overcoat placed him firmly in the same decade. He was heavy and powerfully built, not the type that spends the whole morning exercising at the fitness centre so he can beat the hell out of you: rather the type who lifts his belly up and drops it on your head, which is just as effective. The other seemed older in a way. He was smaller and walked more stiffly, with a slight limp as though he had once injured himself. His face was slightly podgy and he had a white goatee. His blue knitted cap was pulled well down, and the collar of his check lumber jacket turned up as though he didn't really want to be seen.

The demonstrators closed ranks, their faces showing anxiety, irritation and sheer anger. The largest man in the group had moved to the front, seconded by one of the trusties and a couple of new arrivals who looked like students. Evy Berge shouldered her way to the front too.

I was following in her wake when Karin held me back. 'Hang on, Varg, it might be … '

'I've been out on a February evening before, love.'

'Just wait and see what happens.'

'OK.'

The big chap in the winter overcoat spoke with a surprisingly educated Bergen accent, as if he'd been conceived under a rhododendron bush in Kalfaret, the city's poshest district. 'May I ask if you have police authorisation for this demonstration?'

Evy Berge took a letter from her pocket and waved it under his nose. 'Stamped and signed! See here!'

His eyes flashed with anger as he looked at her. 'And how long were you lot planning on keeping us residents awake?'

'Keeping us awake. Get him!' piped up a voice from somewhere a good way back in the group, setting off a ripple of ironic laughter through the others.

'We've got permission to carry on till midnight,' said Evy Berge.

'Why don't you just go home and watch a porn film?' called out one of the girls who claimed to give free blowjobs.

The man stood on his toes and looked over the heads of the people at the front. 'Who said that?'

The girl stood on tiptoe herself. 'Me.'

He glanced from her to her banner. 'Is that an offer?'

'Just come here, and I'll bite it right off!'

He started to push his way towards the back. 'Come here you little cuntlicker, I'll show you … '

The man who looked like a hired bodyguard barred his way. 'Let's just take it easy, now.'

'And what the fuck are you? A eunuch?'

'An off-duty bailiff, if it's all the same to you.'

The two men stood there glowering at each other. They were the same size and looked as though both knew a thing or two. I was itching to give somebody a piece of my mind too. Karin gripped my arm even more tightly.

The man with the blue knitted cap said: 'Come on, Bernhard. You heard what the guy said. It's not worth it. They'll be off by midnight.'

I stood there listening. *That voice …*

I craned my neck to try and get a better look at his face, but there were too many heads in the way. I felt my scrotum shrinking, one of the last instinctive reactions we still have, and a sure sign of danger in the air. *It surely couldn't be …*

'OK then! Cocksucker!' he hissed at the great bailiff. 'You'll be getting a free session for this, I suppose?'

The bailiff followed him out into the street, but Evy Berge set off hot on his heels and stopped him. 'Don't rise to the bait! We've made our point.' She raised her yoke. 'We'll be back! Bet your bottom dollar on it!'

'Leave my arse out of it!' he shouted to them from the other side of the street.

The man in the lumber jacket didn't even turn round but led the way, making for the corner leading to Holbergsalmenningen. I stood there peering at the way he walked. *Once upon a time twenty years ago …*

'Oh, my God!' I said to myself.

'Hm,' said Karin, pulling even closer. 'Think we can go now?'

I glanced round. The group was already breaking up. 'Looks as though the show's over for tonight.'

Evy Berge came over to us. 'Sometimes we've actually had to call the police ourselves. But tonight it went off OK, luckily. Quite a good demonstration, eh, Veum?'

I nodded. 'Thanks a lot.'

'Come on!' said Karin. 'I'm freezing ... '

Later on, in bed at Fløenbakken, when she'd warmed up again, she lifted her head from my chest, looked deep into my eyes and said: 'I can't help thinking of Siren, when I – hear stuff like that.'

I put my arms more tightly round her and gave her a gentle squeeze.

'I just can't imagine what it must feel like to – do it for money ... '

'I can assure you that the girls who sell themselves like that don't feel too good about it either. I've met plenty of them in all the years I've been doing this job.'

'And so young ... '

'Boys too, unfortunately. But they're still a minority. After all, there are fewer gays than heteros when all the chromosomes are finally totted up.'

'But what drives them to it, Varg?'

'Money, quite simply. Many of them to pay for a habit, but others just to buy the right clothes, for example, to keep up with the rest of their girlfriends. And the radical feminists who took part in the demonstration down there are wrong when they say that it's all the men's fault. Prostitution's about power above all. You can afford to buy power over another person for a limited period of time. Even the feeblest man finds there's someone who's even punier than him. Why do you think so many of these girls are eventually raped and abused in their own milieu? Whores are pariahs, Karin; they always have been.'

'And one of them was my sister. I've just never been able to get my head round it! We had the same mother and father, we came from the same background, had the same upbringing … What was it that made her end up like that, while I … ?'

'Who knows? Brothers and sisters are different, aren't they? The genes are not equally divided. But, above all, I think it's a matter of who you go around with, what your friends are like in the years when you're finally staking out the course your life is going to follow. Siren was unlucky in that way, you know that better than I do, whereas you … '

She laid her head back on my chest and mumbled: 'If only we'd known that it was going to turn out like this when we were small, would we have done things any different? Would we have been able to stop what happened? Would we, Varg?'

I couldn't give her the right answer. Nobody could.

It was a restless night. When I eventually dropped off to sleep I drifted straight into a horrible dream. In a hotel room looking out onto doomsday I met the man in the lumber jacket again. Now he pulled off his knitted woollen cap and showed me his face. Only there was no face, just a bare skull, as though it was death itself that was on tour in the provinces and had at last found a grateful listener.

I woke bathed in sweat, unable to drop off to sleep again.

Twenty-eight

TUESDAY WAS A DAY with a calm clear sky, streaked with peach in the east. A pale moon with a little bite taken out of it hung suspended over Damsgårdsfjell Mountain and Lyderhorn.

We walked over the Kalfaret district to town, followed the pedestrian crowds through Marken and on Strandkaien, kissed a hurried goodbye, and Karin carried on down to the Population Register Department at Murhjørnet as I took the stairs up to the third floor, the papers under my arm and keys in hand.

During the previous day, the status of the 'witness' had changed to 'suspect' but anonymity was still maintained. However, according to the newspaper reports, the 'suspect' refused to accept that he was in any way linked to the death, apart from having met Torild Skagestøl 'a few times.' Yet one of the papers quoted a source confirming that the 'suspect' had been seen with Torild 'and another girl' on Thursday afternoon 'at Jimmy's, the amusement arcade-cum-snack bar in the centre of Bergen.'

I leafed back through my notes. Hadn't Astrid Nikolaisen said the same when I talked to her? Yes, there it was ... Torild and Åsa together with 'some bloke or other' ... Helge Hagavik, the mysterious 'suspect'?

I made three mental notes. I should have a word with Astrid Nikolaisen; I should have another word with Åsa and – if possible – I should have a word with Helge Hagavik.

It would take up most of today and go a long way towards helping me forget what day tomorrow was.

◆

The block Kenneth Persen lived in lay on the shady side of the street in the part of town that basks in the shadow of the towers of Vetlemanhattan on Nygårdstangen and is unlikely ever to see the light of day again.

His name was on one of the eight post boxes in the entrance hall downstairs, but as I climbed the stairs, there wasn't a single name on a door anywhere, as if everybody who lived there was a member of Alcoholics Anonymous.

I went from floor to floor, pausing to listen for any sounds that might indicate someone was home, knocked on a few doors where I thought I could hear signs of life, but nobody answered.

Eventually, I realised I'd spent quite enough time on this aspect of the project and left.

In front of the City Station a handful of youths lolled against the concrete wall at the entrance to the pedestrian underpass, smoking, schoolbags thrown at their feet, and making not particularly positive remarks to passers-by.

I went into the waiting room and looked round. The smell of cooking oil and printing ink hung like a ring of self-loathing around the snack bar on one side and a national newsagent's on the other. The garish posters in front of the shops on the first floor proclaimed that the January sales were still on, but the spark had long since gone out of them. I saw no sign of Astrid Nikolaisen anywhere, but in the space of just a few minutes, I observed two drug transactions with no particular attempt to conceal what went on.

I met Sigrun Søvik in the café on the first floor, as arranged.

She was sitting at one of the tables facing Lille Lungegård Lake, in sharp profile against the bright daylight outside. She was wearing the same outfit as last time: a red shirt, blue jeans and a grey knitted waistcoat. On the chair beside her she had hung a greyish-brown, slightly old-fashioned sheepskin jacket with a 'No To Nuclear Power' badge on one lapel.

I waved to her from a distance and fetched a cup of coffee from the counter before making my way over and taking a seat opposite her at the table.

I unwrapped two sugar lumps, popped one into my mouth and took a swig of the piping hot coffee.

Sigrun Søvik followed my movements with her eyes as though I was demonstrating first-class engineering skills, or else because she was overjoyed at being able to put off the evil hour.

I stole a quick look at her.

Her cheeks were surprisingly red, as if she'd had to rush to get here in time. Her eyes flitted to and fro, from my coffee to my face, without settling on either of them.

'You had something to tell me,' I said tentatively.

'Yes, I did ... Afterwards ... it occurred to me ... From what I said, you may have thought something had happened – between Mrs Furebø and Holger Skagestøl ... when they paid us a visit at Radøy.'

I nodded slightly. 'Erm, not necessarily.'

'But I – I *know* that it wasn't the case!'

'Oh?'

She looked at me, alarmed. 'Yes, I mean, I don't *know*, but ... *Was* there something between them, then?'

I had to tread carefully. 'I'm not quite sure what you're getting at ... '

'What I meant was ... At any rate, I know why Torild and Åsa *dropped out*, that's what I meant.'

'And it had nothing to do with ... '

'No! And that's why I thought ... You don't need to bother anybody with all that *now*, after the terrible thing that's happened to Torild ... '

'I see ... ' I nodded at her to go on. '*Why* did they drop out, though?'

'I ... I caught them in the act.'

'Caught them in the act?'

She looked out of the window towards the Electricity Board

building, although it didn't seem to cheer her up much. 'You know, young people at that age, they've just – they're in the process of discovering themselves … And that Friday evening, when everything was supposed to be quiet, I made my usual round of all the tents. I heard … sounds from Torild and Åsa's tent … The light from a torch … I thought they must have been reading or – eating chocolate or … something like that. But when I unzipped the tent and put my head in … '

I waited.

'They were – naked, and they … ' Her eyes swivelled round like a searchlight. 'I've been involved in youth work for many years, I'm not all that easily shocked, but so young and already so depraved!'

'In other words, they – '

'Yes, I'm not going to say any more! Not about what they were doing!'

'All right. But what did you do?'

'I told them off, of course! Separated them and put them in separate tents for the rest of the time, but naturally I didn't say anything to anyone – not to anybody, you understand, until now! I don't want it to get out that something like that could happen when I was in charge! Do you understand?'

'Yes, I do. But I can't see what there is to make such a fuss about either. We were all young once – '

'Not me!'

'No?'

'I mean I never did anything like *that* … '

'No, I'm sure … '

She glanced at the clock. 'I must be off now. I just wanted you to know that *that* was why they dropped out! Because they were embarrassed, of course! They couldn't look me in the eye, either of them, for the remainder of that Whitsuntide camp.'

She stood up and put on her sheepskin jacket. She hesitated for a moment. 'You won't tell anybody, will you? Now that you've heard … '

I gave her a look of reassurance. 'It probably … As you said yourself, they've more than enough to think about without bothering about youthful peccadilloes … '

When she had gone I slowly drank my coffee before heading off in the same direction.

Around Lille Lungegård Lake the flock of ducks had thinned out considerably. Only the omnivorous gulls tottered about on the half-melted ice, pecking around one of the holes near the edge in the hope of finding something to eat. The glass front of Hotel Norge reflected the winter sky in pastel tints. The music pavilion in the City Park was bereft of flower displays, and the beds were covered over with branches from fir trees, to keep the hope of spring alive. Who wanted to die or be buried in February, when life was slowly reawakening, when the new shoots were just beginning to push cautiously through the winter covering and when there would soon be some real warmth in the sun?

Not me, not anyone.

Twenty-nine

I FOUND DANKERT MUUS in his office.

He looked up when I knocked, as delighted to see me as if I'd just trampled all over his tulip beds on a Saturday off.

'Can I have a word with you?'

'If it's absolutely essential.' He looked at me suspiciously. 'I made things perfectly clear, didn't I, Veum?'

'Yes, but this is about something else, actually.'

'Which is?'

'I see from the papers that you're making a lot of headway.'

'Oh yes?'

'The chap you're holding ... You must have some good evidence, since he's been promoted to a "suspect"?'

'In the papers, yes! You mustn't believe everything you read. But I have no comment to make either to you or to anybody else outside the force.'

'He still hasn't been charged, I understand?'

He gave me a long-suffering look 'What was it you wanted, Veum?'

'You don't think it might help if I had a word with him?'

'He's in custody as a witness, Veum. No one is allowed near him without a very good reason.'

'Who's his lawyer?'

'That daft bugger Vidar Waagenes. But I've laid it on the line for you, haven't I?'

I looked at him. Despite the fact that he sounded like himself, it wasn't the same Dankert Muus who sat there. There was something resigned and fatalistic about him as though the only thing that was keeping him going was the red ring on his wall calendar.

I leaned forward. 'I called by yesterday. Helleve gave me the green light to carry out my investigations into prostitution.'

'Did he now?'

'I mean, we know that Torild Skagestøl – '

'Veum!' He closed his eyes at the mere mention of the name.

'Look, Muus, just hear me out.'

He opened his eyes again and nodded. 'All right, then!' he said with a jaded air, sitting heavily back in his chair.

'We know she frequented a number of places we can link with prostitution. I've talked to a person who recognised her as having been with Judge Branch the day he – '

He stamped both feet on the ground and sat up in his chair. 'Veum!'

'And one of the places she used to visit a lot was Jimmy's amusement arcade, which the papers also mention today and which most people regard as being more or less a knocking-shop, and they're not talking about knocking on doors, Muus, they're talking about real *business*.'

I wasn't going to let him interrupt me now. 'A tip-off I've got from some of the Women's Libbers who organised the demo in C Sundts Street yesterday evening also implicates the bar in what used to be the Week End Hotel, now the Pastel, as a similar knocking-shop, and who owns *both* Jimmy's and the Pastel Hotel, Muus? Who else but Birger Bjelland, the prodigal son from Stavanger?'

He gave me a hard look. 'That comes under another department, Veum.'

'Even if it's directly linked with the murder?'

'We-ell … no, maybe not then.'

'There's nothing you lot want better than to finger Birger Bjelland, right?'

'It won't be in my time.'

'If I were in your shoes, I'd have asked Helge Hagav – '

'Who gave you that name, Veum?'

'Er … a press contact,' I lied, quick as a flash.

'Jesus Christ! So the vultures are after their pound of flesh again, are they? *What* would you have asked him about in our shoes, did you say?'

'What he'd got to do with Birger Bjelland. Who it was who got Torild Skagestøl to try drugs, and where they got the drugs from.'

'OK, Veum. I'll take it at face value. Would this be the motive for the murder, according to you?'

'Either that or jealousy.'

'Because she ... ' He made a few illustrative gestures with his hands. 'For example.'

Muus rose, went over to the calendar on the wall as though to get as close as possible to the day circled in red then turned and fixed me with that dispirited look of his. 'But you said you'd come to see me about something completely different, Veum.'

I pushed my chair back slightly to put myself out of his reach. 'Yes. I've come to report somebody.'

He raised his eyebrows. 'Who?'

'I don't know.'

'Exactly.' He gave a deep sigh, went back to his desk and sat down again. 'How do you spell it?'

I reached down into my inside pocket, took out the envelope containing the threatening letter and placed it in front of him. 'Just before the weekend I received this.'

Without saying a word, he opened the envelope and read the page with the death notice on it. Then he looked up again. 'When's the funeral? So I can arrange to be there, I mean.'

I gave a crooked smile from the corner of my mouth.

'You're surely not taking this seriously, are you?'

'Oughtn't I to?'

'Veum ... in the almost forty years I've been in the force, I couldn't count the number of threats I've received, most of them were verbal, admittedly, but quite a few were written ones as well. Never, not one single time, has anyone even come close to carrying out the threat.'

'So you mean I should just forget about it?'

'In any case, we can't offer you personal protection just on this basis. But of course, I can ask the patrol cars to drive down your street a bit more often, if you like. When did you say it was?' He glanced down at the letter. 'Tomorrow. Exactly. That means it'll be Monday or Tuesday in other words.'

'Er, what will?'

'The funeral,' said Muus sardonically. Then he changed his expression. 'Honestly, though, Veum. Do you have any personal enemies, I mean, such bitter enemies that they might send you – something like this?'

I hesitated.

He noticed it. 'Well?'

'Remember The Knife?'

His eyes glinted. 'There've been quite a few with that name. But I guess you mean the one you got sent down that time. What was his name again, Harry Hopsland?'

'I think I *saw* him in town yesterday ... '

'*He* reported *you* once, didn't he?'

'So you do remember.'

'As if we could ever forget it, Veum. That the case was thrown out, I mean.'

'As far as I gather, he's more or less kept to Eastern Norway since he got out, hasn't he?'

'You may be right. If you can give me a minute, I'll go and get his file.'

Two minutes later he was back with a small index card in his hand, partly typewritten, but with handwritten additions in biro and pencil. 'Now, let's see. Yes, that's right. He did six years. Since his release he's mainly remained down in Vestfold, some of the time in the Oslo area. He was mixed up with the people involved in pyramid selling in the early eighties. He's had two charges for GBH, aggravated by the use of dangerous weapons. He got six months for one of them. The other charge was thrown out because

of insufficient evidence. Then he was arrested again in Sandef-
jord in the summer of 1989 on suspicion of pimping at one of the
tourist hotels there, but that didn't get to court either, probably for
the same reason.'

'What about … that time we nabbed him here in Bergen? It
was because he was operating as a pimp and dealing in drugs
at the same time. He was both the chicken and the egg, so to
speak.'

'In that case he escaped being arrested for it.' Muus turned over
the card. 'So you think he might be back here in Bergen?'

'Doesn't it say anything about it on there?'

'No, we don't register absolutely *everything*, you know.' He
nodded. 'But he has family in Bergen, I see.'

'Does he?'

'A son. Ole Hopsland, born in 1971. And he also has two brothers, or step-brothers they must be, actually. That fits in too. The
Persen brothers.'

I nearly shot out of my seat. '*Persen*?!'

'Yes. Know them?'

'No, but I've just … '

'They've been around on the fringes of the criminal underworld
here for fifteen or twenty years. Kalle and Kenneth: what original
names! Kalle works at … ' He paused for a moment. 'Exactly, at
Jimmy's.'

'Precisely.'

'Kenneth's never actually had a proper job, I don't think.
"Seeking employment" – isn't that what they call it nowadays just
so we won't forget that they're jobless, and that some of them will
remain so for the rest of their lives … ?'

'Actually, I've met him as well, in connection with this case.'

'Oh?'

'At the home of one of the girls whom you'll certainly have
questioned as a witness. Astrid Nikolaisen … '

'Yes, we may have. It's Jensen who's dealing with the girls.'

'Apart from the fact that she hasn't showed up at home since – Sunday.

He frowned. 'Not shown up, you say?'

'Yes, I … But it strongly looks as though she's shacked up with Persen.'

'My God. Well, well, well, I'd better get Jensen to check up on this.'

'I can show her where he lives.'

'Just give us the address, Veum.'

'Sure?'

'A hundred per cent.'

I gave him the address in Nedre Nygård. After noting it down, he looked up at me slightly askance. 'What actually happened between you and The Knife that time, Veum? Something to do with a girl, wasn't it?'

Thirty

I PARKED DIRECTLY OUTSIDE Nattland School. There were still ten minutes to go before the bell went for the end of the last lesson.

Yes, it had been something to do with a girl. But not the way Dankert Muus had always liked to think.

During the years I worked in Child Welfare there'd been two cases I'd been particularly taken up with. One of them was Siren, Karin Bjørge's sister. The other was Eva-Beate.

Siren had not worried me all that much. She came from a family who took an interest in her and had a sister who sacrificed some of the best years of her youth to look after her. That everything eventually turned out as it did could not be laid at the door of the family or her sister.

But Eva-Beate had been a different matter. She was from a children's home. Her mother, who was a drug addict, committed suicide when her daughter was no more than three years old, and I never really figured out whether she remembered anything at all about that first chaotic period in her life. Her father belonged to the army of the unknown. He was not even a name in the population register. The attempts made to place her in foster homes failed. She ran away every time. The only place she felt at all at home was in the children's home. Everything was fine while the old housemother was still there. But when she retired new people took over. They tried their best to give Eva-Beate opportunities she hadn't had before, tried to nudge her into school and vocational courses. But by then running away had almost become a way of life for her. She was one of those desperate kids whom nothing could hold, who shied away from the light as often as she could and sought the darkness wherever it was to be found.

To begin with, she was one of those ghostly faces that always turned up when we would check out a building due for demolition as we tried to track down other kids, the ones who were hauled in time after time when the police made a drugs raid. Then I suddenly started to get through to her, as if I reminded her of somebody or other. I invited her home to dinner. Together with a colleague, I went hiking with her in the mountains. Slowly but surely I drew her away from the drugs world and found out who her pimp was. But she didn't want us to shop him. She couldn't even entertain the thought of having to give evidence against him. He does you with his knife, she said. One of the girls who grassed him up was slashed to bits, here ... and here ... and here! She pointed first to one cheek, then the other, then to her breasts.

Then eventually I paid him a visit in person, at his usual table at the back of The Owl one day in October 1973. He asked me to come outside with him, and we walked up Olav Kyrres Street towards Nygårdshøyden. We went into the inner courtyard in front of the old mansion where the Conservatoire used to be, and suddenly he pulled his knife on me. But I was ready for him and kicked him in the thigh, twisted his arm right round his back so he had to let go of the knife. As I kicked the knife away, I gave him one of my lectures. – I can either break your arm, Knife, or I won't. But I know all there is to know about you, and if you don't bloody steer clear of Eva-Beate, I'll tell the police all I know, with a copy to the Devil himself. He gasped: Why the hell don't you do it, then? I twisted his arm a bit further without answering. – Get the fuck off me, he groaned. I'll steer clear of the little slag!

I released my grip on him, and he fell over. I bent down and picked up his knife and put it in my pocket. Eyes flashing like a cornered rat, he said: I'd lock my bloody door at night, if I were you, Veum! I'll come for you one of these days, and I don't give a flying fuck if the whole Child Welfare Department's standing guard over you and holding your hand! – Be my guest, I said, young and cocky as I was in those days.

Meanwhile, things went better than anyone could have expected with Eva-Beate. She really got back into attending school, found a foster family where she felt accepted at last, fell in love and suffered all the usual heartaches: just as life should be for a fifteen-year-old, even if she still had too many memories to have the courage to be fully at ease with her friends. I followed all these developments with great satisfaction, like a proud uncle on the fringes of her life, and several times when I was dealing with cases which seemed at least as hopeless as hers once had, I used her as an example of the fact that there were success stories.

Then all of a sudden, during the weekend of the national Mayday holiday in 1975, she disappeared. Her foster family were beside themselves with worry. I dropped everything I was doing, put on an oxygen mask and plunged deep down into the subterranean world she had frequented before. One day I passed The Knife in the street. He gave me two fingers with an unconcealed look of triumph in his eyes, but when I tried to grab him, he gave me the slip.

A week after she'd gone missing, we heard the first rumours that she was back on the leash again and was on the game. A fortnight after she'd run away from the foster home, she was found.

The trail led to a cheap hotel in the centre of town. Without realising it, I walked past one of the drug police's cameras, went up the stairs to the second floor and barged right into the room they were in without even knocking.

Eva-Beate lay on her back in bed, thighs splayed, and her sex gaping like a bloodhound's muzzle. Her vacant look showed she was completely out of her head, and there wasn't much life in The Knife either as he lay there on his belly, wearing no more than a pair of tiny briefs and with one of his arms draped across her small breasts like a flabby, bloated maggot.

When I walked in he turned round with a sleepy expression on his face. As he swung his legs down onto the floor and reached for the knife that lay on the bedside table, Eva-Beate sat up confused in bed and reached out for him as though she was having a nightmare and wasn't sure whether she was asleep or awake yet.

First I kneed him in the face then broke his arm this time. I dragged him out of the bed and onto the floor and kicked him over and over again until I heard footsteps coming up the stairs, and the two officers from the drugs section came storming in and had to get me in a half-nelson to calm me down. The Knife lay apparently lifeless on the floor in front of me, while Eva-Beate had sunk back into the same position as when I had come in, her sex like a trussed chicken between her legs.

Then we had to start again, right from the bottom. But this time with other people to help her. I never did actually get the boot from the Child Welfare Department. Yet some highly placed individuals suggested I should take some leave for as long as I liked, and I took the hint and never went back

That same autumn I opened my office on Strandkaien. Eva-Beate was not faring so well. She died of an overdose in Møhlenpris a few years later, never having really shaken the habit.

And here I sat again, almost two decades later, waiting for another girl whose circumstances were not quite so dramatic. But I was afraid that Åsa too was teetering on the edge.

The school bell rang, and it was not many seconds before the pupils began to pour out of the low building. I went to stand beside my car so she would see me.

She came out in a little group, yet there was something lonely and dejected about her. When she caught sight of me it was almost as though she was relieved to have an excuse for parting company with them. Nor did any of them show any visible reaction when she said she was off.

'Hello, Åsa,' I said.

She frowned. 'Was it Dad who sent you?'

'No. Should he have?'

'He's fetched me from school every day since – Torild went

missing.' She looked at the clock. 'Suppose he must have been held up a bit then.'

'I just wanted to ask you a question. Shall we sit in the car?'

She glanced up Merkurveien. 'We can just stand here if you like.'

'Last time we spoke … '

'Yes?'

'You weren't entirely honest, were you?'

'Yes, I was!'

'A lot's happened since then, Åsa. You mustn't keep anything back now.'

'Like what, for example?'

I nodded at her new brown leather jacket. 'Your Dad knew you couldn't afford to buy a jacket like the one you two took back. And in the shop, it turned out the jacket wasn't stolen. I'm not surprised he comes to fetch you.'

She looked away.

'Where did you get the money from, Åsa?'

She didn't reply.

I moved a step closer. 'Do you realise what you're doing with yourself, Åsa? With your own youth?'

She turned to face me again, an insolent look on her face. 'It's guys like you who want a piece of it!'

'Guys like … '

'Yes, don't think I haven't seen the way you look at me!'

'I was looking at your jacket, Åsa!'

'Oh yeah, it's the blinking jacket you were interested in, is it?'

'You'd do better to listen to what I'm saying to you, Åsa! You and Torild were with Helge Hagavik at Jimmy's the Thursday she – didn't come home, right?'

'And what if we were? I told you, I went home earlier!'

'So it *was* Helge Hagavik, then?'

'Yes, I … ' Almost immediately her face closed up again. '*Oh shit!*' she said almost inaudibly.

Higher up Merkurveien the whine of a car engine driven at

speed could be heard; it was somebody in too much of a hurry for all the sharp bends. Then it came into view. The white Mercedes swept down towards the school and came to a halt just behind my little Toyota. Trond Furebø pulled on the handbrake, opened the door and was standing beside us all in one movement.

'What the hell are you doing here, Veum?' Without waiting for a reply, he turned to Åsa. 'I was held up five minutes. I'm sorry. I broke our agreement.'

She gave him a look so much as to say this was one thing parents were experts at: breaking agreements.

He turned back to me. 'I asked you a question!'

'You didn't give me a chance to answer.'

'He was making advances to me, Dad,' said Åsa pertly.

I stared at her.

'Advances?! You mean – '

Just long enough for him to land the first impulsive punch – bang – on my chin.

I fell backwards, saw stars, and as I tried to focus, momentarily saw both of them double.

I nevertheless managed to parry the next blow, well enough to adopt a defensive position, and he was no trained fighter. His temper made his voice rise several octaves. 'Goddamn it, Veum, we parents do all we can to protect our children, leave work early, just to get up here to fetch her every day, with all the impact that has on those crucial early evening hours at work, then you come and – '

'Surely you don't believe her, Furebø? Think I'm an idiot or something? I haven't made any bloody advances to her at all! I asked her a couple of questions, and if you don't believe me, then we can all three of us go down to the police station and repeat them there!'

He was calming down now. He kept glancing at his daughter. 'Åsa?'

She looked at him defiantly.

'I asked whether it wasn't true that she and Helge Hagavik were among the last people to set eyes on Torild before she disappeared. She confirmed it. Helge Hagavik's been taken into custody as a so-called "witness" in the case. *He* for one knows a lot more than he's prepared to say. Which makes me suspect that Åsa knows more too … '

He had lowered his fists now. His arms hung straight down at his sides as though they didn't belong to him at all. 'Åsa … '

'I've said all there is to say. Me and Torild were at Jimmy's, and we sat there talking to this guy, I don't know who he was or what he was called, and then Torild got … then there came … But I went home.'

'Then Torild got *what*?' I asked.

'A *telephone* call!'

'From who?'

'How should *I* know? She had to go, she said, to He – to that guy and then – we left.'

As calmly as I could, I said: 'The hardest thing about lying, Åsa, is that it's so impossible to remember what you have said and what you haven't. You're starting to get your wires crossed.'

'Like hell I am! I'm telling you exactly what happened! Torild left, and I left to catch the bus home. Just ask Mum what time I got back!'

'That's right, Veum,' Trond Furebø said quietly. 'My wife confirms that she came home surprisingly early that evening.'

'But it still doesn't explain … I mean, I think you know perfectly well where Torild was going that evening!'

'No, I don't know! I don't!' She turned to her father. 'Can we go home now?'

'Yes, we … ' Trond Furebø pulled himself together. 'Strictly speaking, this is nothing to do with you either, Veum. Get into the car, Åsa. We're going.'

I gave a heavy sigh.

If she was telling the truth, there were only two people who could confirm it. One of them was dead. The other was Helge Hagavik, and he was in custody.

Thirty-one

VIDAR WAAGENES had his office in the premises of a firm of solicitors on the fourth floor of a building in Strandgaten. He was smaller than he appeared in the pictures I'd seen of him in the papers. A dark lock of hair kept falling down over his eyes, and he had developed a practised gesture for pushing it back again.

He was only just over thirty but, despite his youth, had made a strong impression on the bench. So it surprised me that he made such a weak impression in the flesh, friendlier and more compliant than a broker sensing a good investment opportunity

It was nearly three o'clock before he could see me, the hearing he'd been taking part in having ended 'a little early', as he put it, hurrying back from court. His friendly secretary, who had given me a large mug of coffee while I waited, gave him a much larger pile of legal documents, which, to judge by the look on his face, he would be snuggling up in bed with that evening.

He beckoned me into his office, dumped the pile of documents on the ebony-coloured desk, hung his grey overcoat and the burgundy woollen muffler on a coat-rack and offered me a seat in an unusually comfortable chair.

He offered me a cigarette from an elegant case, and when I declined, took one himself.

'How can I help you, Veum?' he asked, lighting the cigarette.

'Helge Hagavik.'

He inhaled the smoke pensively before blowing it out just as slowly. 'I see. In what way, then?'

'I'd like to have a word with him.'

'What about?'

'About what he did after Torild Skagestøl disappeared, among other things.'

'Nothing that has anything to do with that, at any rate – if we're to believe the statement he made to the police.'

'And to you?'

He shook his head. 'I've nothing more to tell you either, Veum, even if I could. Is that all you wanted?'

A sudden suspicion came over me. 'Tell me, who was it that actually hired you to take this case, Waagenes?'

'I was officially assigned. Why do you ask?'

'Well … He hasn't mentioned Birger Bjelland to you, has he?'

'No.'

'The Persen Brothers?'

'No. He stubbornly maintains he found her purely by chance.'

'And you believe him?'

When he did not reply, I added: 'He *knew* the girl personally, Waagenes! They were seen together the day she went missing from home.'

He ran his hand over his forehead, looking tired. 'No, it's just that I haven't got him to talk yet.'

'Maybe that's how I could help you. If only I could have a word with him.'

'Can't you tell me what it is you know? Then I can take it up with him.'

'I'd rather do it face-to-face. I have a reputation for getting people to talk. He might let his guard down more if he thought I was just an ordinary member of the public … '

'I can't let you speak to him unless I'm also present myself, Veum. We'd never be allowed to do that.'

'Course not! But am I to understand you're willing to give it a try?'

'I'll ask Hagavik himself first. I'm going to call in to see him tomorrow morning. Can you try and ring me at about midday during the lunch break?'

'Thanks a lot.'

'Don't thank me too soon.'

◆

I called Karin from my office.

'Personal or business?' she asked.

'Both – sort of.'

'Let's deal with the business first, then.'

'OK. – It's about a guy called Harry Hopsland: about my age, maybe a bit older. I'm trying to find out whether he's registered that he's moved back to Bergen and where he lives, in that case. He's lived here before, you see. And then there's his son, Ole Hopsland, born in 1971. If you could find out his address.'

'OK.'

'The second thing may be a bit more complicated. It's about a chap from the Stavanger area, Birger Bjelland, and he must be round my age as well. As far as I know he came to Bergen about twenty years ago.'

A slightly more distant note had crept into her voice when she said: 'He was the one behind it that time they nearly – did you in, wasn't he?'

'Yep.'

'What do you want to know about him?'

'I wanted to ask you to get in touch with Stavanger if you don't have direct access to their archives via the computer network.'

'Yes we do, within certain limits … '

'I just want to know if he has any close relatives down here.'

'That all?'

'No. Just one more thing; now we're into the personal stuff. Are you going straight home after work?'

'Yes. I was intending to.'

'I'm off to see Birger Bjelland now.'

'No!'

'If I haven't called you by five o'clock, can you do me a favour and call the police?'

Her answer was an ominous silence.

'It's not dangerous, Karin. The guy's a highly respectable businessman, putting the best complexion on it. I just want to talk to him, maybe drop a few depth charges. But don't worry, I'll be over the hills and far away before they go off.'

'Sure?'

'Quite sure.'

But there was one thing this job had taught me. You could never be quite sure. Especially when visiting people like Birger Bjelland.

Thirty-two

THE OFFICES of Birger Bjelland & Co. were located in the old warehouses facing the sea in Sandviken, and someone, Birger Bjelland perhaps, had forked out the cash to get them tarted up. Between the smell of seaweed and tar on one side and exhaust fumes and oil on the other, stood the whitewashed warehouse like a kind of barrier between the traffic in Sjøgaten and the gulls bobbing up and down on the water in Skuteviken.

The name of the firm was painted in large black letters on the front of the building, but the green door downstairs was locked, and there was nothing but a nameless bell and an intercom to suggest someone might conceivably say 'Come in.'

I rang the bell.

A woman's voice answered. 'Yes?'

'I'm looking for Birger Bjelland.'

'And you are?'

'Veum. Varg Veum.'

Silence.

After a while the intercom crackled again. 'That's fine. Second floor.'

The lock buzzed, and I went in.

You can never get rid of the smell of dried fish. Despite the fact that the timberwork in the ceiling looked new, that all the internal walls were freshly painted and the floor covering on the stairs still had no signs of wear, the odour of the warehouse's original purpose still hung there. In a way, Birger Bjelland had chosen the right surroundings for the official side of his business activities. This was the smell of old Bergen's trade links as a bridgehead between north Norway and Europe, Brønnøysund and Rostock.

Two floors up, the stairs ended in a door belonging to quite a different period. Its rough surface stained a mahogany colour and the gilt nameplate bearing the words BIRGER BJELLAND & CO. engraved in black might have been the entrance to any agent's in the mid-sixties.

I opened the door and entered a sort of antechamber, low-ceilinged and with dim lighting everywhere, except above the diminutive desk where a strong fluorescent light pinpointed the woman I had spoken to on the intercom. She was in her early sixties and so neat and trim that she might easily have been a bookkeeper for the Salvation Army, and no one would ever have dreamt of putting a hand either on her or in the till.

The look she gave me was the sort she reserved for someone who owed money, and she nodded towards the next door. 'You can go straight in. He's expecting you.'

I knocked all the same and waited for a few seconds before opening the door.

Birger Bjelland's office looked out over Byfjorden. The old warehouse was so positioned that, if he opened the window, he could cast a line and catch a bite for supper, unless he objected to the high mercury content, of course.

Now he sat behind his desk with one hand concealed beneath it like some arch villain in a James Bond film waiting to press the concealed button that opens the trapdoor and propels the unwelcome guest straight down to the alligators in the basement.

He was not alone. Over by a window, as though he'd actually just been admiring the view, stood one of the hunks Bjelland practically always had in tow. In other contexts they would have been called bodyguards. Not without a certain self-irony, Bjelland called them his 'office managers'. At any rate, this specimen looked as though he'd opened more bottles of anabolic steroids than account books in his time.

Birger Bjelland himself looked slightly like a fish out of water. His small mouth was half-open, and his strikingly pale eyes had an expressionless glassy look. He had a neat little moustache, mousy hair with a high hairline and something I assumed was a wig on top. Even though he was quite slim, there was something rounded and streamlined about him, which betrayed the fact that he was probably more at home in the backseat of a taxi than on an exercise bike.

His refined Stavanger preacher's voice had come back to haunt me in some of my worst nightmares since the first time I'd heard it almost six years before. I'd met him face-to-face in Travparken one day last October when we'd had a few choice exchanges. The next time I met him I'd have been happier to feel I had the upper hand.

'Take a seat, Veum,' said Birger Bjelland, pointing with his empty hand to the large scarlet leather chair that towered throne-like on the client's side of the desk.

As I was sitting down, I glanced over at his office manager. 'Am I interrupting something?'

'No, no. Fred and I were just sitting here chatting. It's nearly time to be going home.'

Fred … I felt my palms moisten with sweat.

The man he referred to as Fred had the same type of moustache as his boss, although his hair was shaven right down to the scalp, and his nose looked as though someone had head-butted it a few times. When I met his eyes this time, it was with a sense of mutual understanding that we both knew where we stood, but that I would never be able to produce any evidence as to who it was who'd paid me a visit in my office the time they'd filled me half full of drink when my system was already awash with Antabuse, and all I could recall afterwards was the tone of Birger Bjelland's accent and the name of his companion: *Fred.*

I looked demonstratively at the clock. 'Yes, I have an appointment too … at five o'clock.'

Birger Bjelland gave me a look of sour anticipation. 'No need to spin it out, then, eh?'

'No.' I tried to lean back in the chair as though I'd only dropped in for a casual chat. 'I've been told,' I began, 'that you're the owner of an amusement arcade in the centre of town called Jimmy's … '

He threw up his hands. 'That's no secret, Veum.'

'Do you know what goes on there, I wonder?'

He leaned slightly forward. 'No-o. What did you have in mind?'

'Well, both myself – and others – have noticed that young girls are recruited for certain assignments … you can guess the sort I'm talking about … at certain hotels in the vicinity. And that they're recruited at Jimmy's.'

'And how is this supposed to happen?'

'Apparently by phoning the manager – Kalle Persen,' I added to show how well informed I was.

Birger Bjelland clenched his fingers and looked disinterestedly at his nails. 'No comment, Veum. How my staff run the establishments I have a stake in doesn't concern me in principle, provided they don't make a loss.'

'You've also bought the former Week End Hotel, haven't you?'

'No reason to deny it. In any case, it was in the papers.'

'The same type of thing goes on there too, centred on the bar and with the hotel rooms even more readily to hand, I imagine.'

He frowned as though something had just occurred to him.

'So you're not bothered what sort of reputation your hotels have either, are you?'

'Reputations can take many different forms, Veum.'

'Precisely. Was Judge Brandt one of the clients, I wonder?'

'I do business with so many people,' he said neutrally, 'but that particular name is one I can't say I … '

'No? You must surely have read the articles in the papers about that girl who was found dead, up on Fanafjell … Torild Skagestøl. Does the name mean anything to you?'

'No, it doesn't.'

'Well, no. Perhaps not the name itself, but as an item of revenue in your accounts?'

'You'll have to talk to – '

'Your accountant perhaps?' I glanced quickly at Fred.

'Yes, he's a man of many parts.'

'I'm sure he is. Helge Hagavik was a regular at Jimmy's. Do you remember him?'

With the patience of a saint Birger Bjelland replied: 'I so rarely visit the places I own, Veum, and when I do, it's always to talk to the staff, rarely to any of the customers. What are your sources for all these assertions?'

'Press contacts – and representatives of a Women's Lib group called Ottar, although why I'm not exactly sure.'

He puckered his mouth as though there was a nasty smell under his nose. 'Women's Libbers?'

'Something like that.'

'They're the worst of the lot, Veum. They paint the devil on a chapel wall if the spirit moves them.'

'For absolutely no reason?'

'For absolutely no reason, Veum!'

I hesitated a moment. Then I said: 'Tell me, something I've always wondered about, what's the main activity of this company of yours, Bjelland?'

He scarcely raised his eyelids. 'Finance, investments of one kind and another, and loans of all types and sizes … You're not after a small loan yourself, are you? Interest rates are low just now … '

'One kneecap instead of two?'

'That wasn't funny, Veum. We run a completely legal business, within the precise limits laid down by the law. Our accounts are impeccable, can't be faulted and our relations with the tax authorities couldn't be more cordial.' As though it was the New Jerusalem he was welcoming me to, he threw up his arms and said in an unctuous, sermonising voice: 'I'm the whitest lamb on God's earth, Veum. There isn't a stain on my reputation. My businesses are run on the highest moral principles.'

'Amen. Hallelujah,' I said.

'Don't be blasphemous,' said Birger Bjelland with a rather dopey smile.

I half stood up. 'So how come your name constantly pops up in connection with all kinds of unsavoury business? How come nine out of ten investments you put your money in are connected with prostitution and illegal sales of alcohol, gambling and other fine arts? How do you explain that?'

'Can you show me the way to Sodom and Gomorrah, Veum?'

I glanced round. 'I thought that's where we were.'

'The ways of the Lord are inscrutable.'

'And which Sunday school did you go to? Agnostics Anonymous?'

He raised his hand indolently. 'Veum, let me give you a word of friendly advice.'

'Please do,' I muttered.

'Don't push your luck, old boy. Don't think that you're somehow untouchable. There's nothing sadder than watching good wine turn bad, as it were.'

'Thus spake the wife of Canaan, too.'

He sighed audibly, looked over at Fred and said: 'Mrs Helgesen's almost certainly gone home by now. Can you see Veum out, right out?'

I stood up and walked towards the door.

'And don't forget what I said,' he directed at my back.

Fred already had his hand on the doorknob when I turned back towards Birger Bjelland. 'Don't forget to watch your back too. Be careful, little foot, where you step. Didn't they teach you *that* hymn at Sunday School as well?'

He made no effort to answer; merely smiled that indolent smile of his, which made me think of a shark waiting to attack.

Fred accompanied me out. Right out. And didn't even say '*Au revoir*.'

Thirty-three

I CALLED KARIN well before five o'clock and assured her that everything was all right. There was nobody behind me in the telephone booth pointing a sawn-off shotgun at my head, and no one had invited me to go for a drive I couldn't refuse.

'Are you coming up here?'

'There's still something I have to do. But if the offer can remain open till about midnight, then ... '

'But no later than that,' she said, in a resigned tone.

'Absolutely no later,' I said.

◆

The Pastel Hotel stuck out from the other buildings in the block like a front tooth painted pink.

The Week End Hotel had been one of those anonymous bed and breakfast hotels with a bar, dancing in the evening and a rear courtyard I had the most unpleasant memories of. The new owners had stripped off all the previous ornamental façade, not that anything had been lost by doing so. On the other hand, they had painted it in a nondescript pale pink colour that fitted the new name like a glove.

It was nearly half-past seven when, fresh from the shower and wearing a casually knotted Tuesday tie, I walked through reception into the bar, where there were not many other people besides a couple of middle-aged men and a not quite so middle-aged lady.

I ambled up to the bar counter, hoisted myself onto one of the stools and ordered a Clausthaler and aquavit. 'Riding the lame horse today, are we?' said the bartender with a crooked smile.

I took a quick look at him. The moustache was apparently the club emblem, even if it looked a bit pricklier than Birger Bjelland's.

'Are you Robert?' I asked when he came back.

He put down the schnapps glass, poured the alcohol-free lager directly into another glass before placing it beside the first, took a cloth and wiped away an invisible spot from the bar counter between us. 'Who's asking?'

I pushed the money over to him. 'Wilhelmsen.'

He looked at the money as though it was counterfeit. 'And why?'

'Your name was recommended … '

He looked at me suspiciously.

'As somebody who could tell me where to find some decent entertainment on an evening off.'

'Stripping and stuff? You'll have to go somewhere else for that.'

'What I was thinking of was … more private entertainment, to put it that way.'

He looked at me with contempt. 'I know you're not the law, and your name's not Wilhelmsen. What the hell are you, then? Journalist? Social worker? From the Church Relief Fund?'

I turned partway round and looked out over the room. 'Keep your voice down, Robert. My wife doesn't know I'm here.'

He walked a few yards away, fetched a couple of glasses and started to wash them demonstratively.

I raised my voice. 'Bit quiet here tonight, isn't it?'

He didn't reply.

'It quietens down in the evenings, eh?'

He moved back in my direction. 'Look, Wilhelmsen or whatever your name is, drink up what you've paid for and go stick your fillings in somewhere else, OK?'

'Loud and clear. Message received. Over and out.'

A woman in her late thirties came into the room, cast an expert eye around her, decided there wasn't much choice and therefore placed herself strategically two stools away from where I was sitting.

With a wave to the bartender, she ordered *the usual*.

I caught her eye in the mirror above the bar, and she didn't look away, as keen not to let go as a child clutching treasured marbles.

The bartender came over with *the usual*, which appeared to be just whisky on the rocks. As he placed the glass in front of her, he said something I didn't catch, and after a suitable pause, she cast another, seemingly casual, glance in my direction.

'Your good health!' I said, raising my glass of aquavit to her. After returning my gesture, she got down from the bar stool and came over to me. 'Lonely?'

'I wouldn't say no to a bit of company.' I nodded towards a table with a few chairs some distance from the bar counter. 'Shall we sit over there, where it's more comfortable?'

The bartender's eyes followed us as we walked across the floor.

There was silence for a moment, as we both tried to decide where the situation was heading. She was wearing a little black evening dress that looked slightly crumpled, perhaps from previous visits. Her face was thin, her hair dyed blonde, and close to, I definitely put her at nearer forty. The phone in the bar rang. The bartender answered it and turned his back to us. 'Did he say anything about me?' I asked.

She smiled faintly. 'That I should watch my step with you. That he thought you were the law. Are you?'

I shook my head slowly. 'No.'

'Not that it matters, if you're here off-duty, I've – met lots of nice policemen here in town.'

'I'm sure you have.'

The bartender turned and glanced in our direction, the phone still in his hand. It looked to me as if he was trying to describe my appearance, which gave me an unpleasant sensation in the pit of my stomach.

'So what do you do?'

'I'm in insurance,' I said, which was not a lie in fact. At some times in the year I was. 'And you?'

She sipped her drink. 'I started out as a guide, at the Old Bergen Hotel among other places. But recently I've moved into – escort services and things like that.'

I looked at her askance. 'Escort services and – things like that?'

'Mm,' she said brightly.

The bartender hung up, but a few seconds later the phone rang again. He answered, listened and surveyed the room. Then he covered the receiver with his hand, looked straight at me and said: 'Veum? Somebody asking to speak to you.'

'I … You obviously didn't hear … The name's Wilhelmsen! It must be for somebody else … '

The bartender met my eyes, gave a crooked smile, said something else into the telephone and hung up.

She looked at me. 'What else are you called besides Wilhelmsen?'

'Svein Vegard. What about you?'

'My friends call me Molly.'

'Oh really? I've heard about you.'

She suddenly looked alarmed. 'Oh?'

'*Good golly, Miss Molly,*' I hummed. '*Sure likes to ball.* Isn't that how it goes?'

'And would *you* like to dance?' she asked, glancing at the tiny dance floor.

'I scarcely think we'll be bumping into anybody,' I said, getting up.

She clasped me tight, her belly pushed forward and with no visible shyness in the way she moved. I could feel the contours of her body more clearly now. Her shoulder blades were like the stumps of severed wings, and there wasn't much flight in her thin upper arms either.

The music came from somewhere in the ceiling, dance muzak where it was the rhythm that counted, not precision.

'What branch of insurance are you in, Svein?'

'I work for myself. Often it's car collisions. And sometimes life as well.'

'So, are you a sort of freelancer too?'

'You could say that. Do you come here a lot?'

She looked around. 'Yes. It's usually quite nice here, a bit later in the evening. Good service.'

'What sort of age group usually comes here, then?'

'A bit older than the usual rowdy discos. And not quite as sophisticated as in most large hotels. It's just right for me, actually. Sort of an in-between atmosphere, if you see what I mean.'

'No young girls then?'

She stepped back a few inches and stared up at my face. 'Is that what you're looking for?'

'No, no. I was just – '

'Or *are* you working?'

I muttered something that was supposed to sound like a denial and pulled her closer.

For a while we danced in silence. It seemed as though she'd calmed down again. Her hair was tickling my cheek, and her breathing was gentle and close to my neck. Then as though by accident one of her hands placed itself on my neck, where she gently began to caress me with her long cool fingers.

'If you like … ' she said softly.

'What?'

'There's a room I can use on the third floor … '

I glanced at the bar. The bartender was no longer alone. He'd been joined by two other fellows. They stood there, leaning discreetly against the bar counter and looking in our direction.

One of them I didn't know. The other was Kenneth Persen.

Thirty-four

'NOT A BAD IDEA,' I muttered into her ear, as I felt my whole body tauten.

The third man at the bar was dark-haired and well dressed, with a slight weaselly look. He was the sort I would always suspect of using a knife. That impression was strengthened by the fact that he had his right hand in his jacket pocket as though it had taken root there.

When they saw I'd noticed them Kenneth Persen turned and said something to the bartender, who nodded and looked at me with *What did I say?* written all over his face.

'What does it cost?' I asked.

Her voice immediately took on a businesslike note. 'It depends on what you want. It starts at a thousand kroner.'

I pulled her closer. 'Is there another way upstairs than through the bar?'

'They're not bothered in reception. I have an *arrangement*.'

'But what if I don't want to be seen?'

'Discretion's guaranteed,' she said, almost without making it sound ironic. 'There are some back stairs, of course, a fire escape. But ... '

Kenneth Persen and the well-dressed weasel had now stepped onto the dance floor, but it was hardly to enjoy a waltz together.

Quickly I said: 'Which room?'

'Four-twelve, but ... '

'You go on ahead, and ... '

Just as the two champion dancers came right up beside us I let go of her and propelled her towards the exit.

'But ... '

'Living it up, are we, Veum?' said Kenneth Persen, who had exchanged his black leather jacket for a slightly more bar-friendly suede one.

I nodded at her to go towards the door, but she didn't take my hint. She remained standing there.

'Where's Astrid?' I growled in order to seize the offensive.

Was it just my imagination, or did his eyes momentarily shift sideways and upwards?

'You know the police are looking for her, don't you?'

'All I know is we've been told to see you out, Veum.'

'Don't tell me … *right* out, eh?'

I looked over at Miss Molly. Suddenly she didn't seem as youthful, and the look she gave me was neither warm nor all that friendly. With a contemptuous little toss of the head she turned back to the bar, apparently on the lookout for new investors to offer her shares to. Starting at a thousand kroner.

Kenneth Persen and his well-dressed companion came and stood on either side of me. 'I wouldn't advise you to resist, Veum.'

'Nor you either,' I said and walked up to the bar. 'I'll just finish my drink.'

As I walked past the bar counter, the bartender boomed: 'See you … Wilhelmsen.'

Miss Molly had managed to haul in a new arrival, ten years older than me and the happy owner of a flashy wallet bulging with credit cards, which he was already showing her with the same pride as if it had been pictures of his grandchildren.

In reception I swung round so fast that the two chaps behind me collided. 'What the f–!' exclaimed Kenneth Persen.

'What room's she in?'

He wasn't all that quick on the uptake, and again it took a while before he said anything. 'Who d'you mean?'

'You know damned well.' I turned to face reception, where a pale, fair-haired youth sat who looked as though he could have been a theology student. 'Astrid Nikolaisen.'

'Niko ... '

He started to look her up in the guest register, but Kenneth Persen stopped him abruptly. 'Knock it off! She's not in any guest book!'

'Here incognito, is she?' I said.

The well-dressed fleet of foot one opened his mouth for the first time. 'Kenneth, our orders were to eject him, not converse with him.'

'What a posh speaker! And where were you educated? Bergen Business School?' I turned back to Kenneth Persen. 'I could call the police, of course. Ask them to come and give the place a once-over.'

'They've no bloody right!'

'They want to speak to her, I said! Was it you who gave her the smack, as well, eh? Get the lass hooked on smack then you can have a freebie whenever you like and look after your old age!'

The weasel's right hand was on its way out of his jacket pocket. It distracted me enough to enable Kenneth Persen to land a punch on my shoulder, sending me tumbling towards the exit.

I grabbed hold of the wall but did not have enough time to turn round properly before receiving another blow, also on the shoulder.

Kenneth Persen towered over me, while the weasel still had his hand in his pocket. 'Got the message, Veum? Making myself plain, am I?'

I needed no further convincing to leave the premises. 'Plainer than ABC,' I mumbled. 'I don't need telling twice.'

I slammed the door behind me and turned demonstratively right, down towards the city centre. At the first corner, I stopped and look back.

Kenneth Persen stood in the doorway to make sure I really left.

But he shouldn't be too sure about that. I was of the old school, the 1956 Bogart model: The harder they fall, the more terrible the vengeance they wreak.

Thirty-five

IT WAS LIKE A GOOD, old-fashioned tailing job.

I'd made a quick tour of the area, popped into a snack bar and bought two hot dogs with plenty of onions to soak up the aquavit I'd allowed myself in the bar, taken my woollen cap out of my pocket, turned up my coat collar and taken up a position in a doorway about a hundred yards from the main entrance to the hotel, with an oblique view of both it and the exit from the courtyard at the rear.

The weather was changing. The wind was gusting from the south-west, and there were snowflakes in the air. The view in front of me became grainy and blurred, like a photo taken on the move.

On a chilly Tuesday evening in late winter there wasn't much custom. A handful of guests, all of them men on their own, arrived with suitcases. A few of them made for the bar and the dance floor. In one or two windows on the upper floors the light suddenly went on and off. Perhaps it was Miss Molly taking the man with all the credit cards up to her room. She surely had a slot he could put his credit card into to debit his account.

After about half an hour a taxi stopped outside the hotel entrance. The door opened, and the well-dressed weasel ran doubled up against the wind into the car. The passenger gave the destination and, indicator flashing, the taxi turned right at the first intersection.

Half an hour later someone appeared in the doorway leading to the courtyard at the back of the hotel. Then the figure bent over, leaned against the wall and disappeared back inside.

I looked both ways, kept an eye on the front and walked across the street at an angle, straight through the entrance leading to the rear courtyard.

Astrid Nikolaisen was leaning over, vomiting behind three dustbins. Her hair was a mess, her clothes looked as though they'd been thrown on in a hurry, and her face was ashen. The strangled sounds coming from her were like those of an animal being throttled, and she was making some twitching, almost spastic, hand movements as she leaned her arm and shoulder against the wall to support herself.

Gingerly, I put my arm round her. 'Astrid, I – '

She jumped as though I'd slapped her. She had a dark unseeing look in her eyes. 'Don't touch me!' she hissed hysterically. 'Don't you dare!'

From inside the building I heard the sound of a window being opened, two voices engaged in a heated exchange then the sound of the same window being slammed shut.

I took her by the arm. 'Come on, Astrid! I'll help you! Don't you remember me? It's Veum … '

She tried to get up. Wiped her mouth with the back of her hand, spat out phlegm and looked at me with fresh eyes. 'Yeah,' she mumbled.

A door banged further along the courtyard. 'Astrid? Are you there?' Kenneth Persen called out.

She grimaced and bent over again. 'Come on,' I whispered, 'let's get out of here!'

I gave her a tug, and she followed me reluctantly out into the street and down towards the busier area of the city.

When we were about ten to fifteen yards from the hotel, I heard his voice again: 'Ve-um! You bastard!'

I pushed her ahead of me. 'Round the corner and up the next side street. The grey Toyota at the second parking meter. Wait for me there.'

Then I turned and stood ready to defend myself, fists raised.

Kenneth Persen stopped in his tracks. He looked around as

though sizing up the chances of having a go at me without being seen. But there were already people on the other side of the street who had stopped to watch us. From the next block a group of youths shouted: 'More blood! More blood!' then broke into raucous laughter.

In low tones, he said: 'You're going to be sorry, Veum! She's *mine*, get it?'

'Better than you deserve!'

'It's not the end of the story yet!'

'Oh no?'

He looked at me, eyes smouldering. Then he made a brutal gesture with his right hand as though finishing me off, turned on his heel and strode off back to the hotel.

The youths from further down the street had moved closer now and were enthusiastically applauding the show. The people on the other side of the street had slowly started to move on, some of them with inquisitive looks in my direction, others with obvious signs of disappointment that the show was already over.

I turned and set off quickly after Astrid Nikolaisen in the hope that she hadn't seized the chance to make off.

Surprisingly enough, there she stood leaning against my car, with her arms resting on the roof and head in hands.

I smiled to reassure her. 'Everything's OK.' I dug out my car keys and opened the door. 'Come on ... Just get in.'

She looked at me with red-rimmed eyes. Her make-up had run down her sallow cheeks in streaks. Her clothes were still in disarray. A corner of her pale blouse was sticking out from under her short bomber jacket and something that looked like the elastic from a black bra was hanging out of one of the side pockets. 'Dirty old bastards!' she spat out. 'The stuff they ask you to do, you haven't a bleedin' clue have you? Makes you puke!'

'Yeah, I noticed.'

She held up the thumb and index finger of her right hand, just an inch or so apart. 'Pathetic little – worms – this size! And then they expect us, expect me to … ' She gagged again. But her stomach was empty. All that came out was horrible rasping groans, which again put me in mind of an animal, this time with its foot caught in a snare.

I felt a slight wave of nausea myself. 'Want to talk about it?'

She looked at me baffled. 'Talk? What the hell good does that do?'

Do you want me to go back and break Kenneth Persen's jaw then? Is that what you're waiting for? 'Come on, Astrid, get in … '

Stiffly, she did as I said. I locked the door after her, went round to the driver's side, opened the door and sat behind the wheel.

We exchanged glances. There was a momentary glint of mutual understanding between us, like a father and daughter who had finally reconciled themselves to a shared fate. Then her look clouded over, and her face closed in on itself.

I looked past her. 'There's still ten minutes left on the meter. Shall we stay here or shall I drive you straight home?'

She shrank away from me. 'Home? I don't want to go home!'

'Your mother's frightened for you, Astrid.'

'Like hell she is. She hates my guts!'

'She does n – '

'You don't know what happened!'

'Yes I do. Everything.'

'What?! Did she *tell* you?' She looked at me wide-eyed.

I nodded. 'She's your *mother*, Astrid. You mustn't think she doesn't care about you.'

'But after what I … '

'She's still so young, though, compared with … You must see that it was normal for her to react like that, but she's forgiven you now, I can guarantee you that. So you can't be surprised that she went off the deep end.'

She avoided my eyes. 'That wasn't how she … I was asleep anyway! Suddenly there he was in my bed, and … I tried to resist obviously, but … It's not *that* easy … He's strong.'

'You can report him for rape.'

'Ha, ha, ha! Who'd believe me, eh? I can just hear Gerd in the witness box … '

'But I believe you, Astrid. And when you explain it to her, properly, I'm sure your mother'll understand as well.'

'Gerd … ' she said, almost with a note of surprise in her voice.

'Had he done it before, Astrid?'

'What do you think? As soon as she was out of the door he'd start pawing me! He knew where he'd got me, what with me being on the safe list and that!'

'The safe list?'

'Yeah. Why do you think people were always asking for us, eh?'

'You mean … because you were on a list?'

'Not just me! Torild as well!'

'And this list … what did it consist of, Astrid?'

'Consist of?'

'Yes, what did it *mean*?'

'That we were safe, obviously! That we didn't have anything you could catch … '

'I get it. Was there a doctor who examined you all?'

She looked away. 'Once a month. I couldn't stand it, but we got paid more.'

Her answer struck me like a thunderbolt. The way she said it. *As though it was a summer job in a souvenir shop.* I had to compose myself before I could continue. 'And what was the name of the – er – company doctor?'

'Dr Evensen. His surgery's in Strandgaten.'

'So, did you all go there in normal business hours?'

'No, always in the evening. And there was never anybody else there.'

'And this Dr Evensen, did he just examine you or – ?'

'Not just. But he didn't always, erm, we didn't always, see what I mean?'

'Yes, I'm afraid so. And … who organised all this?'

She looked down. 'It was K-K-Kenneth who talked me into it. He said … you could earn a real packet if you did.' She pulled a face with a shudder of disgust. 'Dead easy money … Just lie on your back and close your eyes.'

'Listen, Astrid. I know it's not easy to talk about it, but I know most of it already … They would ring you at Jimmy's, wouldn't they?'

'They didn't ring *us*!'

'No, all right, but you got the jobs through Jimmy's, didn't you? Kalle, the guy behind the counter … you know he's Kenneth's brother?'

'Yeah … '

'And then – did you just turn up?'

She nodded.

'Where?'

'Different places.'

'Cars?'

'Yeah, that too.'

'Other hotels, besides the Pastel?'

'Various ones. But mostly it was there. The clients rented the room, and Kenneth took us up.'

'What were they like, the clients?'

Her face set hard again. 'Some of them could be fairly OK. There were a few I thought I recognised, from the papers.'

'Politicians?'

She shrugged her shoulders. 'Don't follow all that stuff.'

'They never said their names?'

She thought for a moment. 'Sometimes they wanted you to call them something or other. But it was just their first names, that's if it wasn't just James or something daft like that.'

'James?'

'Yeah. Can you believe it? But most of them were horrible old bastards, like that one today! I'm dead certain he was a teacher, dead certain!'

'And how were you paid?'

'Cash in hand! But … Kenneth kept most of it, we had to give it to him, you see, and it was no use trying to put one over on him, because he always knew how much we'd got!'

I felt a knot in my stomach. 'But Kenneth … it's not like him to run a show like that on his own.'

'Oh?'

'Was he the one who'd contacted Dr Evensen, for example?'

'It was him who made the appointments, at any rate.'

'You never felt there was someone behind him?'

'Think I cared if there was anybody behind him?'

'What did you do with the money?'

She looked out of the window. 'Bought stuff. Clothes and CDs. Partied.'

'Drugs?'

She muttered something.

'What was that?'

I used to have a puff now and then … and a few tablets. Nothing else.'

'No hard drugs then?'

'No!' She looked me straight in the eye as she rolled up her sleeve. 'Want to have a look?'

'No need. I believe you when you say – '

'I believe you when you – ! You sound just as daft as those social freaks in Child Welfare and places! You're all just as daft, the whole lot of you! You lot don't have a fucking clue about – anything – about what it's like to be young nowadays … ' Suddenly there were tears in her eyes.

I placed my hand cautiously on her shoulder to calm her down. 'Take it easy, Astrid. Take it easy.'

Further up the street one of the parking department's cars drove slowly past, on the lookout for a last kill of the day. I took a quick look at the parking meter. Then turned on the ignition and indicated a left-hand turn.

'How long's this gone on for, Astrid?'

'Since – last autumn.'

'*Before* you were sixteen, then?'

She shook her head firmly. 'My birthday's in August!'

'But Torild's birthday was only now, in January.'

She shrugged.

'Was *she* mixed up in all this?'

Her eyes flashed. 'She was just as daft as me! Don't think that just because she comes from a better-class neighbourhood … She *liked* it, she did! I never have.'

'And the parties, did she go to them too?'

'She was the worst of the lot of us!'

'Smoked dope and took tablets?'

'Till her eyes popped out!'

'Why did she do it, do you think?'

'To get her own back on her parents for what they'd done to her. No doubt about it!'

'Done? How do you mean?'

'When they got divorced?'

The car from the parking department stood there, its engine idling, waiting for me to drive off. I waved wearily to the meter men and drove the car off up the hill. Neither of them waved back.

'The fellow who's in custody for her murder. Helge Hagavik. Did you know him?'

'Haven't a clue who he is. But I bet I know his ugly mug … I told them I'd seen her at Jimmy's with a guy.'

I drove down into Nygårdsgaten and took the outside lane so as not to irritate any drivers behind by driving at conversation pace.

I glanced quickly sideways. 'Do you have any suspicions, can you think *why* she was murdered?'

'No! Unless she … unless it was to punish her.'

'Quite a tough punishment in that case.'

'You don't have a clue what they're capable of, guys like – Kenneth.'

'Oh yes I do, Astrid. I nearly killed one of them myself once.'

'One of … '

'One of that sort.'

I drove over Gamle Nygårds Bridge and moved into the left-hand lane up towards Danmarksplass. Outside the Forum Cinema stood a group of youths about the same age as Astrid. She hardly glanced at them.

I drove along Ibsensgate up to Haukeland and from there down Natlandsveien as far as Mannsverk. There was nothing left to say.

When I'd parked in front of the tower block, I said: 'I'll see you up.'

'There's no need!'

'No, I will anyway.'

'OK then,' she replied, slamming the car door hard behind her.

We went into the tower block, pressed the button for the lift and stood there waiting.

'Would you be willing to repeat to the police everything you've told me this evening?'

She shrugged sulkily. 'Maybe.'

'We could get him put away. Do you realise that?'

A hint of fear came over her face. 'But – what d'you think he'll do about that, though?'

'He won't be *able* to do anything, Astrid.'

The lift came and we got into it.

She pressed the button. 'What about when he gets out, though?'

'We'll get him sent down again.'

'We'll get him sent down again!' she said, mimicking me. 'By then me and Gerd'll most likely be dead – have you thought of *that*, clever dick?'

'That's never how it turns out, you know. Mostly it's just empty threats.'

'Mostly, yeah. But what about the one time they're not empty?'

Yes, what about it? Doesn't that go for me too?

We'd reached her floor now and went out of the lift and along the outside walkway. She rang the bell herself.

'Haven't you got the key?'

'Forgot it, didn't I?'

Gerd Nikolaisen answered the door. Her lip was less swollen now, but you could still see she'd been knocked about. The swelling round her eye had gone down, but the bruising was more obvious than before, despite the thick layer of make-up.

For a moment we just stood there looking at one another.

Then Astrid exclaimed: 'Gerd! Who was it who – ?! Was it that Kenneth?'

Her mother nodded. Her face was like a rigid mask, but there were tears in her eyes, and her neck began to redden.

'Oh, Gerd!' She threw her arms round her.

I half-turned away, as if this was too private a matter for me to be involved in. If I looked up, I could see past Landås and up to Ulriken, where the TV mast stood like a floodlit finger pointing at all of us: Big Brother is watching you. If you step out of line, you'll be pilloried on the *News Programme*.

In front of us lay Mannsverk, a district still quite well lit at eleven o'clock in the evening on a gloomy February night: a random collection of housing blocks of various types and sizes, not unlike a moraine left over from the last Ice Age, the difference being that the New Ice Age lay within us.

'Do you still need me for anything?' I asked.

They looked at me as though they'd forgotten I was there. Astrid's mother said: 'No, but thanks for – finding her.' Her daughter just shook her head.

'You two need to have a real heart-to-heart, about everything.' I looked at Astrid. 'Then I'll tell the police what you've told me.'

The look on Gerd Nikolaisen's face suddenly altered. With one movement she pushed her daughter behind her and came right out onto the walkway. 'I don't want the police mixed up in this, Veum! It's private – we have our private life as well, you know!'

'Understood, but Astrid's just told me that – '

'Astrid!' She turned to face her daughter. 'Tell him you don't want this to go any further!'

Astrid looked hesitantly from her mother to me. 'N-no, when you … '

'It's not about your private life,' I said to her mother. 'It's about what your daughter's been up to the last six months. It's important for a murder case! It's no good brushing it under the carpet!'

'We'll deny everything! We won't say another word! Right, Astrid?' She turned to her daughter for support.

Astrid Nikolaisen nodded feebly, shrugged her shoulders and, avoiding my eyes, went back into the flat.

Gerd Nikolaisen looked at me in triumph. 'So that's that!' she said, putting an end to the matter once and for all, following her daughter and slamming the door so hard that I half expected the neighbours to come out to see what was going on. But when I came to think of it, no, they wouldn't. This was what they were used to.

Getting into my car I looked at the clock again. *Five to eleven.* Fløenbakken awaited me.

I took a good look round before parking the car in front of the low-rise block Karin lived in. But I didn't see a living soul. Not so much as a tomcat on the prowl.

Karin sat up waiting for me, frowning. Somebody or other had rung and invited her to the funeral.

Thirty-six

'A MAN?'

'Yes.' She looked at me unhappily. 'He said he was ringing from the undertaker's, but he didn't sound like an undertaker.'

'Was he from Bergen?'

'Yes. Maybe somewhere near, but I'm not certain. I mean somewhere like Kalandseidet, Arna, it was sort of – something wasn't *quite* ... '

'When was this?'

'Just now – half an hour ago.'

'What did he say? Can you remember as near as possible?'

'He ... The phone rang, and I answered. A man's voice asked: "Is that Karin Bjørge?" "Yes," I said. "You're an acquaintance of Varg Veum, aren't you?" It gave me the shivers, Varg, I was sure something had happened! "Er, yes," I managed to get out, "who am I speaking to?" "This is Nedre Nygård Undertakers," he said. I nearly passed out, Varg!'

'Nedre Nygård? There's no such thing as Nedre Nygård Undertakers, that's for sure.'

'At any rate, that's what he said. It could be Nygård Bros, of course ... '

'Nygård Bros?'

She nodded.

'Well ... ' I motioned to her to go on.

'And then he said: "We've been asked to ring round to all Veum's friends and acquaintances and inform them that the funeral's on Monday, at one p.m. at Hope Chapel in Møllendal."'

'Well, at least there's *hope* then.'

'Then the penny dropped that it was just, that it couldn't be …
So I asked, as calmly as I could, what his name was … '

'And?'

'But he just hung up. I stood there, holding the receiver. Completely numb. It was horrible, Varg! Can you tell me what's going on?'

I held her close as I whispered into her ear: 'They're just empty threats, Karin. Don't think any more about it. Stuff like this just goes with – this line of work.'

'Maybe you should look for another line of work, then?'

'Look, I'll tell you everything.' I told her about the phone call with the organ music and the death notice I'd received in the post, and as I spoke, I felt anger rising in me, a need to find out who it was who was no longer content to threaten me personally, but also my immediate circle, and when I found out, the person behind it had better be in good shape because it was going to be a tough contest, to the bitter end.

She looked at me wide-eyed. 'Did it really say … did it give the date as well – in that – death notice?'

I glanced at the clock. It was already twenty-five to twelve. 'Tomorrow,' I said gently. 'It's Wednesday after all. So, in that respect, a funeral on Monday's quite appropriate.'

'Don't joke about something like this, Varg! Have you … Have you talked to the police?'

'Yes. There's not a lot they can do about it.'

'But couldn't you get a – somebody to keep any eye on you?'

'I'm afraid they don't rate the risk of something happening highly enough for that. The police themselves often receive threats of this sort. If they took everything like this seriously, they'd spend more time watching each other's backs than keeping order on the streets.'

'But what … Have you got anything special lined up for tomorrow?'

'I have to go to Stavanger.'

'To Stavanger!'

'Did you manage to find out any of the things I asked you about?'

'Yes, I – I've got it over here ... ' She walked over to the wall unit and fetched a couple of pages. 'I made some printouts. Here, look ... '

She sat down beside me, and I pored over the first page.

'Look, here,' she said. 'Birger Bjelland's mother, Kathrine Haugane – '

'Haugane?'

'Yes, that's her name. Born in 1912. And look here: *father unknown*.'

'Well, I'll be ... '

'Now she's in a nursing home. "Salvation".'

'Sounds just like Stavanger.'

'Birger Bjelland himself was born in 1945. Then there's clearly a sister, Laura Haugane Nielsen, born in 1948. Married to Ove Nielsen.'

'I see.'

'And here's the other one you asked about ... '

'Yes, here's The Knife. Harry Hopsland, born in 1940. Registered as having moved away in 1981. Moved back last year. Address: Nordre Skogveien. A son, Ole Hopsland, born in 1971. Mother – what does it say?'

'Grete Pedersen, moved to Førde in 1978. They were never married. But his son still lives in Bergen.'

'So I see. Did you find out where he works too?'

'Yes, I ... Digi-Data. A computing firm, obviously.'

I scribbled everything down in my book before folding the pages up and stuffing them into my inside pocket. I put my arm round her and kissed her lightly on the mouth. 'Now I *have* to go to Stavanger tomorrow. The plane could fall out of the sky, of course, but that's a risk you take every time, so ... In many ways, I think it's safer *outside* Bergen than actually in it, that is, if we're going to take this seriously at all, Karin.'

'I certainly took it seriously when he rang.'

'I've been out on a winter's night alone before,' I said to reassure her. But as I said it, I noticed that I wasn't fully reassured myself. Someone had sowed frost in my heart, an ice rose in my breast.

◆

I didn't sleep much that night.

If I *was* to take it seriously, what could I actually do?

Was just one person behind it or more? Had it not been for the fact that the first telephone call had been before I started digging around in the Torild Skagestøl case in earnest, it would have been natural to suspect Birger Bjelland and his entourage. But it was most likely some nutcase who was doing this just to scare people without ever actually trying to carry out the threat in reality.

But the fact that he'd phoned Karin worried me. It meant that he must have a fairly good knowledge of my private life, that he'd also probably tailed me – or us – and found out who she was. But it could also mean that he had the backup, if not of an organisation, then at least of some kind of network.

Karin slept restlessly beside me, mumbled something or other in her sleep and threw out one of her arms.

I reached down to the floor beside the bed, located my watch, lifted it up and pressed the button to illuminate the little screen: one thirty-five.

OK. Let's say I was in real danger. In that case, what in particular should I keep an eye out for?

We were not in Sicily, my office was not on Chicago's North Side, and even Soho had an exotic ring for a private investigator in an elongated country not far from the North Pole. In other words, it was not very likely that somebody had placed a car bomb under my Toyota before I set off for Flesland Airport at daybreak. Nor was there any real reason to fear there might be a marksman behind the bushes in the old school garden waiting to focus his telescopic sights on me as I unlocked the car door.

The likeliest scenario was that someone would have a go at me directly with a small firearm or a knife. The very thought of it made me sit up so suddenly in bed that Karin reached her arm out for me and asked drowsily: 'Is it morning?'

'No, no,' I said softly. 'Go back to sleep. I just have to – get up for a second.'

I got up, padded out of the bedroom, through the hall and into the living room.

I stood at the window, gazing out.

It was a strangely peaceful sight. Bergen at a quarter to two in the morning, scattered snowflakes in the air, the protective ring of black mountains with clusters of buildings here and there, the street lighting like the pattern on a gilded peacock's feather in the darkness. Store Lungegårds Lake had the air of a black lagoon, a horseshoe of ice on its surface like the skin on milk; and in the tall, ugly towers in Vetlemanhattan all the offices were in darkness except one, from the top of which beamed forth the time and the temperature at that precise moment.

There were not many cars out and about, and it was hardly likely that any of them were on their way to me.

My breathing was calm and regular. In – out. In – out.

Slowly I felt the tension in my shoulders lessen. The painful knot in my stomach began to loosen and behind my eyelids sleep beckoned with its gentle elfin wings.

I went back to bed and lay huddled up to Karin, my arms around her in a kind of tandem foetal position.

I did not waken until the clock radio burst into life with a blaring fanfare from the newsroom, keen to share the latest disasters with us before we began another working day.

Thirty-seven

EVEN THE WEATHER GODS were out of sorts on the day I was to die. Intermittent hail showers came lashing in over the city, propelled by a gusting north-west wind, the hailstones drumming against the windowpanes, not unlike the Bergen Boys' Brigade's first spring parade.

Karin gave me a long warm kiss before I left. 'Want me to come down with you?'

'No. But you can keep an eye on me from the window till I've gone.' As a sudden afterthought I added: 'And make sure you look after yourself too. I'll call when I get there.'

Then after a few minutes more I said that now I *absolutely* had to leave, and she reluctantly let go of me as though not quite sure she would ever see me again.

Once more there were tears in her eyes. I didn't know whether I was pleased or not. I didn't like giving others cause to weep.

I opened the main door downstairs cautiously. Not many people were up and about yet. A neighbour from one of the other blocks was on her way up towards Årstadveien, and a middle-aged lady was out walking her dog.

I went quickly out and walked over to the parking space, bending down a couple of times as though to check my shoelaces. When I got to the car I took care not to hang about in one place for too long. I quickly walked around it, brushing off the windows. The scattering of snow during the night at least had the advantage of making me fairly sure no one had tampered with the car, either around the locks or elsewhere since I'd parked it. There were no other footprints but mine around it. All I found was the Hardanger lace pattern of hail from the last shower.

I put the key in the lock, turned it, opened the door, nodded up at Karin and got in.

Having seen far too many American films, I looked round at the back seat to make sure it was empty. It was.

I knew that the critical point was what followed now. Most car bombs were connected to the ignition.

There was only one way to find out. With the door still open (as though that would have helped), I put the key in the ignition and turned on the engine. It started like a sailor's widow at the very first touch.

As I turned out of the car park, I waved up at Karin again. She waved back, but not from the heart. It was as though I could see her worried look even down there in the car.

Up in Årstadveien I turned south towards Haukeland Hospital. I looked in the mirror. There was a steady trickle of cars over Årstadvollen. Up from Fløenbakken came a motorbike, which carefully positioned itself close to the pavement two or three cars behind me. I felt the hairs stand up on the back of my neck.

In Fridalen I turned down through Christiepark, glancing in the rear-view mirror. Two of the cars – and the motorbike – were behind.

At Inndalsveien I waited at a red light. The motorcyclist dutifully stopped, still two cars behind me, although there was more than enough room to pass.

I tried to gain some impression of the rider, but it was still too dark, and he was completely covered by a leather bodysuit and helmet with a black-tinted visor.

The driver behind me tooted irritably, and I shot off so fast at green that my car skidded on the slippery surface, although I quickly regained control. The motorcyclist had no problems.

We stuck to one another like Siamese twins all the way to Flesland Airport. The cars between us might change, but the distance between us always remained the same, two or three cars. But when I drove into the long-stay car park to dump the car off he had suddenly gone.

I parked the car and walked quickly to the terminal building, looking around all the while. It was as though I could still hear the faint vroom-vroom of the motorbike, but it must have been my imagination. I couldn't see anything.

In the arrivals hall people hurried in all directions, intent upon their various business. I took the escalator up to departures on the first floor. Halfway up I had a perfect view of almost everything down on the ground floor, but I couldn't see the black-clad motorcyclist anywhere.

Not long after I was on my way out to the plane. Two or three heads in front of me, I caught a glimpse of a tall lanky figure that seemed familiar. But it was only when he turned around at the top of the steps that I knew for certain it was him. Holger Skagestøl was on the same plane.

He found a seat, and I stopped beside him. 'Mind if I sit here?'

He looked up and frowned. 'Veum? What the hell? You're not tailing me, I hope?'

'Heavens no! I'm going to Stavanger on business.'

'Well, in that case … ' But he stole a suspicious glance at me as I sat down as though he definitely didn't feel quite at ease.

◆

Most people feel a natural pang of anxiety when the doors close, you are asked to fasten your seatbelt, and the plane prepares for takeoff.

This time I felt only relief when the doors closed and I was sure that the man in the motorbike gear was not among the passengers; unless he had made a lightning change in the toilets, in which case he could be anyone. Including …

I looked at Holger Skagestøl.

No. I thought not.

Skagestøl's facial muscles were just as tense as the last time I'd seen him. He was wearing a grey suit and had stowed a light-brown winter overcoat in the overhead luggage compartment.

'On business?' I asked cautiously.

He ran his hand over his forehead. 'Yeah. Directors' Conference of the National Newspaper Association.'

'Several days?'

'Till tomorrow. Of course, I could just have cancelled, given the circumstances, but in a way it might not be a bad idea to have something else to think about.'

'Has a date been set for the funeral?'

'No, the police ... But it'll probably be sometime next week. As soon as possible, I hope.' As though to explain what he meant, he added: 'I mean it won't be *over* till then.'

The plane took off, and we sat there without speaking until it had stopped climbing and was on course, and the signal that we could unfasten our seat belts was flashing.

'You will both be pleased the guilty party was arrested so quickly, of course.'

He shot a glance at me. 'Yes, sure. He still hasn't confessed.'

'No, but they never do straight away. Only when they see the game's up, then ... And then you can't stop them, as if there were some higher power they suddenly had to explain themselves to.'

'There may well be too, for all we know.'

An air hostess came round with a carton of fruit juice and an open sandwich on a little polystyrene tray. 'Would you like a paper?' she asked with a smile.

I shook my head, but Holger Skagestøl said he would. 'Both, please.'

After she had given them to him, he glanced quickly at the front pages, placed one of them in his lap and unfolded the other before opening it and leafing quickly through the first pages with a worried look. Halfway through, he suddenly put the paper aside, took the other one and went through the same procedure with it.

Looking sideways at me and turning so his whole body almost

seemed as if it would keel over, he said: 'For the first time in my life I understand what it feels like to be headline fodder, Veum.'

'New experience, is it?'

'Horrible! You see you're just … I mean, even someone like me stuck right in the thick of it, whom you might think would have a bit of influence over what's written, is impotent, no other word for it. Impotent: he repeated as though to make sure I'd understood.

I nodded.

'Suddenly you understand that you've often gone too far yourself. You go through what others have complained to you about before, I mean, that no one listens to you, that your objections, your pleas for your private life to be protected … well, nobody listens, because you've suddenly become news.' He grimaced as he said it.

Through a few openings here and there in the cloud cover beneath us, we caught a glimpse of a dark fjord and the windswept moorland in Sunnhordland. 'Now I'm scared stiff when I go out every day to fetch the morning paper, *my own paper*, Veum. The Oslo papers are placed on my desk as soon as they're delivered, and I have a knot in my stomach every single day from fear of what might be in them, what pictures they want to use. Just seeing your own daughter, a picture of your own daughter, serialised with its own logo at the top of the news pages! Jesus Christ!'

'It'll die down now that Hagavik's been arrested. A case that's been cleared up doesn't have the same news value as an unsolved one.'

'But he hasn't *confessed*, Veum! That's the devil of it! So long as there's no confession, they're free to speculate about everything imaginable, Satanism or worse.'

'Worse?'

'Yes!' He lowered his voice and, after a pause, said: 'We understand now, after the event, that Torild was mixed up in – all sorts. Drugs … ' He found it hard to get the word out: 'P-prostitution!' With a jerk of the head, like a bird catching an insect in flight, he added 'But it was last autumn she went off the rails! *After* I lost control of her!'

'Are you blaming your wife?'

'I'm not blaming anybody! I'm just stating the facts … As recently as last Whitsuntide, when she was, she was – when we were down visiting her at a guide camp on Radøy … '

'Yes, I heard about that. But your wife didn't go.'

He looked at me in surprise. 'What is it you're referring to now?'

'Your wife wasn't with you when you two went to visit the girls. It was just you and Randi Furebø, had you forgotten?'

'Forgotten?' Again he ran his hand over his brow in that characteristic gesture of his. 'No, but … so *what*?'

'A few months later you and your wife separated.'

At last he seemed to get what I was driving at. 'You mean there was supposedly a connection between, that … No, frankly, I hadn't thought of that.'

He almost turned around in his seat, trying to convince me how wrong I was. 'Listen, Veum. Firstly, Randi and Trond, Sidsel and I have been best friends for years, we've been on holidays together, we've shared dinners and breakfasts, been on school trips and goodness knows what else. Trond and I are *mates*; we share everything. If his car conks out, he borrows mine. If mine's in for repairs, I can borrow his. But *not* our wives; we've always kept *them* to ourselves. Randi and I could have driven to the southern tip of Italy together, we could have slept in the car or in camping chalets together, but it would never even have occurred to me to go to bed with her!'

'Really? She's not *that* unattractive.'

'That's not what I'm talking about either! But she's Trond's wife, don't you see? We're *mates*!'

'And your wife and Trond, do they have such high ideals too?'

'Sidsel and Trond? If it's that Whitsuntide trip you're talking about, Sidsel was in poor shape, and anyway, she's never been all that keen on driving, and Trond had gone hiking somewhere. I don't remember exactly. Secondly, Veum, Sidsel and I split up after many years of wear and tear. There was no single event that triggered it off. It was just a gradual realisation, mainly on my part, that she and I had reached the end of the road, no mistake about it. We were way beyond the last warning sign, if you see what I mean. *Proceed beyond this point at your own risk*. From then on we were up the creek without a paddle. And thirdly, nothing of this has anything whatever to do with what happened to Torild!'

'Apart from what you said yourself,' I added, 'that, because of this, of the new family situation, you no longer had any control over her.'

He threw up his hands. 'And I stand by it. If I'd been at home, this wouldn't have happened.'

I made no further comment on that particular point. To protect their own egos, everyone needed to come up with their own explanations. This was Holger Skagestøl's version. His wife would have hers. My own experience told me that the truth lay somewhere in between.

I tried another tack. 'So … Not that it's any of my business actually, but who left whom?'

'Exactly. Not that its any business of yours!'

After a few moments, he felt unable to leave it at that, all the same. He half turned towards me and demonstratively beat the left side of his breast. 'A heart of stone, you see. There are far too many idiotic deserted men out there with visiting rights to their children once a week.'

'Tell me about it!'

'You won't catch me in that brigade, Veum. I never look back. Never!'

'"Never" is a strong word to use, Skagestøl. Too strong for most of us.'

He snorted, turned aside and looked out of the window.

The plane was making its approach to Stavanger's Sola Airport now. As instructed, we fastened our seat belts, and the plane dipped down through the clouds. The sea lay beneath us, grey and surly, with the look of dishwater. The bathing beaches were deserted and slightly reminiscent of the bones of gigantic corpses picked clean.

Holger Skagestøl leafed idly through one of the papers, apparently irritated with himself for what he had said. We landed not long afterwards.

It might perhaps have been natural for us to share a taxi into town, since, despite everything, we had got to know one another a little. But neither of us made the necessary preliminaries, and eventually, he took a taxi in solitary splendour, while I took the airport bus into town.

Thirty-eight

WHEN YOU TRAVEL by plane from Bergen to Stavanger you just have to accept that you'll spend longer on the bus and in your car than in the air, even when the traffic flows as smoothly into the centre of Stavanger as it did on the day I was supposed to die.

The fields round the city were sallow and bare, and the tops of the trees waved in the wind. Yet even now you could already feel why spring came earlier here than anywhere else in the country. There wasn't a snowflake to be seen, only a few scattered patches up on Ryfylke moors. The sun sliced through the clouds at a sharp angle, cut through the windows of the bus and lay there smouldering on your skin. But when I got out of the bus, the blast from the sea was like the scratch of a dirty claw on my cheeks, and it sent a shudder down my spine. Winter still had the upper hand.

I got off at the cathedral, nodded discreetly at the statue of Alexander Kielland and surveyed the scene. The last time I'd been in Stavanger it had been a modern Klondike, a frenzy of activity, its sudden wealth sending prices through the roof. Now everything seemed to have calmed down again. The place had finally got used to its new status, a place where Neil Young, head held high, could sing 'After the Gold Rush' without being booed off the stage.

Stavanger was one of those places God forgot. Perhaps that was why so many chapels had been built there, in a vain attempt to make contact again. When they had eventually given up, they sold their souls to Mammon instead, even though the old neon letters proclaiming that JESUS WAS THE LIGHT OF THE WORLD still shone like a monument from another age over Breiavatnet Water.

Stavanger was a city I'd felt ambivalent about over the years. From 1966 to 1969 I'd attended The School of Social Affairs there.

To start with, I lived in rather miserable lodgings way out beyond Banevigå. In the year above there was a girl the same age as me from Jørpeland, a place opposite Stavanger. Her name was Beate Larsen, and in a colourful get-together at a sort of collective somewhere out towards Egeland, we ended up in the kitchen like two self-obsessed stand-up comics, oblivious of what was going on around us. The following day we took the bus out to Sola and walked hand-in-hand along the beach even though it was September and summer had long since departed south; and when we got back to town, she invited me up to her room, where we deepened our new acquaintance further. With her white thighs on either side of my head and my face deeply anchored in her fjord, I heard her Rogaland accent like a distant *eenie, meenie, miney mo* in the air above me: Oh yes, yes, oh yes, Varg!

Not many months later I moved into her considerably larger lodgings in Wessels Street. When she finished her course six months later she went to Bergen ahead of me, where she had got a part-time job at the Social Welfare Department, while I carried on commuting backwards and forwards for the rest of the time I was in Stavanger. In the May of my final year we got married, and two years later Thomas was born. Neither of us had even heard of Lasse Wiik then.

Stavanger had been the scene of some of my happiest years, and I could never return to the place without being reminded that happiness is fleeting, and about as easy to hold onto as a moonbeam.

◆

The Salvation Nursing Home was just outside Bjergsted. In a modern glass and concrete building, looking out over Byfjord, I asked the way to reception and was sent three floors up and right. 'The door's locked, it's the Senile Dementia Department, but just ring the bell, and they'll let you in,' the lady in reception called out to me helpfully as I was on my way up the stairs.

I followed her advice, and a little dark-haired nurse with a bright round face and great blue eyes showed me in to Kathrine Haugane, asking: 'Are you family?'

'No, I'm an acquaintance – of her son.'

'You mean Birger?'

'Yes. Do you know him?'

'No, but my brother was in the same class at primary school,' she said with a sudden hint of melancholy as though to emphasise how long ago *that* was.

'They were obviously older than you.'

Her face brightened up again. 'Yes, they were actually. Here we are.'

Kathrine Haugane already had a visitor. On the edge of the bed, with some knitting in her hands and an open magazine beside her, sat a woman in her forties, already grey-haired and with a face upon which life had left its imprint all too early.

'You've got a visitor,' said my companion with a cheerful smile.

The woman in the bed gave scarcely a flicker of her eyelids. The other woman stood up surprised. 'Oh?'

I gave a friendly smile. 'It's … ' I hesitated for a moment. 'Veum from Bergen. Varg Veum. I'm an acquaintance of Birger's.'

'Oh.' She put out her hand. 'I'm his sister: Laura Nielsen. Pleased to meet you.'

'Me too.'

She was a little dowdily dressed, in a red shirt blouse, a brown skirt and a plain white knitted cardigan almost like a raffle prize from the last church bazaar. She wore no make-up and no jewellery. Her eyes were pale blue, almost colourless, and were red-rimmed, as if she was suffering from some sort of eye trouble. There was nothing about her to remind one of her brother, but from what I remembered of the notes in my inside pocket, there was nothing to suggest that they had the same father, quite the reverse in fact.

'You are … Was it Birger who asked you to come and – visit us?'

'Well, I … only if I had time. And I just happened to be on this side of town.'

'*He* hasn't been here for two years!' she said, salivating so much that she had to swallow.

'Hasn't he?'

'Not that I don't see his point, mind you! *She's* hardly going to have much to say.' She nodded at her mother, and I followed her eyes.

Kathrine Haugane lay on her back, the eiderdown tucked right up under her chin so her neck could hardly be seen. Her face was thin and wrinkled, the most prominent feature being her nose, sharp and pointed. Her chalk-white hair was parted in the middle, and her skin was grey and sallow, as if it had lain there gathering dust for far too long and no one had bothered to brush it off. Had it not been for the barely visible movement of her lips, you might have thought she was dead.

'Has she been like this long?'

'It'll be eight years this summer. Completely gone.'

'So, isn't she ever awake?'

'Yes, she is, but when she speaks, its just confused babbling. Not a sensible word to be had from her.' She sat down and took up her knitting again. Then she nodded towards the other chair in the room as a sign that I could sit down now that I'd called.

I glanced at the other bed. It was empty.

She followed my gaze. 'Martha Lovise Bredesen. She died two days ago. They're expecting a new patient tomorrow.' She cast off a few stitches and muttered, almost to herself: 'Oh well, at least *they* won't be troubled any more ... '

Strong white daylight filled the room. On the wall above Kathrine Haugane's bed hung a number of private family photographs. One of them showed a woman sitting with two small children in front of a dry-stone wall in such strong sunshine that it must have been the height of summer.

I nodded at the pictures. 'Is that you two?'

She looked up at it almost shyly. 'Yes, it is ... It was one summer, must have been in about 1950, we were at Nærbø.'

'Birger's the eldest,' I remarked.

'Yes, he is – never been any doubt about that.'

'So was your name Bjelland as well, then, before you married?'

'No, er – I've always been called Haugane, I have.'

I looked through the window towards the islands on the other side of the fjord. 'But … do you have a different father, then?'

She pursed her lips and nodded.

'And Birger's father, was his name Bjelland?'

'No, it wasn't … ' She looked down at her mother, lying there with eyes closed and quivering eyelids as though she was dreaming – or just pretending to be asleep.

Laura Nielsen lowered her voice. 'Birger was born in December 1945. Nobody ever found out who his father was, though there were rumours of course, and the general gossip was that he, that his father was, well, *German*, d'you see?' A bitter look came over her face as she remembered it. 'Mother was working as a waitress in a café at the time, where she obviously met decent people as well as other sorts … So it could just as well have been one of the better-off people in town, couldn't it?'

I nodded at her reassuringly. 'Yes, of course it could.'

'So when Birger was almost grown up and moved heaven and earth to find out who his father was, it could just as well have been – it could just as well have been the chap he singled out. And anyway, he was already dead, so who could deny it?'

'No, I … '

'Both Birger and I copped it at school because of this, I can tell you. But mostly Birger. "Nazi bastard! Nazi bastard!" they would shout, running after him. Now and then he'd come home with a bloody nose after a fight. And it never stopped. It's not surprising he got out of this town as soon as he could. Stavanger's a small town, let me tell you!'

'Bergen's no metropolis either.'

'No, I suppose not – but there was no one who knew him there, was there?'

I raised my hand, nodding at her mother. Kathrine Haugane had suddenly opened her eyes. She was staring at the ceiling with a stern look. 'Birger! Don't do it! Roger! Oh no … ' Then her eyelids closed again, as if operated by some hidden mechanism.

I glanced at Laura Nielsen.

She shrugged her shoulders. 'That's one of her standard lines. One of the scenes she plays again and again. It was clearly some awful thing Birger got up to, which she goes over time after time!'

'Any idea what it was?'

'Not the faintest!'

'But what was it she said … Roger?'

'Roger … It was one of Birger's pals at the time. There were probably up to something together, tearaways both of them.'

'Roger … what?'

'Er … Hansen, I think. He died many years ago.'

'Oh … ' I didn't want to press her any more. It was probably nothing important anyway. 'But after Birger was born … what sort of life did she have?'

'She was an outcast. Even if his father wasn't German, the child was illegitimate, and in Stavanger then – well, that was almost as bad! So she went on public assistance, lived in a home for mothers run by the church for a while, they were certainly good to her there, but the rules and regulations were horrendous for a woman in her thirties, after all!'

'But when you were born … '

'Well, er … by then she was in service down at Nærbø, on a farm, and she met a seaman from the locality. Well, he gave her a child and went off on a long trip and didn't come back till two years later, and how could he know it was his child she'd given birth to? Then she moved back into Stavanger, and we've lived here ever since.' She sighed. 'But I can't complain. I've a good husband and manage fine. Time is working in our favour. Soon there'll be no one left who remembers either Kathrine Haugane or her Nazi bastard any longer. So you can give Birger my best regards and tell him it's just as well he stays away! No one here misses him!'

'Birger? Is it you, Birger?' Her mother had suddenly sat up in bed.

'No, mother,' said Laura Nielsen. 'It's *not* Birger, you can see that!' She looked at me apologetically. 'This happens every time she hears a man's voice. It's the same when Ove comes with me. *She* certainly doesn't forget him!'

Kathrine Haugane looked in my direction with her pale-blue, watery eyes. It was almost as though she was looking straight through me. 'Birger! I haven't breathed a word! Not to a soul! You were at home the whole day! The whole day: right, Birger?'

'Yes, yes, mother!' She raised her eyes. 'It's the same old thing over and over again! Lie down and rest now, mother!' She almost forced her mother back down into bed and gave a sigh of satisfaction when she saw the despairing eyes close again.

She looked at the other bed. 'If only she'd been able to find peace too ... Oh, perhaps one shouldn't wish something like that for one's own mother, but sometimes ... may God forgive me, is it an un-Christian thought?'

'Un-Christian ... But it must ... it must be quite an important event if it's left such a lasting impression on her?'

'Yes, I've no idea what she's babbling on about!' She bent down to tuck the blanket tightly under her mother's chin, who looked to have calmed down again completely. 'So now you can return to Bergen and tell Birger what life's like for us here! As if he could care less.'

'Yes, Birger ... Do you know what it is he does in Bergen?'

She looked at me in surprise. 'What he does ... Business, isn't it?'

'But – what sort?'

'Oh, er ... All I know about him is that ... he could have joined the Salvation Army for all I know!'

'Is that likely?'

'Well, yes, actually. You see, when mother came back to Stavanger from Nærbø and the second great disappointment in her life – at least, as far as I know – she was saved.' Bitterly she said: 'It was probably a travelling preacher who saw her as his Mary Magdalene, I'm afraid, but saved she was, at any rate, and so much so that both Birger and I spent more time at chapel than we did at home from when we were six years old till we were well into our teens. Well, Birger right till his military service. I broke away earlier, but by then mother had started to flag, so it wasn't such a big step.'

I glanced at the clock and stood up. 'Well, I don't think I ought to take up any more of your time now.'

'You weren't! On the contrary, it's made a change. In spite of my harsh words, please remember me to Birger when you see him.'

Not without a pang of conscience, I said I would do so before leaving mother and daughter in a sort of silent symbiosis: one lying in bed eyes closed, the other staring vacantly at the other bed and the hope it represented.

Once out in the corridor, I stopped a nurse on her way past with a bedpan. 'Excuse me but … I spoke to a nurse a little while ago, small, dark-haired … '

'Trude Litlabø?'

'Yes, I don't know … '

'Try at the office.' She pointed towards an open door near the end of the corridor.

I went down and looked in.

Trude Litlabø stood up from her chair in front of a computer screen, as I knocked gently on the doorframe. It was a few seconds before she recognised me. 'Oh, hello! How did it go with – Kathrine?'

'Oh, not so bad. I had a nice chat with her daughter, at any rate. Is she always so yonderly, her mother, I mean?'

'Unfortunately, yes. In her condition you might say she's gone into a room someone's lost the key to and is never going to find it again.'

'But she does see something from the window now and then, doesn't she?'

She gave me a look of surprise. 'Yes, she does. Certain events are engraved on her memory.'

'She said something about a boy called Roger. Remember him?'

'Roger, Roger ... You mean, the one who drowned?'

'Drowned?'

'Er, well, I'm not sure. It's Einar you should have asked about that.'

'Your brother?'

'Yes.'

'Where can I find him?'

'Well, er ... ' A shadow ran over her face. 'He's not all that easy to get hold of.'

'Oh? Why not?'

'He's not – well. I mean ... To be frank, he's in a detox clinic for alcoholics, down in Jæren.

'I'd really like to have had a word with him.'

She looked at me searchingly. 'And why is that?'

'I can't say. But I think it could be quite important actually.'

After thinking about it for a few moments she made up her mind. 'Oh, I suppose it can't ... If only it could make him feel, feel that he *means* something, then ... Here you are ... '

She wrote her brother's name and address on a scrap of paper and pushed it over to me. Then she unlocked the door and let me out of the department, wishing me good luck. I thanked her, went down to reception and ordered a taxi to the railway station.

Thirty-nine

NOWHERE IN NORWAY is the sky so heavy as over Jæren. Nowhere is there so much sea in it. On grey days, sky and sea form as one towards the horizon as though a piece of sky has been folded under the land. On sunny days the sea blows up, and before you know it, it's raining.

That day a thin layer of frost lay on the horizon, a stroke from a feather quill that would remain there even in the darkness of night.

'The stamp of February,' muttered Einar Litlabø, nodding seawards.

'How do you mean?'

'That the sea's never darker than at this time of year. As though the colour from all the winter nights had seeped down here, into a kind of melting pot. That's why we have the heavy storms in late winter, so everything can be released before spring. Didn't you know that?'

He had invited me to accompany him on a short walk along narrow tracks that lay in the most sheltered hollows in the wind-swept terrain and were marked out by sombre dry-stone walls, the timeless boundaries of Norwegian farmland, which were always a bone of contention with somebody or other: the source of hundreds of court cases relating to wills, thousands of arguments between neighbours. He appeared to welcome this break in the daily routine, and when I had told the duty doctor about the period I'd spent in Hjellestad some years before, they had allowed us outside the premises without a permit, in the belief that he was in good hands.

His resemblance to his sister lay mainly in the colour of his hair.

Einar Litlabø had dark, shoulder-length hair with streaks of grey, as if life had passed him by all too fast, and he had never had time to go to the barber's.

His face was thin with deep furrows running from his nostrils down both sides of his mouth. His brow looked permanently wrinkled, and the anxiety smouldering away in his eyes told me why he was here.

'B-B-Birger? Do you want to talk about Birger? Why?'

'Are you still in contact with him?'

'With Birger? Oh no! Not for many years now. That was when we were little. Long before he left Stavanger.'

'But you knew him well then, didn't you? When you were both kids?'

'Y-Y-Yes I did! We were best mates, Birger and me. Best mates.'

'So you didn't mind that the others called him Nazi bastard?'

'Good God, Nazi bastard … Birger was fine though. Our lot came from gypsy stock, actually … Didn't Trude tell you that? No, I suppose she didn't. No.'

'I only exchanged a few worth with her.'

'That's understandable. Gypsies who've settled down and Nazi bastards, they were much of a muchness.'

'You were bullied – or *teased*, as they probably called it then – you and your sister?'

'And all our other brothers and sisters too. There were six of us, no seven, but one of them died when she was little.'

I tried to broach the topic again. 'Who was it who teased you then? Birger Bjelland and you?'

'Well, he didn't call himself Bjelland in those days, did he? It was Birger Haugane then … Yes and who do you think it was? All the good-looking, clever ones, all the ones who had both a mother and father and who were fair-haired, had proper teeth and lots of cash in their school bankbooks. In those days we hadn't so much as five kroner in ours, see?'

'But you gave as good as you got I suppose?'

'Gave as good as we got? They went home with bloody noses and muddied clothes, every last one of them. But who was it got the blame, do you think? Them or us? Who was it that was threatened with being sent to reform school if we didn't behave?'

'There was one called Roger ... '

He clammed up suddenly, glancing over the nearest dry-stone wall and out to sea. For a moment it was as though his eyes took on the colours of what they saw, a mixture of grey and white, with a black pulsating heart that was suddenly beating too fast.

'Roger Hansen, wasn't it?'

He stopped and pointed out to sea. 'See that ... the ship there? When I'm walking here, I often think that it's on board a ship like that I should have been, one that sailed away and never came back. The only problem, though, is that the earth's round, and if you sail far enough away, you always end up back where you started from anyway.'

I nodded in agreement before adding: 'And that's just what our lives are like too. We think time only moves in one direction. Yet it's not just the senile who return to their childhood. Every one of us has to do that at some time in our life, Einar.'

He stood there, looking thoughtful, as if he was somewhere else, in a completely different time from the present.

'He drowned, didn't he?' I said softly.

'What ... ' He swung round to face me. 'Why have you come here, Veum? Who do you represent? What do you want?'

'Do you have any children, Einar?'

'Do I have any ... ' His gaze began to wander again. He looked down as though in search of something for his eyes to settle on. 'Two girls and a boy. Two marriages. I'm still in contact with the boy. I'm not allowed to see the girls. Not till I'm – completely ... '

'In that case, I'm going to tell you a thing or two about your childhood mate and the sort of business I think he's behind in Bergen.'

I told him about the young girls at Jimmy's and the sort of activities they were recruited for. Perhaps I laid it on a bit thick, especially considering how sure I was that Birger Bjelland was the moving force behind it all, but it struck home. As I told him bit by bit, his look gradually steadied, and his face somehow became even more lined and almost emaciated-looking. 'It could have been one of your children, Einar; it could have been – mine.'

He turned his back to the sea and looked in over the land, as if there was more hope in the Norwegian bedrock. 'I think we should turn back now.'

We set off again.

'Who told you about – Roger?'

'Kathrine Haugane.'

He looked at me quickly as though to see whether I was serious.

'In her way.' I tried to imitate her voice: *'Birger! Don't do it! Roger! Oh no ... '*

'So she ... ' He looked at me wide-eyed. 'So she saw it too!'

'Saw what, Einar?'

He hesitated for a few more moments. Then it came, slowly at first, as though he had to reconstruct it all, then quicker, bit by bit, as he got into his stride. 'We were seven years old, in the first class at primary school. I called on Birger, to play with him. But there was nobody at home. So I walked down towards Mosvatnet Lake, we often used to play there. This was in January, and there was ice on the water. Suddenly, I saw the two of them, Roger and him, a long way out. Then suddenly something happened. I think they started to quarrel. In any case, Birger shoved Roger so hard that he – fell, like this, forwards, and then ... Then the ice broke, and he fell through it.'

He swallowed heavily. But I didn't give him a helping hand this time. This was a story he had to tell in his own way, for now. 'I ... Roger bobbed back up again, waving his arms, but Birger, he just turned his back on him and ran off. At first, I thought he was perhaps going to fetch one of those life-saving hooks that had been placed around the lake, but then … he just vanished, ran off home, I think. And so did Roger. Vanish, I mean. He didn't come back up again.' He averted his eyes from me with a look of someone asking for forgiveness. 'We were so young, you see! It all happened so fast. One moment it had happened. The next moment all was calm again. Just a hole in the ice. As though nothing had … '

'So you – didn't say anything to anyone either?'

'No, I … When the police started looking for him later that day, there were some other people who'd seen him on his way down to Mosvatnet Lake, and when the police found the hole in the ice … they soon found him. And not many questions were asked afterwards either. It was only a child, after all! Just an accident!' Pensively, he added: 'But the fact that Mrs Haugane also … Why on earth do you think *she* didn't do anything?'

I shrugged. 'Who can tell, so many years after? She had first-hand experience of what it was like to be an outcast and hounded like a dog. Perhaps she recognised her own tormentors in those who tormented her son. Because Roger *was* one of those who used to tease him?'

'One of the worst. No denying *that*.'

I glanced sideways at him. 'And you've carried this around with you all these years?'

The pain in his face was clear to see. 'Not just that … '

'Not just that. Is there more? Involving Birger?'

'It's only a theory. But that's how it is, isn't it, the first time's the worst?'

'Do you mean that he, that – there were *others*?'

In the distance we could see the institution he was on his way back to, looking like a school building on top of the hill.

'There was quite a bit about it in the papers when it happened, but there was never a *case* about it.'

'Oh?'

'It was the year he was doing military service. At Evjemoen. There was a soldier who was killed by a stray bullet, or whatever you call it, when the barrel gets blocked with snow so the whole rifle explodes.'

'And then?'

'Well, it's just not something that happens every day. The chap who was killed was one of the same lot who used to tease him at school, look … ' He opened his left hand and showed an oblique scar on his palm. 'I still have a scar from his sheath knife! And Birger was in the same section as him.'

'You mean that it was *him* who blocked the barrel?'

He nodded. 'Maybe.'

'What was the soldier's name?'

'Ragn … Ragnar Hillevåg.'

'And roughly when did this happen?'

'You can find it in the paper, but – but I did my military service in 1964. I think it was the year after.'

'But it's only supposition, surely? It was never mentioned afterwards?'

'Well, just that many years later, in a bar in town, I got talking to one of the others who'd been in the camp at the same time. And he said the atmosphere was very tense among all the recruits from Stavanger right through basic training school, and that was because Hillevåg was rubbing salt in old wounds.'

'Not just with Birger, then?'

'That's right, but … it was only Birger who'd killed anybody! I mean and *I'd* seen it!'

We were back now. He looked in at the lights from the dayroom as though regretting our walk and was now solely intent on parking himself in front of the TV and forgetting everything.

'You don't have to carry that burden alone any more, Einar,' I said comfortingly. 'As you said yourself, you two were only kids. Kathrine Haugane should have known better. But what does one not do for one's children?'

He nodded. 'The children are the writing on the wall for us, Veum.'

I started. 'The writing on … How do you mean? The writing on the wall means a signal, a *warning*.'

'And that's just what our children are. If they go off the rails, so do we. And I'm not saying it's our fault, if things go wrong. It can just as easily be – ha! – society or the age or just something in their make-up, a tendency they've inherited from far back … '

'The sins of the fathers?'

'I don't know. All I do know is that when things go wrong with those who are new to life then everything else goes to pot as well! *Weighed in the balance and found wanting*, eh, Veum? Weighed in the balance and found wanting, every last one of us.'

Forty

I CALLED VIDAR WAAGENES from Sola Airport in Stavanger. He was in a meeting, but his secretary had a message for me: *Thursday, twelve o'clock at police headquarters.*

While waiting for the first evening plane, I ate a lukewarm stew in the cafeteria, drank a cup of coffee and leafed through a crumpled copy of one of the morning papers, where yesterday's news was equally lukewarm.

The day's events had blotted out all thought of what date it was. But now, as I was about to head off homewards, it came back to me like a boomerang, so forcefully that even in the departure hall I started to look round for people I knew. But I saw no one.

The plane to Bergen was full. In the seat beside me sat a man in his thirties with rimless reading glasses and a briefcase. He looked as though he was planning to go through the whole year's accounts in the bare half hour we were in the air and didn't glance in my direction so much as once.

Nobody else set any alarm bells ringing either, and the only turbulence we experienced before Bergen's Flesland Airport was the strong gust of wind on the port side just before we landed.

I was about halfway down the queue to leave the plane. Descending the stairs to the arrivals hall, I scoured the whole area while I still had a bird's eye view of it. There was nobody to meet me, and nobody I thought I recognised either.

As I had nothing but hand luggage, I made quickly for the exit. And I was not the only one. Most of us were carrying little more than a briefcase.

Outside it was dark, with a biting wind, a good bit colder than in Stavanger. Quite a few people besides me had left their cars in the long-stay car park. In a way, it was reassuring to have company. But on the other hand … who were they all?

I found the car and gave it a quick once-over to check the locks and the windows. Then I opened the driver's side door, took out the ice-scraper, scraped a thin layer of ice from the windscreen and got in, put the key in the ignition key and turned it.

The Corolla started like clockwork, just as it had done all the years I'd owned it.

I looked both ways before moving gently off.

Going down the airport road I kept a constant lookout behind. If there were any motorbikes on the road that evening, they were certainly nowhere near here, and if he'd transferred to a car, I had no idea which one it was.

The radio wasn't properly tuned in, and I hit the search button. A local radio station issued a warning about icy roads in Bergen and the surrounding area and urged people to drive with caution and adapt their speed to the conditions. I did so immediately, to the great annoyance of the drivers behind. But then it was unlikely that any of them had received their own death notice in the post either.

Rather than opting for the motorway, I took the Nesttun exit and drove into town along Fanaveien. Between Nesttun and Paradis, I was stuck right behind a large, dark-blue van. Along the paths around Tveitevannet Lake people were already taking their evening constitutional, and I turned off up Hagerupsvei towards Landås.

It was a quarter to eight when I turned down Fløenbakken. I counted the traffic humps going downhill, looking both ways all the while. In the car park in front of Karin's block there was just room for one more car, but it was a tight squeeze.

I had no idea where the juggernaut came from. I was just in the process of wriggling out of the car when it lumbered over the nearest traffic hump with a roar of its engine loud enough to put the wind up a bull elk. It swerved violently to the left before the brakes were slammed on with a screech that reverberated right through my bones. I glanced up at the driver's seat. High up there behind the wheel, like a raised up *deus ex machina*, I glimpsed a shiny black motorbike helmet.

I closed the door in a desperate attempt to get out round the car. When he hit his target, my hand was still on the door handle.

There was a deafening bang, and a sort of shudder ran through me. As the car was catapulted forwards through the fence and up into the air, I still couldn't grasp exactly what had happened. The car door was snatched away while my fingers were still clutching the handle, and I sailed in a large arc towards the prickly Berberis bushes that encircled the whole parking area. Instinctively, I tried to shield myself with the door, as though crash-landing a flying carpet. Bits of car rained down all around me.

Forty-one

SOUNDS CAME from all sides.

A woman screamed hysterically from one of the windows above. A man let out a high-pitched bellow of rage. A dog howled, and I heard footsteps running from several directions. Somewhere nearby I heard a motorbike being revved up and gradually fading away; then in the distance the sound of sirens.

There was a strong smell of burnt rubber, oil and petrol.

A voice called out: 'Hello? Anybody there?'

I stuck my head up above the bushes, still holding the handle of the car door in one hand. For a moment there was a deathly hush around me.

Then Karin emerged from the dark crowd of people streaming towards me. 'Varg! Are you hurt?'

'No, I … ' Apart from a feeling of tenderness between elbow and shoulder and the sensation that someone had used a vegetable grater on my face, I felt surprisingly all right. But when I shook my head to say that everything was OK, there was an echoing sound I'd never heard the likes of before, and with it came stabbing pains, as sharp and piercing as my voice had just sounded. I leaned forward and covered my mouth, overcome with sudden nausea.

'Hey, you!' shouted the same man's voice as before. 'Was it you driving that truck?'

'N-no,' I mumbled.

'No!' shouted Karin, relaying me.

'Well, who the hell was it, then?'

The sirens had now reached Fløenbakken. With an effort, I straightened up, and for the first time took a proper look round.

The place looked as though a bomb had hit it. The vicar's wife from Fana would never recognise her Toyota now. It didn't take much imagination to see that they were quite angry, as were the owners of the two cars I'd parked between.

True, one of them had only had one side of the rear torn off, yet I doubted whether it would ever be driven again. The other two looked more like accordions than cars, while the crash had hammered mine into a ball, now lying on its roof among the bushes, no more than half a yard from where I'd landed myself. The car that had been beside it wasn't a pretty picture either. Doors, lamps, lights and the remains of bumpers lay scattered over the whole area.

The juggernaut towered monster-like over the whole scene. The driver's door was hanging off like a torn ear, but there was no doubt who had emerged victorious from the collision.

'Veum … is that you?'

'Yes … '

I recognised the two police constables from before. Ristesund and Bolstad were the sort you could talk to. Both were from west Norway, both had moustaches. Bolstad's was reddish brown; Ristesund's black.

'Any idea what happened?' asked Bolstad.

I gestured vaguely with one hand. 'Somebody or other who ran amok with an articulated truck.'

Ristesund glanced at the truck driver's seat. 'Damn right he ran amok. And then? Just vanished into thin air?'

'I wasn't – exactly – all there … '

'Can't you see he's hurt?' said Karin irritably.

Bolstad took out his notebook. 'So did you witness what happened?'

'No. I just live here!'

'Is any of this your car, Veum?' asked Ristesund.

'That,' I mumbled. 'What's left of it.'

He gave a little chuckle. 'Hope you're insured.'

'It's insured up to the hilt. Will that do?'

'Was it you they were after?' said Bolstad.

I looked round and said softly: 'I'd keep my voice down if I were you, with all these car-owners right next to us.'

'But?'

'I went down to see Muus a few days ago to tell him about a threatening letter I'd received. You could say I've just received another, with a genuine first-day issue stamp on it this time.'

'Any idea who might be behind it?'

I made a vague gesture. 'No more than last time.'

I noticed Karin's eyes on my face. I looked down. She knew me better than Ristesund and Bolstad did.

'And you didn't see who did it? Who it was, I mean?'

'God, no. It all happened so fast. I was just getting out of my car, and bang! If I'd still been in the car, there wouldn't be much of a peep out of me now.'

'Nothing that might help to identify him?'

'He was wearing a helmet.'

'Helmet?'

'And … as I lay spread-eagled over there in the bushes, I heard a motorbike being started up.'

Bolstad walked over to the patrol car. 'I'll put out a call to tell the other cars to keep an eye out for a motorcyclist. And also to run a check on the number plate of – that thing.'

Given the cold, most of the neighbours had now satisfied their curiosity. The only ones left were the two hapless car-owners and a woman I assumed was married to one of them. They stood there shaking their heads, while carrying on a hushed conversation, now and then scowling at Karin and me.

Bolstad returned. 'The articulated truck belongs to a firm in Åsane. They're ringing the boss now to find out whether it's been stolen.'

Ristesund looked at me. 'I think you should pop down to A&E, don't you?'

'Yes, you should,' said Karin quickly.

Bolstad agreed. 'We can ring for a taxi. Unfortunately, we still need to hang about here for a bit. If you think of anything else, don't forget to contact us.'

'No, I – I'm due to call in at headquarters tomorrow morning anyway. We can talk about it then.'

'Are you going to ring now?' said Karin in a worried tone. I didn't mention it, but I seemed to hear her words twice, like an echo.

◆

At Accident and Emergency, they thought I'd come out of it surprisingly well. There were no fractures in the arm, and as for my head, it was little more than slight concussion. If I took it easy for a week, the symptoms would just disappear.

I didn't nod because it hurt to do so. Nor did I shake my head. I also avoided Karin's eyes.

A week – that was an eternity by my reckoning. Anyway, I had an appointment: *Thursday, two o'clock, at police headquarters.*

They attended to the cuts on my face from branches and thorns and dispatched me back into the world without any further advice.

As we stood waiting for the return taxi afterwards, I said: 'I think I'll go back to my place this evening, Karin.'

'But why – ?'

'I have the feeling your neighbours won't be all that pleased to see me again.'

'I don't think you should take that – '

'Besides, I don't want to expose you to any danger.'

The taxi arrived. 'I'll come with you,' she said.

The taxi ride home was enough to make me feel sick again. The outer door downstairs was locked. All was in darkness in the flat of the widower on the ground floor.

When I let myself in upstairs I opened the door carefully and took a good look around before stepping inside. But no truck stood there on the kitchen floor ready to go into action as soon as I showed my face.

As we sat on my old sofa, bought in a sale in 1974, each with a cup in our hands, she gave me a worried look. 'You look – furious, Varg.'

I clenched my fist. 'I *am* furious.'

'Because of – what happened tonight?'

'That too … but mainly because of what happens to girls like Torild Skagestøl … Damn it, there's a far bigger network of shady clients out there than there is of people trying to help, for God's sake. Hotel staff, doctors, taxi drivers and pimps – and then guys like Birger Bjelland, our Pontius Pilate from Stavanger!'

'Did you find out anything down there?'

'Yes, I did actually. I'm going to get him this time, Karin!'

'But not for a week!'

'Not before tomorrow anyway … '

She looked at me reproachfully. 'Varg … '

I put my hand over her mouth. Our eyes met. Then I put my face close to hers, placed my hands on either side of her head and held it tight. I was fifty; she was a few years younger. There was no landscape that gave me such peace to walk in as hers.

Thou art fair my love … Thy lips are like a thread of scarlet … Thy temples are like a pomegranate … Thy breasts are like two young roes that are twins, which feed among the lilies … Until the day break and the shadows flee away, I will get me to the mountain of myrrh, and to the hill of frankincense … Thou art all fair my love there is no spot in thee …

Later, when she had fallen asleep, I once again lay listening to the sound of her breathing, yet could not fall asleep myself.

Sleep is the prelude to death. If you stay in bed too long, there is no telling what might happen.

Forty-two

I AWOKE to find her standing beside the bed.

Her voice sounded as though she was in an aquarium. 'Varg? How do you feel?'

'Like Jonah in the belly of the whale. Are we there already?'

'You were sleeping so soundly that I hadn't the heart to waken you. But I must be off now.'

'Have you had your breakfast?'

She nodded. 'You'll take it easy today, won't you? Promise?'

'I'll try not to get too worked up. I'll move slowly and breathe deeply in and out. More than that I can't promise, not hand on heart, until the lid is screwed down tight on this case for good.'

She sighed. 'Well, I should be used to problem children, shouldn't I? So … '

I smiled reassuringly at her.

'You look terribly pale.'

I felt pale too, and scarcely had she closed the door behind her than I was in the kitchen cupboard looking for the strongest headache tablets I could find. And I didn't leave any behind. To be on the safe side, I put the whole bottle in my pocket when I left.

There was no one waiting for me outside. Light snowflakes were falling from a leaden sky, and it was just cold enough for the snow to lie like a shroud over the rooftops.

I opened the letter box and took the post up with me to the office without looking at it.

As I stepped into the office, I glanced at the answerphone. No messages. Then I leafed through the post. Nothing of interest.

Like an aftershock, it dawned on me that it was the silence that was the most threatening thing. It was as though …

As though I no longer existed, as though I was already …
Dead.

Then I called the insurance company and told them what was left of my car. They were none too pleased. But, according to the contract, it was *of course* quite in order for me to have a hire car, *provided* I needed it for my job. Which I did, and they told me which hire firm to get in touch with. After I'd rung off, I felt sure they'd immediately added my name to the client blacklist. At any rate, they'd hardly be rolling out the red carpet next time I called in.

I locked the door carefully as I left.

◆

The hire car was an Opel, and I was in no fit state to adjust my driving in the twinkling of an eye, so I lurched in fits and starts round Nøstet and over Puddefjord Bridge before gradually getting the hang of the new pedals.

Digi-Data plc was one of the firms in a cooperative housed in a refurbished factory in Laksevågsiden. The secretary in reception shot a discreet glance at the cuts and scratches on my face and asked whether I knew which was Ole Hopsland's office. No, I said, and she accompanied me right to his office and held the door open for me.

A young, fair-haired man with a pale face and large round glasses looked absent-mindedly up at us as we came in. I thanked the receptionist for her help and checked that she was on her way back to reception before introducing myself.

'It's Veum. Varg Veum. And don't pretend you've never heard the name before.'

He turned beetroot, and his eyes started to flit about. Before answering he fixed them on a point on my shirtfront. 'Wh-what do you want?'

'Even the best joke can go too far, right?'

'I-I don't know … '

'Oh yes, you do. And if you insist, we can call the police and ask someone with the proper know-how to come up here, dismantle your computer and take a free trip on your hard drive to see what they find. OK?'

'Th-there's no need.'

'Isn't there? Good. OK, so out with it and make it snappy.'

He stole a quick look at my face, long enough for him to see the cuts and bruises and the look of contained fury in my eyes, before glancing quickly back down again.

'Th-there's nothing to tell.'

'Oh no? OK. Let me repeat what I just said. I can call the police and – '

'OK, OK, OK I've got it! It was just the old man who … He said he wanted to play a trick on you.'

'Me?'

'Yeah.'

'Did he tell you who I was?'

He shrugged. 'An old friend, he said.'

'So he's in the habit of posting death notices to his old friends, is he?'

'It was just a j-joke.'

'Yeah. Nearly killed myself laughing. Maybe that was the idea?'

He looked away without saying anything.

'Does your dad still drive a motorbike?'

'Yeah, he … Why?'

'Oh, just wondered … It's a long time since I've seen him. Maybe I should pay him a visit, before the burial, if you see what I mean … '

He looked at his monitor as though he might be able to creep into it and hide.

'You've never done time, then?'

He made no reply but shifted uneasily.

'That'll soon change if I get another letter like that. Got it?'

He nodded.

'And if you see your dad, don't say hello from me. I'll tell him personally.'

Forty-three

DR EVENSEN'S WAITING ROOM was half-full of people, but there were no young girls among them. His secretary looked at me sceptically through the window into her office. When I went over to it she slid the hatch aside and waited expectantly. She was a woman in her forties, with dark-brown hair and the glassy look of someone wearing contacts.

'Is Dr Evensen in?'

'Yes, but we're not accepting any new patients.'

'I just wanted a word with him.'

She glanced towards the other waiting patients. 'As you see, there are a lot of people waiting to see him.'

'Give Dr Evensen a call and tell him it's about Torild Skagestøl.'

'Torild Skage ... '

'Sound familiar?'

She hit a few keys and looked at the screen. 'She's not a patient here.'

'Astrid Nikolaisen, then?'

'No. She isn't either. What's this about?'

I leaned closer to the hatch and lowered my voice. 'You can tell Dr Evensen that a man called Varg Veum is here, and that he'd like to talk to him about Torild Skagestøl, Astrid Nikolaisen and all the others. And if he feels he'd rather not talk to me, tell him in that case I'll come back with the police.'

She looked at me in alarm before slamming the hatch shut just an inch or so from the tip of my nose, lifting the phone, keying in a number and after a moment's wait, starting to speak.

When she had finished she looked as though he had berated her and only opened the hatch wide enough to tell me that Dr

Evensen would see me as soon as he had finished with his current patient.

The other people in the waiting room, who had followed the episode with more or less unconcealed curiosity, looked at me, disgruntled. An older lady stood up and went over to tap on the windowpane. When it was opened she barked: 'What's the idea? I've already been waiting over an hour!'

'Yes, I'm really sorry,' said the receptionist with obvious signs of strain, 'but there's … Unfortunately, we're running a bit behind, and some – cases just *have* to be seen first! I hope you understand …'

'Bah! Some cases!' On the way back to her chair the lady looked me up and down. 'You're a politician, I expect? They always come first in the queue, don't they?' she said to the others with a look that suggested she was expecting a round of applause. But all she got was the nervous rustle of a magazine and one or two nods of approval.

Not long afterwards an elderly gentleman with a surprisingly red nose and shirt open at the neck emerged from the surgery. The receptionist opened the hatch and nodded to me. 'Your turn.'

Considering the looks that followed me in, I might well need a doctor myself soon. But in that case, I would go to a different one. The only thing Dr Evensen looked as though he might consider writing out for me was a one-way ticket to the nearest mortuary.

He sat behind his desk, his face about as expressive as a cod's head down at the fish quay. He was about my age, two or three years older perhaps, but with a good deal more grey in his thin swept-back hair. He was wearing a white doctor's coat with a stethoscope protruding from one of the pockets. His glasses were old-fashioned, with dark brown, almost black frames; he had thin lips and a cold look. The only sign of nervousness was the way he silently drummed his fingers on the desk.

'I didn't catch the name,' he said, repeating slightly as though seasick.

'Veum,' I said, still standing just inside the door.

'And what was it you wanted?'

'I wanted to discuss something called "the safe list" and a few young women, one called – '

'And on whose authority have you come here?'

'On the greatest authority in the world,' I said. 'On the authority of all who have children!'

He looked at me lugubriously. Then he nodded towards the chair as though I were a patient to whom he had to give a sentence of certain death.

I sat down. 'I think you know what we're talking about. There's no point beating about the bush. Torild Skagestøl is dead, one of the other girls has spilled the beans. The only thing that might help you now, once the police get going, is whatever Birger Bjelland had over you.' He didn't react to the name at all. His look remained just as dead and glassy as before. Then he lifted the receiver and keyed in an eight-figure number.

Faintly I heard a woman's voice answer.

'Dr Evensen here. Is he there? Yes, it is. Thank you.'

He looked at the window. It was still snowing. The roar of the traffic from Strandgaten sounded strangely muffled. I wondered whether it was on account of the snow or whether he had particularly well-insulated windows.

'Yes, it's er ... – I have a chap here called Veum. He – '

It was a man's voice this time, and it didn't sound any too pleasant. I noticed that a few beads of sweat had appeared on Dr Evensen's brow.

'What? Yes, he's sit – ... He claims he knows everything. He even says ... Yes. No. I see. I'll count on that, then. Goodb –' The connection was broken with a sharp sound at the other end.

Then he turned to face me again. 'I've nothing to say. If the police come, I'll insist on my lawyer being present.'

'Maybe your lawyer should also have been present when you were examining those girls in the evenings?'

'I've told you I'm not saying anything.'

'You've already said more than enough. That telephone conversation … the *safe* list!' I leaned forward so abruptly that a sharp pain stabbed through my head like an icicle. 'Oh God!'

He looked at me with no trace of sympathy.

'I've squashed people like you before,' I said, 'so don't feel too safe! *Doctor*? Don't make me laugh! If Hippocrates had turned up here he'd have stopped in his tracks and turned tail. Did you never stop to think for a second that you were dealing with young girls – children? That they had parents who were concerned for their welfare?'

His look of embarrassment signalled that I was the one making a fool of myself. 'I think you should go now, Veum. My waiting room's full of patients, and – '

'And I've a good mind to go out and tell them what kind of a doctor you really are, *Dr* Evensen!'

'If you do that, you'll hear from my lawyer, let me tell you! Is that clear?'

'I have a lawyer myself, Evensen. Just wait till you see the newspaper headlines the day we go to court. I shan't be the one losing my clients, you can be sure of that!'

His eyes followed me right to the door like cold clammy fingers on my neck.

His secretary did not look too charming either, and crossing the waiting room was like skiing across Greenland in a howling midwinter gale. As I passed the indignant lady from earlier, I glanced sideways and muttered: 'I can count on your vote then, can I? Is that a promise?'

Forty-four

I MET VIDAR WAAGENES in the police station.

'What on earth's happened to you?' he asked, nodding at my face.

'A car accident.'

'Serious?'

'Mainly for the car.'

As we walked down the stairs to the remand cells, he said: 'You've been engaged *pro forma* to assist the defence in their work. But I wasn't thinking of paying you any fee, just so we both know where we stand.'

'Are things that tight?'

'Not if you should turn up something I can use. In that case, I'll be willing to discuss it. Fair enough?'

'*D'accord.*'

The police sergeant in the remand section checked our papers thoroughly before letting us into the cell where Helge Hagavik sat reading a popular men's magazine of the kind which mainly concentrated on hunting, fishing, crime and naked women.

Helge Hagavik was both larger and in more impressive shape than I'd anticipated. His hair was light blonde, short and curly, and his skin still had a faint trace of colour from the solarium. He looked well built: no bodybuilding fanatic but not a skinny long-distance runner either. When he stood up I saw that he was nearer six foot one, with clean regular features. It wasn't hard to understand that this was the sort a sixteen-year-old girl could have fallen for.

'Hello, Helge!' said Vidar Waagenes with forced heartiness. 'This is Veum, who thinks he may have something to contribute, to your case I mean.'

Helge Hagavik eyed me suspiciously. 'How exactly?'

'I'm a private investigator. I was hired to find Torild when she went missing from home.'

This did not make him any less suspicious. 'What might you be able to contribute?'

'A few facts I've gathered during my investigation.'

'Shall we sit down?' Vidar Waagenes suggested. He had brought in a Windsor chair, which he pushed over to me, himself sitting on the bunk beside Helge Hagavik.

'And what facts are those?'

'Are we agreed that you knew Torild Skagestøl?'

He looked at his defence lawyer, who nodded. 'Yes,' he muttered.

'Where did you meet her?'

He shrugged. 'Somewhere in town. At a pub or a disco.' His eyes glazed over. 'I don't remember exactly.'

'Not at Jimmy's, then?'

He bit his lower lip nervously. 'No, not – there.'

'But the two of you did meet there later?'

'Yes, but that was only because I worked there a bit.'

'Doing what?'

'Oh, tidying up and washing the floor, emptying the game machines and stuff.'

'So you're not at school?'

'No, I dropped out.'

'How old are you?'

'Eighteen.'

'Which school did you go to?'

'Sixth Form College. Doing marketing. But I got sick of it. There was too much homework, and I was pissed off with school.'

'So how did you get this job at Jimmy's?'

'I train a lot. Pump iron, go running and cycling, windsurfing, downhill skiing, anything that's a buzz. I met the brother of the bloke who runs Jimmy's down at the fitness centre … '

'Kenneth?'

He moved his head slowly from side to side as though he was exercising his muscles there. 'Yeah.'

'All that ground's been covered, Veum,' Vidar Waagenes broke in. 'Helge's admitted he knew Torild. Also that they were going out together for a while. But to conclude from that – '

I interrupted him. 'Were going out together for a while? So was it over?'

Helge Hagavik looked almost embarrassed. 'Yes. – From my side at any rate.'

'But the two of you were seen together last Thursday.'

He blinked with both eyes. 'Last … '

'Yes, the week she disappeared! You were one of the last people she was seen with. And it was you who – found her. The police aren't stupid, you know. It's not without *reason* that you're in here.'

'Veum,' Vidar Waagenes began to say.

'But I didn't kill her … '

'No, I don't think you did either.' I let my words sink in to both of them for a moment before adding: 'So it's all the more important for you to tell the truth! Don't you understand that? However painful or difficult it is.'

'Yes … I could never have killed her … '

'No? How long did you go out together?'

He wagged his head a little. 'A couple of months.'

'When?'

'Last autumn.'

'And were you *really* going out together? You know what I mean, don't you? Did you go to bed with her?'

He looked down. 'She said she was sixteen! She looked older than she was!'

'In other words, yes. And when did it end?'

'Well, it didn't really end, as such.' Suddenly, he looked right into my face. With a slightly cocky smile he said: 'I don't believe in the big love affair. I had a few others besides her.'

'Other girls? The same age?'

He nodded before quickly adding: 'And older ones! You meet them at the fitness centre, anorexic-looking forty-year-olds who go to aerobics to keep their figure. They fall like flies if you just look at them.'

I smiled to myself. They say that the way to a man's heart is through his stomach. But the way to some men's hearts is to appeal to their vanity. I'd found Helge Hagavik's Achilles Heel. Now all I had to do was apply some pressure.

'You've had a lot, then?'

'Couldn't count them!'

I tried to look both impressed and jealous. In fact, it was not that difficult. 'What was your impression of Torild?'

He took on a man-of-the-world air. 'She couldn't get enough. Well, that's how they are at that age, isn't it? Once you turn them on. But she wasn't very experienced.'

Against my will, I felt myself starting to seethe again inwardly. 'But you weren't the first she'd had sex with?'

Although slightly reluctant, he was forced to admit this. 'No, she wasn't a virgin.'

'Did she say anything about who she'd been with before?'

'She muttered something about a boy in her class. It hadn't been much to write home about, apparently.'

'I'm sure it wasn't. Compared with you.'

He looked suspicious again. *What was I driving at?*

'But back to the day she disappeared. Thursday, February 11th. You met her at Jimmy's … '

'Yes. But we just sat and talked. It was her and that friend of hers, Åsa … '

'Have you done it with her too?'

'Eh? Åsa? No, she was a bit too … And besides, she didn't inter-est me. I don't take everything that's on offer, you know!'

I leaned forward slightly. 'You obviously know what goes on at Jimmy's?'

'Goes on?'

'Yes, since you've worked there and everything. The police know about it, and so does everybody else. The phone calls from the bar at the Pastel Hotel. The girls who're sent out on – assignments. Torild was involved in that too.'

He scowled at Vidar Waagenes. 'And?'

'There's something I'd like you to know, Helge. That is, if you don't already … Who was it you said runs Jimmy's?'

'Kalle … '

'But he doesn't own the place.'

'No … ' He felt he was on less certain ground now.

'Anybody can call the Companies Registration Office in Brønnøysund and find out who the registered owner is, so you might just as well say it.'

His eyes flitted about, but he said nothing.

'Birger Bjelland, right?'

Vidar Waagenes glanced at his client. 'You knew that, didn't you, Helge?'

'Yes, I – gave them a hand now and then. I've got my driving licence, haven't I?'

'A Ford Sierra. Second-hand.'

'Impounded by the police for forensic tests,' said Waagenes.

'Are you saying you were a chauffeur for Birger Bjelland?'

'Him as well. I drove them, when they were going to play poker and stuff.'

'Birger Bjelland and who else?'

'Er … Fred, Kenneth, Kalle … '

He shrugged his shoulders and looked at me askance.

'Listen … No, let's start at the other end. Tell me about how you found Torild.'

His jaw clicked. 'I've told the law that hundreds of times!'

'And me,' said Vidar Waagenes, but I could tell from the look of him that he wanted to hear it again. 'But all the same, Helge, it won't hurt to tell Veum as well.'

'OK then!' His look became distant again. 'So … I was out

jogging last Thursday. I still live at home, and I often run up towards Fanafjell to push myself a bit, up steep hills.'

'Sounds reasonable.'

'But then, maybe it was something I'd eaten or some tablets that had disagreed with me, you see, I take a fair amount of – body-building products. So I had to – have a shit. And I didn't much like the idea of crouching down just at the side of the road, so I walked down the slope on the right, and down in the bushes I suddenly saw that someone was lying there.'

'So you were surprised when it was also somebody you knew?'

'Surprised? I was stunned. And I immediately realised what it would make me look like. But shit, I said … '

'Literally.'

'I couldn't *not* report it either!'

I scratched my cheek. 'But you do realise the situation you've placed yourself in, and I don't mean vis-à-vis the police but in relation to Birger Bjelland & Co?'

'No, I … '

'By "finding" Torild Skagestøl the way you did, it means that, through you, the whole operation could be exposed.'

'Operation?'

'And I guarantee you that lot don't treat squealers with kid gloves.'

'Squealers! I'm not a grass!'

'Oh no? You could say it looks pretty much like it though! And I can guarantee … you won't be safe anywhere. They have their people, not here maybe, but when you're taken to prison to serve your sentence … They'll get you then, Helge. You can count on it!'

He turned back to Waagenes. 'But I only *found* her!'

Vidar Waagenes sighed. 'Yes, that's been your story all along, Helge. But if it's true that you're so closely connected with them … then Veum's right. The only thing that can help you is to tell the truth. If you're lying, you're simply in danger of being sentenced for something you didn't do. Don't you see that? The police have very strong clues, there's no denying it.'

'You're my defence lawyer, aren't you?'

'Yes I am, but we're not in court now, Helge. Any defence lawyer would say to his client that, when we're talking between ourselves, you have to put all your cards on the table. Understand? That's the only way we can help you.'

'If what you say is true, it doesn't make any odds whether I say anything or not. I've had it, in any case.'

'But you admit you chauffeured for them,' I said quickly. 'So why can't you admit that you did so on that occasion too? I mean, that you drove Torild's body up there, alone or with somebody else, and dumped her, and that later your conscience started to bother you ... You'd been going out with her, so she must have meant *something* to you! ... And that's why you pretended to have found her. But you weren't the one who *killed* her, were you?'

I'd seen people crack before. It follows a fairly regular pattern. After they've stuck to the same lie for days, weeks even, someone suddenly finds a fissure in the dike and hammers in a wedge then the whole house of cards collapses, and they make a clean breast of it, often in a surge of almost heart-rending relief.

Helge Hagavik's macho mask crumbled like clay. He wept like a child, Vidar Waagenes having to put his arms round him and do what he could to comfort him. In other circumstances it would have seemed comical: dapper little Vidar Waagenes with his dark boyish hair, arms round the big blonde child weeping away what was left of his solarium tan onto his lawyer's breast.

Meanwhile, I sat motionless on my chair with the same bitter taste in my mouth as always on such occasions. Did triumph always taste so bitter because you knew how many people's fates you had trampled on to achieve it?

When he eventually looked up at me again, he was red-eyed, his cheeks bloated with weeping. He looked like a six-year-old who'd been given a rocket for being naughty at school.

'So tell me,' I said. 'What happened to her?'

'She ... I stayed behind at Jimmy's after she ... I sat in the room at the back with Kenneth drinking coffee and watching TV. They've got Eurosport. – There was a phone call. Something had happened – so could we come and clear up?'

'Who was it who rang, did you say?'

'Dunno.'

'And what happened then?'

'We went up, and there she lay.'

'Torild?'

He nodded.

'And was she dead?'

'Yes! She was dead. No doubt about that.'

'It must have been a terrible shock for you.'

He shrugged. 'Well, yes … '

'But – so was there nobody else in the room?'

'No, just her. She was lying on the bed, naked, and we – we saw straight away, her eyes, wide open … '

'Did the two of you find out what had happened?'

'No. Some of the clients could be a bit rough, you see? Kenneth said it was definitely somebody who'd completely lost it.'

'And … but who let you in?'

'To the hotel? Kenneth had a master key.'

'Kenneth? So which hotel was this?'

'The Pastel, of course! What did you think?'

'And which day?'

'Thursday! Well, that was when it happened.'

'Not Friday, then?'

'Friday? It was *Thursday*! Believe me, I *know*!'

'OK. So how did the two of you carry out your assignment?'

His mouth started to tremble again. 'Kenneth had one of those plastic bin liners. We got her into it, carried her down to the car, put her on the back seat and drove off. We talked a fair bit about what we were going to do with her, whether we should dump her in the sea or … But then we decided to take her up there, to Fanafjell, and it was Kenneth's idea that we should c-carve a

Satanist emblem onto her skin, to put people off the scent. She was dead anyway, so it didn't make any odds to her!'

'So that's what you did?' I said, surprised at how calm my own voice sounded.

He nodded.

'And then?'

'Well, afterwards … I drove Kenneth into town, before I drove back … Oh yes, I made a detour via Ulven and Lysekloster that time … '

'Worried she might suddenly be at the roadside thumbing a lift, were you?'

Vidar Waagenes gave me a long-suffering look. 'Helge … ' He opened his briefcase and took out a brown envelope. Then he unfolded a form, cleared his throat discreetly and glanced round a trifle pompously before continuing. 'I've received a copy of the final report from the Institute of Forensic Medicine regarding the cause of death and including the results of various other tests.'

He paused. Helge Hagavik sat there, looking at him in silence. He glanced from one of us to the other before continuing: 'From this it emerges that Torild Skagestøl died from suffocation, probably from somebody pressing a pillow or similar object against her face. The Satanist emblem was definitely carved onto the body when she was already dead, et cetera, et cetera. We don't need to go into every detail. But there's one thing you need to be aware of, Helge, according to what you've told us both today and before.'

He paused for effect before fixing his eyes on his client, saying: 'According to this report here, Torild Skagestøl was HIV-positive.'

Raw fear spread across his face. 'HIV? But, but she was on the safe list!'

'Exactly,' I said. 'The safe list … '

Forty-five

'LET *ME* TELL MUUS,' said Vidar Waagenes, as we made our way back upstairs. 'I mean, that my client's willing to make a full confession of complicity after the victim was killed, but that he insists he had nothing whatever to do with the killing.'

'I think he's going to be over the moon – Muus, I mean.'

'But tell me, Veum, what was that about – Friday?'

'Friday was the day Judge Brandt died, at a hotel in the centre of town, after being with a young woman. It was a false trail.'

He paused on the stairs. 'Maybe not.'

'No? Why not?'

He tapped me on the chest with the brown envelope from the Institute of Forensic Medicine. 'If Judge Brandt was in the habit of going with prostitutes ... If I'm not much mistaken, he was part of an exchange trip to Central Africa last year. An initiative aimed at trying to promote our Western legal systems down there.'

'You mean, that he ... That we're talking about a source of infection?'

'If I'm not much mistaken, Scandinavian statistics show that there's a remarkably high incidence of HIV-positives among heterosexual men who've had sex with prostitutes during trips to Africa, not least in the central regions.'

'So he brought something back home with him, then?'

'But whether this has anything to do with *this* case, I've really no idea.'

'Everything or nothing, probably.'

In the Personal and Violent Crime Department Dankert Muus was waiting for us with a face like thunder. 'So what in hell's name have you two managed to dig up? Been keeping bad company, Waagenes? I mean, even *worse* company?'

'Veum's helped me get my client to talk. He's ready to confess, Muus.'

A look of reluctant acknowledgement spread over the chief inspector's normally grim face. 'Well, I'll be!'

'But not to the actual murder,' Vidar Waagenes quickly added. 'Just complicity afterwards.'

His enthusiasm collapsed like a burst balloon. Muus eyed the lawyer with suspicion.

'Does this mean that he knows who did the murder, then?'

'A client,' he claims.

'Oh? But in that case, is there anyone who knows who the client was?'

'There may well be,' I interrupted. 'As you know, I've already made a number of inquiries around Birger Bjelland & Co.'

'Oh? And?'

'If we get Helge Hagavik to repeat what he's just told us, then all we need do is call in Birger Bjelland for a – what shall we say? – chat? And I may also be able to add something further.'

'Such as?'

I recapped most of what I'd found out. About the Persen brothers and Jimmy's as the intermediary. About the guy called Robert in the bar at the Pastel Hotel and what went on in the rooms there. About Astrid Nikolaisen and the safe list. And lastly, about Dr Evensen, whom I advised them to contact as soon as possible, with or without a lawyer present. The only thing I didn't mention was what I'd found out about Birger Bjelland's background in Stavanger. Those cases were long past their sell-by date, and anyway, it was not certain they could be investigated at all now and were perhaps better kept up my sleeve as evidence in a formal prosecution.

'You've certainly not been dragging your feet, Veum, I must say. What about … I heard you'd had an accident?' He nodded at my face. 'D'you think it's connected with all this?'

'Only indirectly, if at all. I told you about it last time I was here. And I showed you the letter I received. Now I've seen all I need to in the person of Ole Hopsland, The Knife's son. I can't prove that The Knife was at the wheel, of course, but his fingerprints are the first thing you people should look for. If you find them, I'll be happy to give you the threatening letter, with the envelope and the whole shooting match, and press charges right away.'

'The truck was stolen anyway. We've established that much.'

'When was that?'

'Sometime after five o'clock yesterday, from a depot in Åsane.'

'Any witnesses who saw it in Fløenbakken?'

'No, not yet. Not that that necessarily means anything. At that time of day you could park in Fløenbakken without anybody noticing.'

'Well … I've said my piece. I'm making a few discreet inquiries myself in connection with the case. To return to Birger Bjelland, something else cropped up as a result of the report from the Institute of Forensic Medicine.'

His eyes narrowed, and he looked at Vidar Waagenes. 'Isn't that confidential?'

'I've, er, engaged Veum to investigate a few things for me. In my view, that makes him entitled to examine all the documents in the case.'

'We might not have shared that view here.'

'Can't we forget that, Muus? I *have* seen it. Listen. Let's say that Dr Evensen reported Torild Skagestøl's positive HIV test to his bosses, and let's say between ourselves that they're Birger Bjelland & Co. The consequence is that they have to get rid of her, which they do.'

'But – not by pretending it was a client who did it, surely? That would blow the whole set-up wide open?'

'It was Helge Hagavik who claimed it was a client who did it. Don't forget where he found her! On Fanafjell, with a Satanist emblem carved on her backside. They did their level best to distract attention from the game they were involved in. It was Helge Hagavik who cracked and who, in an almost touchingly naïve way, pretended to have "found" her while out jogging! They hadn't reckoned with that. A guilty conscience doesn't rate very highly with that lot.'

'So you maintain she was got rid of because she was HIV-positive?'

'I'm just saying it's a possibility. They couldn't let her carry on if she was a source of infection, given the risk of exposure. Remember, we're not talking about some half-baked street prostitution racket here, Muus. We're talking about a first-class service with judges and certainly many other prominent figures on the list of clients!'

He nodded: 'We'll have a word with that doctor. And if we feel we have enough good evidence, I think we'll invite Birger Bjelland to come in for a little chat too.' He rubbed his hands with glee. 'I can't say I'm not looking forward to it. That would be some way to bow out, getting that fish put away!'

'Bow out?' asked Vidar Waagenes.

I pointed at the red circle on the wall calendar. 'Inspector Muus is retiring soon. Next time we call in he might give us a piece of his retirement cake.'

Forty-six

BACK AT THE OFFICE I called Laila Mongstad to tell her what I'd found out about Birger Bjelland. But she was busy with another case and hadn't time to talk to me. 'I'll ring you tonight, Varg,' she said quickly before hanging up.

Then I drove up Nordre Skogveien to the address Harry Hopsland had given in the population register. The block he lived in was a beige low-rise building with brown-painted doors, and I found his name on one of the letter boxes.

That was the closest I got.

A middle-aged female neighbour with large bags under her eyes and a nervous cigarette at the corner of her mouth confirmed that it was a Hopsland who'd moved in quite recently. 'But usually we don't hear a peep out of him. He's as quiet as a mouse, except when he's revving up his motorbike.'

'Where does he keep it?'

'At the back.'

'There was no motorbike there just now.'

'Wasn't there? In *that* case, he's out.'

My headache had come back with a vengeance. I drove home, took a further dose of painkillers, called Karin and told her I was going to lie down, that she had no need to worry and that I intended to take it easy.

It was dark when she rang, waking me.

When she heard my gravelly voice, she said: 'Oh, were you still asleep?'

'Yes, I must have been. What's the time?'

'Ten p.m.'

I moved my neck slowly to make sure it had not seized up completely. 'I must have slept like a log.'

'Well, I'm sure it'll have done you good.'

Having made certain I was planning to sleep on, she wished me good night and hung up. Gradually I drifted back to sleep, but shallower now, as though I no longer really needed it.

Laila Mongstad rang at eleven. Her voice sounded tense. 'Varg? Can you come down? There's something I have to show you.'

'Down – to the office?'

'Yes. It wasn't Halstein Grindheim, after all.'

I still felt rather groggy, and my arm had begun to ache. 'Wasn't it? So who was it then?'

'Are you coming?'

'Yes, sure. But you'll have to give me half an hour.'

'I'll wait. Meanwhile, I can … See you then.'

'Bye.'

I took a quick shower, put on a clean shirt, walked up to Blekeveien and got into my car. I parked on the hill beside the newspaper offices and walked round the corner to the main entrance. At the door I ran into Sidsel Skagestøl on her way out.

I stood aside, and she looked up. 'Oh!' she said with a start. 'It's you.' She remained standing in the middle of the doorway.

'How are things?'

She looked away. 'Well … Holger isn't in, if that's who you're going – '

'No, it wasn't actually. And you?'

It seemed as though she felt the need to explain why she was there. 'There are so many things to see to, and I reckoned … It was something I thought of, but he'd already left. And I'm not going to where he's living.'

'Why not?'

'What if he had someone there?'

'A woman?'

'Yes.' She looked out at the street. 'Well, I ... ' She nodded towards the Grieg Concert Hall. 'My car's over there. Good night.'

'Good night.'

I stood there, watching her walk away for a moment. Then I went into reception.

The receptionist looked at me suspiciously. 'Do you have an appointment?'

'Yes. With Laila Mongstad.'

'OK. I can ring her and – '

'She's expecting me.'

'Yes, but all the same. Here.' He handed me a guest badge, and I fastened it dutifully to my coat lapel.

He was still holding the telephone. 'She's not answering.'

'She hasn't left, has she?'

'Oh no. Just a moment, I'll ask in the editorial office.' He rang another number while keeping a careful eye on me. 'Yes, hello, it's reception. Is Laila there? – No? There's someone down here who says he has an appointment with her.' He turned towards me. 'What's your name?' he asked.

'Veum.'

'Veum. OK. Fine.' He replaced the receiver and nodded to me. 'Furebø's coming down to fetch you.'

'Furebø?'

'He said he knew you. In the evening we don't let people go up to the offices unaccompanied. We've had our fingers burned over that before.'

The lift opened, and Trond Furebø emerged. 'Veum ... I'll escort you up.'

We both entered the lift, and he pressed the button for the fourth floor. 'Sorry about the formalities, we've no option but to follow the rules laid down for us.' He glanced at the door. 'I assume it's not about Torild?'

'No, no,' I said gently. 'It's about something completely different.'

The door opened, and we walked out of the lift.

'I can find my own way now.'

'Actually, I really wanted to talk to her about a case she was working on earlier today.'

He walked along with me down the empty corridor.

An office door opened, and a man came out with a computer printout in his hand.

Trond Furebø slowed down. 'Holger! What the hell? Were you in the office? Sidsel's just been here, asking for you, but we – couldn't find you … '

Holger Skagestøl looked away, embarrassed. 'I wasn't up to … So I … ' He nodded towards the empty office he'd just come out of. He looked at me. 'What are you doing here?'

'I've got an appointment with Laila Mongstad.'

'Oh? In connection with … '

'Er … ' I said, repeating the not entirely accurate assertion that it was about another case.

'Well, I'd – better be getting back to work.' He walked past us heading for the stairs down to the main editorial office. 'Are you coming, Trond?'

'Yes, I'm just escorting Veum … '

We walked on.

The swing door closed behind us. In the large open-plan office most of the desk lamps were switched off. Only a couple of computer screens were still on.

Over at Laila Mongstad's desk, both lamp and screen were on.

'Laila?' called Trond Furebø. 'Are you there?'

There was no reply.

I walked faster. 'Laila?'

He saw her first – and stopped dead in his tracks. 'Laila?' he said for the third time, like a kind of exorcism.

I carried on into the room, unable to stop until I had placed my fingers on the side of her neck to feel for her pulse.

My heart was pounding in my chest, and my fingers were as cold as ice against her skin.

Laila Mongstad lay slumped over the desk in an awkward twisted position, as if trying to avoid touching the keyboard.

I looked at her screen. One of her hands still lay on the keyboard, pressing down one of the keys, where she had written a last message to the world: kkkkkkkkkkkkkkkkkkkkkkkkkkkkkkkkkkk kkkkkkkkkkkkkkkkkkkkkkkkkkkkkkkkkkkkkkkkkkkkkkkkkkkkkkk

I turned and looked at Trond Furebø.

He stood there, staring, hands at his sides, with an expression of utter horror on his face: 'Is, is she – ?'

'Yes. I think you'd better go and call the police.'

Forty-seven

ONLY WHEN I was alone with her did it seem to dawn on me what had happened.

I stood there with a feeling of paralysis, impotence and rage, as if slowly filling up with filthy brackish water, a dark and disgusting liquid I would never manage to wash myself clean of.

She lay head on one side, her reading glasses on the desk, staring glassy-eyed, still wearing a look of disbelief. From this angle you could see a lightly camouflaged crown on the back of her head from which her hair grew in a kind of whorl, and the hint of silvery grey at the roots showed she would probably have been going to the hairdresser's again soon.

It was impossible to say whether she had been jumped from behind while working or had been murdered as a result of an argument. But it was not very likely in those empty offices that someone had crept up on her without her hearing something and turning round to see who it was. That is, unless she had been so engrossed in what she was doing that …

I leaned forward and read the file name on the screen: BJEL-LAND.DOC

'Oh Jesus wept,' I said to myself.

Trond Furebø came back. 'They're on their way,' he said grimly. 'I've informed the editor too.'

'So long as you haven't tipped off the other papers … '

He looked at me in disgust.

'I'm sorry, I didn't mean it – like that.'

'Did you know her, Veum?'

'Yes, we were – old friends.'

The door leading into the editorial offices flew open, and Holger

Skagestøl came in. 'I can't believe what I've just heard! It can't be true!'

We didn't reply, but watched him as he saw the evidence with his own eyes. He stood there in front of Laila Mongstad with an expression that mirrored some of my own emotions: fury, impotence and dull shock. 'It can't be true!' He looked round helplessly. 'In here? Here in these offices?' He turned towards me. 'What's it all about, Veum? Did it have something to do with – Torild?'

'I don't know. I looked at Trond Furebø. 'What case was she working on? I mean, earlier today.'

'A child welfare case. It was her pet subject. If she ever got wind of a child in distress, she went to work like one possessed and wouldn't rest till she'd got at the truth.' He looked down at her, shame-faced, as though feeling he had said something wrong. 'What … what d'you think can have happened?'

'Somebody's been a bit too rough on her,' I said grimly. 'Maybe she didn't see eye-to-eye with the desk about splashing it all over the front page?'

'Veum!' exclaimed Holger Skagestøl, and Trond Furebø followed him with: 'I don't think I like your tone of voice.'

'No, there's something about sudden death that makes me put my foot in it and say silly things. Just can't help it.'

Skagestøl looked down at Laila Mongstad's short neck. 'She was a first-class reporter. Never let go until she'd got to the bottom of a case, and the copy she handed in was unbelievably well researched.'

Hearing loud voices out in the corridor, we all looked up at the door to see Atle Helleve, Peder Isachsen and a uniformed officer coming in.

Helleve said a curt hello to me. 'I've let Muus know. He's on his bike.'

'That must be a sight for sore eyes.' Oops, I'd done it again.

Isachsen looked at me angrily. 'To what do we owe the pleasure this time?'

I ignored him and turned to Helleve. 'Laila Mongstad. A

reporter. I talked to her on the phone only a short time ago. When I got here, there was no reply when the man on reception paged her. Furebø accompanied me up here, and we – found her like this.'

Trond Furebø nodded in confirmation.

'And what did you talk to her about, Veum?'

I pointed to the computer screen. 'About that man there.'

He scratched his beard and leaned forward. Then nodded grimly.

Isachsen was reading over his shoulder. 'Who? Birger Bjelland?'

'Think there could be any connection?' asked Helleve.

'I wouldn't rule it out.'

Helleve glanced at Furebø. 'Any chance of a printout of the file?'

'Yes, sure. I can – '

'But preferably from one of the other computers,' said Helleve, interrupting him. 'We need to have this one examined for prints first.'

'That should be OK,' said Furebø, glancing at Skagestøl.

'But officially we ought to wait till the editor gets here – and let him make the decision.'

Helleve nodded.

'Check the Delete key first,' I said.

'You mean whoever did it may have tried to wipe something?'

'Yes.'

'Helleve!' came a sudden shout from the door. It was another uniformed officer who had appeared. 'One of the windows leading to the courtyard at the back is wide open, and there are footprints in the snow!'

Helleve walked over to the nearest window. 'How would you get out of there?'

Furebø looked at him thoughtfully. 'Through our own back gate, but it's very secure and protected against people climbing over it, as well. Then there's the University's Social Science building and St Paul's School.'

'The footprints lead that way,' said the officer, pointing north.

'Then it looks like St Paul's,' said Skagestøl. 'If you're agile, it's possible to get up to the yard from there.'

'Up to?' I asked.

'Yes. I mean, it's harder to get into this place in the evening than it is to get *out* of it!'

Helleve butted in again. 'So you think whoever did it may have got in that way too?'

Skagestøl looked at him, puzzled. 'Oh? Look, I've no idea!'

The inspector turned back to the constable. 'Did you have a close look at the footprints?'

'It looked as though there was only one person. One set leading in, and one back out.'

Helleve looked at Skagestøl, who muttered: 'Yes, that's more or less what I meant.'

The detective beckoned to the other officer to come over. 'Can you tell the patrol cars to keep a lookout for anything that moves in this neighbourhood? Mainly up towards Nygårdshøyden, I think. It's easier to give people the slip there,' he added, as if one of us had asked him to justify himself.

Then he turned back to the first officer. 'Go down and secure the window and the area around it until we've carried out the necessary technical investigations.'

The officer nodded, turned and set off towards the door, where Isachsen had his work cut out trying to keep the editorial staff on shift at a suitable distance. 'We must thoroughly investigate the scene of the crime before we let unauthorised persons anywhere near.'

'Unauthorised!' boomed Bjørn Brevik's voice. 'This is a news case, and it happened within this paper's very walls. Here *we* say what goes!'

'Over my dead body,' snapped Isachsen.

'Just wait till Muus gets here,' muttered Helleve. 'He'll eat him alive.'

Trond Furebø cleared his throat. 'I'll have a word with him.'

'Do you need me any more?' asked Holger Skagestøl.

'No,' said Helleve curtly. 'But don't leave the premises until we've registered who was here when it happened.'

'But is there really any need … ?' Skagestøl glanced at the window and the back courtyard.

'Yes,' said Helleve even more curtly.

Holger Skagestøl glowered in my direction before he went, as if to suggest that everything was surely my fault.

'Well, he certainly didn't do it personally,' I said.

Helleve looked at mc. 'Who?'

'Bjelland! He always gets somebody to do his dirty work. But if you lot find out who did it, you can nail him good and proper this time.'

He stood there, notebook in hand. 'Want to wait till Muus gets here, or have you said all you have to say for now, Veum?'

'Have you got it all down?'

'Yep.'

I glanced at the window. I could hear the distant beat of war drums. Mother headache was coming on. 'In that case, I think I'll go home. You know where to find me if anything crops up.'

'OK. Dismissed,' said Helleve and turned back to Laila Mongstad.

I took a last long look at her. But that wasn't how I wanted to remember her. I wanted to remember her as the promise I'd once held in my arms, the warm eyes, the big smile, the soft lips. I wanted to remember her as she was when alive, not as an empty shell. I wanted to remember her.

◆

But I didn't get off scot-free, after all.

I met Muus in the corridor with the police doctor at his heels.

'Veum,' he growled from a few yards away.

'Why don't you slow down a bit? Wait till I've retired, for God's sake! Don't find us any more of them! How many times do I have to ask you?'

'This is something I'd rather not have found, Muus.'

'Give this man a shot of embalming fluid,' he said to the doctor as they passed.

'Is it any good for headaches?' I asked, but neither of them bothered to answer.

I took the lift down, handed in my visitor's badge at reception and was duly checked out under the beady eye of a zealous officer.

Once outside I stood and filled my lungs with one deep breath after another.

It had stopped snowing. On the other side of the road, the Grieg Concert Hall looked more than ever like a ship that had run aground. Behind the Concert Hall, Fløifjellet, Vidden and Ulriken rose up like peaks of meringue dusted with icing sugar. The television mast up on Ulriken belonged to the same family as the Concert Hall: a rocket that had never been launched, a monument to a space programme no one could afford to carry through.

New snow with fresh tracks.

I wondered ...

But not long enough to stop me walking up the hill, getting into the car, swallowing two headache tablets and driving home.

I parked on the steepest part of Blekeveien, lucky to have found a space between two other vehicles.

Outside the main entrance I stood fumbling a bit with the keys. Perhaps that was why I didn't notice them until they were right behind me. Kenneth Persen grabbed my arm and twisted it behind my back in a police grip. Fred held something sharp and cold against my neck, growling: 'Bit bloody late aren't you, Veum? We were starting to think you wouldn't turn up.'

'What do you want?'

'To invite you for a drive,' said Fred.

'Your last trip,' Kenneth Persen added, giving my arm an extra twist for luck and making me wince with pain.

Forty-eight

'WELCOME TO The Short Stay Hotel, Veum,' I heard Birger Bjelland's voice say, as his two henchmen released their grip on me and sent me flying headlong onto the dusty concrete floor. The bright torch he had pointed straight in my face had blinded me so it was impossible to see anything more than his silhouette.

I turned partway round.

Fred and Kenneth Persen shone their own torches into my eyes. One was standing on either side behind me, so that I found myself in the middle of something like an equilateral triangle. There was no doubt about who was in control of the situation.

They had put me on the floor in the back of the car, but we hadn't driven far, and when they led me from the car over to the derelict factory building, I'd seen where we were. We were on an industrial site in Sandviken, right on the edge of the sea, behind a tall wire fence and on something that looked like a building site, apart from the rusty remains of pulleys, cranes and signal towers. The ground-floor windows of the large, greyish-white building were securely boarded up. Higher up, dark holes gaped where the windows had been smashed.

'Have you checked whether he's wired?' asked Birger Bjelland. 'No bugs anywhere?'

'No,' Fred muttered behind me.

'Get to it, then!'

Kenneth Persen kept his distance, while Fred searched me with a zeal that suggested it turned him on.

'Pack it in,' I mumbled 'You've no chance with me, you know.'

'Shut it or I'll pull it right off!' he hissed back. Aloud, he said: 'He's clean, Birger!' Then he moved away.

The adrenaline pumping through my veins was like a tidal flow inside, a kind of dizziness, exhilaration almost. I felt the slight aftertaste of the headache tablets mingle with something new and sour, straight from the stomach.

I turned my face slowly in the direction of Birger Bjelland. 'What is it you want?'

'I thought you were interested in hearing about my plans, Veum.' Although still sounding as sanctimonious as ever, this was nevertheless the voice of someone about to either excommunicate me or banish me straight to hell.

'Which plans?'

He swung the torch around. The beam swept over the walls, the concrete staircase leading up the building and the marks left on the floor by dismantled machinery, before ending up on my face again.

'My hotel plans. I thought you'd heard about them. "Hotel Seaside" I thought we might call it, and it's going to be quite some hotel, I promise you. A view over Byfjorden, an indoor swimming pool on the top floor with sliding glass doors that can open out to form a classy sun terrace when the weather's right … '

'Just for a day?'

'Deluxe suites and ordinary tourist rooms, a restaurant with a dance floor and gourmet corner, a gambling area in the basement, all within the law of course … '

'Of course.'

'But we're not going to start work until we've got the finance sorted out, an alcohol licence and full backing from all the local bodies.'

'No problem for you when you can pay *under the counter*.'

'It's getting harder and harder with your sort going round town every blessed day, spreading shit about me!'

'Oh, so that's what you wanted to talk about.'

The cone of light bobbed about again. 'Every single day this godforsaken dump stands empty I lose money on it!'

'Most people make duff investments now and again. Some more than others, of course.'

He moved closer, and the light became harsher. 'Each time you badmouth me to the law, it makes it that bit harder for them to recommend issuing an alcohol licence; and I do get to know when you've been down there, Veum, don't worry!'

'Isn't Isachscn one of your poker gang?'

'Each time there's some shit about me in the papers, it becomes harder to get credit from government loan bodies.'

'But you *can* get rid of reporters, can't you?' When there was no reaction from him, I added: 'Anyway, I thought you were into loans yourself, with an interest rate well above the knees you've capped when the loans aren't paid back.'

'Go on, talk away, Veum, nobody's going to hear any more from you, anyway.'

'Oh no? Don't be too sure about that! You've heard of letters, haven't you?'

After a little pause, he said: 'And who've you written to? His Majesty?'

'One thing you can count on is that it'll go to the right places, if anything happens to me.'

'If anything happens to you? *I* can't accept responsibility for what might happen when you're out for a stroll some dark winter's evening.'

'To put it another way, Bjelland, you *do* have responsibility now. Because whatever the hell happens, and whoever the hell actually does it, they'll lay the blame at *your* door. So you ought actually to look after me from now on.'

There was a clear hint of uncertainty in his voice now. 'So what's supposed to be in this letter, Veum?'

'A detailed report, from A to Z. Want to hear the short version?'

No reply. I took it as a 'yes'.

'For example, it deals with the operation you've built up round

Jimmy's and the Pastel Hotel. How you recruit the girls, how they operate, who the clients are … '

'You know damn all about it, Veum!'

'Sure about that, are you? I know quite a lot. I know all about the safe list. You were on the phone yourself when I was talking to Dr Evensen, I've talked to Robert at the Pastel Hotel, Kalle Persen at Jimmy's – but more important than all that, there are girls who are willing to talk. Girls who've had enough. Not least because of what you did to Torild Skagestøl. You put the fear of God into them.'

'I … we didn't do a damn thing to Torild Skagestøl.'

'Oh no? Sure about that?'

He spontaneously lowered his voice. 'Why the hell do you think we went to such lengths to camouflage the death?'

'Yes, and as chauffeur you chose a beginner who cracked long before anybody had even *thought* of checking up on him!'

'That bloody dope won't get much older.'

'Oh no? You'll take care of it, will you?'

Again he chose to remain silent.

'So who did it? A client? You must all know who she was with that day?'

Still no answer.

'Or was it that one of your trusties, such as one of the two super-men behind me, was the client, killed the girl – and left others to clear up the mess? Who do you trust most? Fred with no surname? Or others? A hired gunman from Oslo perhaps? A normal favour between colleagues?'

'Why on earth would I want her dead? If what you say is true, she was a source of income for me!'

'Because she was HIV-positive, yet still on the safe list, a potential source of infection and a cursed nuisance to the whole organisation.'

'That's just bollocks, Veum. If this is all the ammo you've got in this so-called letter of yours, then … '

'Oh no, there's a lot more than this, Bjelland. Want to hear?'

No reply.

'The problem with you, as regards the police and the press too in a way, is that they've never found anything they can put their fingers on. You buy and sell, go bust and start up again, hotels and bars, amusement arcades and so on. Everybody knows that you're right at the top of the dirty money market in this city, with interest rates you *could* write to His Majesty about; but nobody's so far managed to dig up any real dirt on you. Till now.'

The silence was more ominous now. You could hear his soles shuffling about, the crunching gravel under them sounding like teeth shattered against a midnight pavement during an evening on the town.

'Regards from your mother, Bjelland, by the way. And from your sister. And maybe from a few other people I talked to down there.'

'Have you been in – Stavanger?' he said as though it was like climbing Mount Everest.

'It doesn't take very long,' I said. 'Half an hour in the air, and you're there.'

'So what the hell did you get out of mother?'

'Obviously you knew she was an eyewitness.'

'Eyewitness? What to?' In his confusion he reverted to a Stavanger lilt.

'Or didn't she ever tell you that?'

He pulled himself together, and the Stavanger lilt disappeared. 'To what, I said?!'

'To what you did to Roger Hansen, that time at Mosvatnet Lake, or have you forgotten about that?'

The silence lay between us like a fuse. All it needed was a spark to ignite it.

When he spoke next his voice was so low that it was barely audible. 'It was a mishap – an accident – and even if it wasn't, that case is so old it's got hairs on it … '

'Maybe so. But it's still an aggravating factor. And what about

Ragnar Hillevåg and the stray bullet at Evjemoen Military Camp? That case has got hairs on it too, I suppose?'

He continued to speak in the same low voice with a growling undertone. 'You've been very thorough, I see.'

'I could have written a whole book about you, Bjelland. But I left it at a four or five-page report. On top of those other things ... '

'What other things? I had nothing to do with Torild Skagestøl, I said!'

'And what about Brandt?'

'The judge? Oh, him ... '

'Yes? He died while he was with one of your girls, didn't he? Or did your lot give *him* the push as well, because he was the source of the HIV infection?'

'Brandt? Don't make me laugh!'

'And last of all, there's Lalla Mongstad, who was maybe on the edge of a breakthrough in the investigation she and her paper had been carrying out into your activities for months ... '

'That reporter slag? What about her?'

'As you say, what about her, Bjelland? Was *that* really necessary?'

'I haven't come here to solve riddles, Veum!'

'No, so you said. But now I've seen it, this hotel of yours. You've told me about your plans, and I've told you a few things too.' A cold gust of wind funnelled down my neck. 'So – what now?'

He shifted his weight, but the beam from the powerful flashlight remained full on my face. His voice was grating. 'Like I said, Veum, I can't take responsibility for what happens when you're out for an evening stroll.'

'But the letter, Bjelland, you're forgetting the *letter*!'

'I've ridden out so many storms. My lawyer'll sort this one out as well.'

The beam now came from beside me. I stood pinned in the middle of the floor by the light.

I could try jumping to one side, of course. But I was blinded. It would be a piece of cake for them to catch me again.

They were moving towards the door now. I turned slowly round following the light.

I felt unsure of myself. What were they planning to do?

The door opened, and a gust of fresh air blew in. Despite the fact that the sharp beams of light were still being shone in my face, I saw them now: three silhouettes in the doorway.

'Feeling lonely, Veum?' Birger Bjelland shouted.

Now it was my turn not to answer.

'Don't worry. One of us is staying behind. Somebody who's dying to meet you again. So much so that he's actually announced it, he says!'

A cackle of raucous laughter followed them out. The door slammed shut, and I heard the heavy bolt being shot on the outside.

Suddenly the light was out of my eyes. Blinded, I took a few steps sideways. Somewhere near me I heard a sound.

Forty-nine

I BENT DOWN, kicked off my shoes and quickly made off in my stocking feet. Then I stopped and held my breath, meanwhile carefully massaging my eyes, trying to erase the image of two white discs from the retinas.

I stood and listened.

Where had the sound come from, and what had I actually heard?

Did he have a torch like the others, which he was about to switch on? Or was he counting on having the upper hand for long enough to carry out the sentence, so that it would be all over before I could see properly again?

Should I try and talk him out of it?

But wouldn't my voice betray where I was?

I tried to remember how the place looked from my glimpse of it in the light from Birger Bjelland's torch. Bjelland had been standing about there, and the stairs leading to the upper floors had been – ten to fifteen yards behind him.

But had there been a stair rail? Or was it just a large open staircase?

What was he planning to kill me with? A firearm? With the weapon from which he'd got his nickname? Or with his bare fists?

Again I heard a faint sound, a movement in the darkness.

Instinctively I moved away from the sound. I tried to steal away, but the faint crunch of the gravel on the concrete floor betrayed where I was.

I opened my eyes wide and breathed as calmly as I could. Just as I felt I was starting to make out some shapes around me, it became darker. I heard the sound of heavy steps suddenly very close. Automatically I bobbed down and threw myself to one side.

He swore to himself as he lurched past me. I scurried away on tiptoe towards where I thought the stairs were. One of my feet brushed against something hard and sharp – a nail? – pulling with it the object it was protruding from.

I quickly bent down, seized something that felt like a piece of plank and ran my fingers over lumps of dried cement until I came to the nail. I set off again.

'Veum!' he yelled behind me. 'You haven't a chance, Veum!' She'd been right. His accent was from somewhere just outside the city.

I didn't give him any extra chances either. I kept quiet.

I'd reached the stairs now, my toes touching the first step. I moved my left hand, feeling for the wall.

There ...

With the bottom of my arm against the wall, I followed the stair upwards to the first corner, then on towards the right until I came up against another wall, then right again.

Down below I heard heavy steps on the stairs. 'You're not going to get away, you bastard! I've got you now!'

I was on the first floor. From a window high up a faint glimmer of light fell into the great empty room. Just inside the doorway stood a large metal drum. I put my foot against it and pushed. With a colossal din it tipped over and rolled down into the room below.

Under cover of the racket I carried on up.

It had the desired effect. Confused, he stood in the doorway listening to the sound of the rolling drum.

'Veum! Come on out! I can see you!' he shouted.

But I didn't come out. Not for him. I was already on the second floor. And now I could see where I was.

Here were the large broken windows, gaping nakedly out at the night. The sea air buffeted me through the long corridor leading into small individual rooms in what had probably once been the administrative wing of the factory.

I walked down the corridor and stood looking round me.

He must have changed tactics. Now I could no longer hear him.

I walked to the end of the corridor, where an entire pane of frosted wire glass hid the view. *Surely there must be some back stairs somewhere?*

Suddenly, there he was at the top of the stairs, a huge shadow in the dimness. I glimpsed something in one of his hands. In the other, there hung …

He was breathing heavily

… a bicycle chain?

We stood there, staring at each other like two boxers each in our corner of a ring, kept apart by our mutual fear of one another.

I felt utterly vulnerable as I stood there in my stockinged feet and with nothing to defend myself with but the pathetic bit of wood with the sharp nail in it.

'It's the end of the road, Veum.'

'Literally. Can't we say it ended in a draw? Then we can part and still remain good friends.'

'When the fuck were we ever good friends?'

'Well, you may be –'

'All the years I was doing time, I looked forward to this moment, when you and me would meet again, in a dark room, with nothing else to do but settle old scores.'

'I've none unsettled – '

'But *I* have!' He came a few steps closer.

I clutched the plank tight. 'So you were part of this plot too, were you, Knife?'

'I haven't been in any fucking plot! I came back to Bergen to live. But before I can really feel at ease in the place there's something that has to be got rid of, a rat that has to be exterminated, and that is – ' He waved one hand at me so the bicycle chain rattled.

I lifted the plank. 'You shouldn't believe what the old folks say. This town is more than big enough for the two of us.'

'It's too late for me, Veum.'

'Yes, maybe it is. Pity your aim wasn't better yesterday evening.'

'Is it?'

'And the same goes for your son! He's going to be done for complicity!'

'Nobody's ever going to see the connection!'

'Oh no? Muus knows about the threatening letter! And what'll happen when they find your fingerprints in that truck you stole?'

'Bjelland promised he'd give me an alibi. He … '

' … is an expert in stuff like that from way back. Yeah, I know that, thanks.'

Suddenly, unexpectedly, he lunged forward. He swung the bicycle chain in the air in front of me while holding his knife well out to the side, in the death position, raising the point upwards.

I shielded myself with the plank. The bicycle chain got caught on it, and I gave a sharp tug to try and make him lose balance. With only partial success.

I moved forward to try and get round him. He snatched the bicycle chain back, and now *I* lost my balance. The knife flashed, I grabbed onto the nearest doorway, held on – and was hurled sideways into the room.

A cold blast of sea air hit me. With a shock I realised that the office had no end wall. I stopped and stood there swaying, overcome with sudden vertigo. Slowly I turned round.

He was standing in the doorway, baring his teeth in something almost like a smile. 'Now you're in the trap!'

I could see his face plainly now. He was wearing the same dark-blue knitted cap as the evening I'd recognised him in C Sundts Street. His features were just the same, as heavy as they had been in 1975, only tauter and more drawn, like a rubber mask discarded as a reject. His close-cropped hair looked completely white. His eyes had a feverish cast, as if he was on something, unless it was just a reflection of the mad existence he led.

The room was like a long narrow cell. One step at a time he came towards me, holding his arms out from his body: knife in one hand, chain in the other.

Now survival was all that counted.

I lashed out with my foot at his groin but missed, kicking the inside of his thigh instead. But it was enough to make him lose his balance, and he fell, first against the wall then towards me. In desperation, I swung the plank at the hand holding the bicycle chain.

The yell told me I'd struck home with the nail.

As he tumbled past me, he jerked his arm back so hard that the plank slipped from my grasp.

For a few absurd moments we stood there swaying, his face contorted with pain and the knife jerking about in his uninjured hand. In the other, he still had the bicycle chain. The plank with the nail lay on the floor between us. For a moment I wondered whether I might be able to reach it.

Then, almost in a reflex action, I took two quick steps forwards and gave him a sharp kick in the belly so that he fell backwards. Immediately I bitterly regretted it.

He threw up his arms for a second or two, clutching desperately around him. Then down he plunged backwards through the gap in the wall.

For the briefest of moments our eyes met, and I knew, without a shadow of a doubt, that that look would haunt me for the rest of my days.

'Ve – !' he managed to shout.

Bewildered, I stuck out my hand, but too late.

He was gone. His long-drawn-out scream was abruptly silenced.

For a long time I simply stood there. Then slowly I walked up to the gap in the wall, held on tight, stuck my head out and peered down.

He lay on his back on the quay in front of the factory, motionless.

The wheel had turned full circle. The death notice had been accurate. Only the name was wrong.

◆

I found my way back down to the bottom of the staircase, but it was some time before I came across my shoes. Afterwards, it took me barely ten minutes to get out through one of the broken windows on the first floor.

I walked round the building and onto the quay. Harry Hopsland lay there with the back of his skull smashed and a mixture of blood and brains like a clumsily drawn halo round his head. His eyes were glazed and unfocused as though he was in the dock listening to the first of a long list of charges being read out to him. I had no need to hurry to call an ambulance. He had reached his destination.

I wandered up as far as Helleveien before managing to flag down a taxi. The driver shot me a quick glance when I asked him to take me to the police station.

In the police station I met an inspector by the name of Paulsen whom I'd met in passing once before. He was clean-shaven, with mousy-coloured hair and was not completely lacking in common humanity.

When I told him about Harry Hopsland he immediately called for an ambulance and asked for a patrol car to be sent out. When I told him about Birger Bjelland it was the last straw. 'I'll have to ring Muus about this,' he said.

'Can I report back tomorrow, d'you think?'

He gave me a worried look. 'Need any help?'

'No, but a good night's sleep would be great.' I wrote down a phone number on a notepad. 'You'll be able to reach me at this number here.'

He nodded. 'OK. I'm sure it'll be fine. We know where to find you.'

'Oh? I wish I could say the same.'

Then I went off towards the phone number I'd given. I rang before letting myself in.

Fifty

'WE REALLY MUST STOP meeting like this,' she said the next morning, leaning over to my side of the bed and running her fingers gently over the scratches on my face.

I grimaced.

'I mean it!' she said. 'One of these days I'm going to be called in to scrape you up off the ground in little pieces.'

'So long as you don't lose any of them,' I said, trying it on.

'That's not funny!'

I ran the tip of my tongue over my dry lips. 'Shall we make some coffee?'

'But there's no point trying to talk any sense into you! You're just like – ' She stopped herself, but I knew what she'd almost blurted out: *just like Siren.*

'That – reporter who was murdered. You knew her very well, didn't you?'

'Not as well as this.'

'Do you, do they know – who did it?'

I looked aside. *Did we know, actually?*

'If it turns out to be my fault that she … it'd be two deaths in one day I'd be responsible for.' I looked up at her awkwardly. 'I think I feel the burden of them on my shoulders already.'

The light outside her windows was sharp and white. The temperature had suddenly risen ten degrees, yesterday evening's layer of snow had melted, through the open bedroom windows the twitter of birds could be heard from the trees in the old school garden, and there was an unmistakable feeling of spring in the air. February was on the way out. March was just round the corner, full of expectation like a young girl on the way to her first date.

Besides, it was Saturday; and we could linger as long as we liked over breakfast. We made bacon and eggs, sliced up some tomatoes and let them sizzle a little in the fat before putting them on our plates. We drank low-fat milk and coffee, ate slices of bread with honey and rosehip jelly, divided the Saturday paper in two and read it so slowly that it almost looked as though we were looking for something quite out of the ordinary; a code hidden in the text.

Laila Mongstad had made the front page again, but this time without her by-line. They hadn't even revealed her name. For the time being, the case was being linked to what they called a 'break-in at the newspaper's offices in the evening.' It was still too early to establish whether it had been pure chance that it was a 'journalist on the evening shift' who was the killer's victim, or whether the attack was aimed at that journalist personally.

All I found on the other case was a little one-column announcement that ran:

Man found dead in Sandviken

A man in his fifties was found dead late yesterday evening, the victim of an accident on an industrial site in Sandviken. The deceased was already known to the police. The duty police officer, Inspector Arvid Paulsen, would not comment on the death other than to say that the usual investigations would be carried out.

Karin pushed her part of the paper across the table to me saying: 'There's a death notice for that judge here.'

'Oh?'

I turned the paper and read:

My beloved husband, our dear father,
grandfather and brother

HERMANN CHRISTOFFER BRANDT

Suddenly departed this life today.
Bergen, 12 February.

Tora,
Elisabeth – Lars, Henning – Live,
Ole-Petter, Terje, Anne,
Elisabeth, Gro Therese,
Hugo Andreas.

No flowers. Private Funeral

'Tora,' I said almost to myself, 'T for Tora.'

She looked at me over the top of her coffee mug. 'What are you talking about?'

'Oh, just thinking aloud.'

After breakfast I took a long warm shower while Karin was out buying more papers. In the Oslo tabloids the killing of Laila Mongstad was given full coverage, and she was named too. They had also dug up a ten-year-old photo of her from a Press Association directory. One paper carried a full interview with 'a colleague on the evening shift', Bjørn Brevik, who said a possible connection between the murder and the fact that Laila Mongstad had been working very hard for several months on exposés of what he referred to as 'the Bergen underworld' couldn't be ruled out. The paper's editor would not comment on the death at all, other than to say that he 'found it shocking and highly regrettable'.

The death in Sandviken was not mentioned in any of the papers.

It was past one o'clock when there was a call from the police station. 'Veum? Muus here. We've arrested Birger Bjelland. Do you think you could come down and make a full statement?'

'Now? Right away?'

'Any reason to postpone it?'

I gave Karin an apologetic look, mumbling: 'No, I suppose not.'

Half an hour later I was down at the station, where Muus met me looking as though he'd been awarded the Royal Golden Order of Merit. In fact I couldn't ever recall seeing him in such good spirits. 'We've got him this time, Veum!'

'Let's hope so.'

I accompanied him up to his office, where Atle Helleve sat reading a paper while waiting.

'No Saturdays off for you either?' I joked.

With a sigh he folded the paper. 'Far from the madding crowd on a day like this? Not likely!'

'My goodness, a well-read policeman,' I added.

'We come in all shapes and sizes, you know.'

Muus looked slightly lost for a moment. 'Let's not waste any time. Sit yourself down, Veum, and let's go through all the details.'

And that's exactly what we did.

Again I went over everything I'd dug up about Birger Bjelland's operation, the safe list, Jimmy's and the Pastel Hotel, Dr Evensen and Bjelland's other henchmen.

This time I added what I'd unearthed in Stavanger, if only to colour in his background.

Helleve was doing the note-taking. He wasn't just well read but an ace on the keyboard too.

When I got to the events of the previous day they really started to prick up their ears. The battle with The Knife brought out a hint of the old Muus again. He leaned forward, bared his teeth and said: 'That sounds like what the legal people usually call "involuntary manslaughter", Veum … '

'It was *self-defence*, ' I said.

' … not least considering the history you two have – between you, I mean.'

'Well, if we're going to consider their whole life story,' Helleve started to say.

Muus cut him off. 'On the other hand … it would be one hell of a lot of paperwork.' He glanced at the magic red circle on the wall calendar.

I followed his eyes. Then I looked at the date on my digital watch: February 27th. 'Well, I'll be damned, Muus! Congratulations! Is this, can this really be, your *last* day?'

He looked at me equivocally. 'In principle, yes, Veum, but I'm afraid there's going to be a certain amount of paperwork to do next week, on overtime, so to speak. So, in other words, I think we can say thanks for seeing The Knife out, but … ' He leaned slightly to one side and fixed me with his eyes. '… if ever I hear you're mixed up in anything like this again, Veum, I'll come back out of retirement even if I'm already on the other side, right?'

I nodded, uncertain how grateful I should appear. 'But … What about the murder of Laila Mongstad? Have you found out anything there?'

'Nothing definite yet.'

'What about the cause of death?'

Muus let his eyes rest on me for a moment before deciding to reply. 'A heavy blow to the back of the head that must have knocked her out. After that she was just strangled.'

A shudder ran through me. *Struck on the head – and strangled … The neck I had …*

Muus went on: 'We're investigating Birger Bjelland's entourage for this too, of course, starting with the file that was in her computer. But for the time being we're keeping an open mind.'

'It was like Piccadilly Circus down there late on, according to the receptionist's register,' said Helleve.

'Yes, I met – one of them.'

'Who was it?'

'Sidsel Skagestøl.'

'That figures. She was there – but came away empty-handed. Furebø's wife and daughter called … '

'Did they? When?'

'Just before you arrived. They'd been at the cinema and called in to see whether he was ready to come home with them.'

Half lost in thought, I said: 'It was something she said when she phoned … '

'Who?'

'Laila Mongstad. *It wasn't Halstein Grindheim after all.*'

'Grindheim? The politician?' Muus cut in. 'So who was it?'

'That's just what she was going to tell me. That's why she asked me to come down.'

'So what the hell did she mean?'

'She was poking around in a case, and Grindheim … she'd identified Grindheim thanks to a photo of his car.'

Muus glanced at Helleve. 'Didn't we seize an envelope with photos in it down there?'

'Yes, I've got them under lock and key. I'll go and get them.'

While he was out, Muus look at me searchingly. 'Grindheim, Grindheim … Was this the same case, Veum?'

'Yes, but as she said, it wasn't him… '

'No, as she said … but she's dead, isn't she?'

'Tell me, Muus, do you think you've really time to retire?'

'Don't tempt me, Veum. Don't tempt me … '

Helleve came back with the pictures. I recognised them at once and quickly leafed through them till I found the right one.

I placed it on the table in front of them and pointed. 'The car registration number.'

'Could she have been mistaken, do you think?' asked Muus.

'If it was the number plate that identified Grindheim, then …
The number eight there, for example, is so unclear it *could* have
been a three,' said Helleve.

I looked at them. 'Can we give it a try? Check it against the
register of numbers?'

Belleve already had his hands on the keyboard and his eyes on
the screen. 'But there's only Bergen and the county of Hordaland
here. It was a Bergen number, though, wasn't it?'

I nodded.

He typed in a few codes before the number itself and sat waiting,
as the computer searched for the answer.

When it came up on the screen he sat there staring at it
speechless.

'Well?' said Muus impatiently, starting to get up out of his chair.
'Who was it?'

'Holger Skagestøl,' said Atle Relleve, turning wearily back to
face us with the look of someone who has seen it all.

Fifty-one

'WE'LL DEAL with this part of the case ourselves,' said Dankert Muus, looking at me sharply.

I nodded gently. 'You hardly need to tell me that.'

Muus glanced at Helleve. 'Do we know where he lives?'

Helleve searched through his papers. 'He's rented a basement flat from a colleague on the paper ... at Bones.'

'Then let's go and take a look, the sooner the better.'

'Do we know what we're going to say?'

'We'll think of something.'

I stood up. 'Have a nice day, Muus. For the rest of your life.'

'Without you, Veum,' he said with a blissful smile. 'Without you.'

◆

In the car on the way up to Årstadvollen I had so much on my mind that I felt completely at sea. *Holger Skagestøl, as a punter, in the same outfit as ... But how did that fit in, and what had it got to do with all the rest? Had he, through a misunderstanding, paid for the services of his own daughter? And in that case, had he... Wasn't it Birger Bjelland and his cronies, after all? Had Helge Hagavik been right: that it was a client?*

When I got to Fløenbakken I did not turn right but carried on heading south.

I passed the tower block at Mannsverk without pausing, and at the top of Birkelundsbakken turned right.

I looked at my watch. Quarter to four on a Saturday afternoon.

Was there anyone in the Furebø family sitting waiting for the football pool results, I wondered?

I parked the car behind the white Mercedes in the driveway.

It was Randi Furebø who came to the door, as immaculately turned out as usual. This time she was wearing a simple grey skirt with a waist-length black waistcoat.

She struggled to control the look on her face when she saw who was at the door.

'I'm sorry to disturb you,' I said, 'but I really must have a couple of words with Åsa again.'

'A couple of words?' she repeated sceptically.

And in a way she was right. I'd probably need more than a couple of words.

'Is she at home?'

She nodded and stepped passively aside. 'She's in her room.'

'Is it all right to speak to her there?'

'Yes, yes it is … '

From upstairs I heard the voice of Trond Furebø. 'Who is it, Randi?'

'It's … ' She had to raise her voice. 'Veum!'

Furebø was already on his way down the stairs. 'And what the hell does he want?'

'I need to have a couple of words with Åsa,' I said again.

He was wearing a kind of jogging suit of shiny, dark-blue material. The top hung open. Underneath, he was wearing a white T-shirt with the words 'Bergen Run' and the names of some major sponsors on it. 'Not unless we're present!' he said sharply.

I shot a sideways glance at his wife. 'If you think it's a good idea … '

'We want to know everything!' she said quickly, looking as though she was on the verge of tears. 'It's pointless to keep anything back now.'

Trond Furebø gave a toss of his head. 'We'll go upstairs. Can you fetch her, Randi?'

She nodded, and I followed Furebø up to the spacious sitting room. I was right. The TV was on, and Furebø had already set himself up in a comfortable chair, with the pools coupon, a bottle of beer and a bowl of potato crisps. Now he swung the chair partway round, turned down the volume and looked at me with an irritated expression. 'Is this really necessary, on a Saturday afternoon, Veum?'

I sighed. 'Not if I could help it.'

'Who the devil can help it, then? Our Father who art in Heaven?'

'That's two you've mentioned already.'

Åsa and her mother came down the stairs, Åsa looking like a sulky child, her mother en route to eternal martyrdom.

'Hello, Åsa,' I said in yet another attempt to keep the tone light. It wasn't easy.

She simply pulled a face but said nothing.

Randi Furebø glanced at her husband. 'Shall I put on some coffee?'

Furebø shook his head sternly. 'He can have a beer if he likes.'

'He's driving, so he'd prefer a Clausthaler,' I said.

Randi Furebø nodded and went out into the kitchen.

'Veum says he has a few questions to ask you, Åsa,' said Furebø.

She glanced in my direction but without actually looking me in the face. She was wearing light blue jeans and a white, full-length blouse. She looked as if she'd just washed her hair, as the ends were still wet. The only thing that jarred was the closed stony expression on her face.

'I'd like to talk a bit again about the day Torild disappeared – and the day after,' I began cautiously.

'The day after?'

'The Friday.'

She looked at her father. 'I was grounded from that Friday onwards.'

Randi Furebø returned from the kitchen with a glass and an open bottle of Clausthaler on a white tray. 'Well, not grounded,' she said. 'It was because we were anxious about you, Åsa!' She glanced at me while putting the tray down on the table beside me. 'We'd no idea what might have happened!'

'No … thank you,' I said, pouring myself a glass of alcohol-free beer. 'And from when were you grounded?'

'After I got home from town. There was no school that day.'

'It wasn't till the afternoon that we heard Torild hadn't come home,' her mother added.

Trond Furebø cleared his throat. 'Listen, Veum, what's the point of this, anyway?'

I kept my eyes fixed on Åsa. 'The day before, you and Torild were at Jimmy's when she received a phone call, weren't you?'

She twisted about on her chair.

'Weren't you?' I said again.

'Yes.'

'You knew where she was going, didn't you?'

'Didn't you, didn't you? How could I know?'

'You'd received phone calls like that yourself a few times, hadn't you?'

'Veum!' Now it was her mother's turn to react. 'What are you insinuating? This goes far beyond – '

'Just look at her! She's blushing with – ' I stopped myself just in time and turned to speak to Åsa in a much gentler tone. 'You could make money out of it, couldn't you? Far more than you could expect to get at home, however much you badgered them to raise your allowance.'

Furebø slammed down his glass. 'Are you trying to … ? How dare you come here and … '

'It was Torild and Astrid who … I just went with them,' said Åsa faintly. 'I'm not like that.'

'But they were?'

She nodded.

'They were on drugs, weren't they?'

'No. Just – tried them.'

'Tablets?'

'Helge had got hold of some stuff from England, some pills that were supposed to give, to make you, even when you … '

She looked shiftily back and forth from her mother to her father.

'Even when you … ' I repeated.

'Even when you did it on your own!' she burst out.

I glanced quickly at Furebø. 'Ecstasy.'

'What's that?' barked his wife crossly.

'Tablets that are supposed to increase libido, or so it's claimed. Especially popular at so-called House parties. There hasn't been much of it in Bergen yet, but in Oslo it's been around for a number of years now.' Bitterly I added, 'But it doesn't increase the sex drive, Åsa! It just does your head in, makes you a nervous wreck and so out of it that … Abroad there've been a number of murders under the influence of stuff like this. So it probably won't be long before we have the first one here. If we haven't already.'

'Maybe *this* was what that Satanist had taken?' said Randi Furebø weakly, as if to change the subject.

I looked at her askance with a crooked smile, so as not to give her too much hope.

'The day after, the Friday, you were at Jimmy's again. But then neither Astrid nor Torild was there. Was that why you said that you would do it?'

'I'm not like that! I couldn't know!'

'But they tempted you with the promise of good money, eh?'

She looked down then sideways, up at the ceiling, everywhere but at her parents.

'Don't tell me it was your first time!'

'No, course not! I'd done it before! But I wasn't like that! I didn't do it all the time! I tried to stay out of it!' At last she glanced at her parents: 'Do you understand?'

Randi Furebø just sat there, staring at her, as pale and lifeless as a wax doll. Trond Furebø was ashen-faced. His silver hair no longer became him. His boyishness had vanished. In the last five minutes he seemed to have aged ten years.

'Understand?' he murmured. 'How can you "understand" something like that? Your own daughter.'

'Åsa!' her mother whimpered as though she was in pain and the pain had been inflicted by her daughter.

'It was you who was with Judge Brandt when he died, wasn't it?'

She nodded. She was still struggling to hold on to her mask.

'They found a bottle of tablets in the bathroom. Did you take them – to make it easier to go through with it?'

The dam burst. And she broke down, weeping uncontrollably. Tears poured from her eyes and nostrils as she sobbed: 'He ... he was repulsive! The old pig! He was wearing – women's underwear – and he wanted, I had to take my clothes off and put on something he'd brought with him, in leather and jackboots and, and a sort of whip, and he made me, he crawled round on the floor, and I had to kick and whip him, and in the end he wanted, he lay on his back with his legs in the air like a little baby, and, there was an opening in – I was supposed to sit on top of him and pee on him!'

Her mother let out a loud gasp. Her father clamped his jaw shut so hard that it cracked.

'But I couldn't do it!'

'That's something at least!' exclaimed her mother as though even the smallest chink of light was worth seizing upon.

'And as if that wasn't enough he, he had a bad turn, a sort of attack, and that was it!'

'He died, you mean.'

'Yes! I didn't know it at the time, but I ... '

'And what did you do? Did you call for help?'

'I ... ' She shook her head. 'I pulled off those horrible clothes, put my own back on and just ran off ... '

'Where to?'

'Back to Jimmy's and told them ... '

'Told who?'

'Kalle and Helge! They ... they took me into the room at the back and said I wasn't to worry, said I should just forget about it and that they'd take care of everything, then they phoned somebody, and I ... I came home.'

'You came home,' I said lamely. 'And were grounded?'

She nodded.

'Without saying a word about it?'

'You don't think I'd say anything … ' She looked away again. 'About *that*?'

'But you were grounded, all the same.'

Randi Furebø opened her mouth – and closed it again.

I looked at her. 'Why?'

She gestured vaguely and glanced at her husband. 'Well … we didn't know what had happened to Torild … '

'Yes, that's true. But, all the same, didn't the two of your trust her?'

'Trust Åsa? Do you think there was any reason to after what you've heard today?' She looked at her husband again as though waiting for him to say something.

But Furebø just stared at his daughter as though she was a total stranger who had forced herself upon his attention and demanded to be taken seriously.

'That episode with the leather jacket … '

Furebø looked at me and snapped: 'Yes? What about it?'

'I don't quite see the connection.'

'There wasn't any connection! This … My daughter, who stands here before you, I almost said, stole it. I insisted she should take it back, and – '

'But the manageress was sure it had been bought and paid for.'

'Sure? She was a complete dope! It was several weeks since it had happened; how could she be so sure?'

'Several weeks? It was just last Wednesday that I went there for the first time, and on that occasion – '

'So what?'

I turned back to Åsa. 'What's your version of the story?'

'About the leather jacket?'

'Yes.'

'It … ' She shot a quick look at her father again. 'What he says is true. I'd stolen it.'

I looked at her gently. 'Listen … everything else is on the table now, Åsa.'

'They *know* how you – earned a bit extra. Can't you just as well admit that you *bought* it, as the lady said, with money you'd earned – doing that?'

'Yes, but … it was just that Dad hadn't seen the jacket before – the day you … '

I looked at Furebø again. 'Was *that* when you understood – or at least suspected, what Åsa was mixed up in?'

'Yes, I … '

His wife gave him a hurt look. 'You didn't say anything to me about it!'

'No, I didn't want you to … '

'But all the same she'd been grounded from the Friday, five days before.'

'Yes?'

Both of them looked at me for an answer. Even Åsa turned her attention to something other than her own dark conscience.

I hadn't taken my eyes off Furebø. 'No, not because Torild had disappeared but because you knew why she had disappeared, and perhaps even what had happened to her?'

'What?!'

Randi Furebø looked at her husband uncomprehendingly. 'Trond? What is he talking about?'

I leaned forward and stared at him. 'Where were *you* on Thursday evening, Furebø?'

'At work, as always!'

'We can check up on that. It's not completely impossible that you too went into town on a little errand, isn't that so?'

'Out on … Trond!'

'The police are with Holger Skagestøl at this very moment. They've identified the car from a photograph. He's been caught *in flagrante* as a client in the area.'

'Which car?'

'Holger!' Randi Furebø looked from her husband to me. 'Now I think I've taken leave of my senses. I just can't imagine Holger would go to a – prostitute.'

'Can't you? What about your husband, then?'

'Veum! That's completely unwarranted!' Furebø cut in.

'Is it?' I turned my attention back to him. 'Oh yes. Holger Skagestøl told me, as an example of what good friends the two of you were, that you often swapped cars, if the other one's car was in for repairs. Was that the case one January evening when you picked a girl up in his car? – This is what Laila Mongstad had got wind of. Actually, she perhaps still thought it was Holger. Did she ring you to ask you what you thought? Did you realise that if Holger were faced with these charges, he'd send the ball back to you?'

'She … But what about … You're forgetting the break-in – from outside.'

'It's the easiest diversion to create for someone already in the building. One set of footprints in one direction, one in another. But there was no one who said the footprints could go out and then back in, and not as we were supposed to think: in and then out again.'

'These are just loose accusations.'

'The police will get them to stick.'

'So I'm supposed to have … ?'

'You knew what Åsa and Torild and their friends were up to, because as a client you'd had Torild the same evening she was killed, and that was why you were so insistent that Åsa should be grounded from the following day. But you couldn't prevent her from going into town that morning, because there was still nobody who had the faintest *inkling* of what had happened to Torild. But from Monday onwards you collected her from school, didn't you?'

Now the expressions on the two women's faces were quite different. Åsa looked at her father with the same sort of naivety he had looked at her with a few minutes before. As for Randi Furebø, tears ran silently down her cheeks.

'Trond … Yes, it's true … everything he says fits … You weren't home at all that evening. There was something restless about you at breakfast the next morning. Don't you remember me asking you if something was bothering you at work? You were furious when you heard that Åsa'd been in town that day, and from Monday onwards … Everything fits!'

I leaned back in my chair a little, sipped my beer and looked expectantly at Trond Furebø.

He sat there, almost apathetic, ashen-faced, his lips strangely crooked, almost like a stroke victim. Finally, he turned to look at his two women and said hoarsely: 'Can't the two of you leave us for a bit? Can you go downstairs? I have to talk to him about this alone.'

Fifty-two

THE TWO WOMEN walked towards the stairs leading down to the ground floor. Randi Furebø attempted to put her arm round her daughter's shoulder, but Åsa shook her off with an irritable sideways glance as though it was all her mother's fault.

Trond Furebø's eyes lingered on them, and he did not look back at me until he heard the door downstairs close behind them.

The look he gave me was strangely distant, as if he stood at the end of a long dark corridor and could only just make me out at the other end.

When at last he spoke, it was so softly that I had to lean forward to catch everything, yet there was no doubting the intensity of his voice. 'Oh my God, Veum, what a high price a man has to pay!'

'For what?' I said calmly.

'For this whole accursed life! For trying to elbow a bit of breathing space in his life, to have butter on his bread for once.'

'Has it been that hard for you?'

'Hard? You don't have the faintest bloody clue! But sit in judgement over others, you can do that all right!'

I shook my head slowly. 'I've never – at least, hardly ever – sat in judgement over anyone. I can even accept prostitution as a phenomenon, provided they're responsible grown-up girls. But I have no time at all for the pimps who make a packet out of – ha ha! – "protecting" them, and I've just as little time for people who buy young girls barely over the minimum age of consent and get them to do unspeakable things with them!'

'I didn't get them to – all I bought was pure clean sex, to make up for what I no longer got even the faintest whiff of here at home!'

'Pure clean sex, as you call it. Can't buy me love, is that it?'

'Love!' he said with contempt. 'It's something young girls read about in their magazines, see at the cinema or hear about on records. The reality's quite different.'

'The reality is your best friend's father who pays to go to bed with you – is that how it's supposed to be, according to you?'

He looked away. 'You've misunderstood me there, Veum!'

'Have I? Let's get down to brass tacks, then, shall we? It was at the Pastel Hotel, wasn't it?'

He nodded. 'I – didn't have much time, two hours at the most, but I'd reserved a room as I … '

'Usually did?'

'Not as I usually did! But like a few times before. She … Reception rang to say she was on her way up. When there was a knock at the door … it was just as much of a shock for both of us, but obviously, in a small city like this, it's not all that unlikely that one day you'll run into somebody you know in this game, is it? I mean do *you* know who's behind all the contact notices you see in the papers? Eh?'

'Yes, and then what happened?'

'She … To begin with she wanted to go, but I pulled her in, closed the door and held her close … "Uncle!" she said … That's what she'd called me from when she was little … I said: Forget who it is, just do what you usually do, and I'll give you a bonus, you can have – anything you like!'

He scrutinised my face as though looking for some understanding. 'You must realise, it was such a strange … It was as if … ' He glanced in the direction of the stairs leading down.

I helped him along: 'As though it was your own daughter you … '

'Yes! She said: "Let me go!" But I said: Do you want me to tell your mother and father? She stood there like a statue as I undressed her. I laid her down on the bed, threw off my own clothes, forced her to touch me, as I kissed and caressed her, before I … ' He pursed his lips. ' … had intercourse. She … '

'Yes?'

'She lay there, weeping under me; it was – horrible.'

'The two of you were … Somebody told me once that the Skagestøl family and the Furebøs were so close that it was as if you were father to their children and – vice versa. Seen in this light … '

'Yes! That was just it. I admit it – it was an incredible turn-on. But it made me feel the sort of self-loathing I've never experienced before.'

'And then … '

'Then … ' The words were harder to get out now. 'She just wept and wept, and it was as if, as if I needed to hide, to blot her face out … '

'And this is what you did by … '

'I grabbed a pillow, covered her face and – pressed … She resisted, but I thought: she's going to blow the whistle, she's going to tell somebody or other, Ma, Randi, Holger … I … So I pressed harder and harder until eventually she lay still … Do you understand?'

I felt a sharp pain in my chest, a sort of muscle spasm. 'I understand what you're saying, but I … Yes, psychologically, I can even understand why you did what you did … But to understand, to really understand it, Furebø, entails so much … You can't expect me to. What you need for that is a priest, not a private investigator.'

He made an effort to pull himself together, sat up straight and looked around him as though relieved it was over with.

'And afterwards … what did you do?'

He looked up at me surprised, as if he thought it was a silly question. 'I rang down to the bar, explained the situation to Robert, told him there'd been – an accident and that obviously I was willing to pay any extra expenses the hotel might incur … He said there was absolutely no need, it was one of the drawbacks of that business … then I heard nothing more about it until I, well … You know the rest.'

'And you've not heard from them since?'

He shook his head firmly. 'Not a word … ' He looked shifty. 'But I … I must confess I didn't expect to get off scot-free there either. There's a price to be paid for everything,' he said with a cynical little smile as though, in spite of everything, it had actually been worth it.

I stood up. 'Well … I suppose you'd better stay here till the police come,' I looked at him thoughtfully. 'You'll find out what the punishment will be in due course.'

'Punishment?'

'The first thing they'll do is take a blood sample.'

He paled. 'What do you mean? A blood sample?'

'Well … ' I didn't elaborate. 'Perhaps you ought to tell Åsa and your wife first?'

'Tell them *what*, for God's sake?'

'Everything. As much as you can.'

He gave me a strained look. 'You can … Can you ask them to come up … '

I nodded. Before leaving I took one last look at him. He filled up his glass with beer and sat down in the chair in front of the TV where the football match had long been in progress. But he didn't turn up the sound, and it didn't look as though he was all that interested in the result now. In any event, it would be a long time before he would enjoy any win on the pools.

I went downstairs and knocked on the door of the room where Åsa and her mother were sitting, Åsa on the sofa and her mother on one of the chairs, both looking dejected and not exchanging a word. From the radio a Saturday voice was discussing a book they would never read and were scarcely interested in anyway.

'He'd like to talk to you now,' I said, and they rose mechanically as though it was an appointment with a gynaecologist.

As she passed me, Åsa snapped: 'It was all Sigrun's fault!'

I stared at her. 'Sigrun Søvik? The Guides leader? How do you mean? Because she – surprised the two of you?'

'Did you know about it?'

'Yes, she told me she caught the two of you in … Well … '

'Caught us! We weren't doing anything wrong! We're not *like that*, we just wanted, we were just examining one another, feeling what it was like when somebody else, where it felt good if somebody … Did she tell you *everything*? What happened afterwards as well?'

'Afterwards? She said she reprimanded you and placed you each in separate tents.'

'And was that it?'

'Was there more?'

'Oh yes! She told us straight that either she'd tell our parents or … Well, she'd have to punish us, she said, with a disgusting grin!'

I felt that strange stabbing sensation in my chest again. 'And then … '

'We had to go to her tent, first Torild and then me, and do the same to her as we'd done with – while she – *as a punishment*, right?'

Randi Furebø opened and closed her mouth like a fish. 'What on earth, Åsa!' She looked at me. 'Can you credit that this sort of thing goes on!'

I kneaded the recalcitrant heart muscle with my knuckles. 'So was this how you two learned to barter your bodies?'

She looked at me defiantly but said no more.

Randi Furebø tugged gently at her daughter's blouse. 'Åsa … I think we'd better … ' She glanced upstairs.

With a last look at Åsa I mumbled: 'I'll show myself out.'

Neither of them accompanied me to the door but stood watching me as if to make sure I really left and had no more surprises up my sleeve.

Once outside the door I ran straight into Helleve and Muus. Muus looked at me like thunder: as though about to yell *Veeeeeeum!* But when he remembered what day it was he thought better of it, raising his eyebrows and saying quite calmly: 'Veum?'

And as calmly as I could manage, I said: 'He's confessed everything. As I'm sure he will to you too.'

They stood there looking at the house. 'Furebø?'

I nodded. 'Furebø.' Then I turned to Helleve: 'You couldn't just move your car a bit, could you, so I can get out?'

At the top of Birkelundsbakken, Bergensdalen broadened out to its full width. It was the season for spring-cleaning. The city needed a clean in a caustic bath of white spring light. But the trouble with spring is that it throws open all the windows inside you, including those you'd rather leave shut forever.

Down in Mannsverk some young girls stood waiting for the bus in close, intimate little groups. I couldn't help thinking: What were they up to? Where were they going? To a boyfriend in the same class, to their best friend's father or to an old bloke in women's underwear crawling about on all fours and asking them to – ?

But life is like spring. It comes and goes. And suddenly it's autumn, and you're going to die. Did they give it a single thought as they stood there laughing? Did they?

One of them looked at my car and pointed. Another gave me two fingers, while a third stood with her hands in her jacket pockets and looked at me thoughtfully as I drove past as slowly as if I was on the way to somebody's funeral, as slowly as if somebody or other had just died.

In Fløenbakken I turned down left. It wasn't autumn. Not yet.

NEW FROM EUROCRIME

THE WOMAN FROM BRATISLAVA
Leif Davidsen
Translated from the Danish by Barbara J. Haveland

Spring in 1999. NATO is bombing Yugoslavia when the impossible happens. One of their indestructible fighter planes is shot down. Someone has obviously been leaking information.

In Bratislava, Teddy Pedersen, a middle-aged, Danish university lecturer, receives a visit from an Eastern European woman who turns out to be his half-sister. Father to both of them was a Danish SS officer who had officially been declared dead in 1952, but had in fact lived on in Yugoslavia for many years. In Copenhagen, Teddy's older sister is arrested on suspicion of being a Stasi agent, and a murder leads Teddy – and the Danish intelligence service – to investigate the relationship between these two – the woman in Denmark and the woman in Bratislava. The link between them proves to have far-reaching personal and political consequences.

'One of Denmark's top crime writers' *Sunday Times* on *The Serbian Dane*

978-1-906413-35-4
£7.99

AT CLOSE QUARTERS
Eugenio Fuentes
Translated from the Spanish by Martin Schifino

Fuentes makes a sociological portrait of the present, and analyses the secret reasons that may push one to commit murder.

Every day Samuel watches as a woman drops off her two children at the bus stop. He is so fascinated by her that, one afternoon when he cannot be at his window to observe her, he leaves his camera programmed to take pictures of her picking up the children. Later, when he looks through the pictures, he sees an unexpected event that has been photographed. That day, on the corner, a group of teenagers provokes one of the neighbour's dogs, which ends up killing one of them. Samuel decides to approach the woman. Her name is Marina, she is recently separated, and the daughter of a high-ranking officer, Captain Olmedo, who is in charge of dismantling the city's military headquarters, and who is found dead in his house, with a bullet from his own gun, through his chest. His daughter does not believe the official version of the suicide and she hires Cupido, a peaceful detective who will discover hidden secrets as well as the tense relationships of those that surround them. He will investigate Olmedo's military colleagues, his daughter's ex-husband, and even the anaesthetist who cared for his wife during her plastic surgery. There are reasons that make all of them suspects.

'Old fashioned, character-led who-dunits uncovering the dark side of secret Spain' *Observer*

978-1-906413-36-1
£8.99

SPIDER TRAP
Barry Maitland

**Old skeletons, new murders – Brock and Kolla must catch
Spider.**

Skeletons are discovered in a wasteland behind Cockpit Lane, an
area of inner South London, and DCI David Brock and DS Kathy
Kolla of Scotland Yard's Serious Crimes Branch are called in to
investigate.

The discovery that the victims died during the Brixton riots,
over twenty years before, lead Brock and Kolla on a dark and
dangerous journey in which past and present come together in
an intricate web of deception and intrigue as Brock encounters
a formidable old antagonist, Spider Roach. In a desperate search
to find a crucial piece of evidence, Brock and Kolla unknowingly
set in train a series of events that erupt in a shocking, violent
conclusion.

Written with Maitland's characteristically vivid sense of
character and place, *Spider Trap* is Maitland at his scrupulously
plotted, complex and compelling best.

'Maitland gets better and better, and Brock and Kolla are an impressive
team who deserve to become household names' *Publishing News*

978-1-906413-37-8
£7.99

LORRAINE CONNECTION
Dominique Manotti
Translated from the French by Amanda Hopkinson and Ros Schwartz
Winner of the CWA Duncan Lawrie International Dagger Award

In Pondange, Lorraine, the Korean Daewoo group manufactures
cathode ray tubes. Working conditions are abysmal, but as it's the
only source of employment in this bleak former iron and steel-
manufacturing region, the workers daren't protest. Until a strike
breaks out, and there's a fire at the factory. But is it an accident?
The Pondange factory is at the centre of a strategic battle being
played out in Paris, Brussels and Asia for the takeover of the
ailing state-owned electronics giant Thomson. Unexpectedly, the
Matra-Daewoo alliance wins the bid. Rival contender Alcatel
believes there's foul play involved and brings in the big guns
led by its head of security, former deputy head of the national
security service. Intrepid private cop Charles Montoya is called
to Lorraine to investigate, and explosive revelations follow –
murder, dirty tricks and blackmail.

'French crime writing at its best' Ruth Morse, *TLS*

978-1-905147-61-8
£8.99

CHE COMMITTED SUICIDE
Petros Markaris
Translated from the Greek by David Connolly

Since the night Commissar Haritos had the brilliant idea to
offer his chest as a shield in order to save Elena Kousta from
a bullet fired by her stepson, his life has changed radically.
Haritos's long convalescence has given his wife the opportunity
to take control and, now, subdued and tamed, he witnesses a
shocking suicide captured live on TV. The victim, Iason Favieros,
a former revolutionary activist who had been jailed during the
dictatorship of the Colonels, had built up a sprawling business
empire in a surprisingly short period of time, including Olympic
contracts. This tragedy is quickly followed by the suicides of a
well-known Greek MP and a national journalist – at his own
party. With the police and the press left groping in the dark,
Commissar Haritos is under pressure to solve the mystery that is
lurking behind this series of public suicides, unveiling the secrets
buried in the victims' past.

'Haritos himself is an intriguing find: zealous in his work, more in
love with his wife that he will admit, suspicious by training, his only
relief from work being the hours he spends learning new words in his
dictionaries at home' *Washington Post*

978-1-906413-34-7
£8.99

THE CONSORTS OF DEATH

Gunnar Staalesen

Translated from the Norwegian by Don Bartlett

'I got a telephone call from the past.' Thus begins the thirteenth novel in the series about Bergen detective, Varg Veum.

It is September 1995, and Veum is in his office when a telephone conversation takes him back twenty-five years, to a case he was involved in while working as a child protection officer, during the summer of 1970. A small boy was separated from his mother under tragic circumstances. But that had not been the end of it. In 1974 the same boy had surfaced in connection with a sudden death in his new home. And then again, ten years later, in connection with yet another case: a dramatic double-murder in Sunnfjord. The boy is now an adult, and on the run in Oslo, determined to take revenge on those responsible for destroying his life, among them the former child protection officer, now detective Veum.

'Popular Norwegian series featuring private eye Varg Veum, an upmarket Scandinavian Philip Marlowe' Maxim Jakubowski, *The Bookseller*

978-1-906413-38-5
£7.99